ABSENCE

Mist and Shadow

by

J.B. Forsyth

Copyright © 2016 J.B.Forsyth
All rights reserved

ISBN: 1533486123

Absence

For Mum

Thanks for everything

Acknowledgement

Thanks again to Lindi for all your encouragement and support

It Lies Amongst the Flowers

Suula led them through the forest for most of the afternoon. At times she took them up steep slopes or along dried river beds when easier passage was clearly on offer. It was a tortuous and erratic route that Kye would have found strange if not for Ormis's demonstration with the bramble bush. He found himself studying every plant and tree she turned from, trying to guess its potential danger. At one point they came to a carpet of dandelion clocks; much the same as any he had run through with Emilie, kicking up blizzards of seeds. He saw nothing alarming in their delicate heads, but Suula took them on a near right angle to avoid them. Danger it seemed was all around and it engendered him with a simmering trepidation that focused him like a tightrope walker. And if that wasn't enough, there were several occasions when he felt something watching him from the trees. But when he looked there was nothing there.

It was late afternoon when Suula stopped and made a quick gesture with her hand. They all froze except for Kye. He was looking off into the trees and continued to walk until his chest struck Ormis's outstretched palm. The exorcist put a finger to his lips and conjured a black warning in his eyes. Up front, Suula crept forwards on her own then disappeared from view; leaving them listening to the birds.

When she returned, she stepped out of the woodland right in front of Kye, giving him a start. She was wearing the same boots they all wore, but hers were functioning like cat's paws. 'They stopped,' she said. 'There was an incident with the girl and a toruck was killed.'

Kring stiffened. 'Was it Karkus?'

'No. He left with the other one about an hour ago.' The giant was bracing for bad news and his hulking frame relaxed only a little at this. His brother was alive, but one of his countrymen was dead. 'And there's something else - but it's best if you see.'

She led them through a stand of hazel, to a strip of forest abundant with bluebells. The toruck was there; slumped at the foot of a big maple - his dead eyes fixed on a black coffin that lay open in the flowers. Kring went to him, prompting Kail to level an arrow at his back. But Ormis raised his hand in a restraining gesture and he lowered it.

'His name was Rox,' said Kring. 'Karkus grew up with him.' He knelt, closed the toruck's eyes and reached around the back of his head. When he brought his hand out it was covered in blood. 'Fractured skull.'

'They were carrying the girl in the coffin,' said Suula, 'The one at the back fell and this one dropped his end and spun around; drawing his swords. Something struck him – lifting him off his feet and launching him against the tree.' She spoke with certainty – as though what she was saying was playing out in front of her. And the soldiers appeared to believe every word.

As she talked Kring's hand wandered towards one of Rox's fallen blades, but the tip of Rauul's sword came down and clinked the hilt before he could grab it. The giant gave him a dark look and got back to his feet.

'The largest of the three was guiding them,' Suula continued. 'He ran back, took the girl from the coffin and threw her here, where he cut the little finger from her left hand.' She sidestepped and pointed to a depression in the bluebells. 'It lies amongst the flowers.' They all stared; shock and disgust clear on every face.

Ormis went to the patch of bent bluebells and parted the stalks. A curled finger was nestled within – its fingernail shining in the light and the congealed mess at the other end glaring like a bloody eye.

Kye stared and stared, hardly able to comprehend what he was seeing. He knew they were tracking killers, but the sight of Della's little finger transformed them into monsters. Unbidden, his imagination began to assemble a scene in which they were cutting it off and he turned away, hurling the contents of his stomach over the flowers.

Kring's eyes burned the ground around the finger, his face betraying the painful turmoil he was suffering inside. And when he spoke it was like he was addressing the forest itself. 'It cannot be. Karkus would never do such a thing… Not him. Not ever.'

'He punished her for killing Rox,' said Ormis.

Kring went to the finger and dropped to his hands and knees, poring over his brother's alleged crime as if looking for evidence to absolve him.

But it was a show.

Like most of his countrymen, Kring was a sleight-of-hand master. Whenever he quaffed a few too many in the Moon and Cobbles he would awe the patrons with his talents – making coins vanish beneath upturned flagons and reappear behind someone's ear or under their hat. And when they asked how he did it; his standard slurred reply was that he had twice their number of hands and each one was twice as big. Now, as he made a show of examining the finger, he palmed a stone with the hand he was using to bear weight. Then he sat back on his heels and got to his feet. As he reached full height he spun on Kail, throwing the stone with a flick of his wrist. The soldier was only ten feet away, but like the others, his mind had wandered at the sight of Della's finger and he was caught off guard. He flinched as the stone clocked his forehead and staggered away. Kring lunged, stepping around the back of him and lifting him up like a shield. He slid Kail's sword free and the point was against his neck before the others unshouldered their bows. With his feet dangling Kail looked like a runaway child caught by a monstrous parent, and he looked at Rauul over the giant's thick forearm with something like an apology on his face.

'I don't want to fight,' said Kring. 'I can't deny what's plain to see and all I want is to help put things right. To get that wee girl back and undo what's been done to my brother... Let me go on as one of your company and with my countryman's swords.' The soldiers held their arrows levelled, waiting for an opening. 'If I wanted to harm you, this would be my best chance.' He lowered Kail's sword and pushed him away, leaving himself wide open. The Elite Guard had clear shots now, but were waiting for Ormis's signal.

'Come on! Put me down or let me go on with the means to defend myself.'

Ormis was not a man to be rushed and he regarded him for some time; hundreds of cogs whirring behind his eyes. 'Very well,' he said finally. 'Take his swords – but leave the daggers.'

Kye was stunned. He hadn't expected Ormis to agree and by the look of them, neither had the Elite Guard. Their eyes flicked to Rauul now and it wasn't until he gave them a nod that they lowered their bows.

Kring took the swords, slipping them into his empty scabbards under their watchful gaze. 'I need to bury him.'

'We haven't time,' Ormis replied.

'It's not our way to leave him like this.'

'Karkus left him.'

Kring's eyes flashed as if he'd been stung. But when he spoke again his voice was surprisingly level. 'It won't be long before something finds him.'

'He's dead... The girl might still be saved.'

Kring looked from Rox to Della's severed finger and all protest left his face. 'Give me a minute then.'

The exorcist nodded. 'A minute is all.'

He positioned Rox flat on his back and folded his arms over his chest. When he stepped away, Kye saw that the tattoos on the dead toruck's forearms were now lined up, forming a row of five symbols. Kring bowed his head, crossing his lower arms in a big X to form a single larger symbol from a different set of tattoos. Kye realised he was intruding on a private ritual and turned away, feeling suddenly embarrassed. He was in time to catch the end of a silent communication between Ormis and the Elite

Guard, from which he could tell the soldiers were unhappy with the exorcist's decision. The giant had his swords, but they were going to be watching him even closer now.

When Kring was done they fell in line and resumed their eastward march, leaving Rox and Della's finger to the woods and whatever came crawling.

Eavesdropping

Della sagged as the big toruck bound her arms and legs; burning her skin as he tightened the knots. But she was in no mood to struggle and barely felt it. He had carried her to this place with a knife to her throat; no doubt fearing a repeat of her earlier performance. But he needn't have worried. She was so appalled by what she had done she spent the whole time staring at the forest floor as it sped away beneath her.

She had killed a toruck by lifting him off his feet and smashing him into a tree. She hadn't meant to, but she was so angry she lost all self-control. What she remembered was wanting to *hurt* him; but not to kill him. Her father had taught her never to go Absent while angry, because venting on the Membrane risked effecting the physical world. Things could get broken and people could get hurt. It was a warning she had all but forgotten about, for up until now it had been impossible to go Absent when she was even the slightest bit angry. Her preparations ensured she was calm for transition and once on the Membrane her time was usually spent in blissful release from the poison.

She looked down at the raw stump of her little finger and the transparent salve that covered it. There was no real pain - just a vague throb that worsened as she looked at it. The shadow was looking at it too and she could feel its gleeful approval in stark contrast to her dismay.

'Ah your finger,' said a voice behind her. 'Karkus told me what you did. Tell me, what kind of witchcraft allows you to take leave of your body?'

'Izle said no questions,' the big toruck said in gruff reprimand. A period of silence followed through which Della watched an ant scurry across the stone floor.

'My name is Griglis and I'm here to ensure you don't misbehave again. You might be thinking of repeating what you did back there in the forest. But the flies buzzing around your head are fieraks and if you slip your body they'll light you up like a beacon.'

Della looked around, through a ball of darting flies. She was in a circular dungeon, lit by a pair of alushia torches. Barrels were stacked against the wall and the big toruck who cut her finger off was sitting on one. The blade he had used was resting on his lap and the sight of it got her finger throbbing again. She turned to look at Griglis. His gaunt face was a haven of shadows - an angular scaffold for sunken eyes that glittered in the torchlight. 'If Karkus sees so much as a flicker -' His threat sheared off as their eyes met and he flinched away in what appeared to be shocked recognition. And his reaction was matched by the shadow. She felt it jerk down inside her; like it had been caught peeking over a wall.

Griglis looked over to Karkus as if to confirm an insight, but the giant gave him nothing. When he spoke again there was a waver in his voice. 'If Karkus sees so much as a flicker of spirit light, he'll make good on his promise and cut you again... Understand?'

Della nodded. He continued to stare at her, but not to punctuate his words. His surprise was gone and he was looking at her like she was a wish he had just spoken down a well. He made an awkward gesture to Karkus and left, his footsteps speeding up on the stairwell until it sounded like he was running.

She lowered herself to the cold floor and rolled onto her side, facing away from the toruck and his glinting knife.

What was going on?

Griglis and the shadow had seen one another and it was clear they were both rattled by it. The shadow had gone back into hiding; its fear like an afterglow in the place it had vacated. Griglis's reaction was more difficult to interpret. He was shocked at first, but something more complicated had evolved in his eyes. No one had ever looked at her in such a speculative way and it gave her the creeps.

A few hours ago, she thought they were going to bury her alive. Now, with a cooler head, it made no sense. If Kye had told the exorcists about Absence, they wouldn't put her in the ground without studying her first. Griglis was most likely one of their interrogators and the coffin, just a convenient method of transportation. She had to escape. There were stories about what the exorcists did to people in their dungeons and it would be her turn to endure their hot irons and choking ropes when he came back.

But how could she escape? She was tied up with a toruck glaring at her and there was a ball of fieraks knitting the air; ready to give her away the moment she went Absent. She was losing hope when one of the fieraks bounced off a barrel, giving her an idea.

She tucked her hands under her head and curled up as though settling to sleep. Then she shut her eyes and started her preparations for Absence. But no sooner had she begun, she was ready - floating inside her body like driftwood on the surface of a lake. She remained in place; shocked by her sudden transition and unable to understand how it had happened. Her mind clearing rituals were usually essential to the process and she had never been able to bypass them. But strange as this was, it served her purpose now and she wasted no more time thinking about it.

She had left her body thousands of times and on every occasion had *risen* from it. But this time she directed herself downward; through the stone floor and into the earth. It felt totally unnatural – as different as swimming down instead of up. But once clear of her body, her movement became effortless once more. She descended for several seconds before rising to a vertical position and accelerating away through the forever darkness of deep earth. And after a count of ten she angled up into the forest.

She revolved as though skating on ice and saw the outer arc of a crumbling wall. Behind it was the solitary tower she had come from. She had escaped in Absence, but while her body lay in its dungeon she was still its prisoner. She stared at it for some time, trying to place it. But in the end she had to conclude she had never seen it before. *Strange* she thought, given she had lived in every corner of the Westland. She drifted over the wall and hoping for clues, began to circle it. But when its highest balcony came into view, she froze. Upon it, gilded in the low light of the setting sun was Griglis. And floating in front of him was a ghost.

All at once she felt exposed; a reflex brought about by the presence of another spirit. Such approximations were dangerous and were to be avoided at all costs. She backed up until she was out of sight. Under any other circumstances she would have fled, but she sensed the importance of hearing what they were saying. So she drew close to the tower and made her way slowly around, minimising the distortion on the Membrane. Gradually the voices resolved into clarity.

'How many of them?' asked Griglis.

'Eight: Four soldiers, a tracker…'

'What is it?'

Della ran cold. Despite her care the ghost had sensed her as easily as a spider senses a fly on its web. Her instinct was to flee, but she forced herself still. A hasty retreat would be the equivalent of struggling on the web and would give her location away. So she waited, knowing it had only to drift a few degrees around the tower to see her.

'There's a spirit close by.'

'Never mind that now. When you're done you can sweep the area and take your fill. But for now you must stay focused. You said there were eight?'

Della relaxed a little.

'Four soldiers, a tracker, an exorcist, a toruck and a boy.'

'A boy?'

'Yes, and he's twum. Sensed me from over fifty yards away.'

'Did you recognise the exorcist?'

'No.'

There was a long pause when all Della could do was listen to the breeze.

'Did they come through the Wall?'

'I don't know. But their tracker is skilled and she followed the torucks as if they were dripping blood.'

'We must assume they're coming for the girl… How long before they arrive?'

'It won't be tonight unless they walk the mist.'

'Good. I'll send our old friend out to them. Put such things beyond doubt. Follow him, make sure he does a thorough job then report back.'

There was no more talk, just the sound of boots receding into the tower.

Della waited for some time before she dared to move and when she did she drifted down the tower as slowly as a strip of gauze cast from the balcony. She reached the cobbles and accelerated into the forest again, rising into the canopy of a large hornbeam. And as she looked out through its foliage she considered what she had heard.

An exorcist, a toruck and a boy. It had to be Ormis, Kring and Kye. She was sure of it. And if they were here to rescue her, then who were the people holding her prisoner? The answer came in a flash. The man behind the whispers – the one called Izle. His monster had failed to get his shadow back so he had sent the torucks to snatch her from the gaol.

She had to warn Kye that Griglis was sending someone to kill them. But she had no idea where to look for him. She rose up again, hoping to get her bearings from her surroundings. As she broke the canopy she saw what hadn't registered before: the forest was huge and it ran all the way to the horizon. She stared, bewildered. She had travelled the length and breadth of the Westland and had never seen a forest anywhere near this size. But then she looked towards the setting sun and realised what was wrong. For most of her life she had watched it rise over the mountains – but here, it was setting behind them.

…unless they walk the mist.

She had been so surprised to hear about a rescue party the spirit's words had gone right over her head. But the significance of them hit hard now. The torucks had brought her over the mountains – into the great forest and jungle of the Wilderness.

Awakening

Griglis stood on the tower's broken steps, staring across the courtyard. He had spent the last few days pacing the tower in nervous frustration, but now, as the implications of what he had seen in the witch's eyes were sinking in, he felt a flutter of excitement.

He had been in the service of Izle Rohn for a long time now. How long he couldn't say. His best guess was more than ten years, but less than thirty. The trouble was, most of his time in the Eastland had passed in the soupy awareness of mental servitude.

Of the fifteen exorcists who Izle had taken into the jungle he was one of only two that remained. And he, like the rest of them had trusted his then High Exorcist, believing his deep scours to be a necessary part of training. He knew now that they were no such thing. Izle had used his scours to subjugate them - ploughing their minds and sowing them with the seeds of servitude. He had taken each of them in turn, ensuring his complete dominance before moving on to the next; starting with the novices and working up through the ranks. And it might have gone all the way to the top if Kass Riole hadn't discovered what he was doing.

Years passed and he served Izle with the rest; shoring up defences in the glass tunnels, fashioning weapons, foraging food, snatching quaggar from their villages for scour development and more recently, snaring jungle horrors for new experiments.

But over the last year Izle's power over him had waned. His memories, reason and autonomy sprouting from his servile mind like stubborn weeds – a rebirth he had come to think of as his awakening. As far as he knew he was the only one of the fifteen to have undergone such a change. He had thought long and hard about why this was so and was at first convinced it was due to a superiority of mind. But as his reason sharpened, he understood the truth of the matter. He was one of Izle's first conquests and as such he had been subjugated by an unrefined process. Those who were enslaved thereafter, were done so with a sharper tool.

But he hadn't come through the process unscathed. He looked at his pale hands and the veins that pulsed with green mist light after dark. The Wilderness had polluted him and the process could not be undone. He was enlisted into the ranks of the Caliste as a bright and noble young man; but that person was dead. The mist had poisoned his blood and now there was a fist of jet where his heart used to be.

His awakening had been a slow process. But he was glad of it. Any faster and he would have been unable to adjust from the unquestionable obedience expected of him, to the pretence of it. Izle's voice was once an undeniable authority, emanating from the centre of his head. But over the years its power abated until he heard it the same way he heard any other voice. His awakening was now complete and every day was an effort to keep it secret. It was hard to exhibit the right degree of deference and to acquiesce to all that was asked of him. He was sure to be discovered soon and if Izle wasn't so obsessively focused on Irongate, he would have been already. He had thought of escape, but with all the spies Izle had at his disposal, he wouldn't get very far. His only hope had been to abandon him after they crossed into the Westland, when he was too involved with the Reader Ceremony to pay any attention.

But one look in the witch's eyes had changed everything.

Four days ago they were gathered at the tower and ready to move. Izle's plan was going well. The King of the Westland was dead, and if the protocols of Irongate were observed there would be one week of mourning before a Reader Ceremony was called. Raphe was already in Irongate and would soon be in a position to assure Izle an advantageous position among the hopefuls.

Only one thing remained to do.

Kass Riole was expected to recall the exorcists once Raphe started all the trouble. Their numbers had dwindled in recent years, but collectively they were a threat that couldn't be ignored. Izle's plan was to eliminate them before they could assemble and organise. For this task he had employed one of his Eastland conquests – a remarkable creature able to mimic the form of anything it touched. It was a creature perfectly suited to infiltrate the Westland, but how it was supposed to find and deal with such a widely dispersed order was a detail that hadn't been shared.

Izle guided the shape shifter from the top of the tower by sending his scour after it in a thin ribbon. It was a technique developed over many years through tireless experiments with quaggar captives. He had been there to witness Izle's breakthrough, when he managed to maintain a scour on a quaggar boy after lifting his fingers clear of his face. After that he had worked to increase the distance over which he could exert his influence. The distance now appeared to be limitless. He could project an invisible ribbon of consciousness across many miles – a stream of whispers that could be heard if you were close enough.

Absence

Two days after Izle sent the shape shifter over the mountain Griglis felt a meteoric pulse in the whispers, followed by a shriek from the top of the tower. He bounded up the stairs two at a time and thumped on Izle's door. Not because he cared what happened to him, but because it was expected. Izle sent him away without opening the door, giving orders not to disturb him again for any reason. The whispers resumed shortly afterwards, but they were much weaker than before.

When Izle finally came down, he brought with him a change of plan. The mountain crossing was to be postponed as the shape shifter had discovered a powerful witch who was a threat to their success. Karkus was to acquire the witch from Irongate with any means necessary and bring her to Joebel. And once she was taken care of they would proceed with their original plan. He was ordered to wait at the tower for Karkus and to assist in the witch's safe transit to Joebel. But under no circumstances was he to touch or even question her. He was to speak to her only to give instruction or reprimand.

The unelaborated threat from the witch and sudden change of plan had intrigued him, but he neither probed his master or expressed interest. He simply nodded as if it all made sense and got on with his preparations. But there had been much to think about.

When Izle came down from his room he looked twenty years older; lowering himself from step to step with a shaky hand braced on the wall. He looked so pathetic and vulnerable that he was gripped by an almost undeniable urge to spring up the steps and plunge a dagger into his chest. But Karkus was standing right beside him and he suppressed the urge, forcing himself to wait patiently. If Izle had looked at him during those few seconds his eyes would have betrayed everything he was fighting so hard to conceal. But by the time they were face to face, he had hidden it all away behind a placid screen of deference.

Something had gone seriously wrong and he had been left alone in the tower to fester on what it might be. But now, after all the waiting, the witch had arrived with the answer in her eyes.

When she looked at him it was like looking at Izle. He couldn't say exactly what it was in her startling blue eyes that gave him that impression, except that he felt his old master's cold glare upon him. And he'd had that feeling before, whenever he looked into the eyes of the quaggar captives while they were under the influence of Izle's extended scour. The feeling was so strong he had looked at Karkus; sure he must have seen the same thing. But he hadn't. Perhaps, he thought, a toruck's coarse intellect was insensitive to such things. When he looked back at the girl, the feeling was gone and all he saw were the frightened eyes of a little girl far away from home.

It hadn't taken long to imagine what had happened. Izle's extended consciousness had crossed paths with the witch and part of him was now trapped inside her. He was divided and weak and had retreated to Joebel until he could take back what she had taken from him.

He smiled at the revelation - the smile of a cutthroat who hears the footsteps of his intended victim. For such a reunion was never going to happen. At the first opportunity he was going to reach inside the witch and burn Izle's consciousness right out of her; leaving him in a permanent state of vulnerability. A situation he would fully exploit. The only problem was getting access to the witch. He only needed a few minutes with her, but Karkus was guarding her like a dog. He still had hope though. There were many miles between the tower and Joebel and there would be plenty of time for an opportunity to present itself.

He forced his mind back to more immediate concerns and looked across at the well, feeling the first wave of revulsion for what waited within. He descended the steps and crossed the courtyard. He had come through his awakening to find himself, not in the service of an exorcist, but some other sort of practitioner. Izle had perfected his scour techniques and now he was using them in conjunction with spirit melds - forging subservient entities by binding the souls of his followers to those of jungle horrors. One such example waited in the well. He still found it difficult to believe that the mind powering the crawling ensemble at the bottom of the shaft was Tyrus – one of the exorcists with whom he had once shared a dormitory.

There was a strong possibility he was next in line for a similar fate. A few weeks ago he had helped Raphe and the torucks set a trap for a giant moleworm. They had set many such traps before, and whatever they caught soon became one half of a spirit meld. The other half being one of the remaining exorcists. Of the original fifteen, only Raphe and he remained. And given that Izle had entrusted Raphe with important duties in Irongate, he had seen his name written clearly on the moleworm's slippery back. So when the trap was completed he sabotaged it, pulling the linchpin free and severing some of the big ropes the torucks had fixed in place. He earned himself some time that day, but he didn't have forever.

He pulled the bolt on the well's flaky iron cover and flipped it over, stepping back as it squealed on its hinge and clanged down on the other side. There was no need for the cover, as the vile ensemble at the bottom would wait until called. But he was glad it was there. It eased his mind to have a lid on his old friend. He inched toward the rim, angled back like someone looking over the edge of a cliff. Twilight reached into the well, but it had not the strength, or perhaps the stomach, to illuminate the bottom.

'A party of eight are tracking Karkus here,' he said, projecting his voice into its black throat. 'They are a few miles to the west. Find them and kill them.'

Beyond the reach of the light something seethed in the shadows. It was more than enough for him. His message had been received and it was time to go. He turned from the well as it rose from the depths, clicking against its stone lining like pine needles spiralling on a wind. As he hurried back to the tower, something vile poured over the rim. It constructed itself from hundreds of tiny bodies and thousands of little legs, before setting off through the broken gates in a skittering run.

hhhhhhhhhh

The forest was thick with shadows when they entered a diamond shaped clearing. Suula was waiting for them - her lithe form poised on top of a fallen tree. Ormis saw the question in her dark eyes, gave her an approving nod and signalled the rest to make camp.

'You'll find a hammock in your backpack,' he said to Kye. 'Lash it between those oaks over there and I'll check your knots when I'm done with mine.'

Kye frowned. 'What about Della? It's not dark yet.'

Ormis tipped his head to the canopy. The sun was low in the sky and its rays no longer touched even the highest leaves. 'The shadow of the mountains is upon us and it continues east. When it reaches the Abyss the mist will come and to walk through it is folly. Karkus knows this, and he'll be making camp too. If we set out at dawn, we'll lose no ground on him.'

Kye had never heard of the Abyss and he wondered how the exorcist could be sure a mist was on its way. He was about to ask when Kring joined them. 'I'll help the lad with his hammock.' Ormis regarded him for a moment before nodding consent and going about his business.

Kring led Kye to the oaks and took the hammock from his backpack. Then he circled each of the trees, inspecting the foliage and shaking some of the low branches. Once satisfied, he flicked the hammock out and laid it on the ground. He caught Kye staring at his tattoos and straightened.

'You're wondering what they mean?' he said, holding all four arms out from his sides. 'They mean nothing until we bring them together like this.' He aligned both of his left forearms in front of his chest making a strange symbol from two of his tattoos. 'See... I can't tell you what it means though, cos it's our secret. But I can tell you this much. We form some symbols for love and others for war... Some can bag me a mate and others can get me a belly full of steel.'

'What about the symbols you made for your friend?' Kye asked, referring to the way Kring had arranged the dead toruck's arms.

'It's our secret remember.'

Kye blushed, but Kring just smiled again. He turned away and began lashing the hammock to one of the oaks, his big hands making quick work of it. 'It was a nasty thing you had to see back there,' he said as he took up the other end. The image of Della's severed finger had plagued Kye for most of the afternoon and the mere mention of it brought it back with vivid brilliance. 'He shouldn't have cut her like that, no matter what she's done... It's not our way.' He finished the lashings then fixed Kye with a look of ferocious sincerity. 'I don't know what's going on with my brother, but I promise to do all I can to help get your friend back.' He crossed his lower forearms, one palm facing forward and one facing back, making another symbol. Kye didn't need to be told what it meant, because taken with his solemn face and blazing eyes it was obvious. It was a way of sealing an oath - like spitting on hands before shaking, or writing in blood.

Kye felt a need to respond, but all he could do was shift his weight and give the giant an awkward nod. But Kring seemed satisfied. He turned back to the hammock and tested it by leaning into the centre of its droop. 'All done,' he said, stepping away. All we have to do now is wait.' He placed a callused hand on Kye's shoulder and turned him around. 'If you look to the east, you'll see the mist when it comes.' The light was draining from the forest quickly now, the leaves turning a darker green and the trees becoming pillars of shadow.

'I can't see anything,' Kye said, after staring for some time.

'Patience lad. It won't be long now.'

And it wasn't.

The words had just left the giant's mouth when the mist appeared between distant tree trunks - a broken band of pulsating green light that became a swirling carpet of knee deep mist. Wispy tendrils led the charge, snaking around trees and bushes and turning them into islands in a huge witch's broth. As it billowed into the clearing Kye saw faces with yawning mouths and orb like eyes boiling up on its leading edge. He jerked away and would have fallen if Kring hadn't grabbed him.

'Steady on lad. No need to panic as long as you keep your feet. Your boots and britches are soaked in alushia sap and resistant to it.'

Kye looked down at them, remembering the strong smell of pine and rose petal when he first put them on. The mist was running through his legs now like an eerie river. Its perpetual light pulsed in a steady rhythm; radiating one moment and contained the next - a constant cycle that chased shadows up trees and let them down again. He turned to watch it roll west and got a fright. The others were looking at him just as the mist was at the top of its pulse and it gave them the look of undead warriors. The effect was lost when shadow reclaimed their faces and some of them looked away.

Ormis came over and the three of them stood in a line, looking east.

'The mist is the poison that perverts the land,' he said, his face glowing sickly green in each pulse of light. 'Hypnotic isn't it? But if you stare into it too long, you'll forget who you are and what you are doing... Stand quiet now and hear its foul breath.' Kye listened and after a few seconds he heard a constant exhalation, as though the exorcist had put a seashell to his ear – *hhhhhhhhhh.*

'Up from the Abyss it comes, pouring out all night long. And when the sun rises every last wisp soaks into the land, perverting all life this side of the Wall. The vegetation has learnt to thrive on the mist and needs neither sunshine or rain. In Rockspur they have grown trees in dark rooms without water or soil - placing seeds in empty pots and feeding them nothing but mist... There are no seasons here. In the dead of winter, when the streets of Irongate are covered with snow, the forests and jungles of the Eastland continue to flourish.' He lifted an arm to point. 'See where the mist spirals down around the bushes, and at the base of that tree?' Kye nodded dreamily, thinking how it looked like water draining from a basin. 'Some of the flora has developed a greater thirst than others. The shredder you saw this morning is one such plant. We've been avoiding others like it all day.' There wasn't a sound to challenge the exorcist's voice and it had the tone and gravity of a fireside storyteller.

'But don't be fooled into thinking such clues make the mist safe to walk. There are creatures that hunt beneath it and use it for cover. The only thing to do once it comes, is to find safe ground and stay there till dawn.' He walked away leaving him alone with the giant once more.

'Jump into your hammock,' said Kring after a time, 'and let's see how well it holds.'

He wrenched his gaze from the mist and staggered. But Kring kept him from falling again. 'Remember, don't go staring at it lad. If you have to look then keep your eyes moving the whole time.'

He jumped into the hammock, feeling a flutter in his stomach as it twisted against its lashings, nearly discarding him into the mist.

Kring laughed. 'Just takes a bit of getting used to that's all.'

'Where's *your* hammock?' he asked once he was settled.

'I don't need one. Us torucks sleep on our feet. Besides, even if they could take my weight, I'd likely get tangled up.' He lifted his four arms in explanation. 'Now try to get some sleep.' He trudged away, making a trail of disturbance in the mist.

Ormis came over soon after. 'Heed our words and don't look into it too long... The soldiers will keep watch, but if there's any trouble in the night, move to the centre of the clearing and stay there. Understand?'

He nodded and the exorcist strode away and climbed into his hammock. He tilted his hat down over his face and folded his arms, his ring pulsing in synchrony with the light. Kye realised then that there was mist trapped in its gemstone. But given what the exorcist just said, he couldn't understand why he wanted to wear such a thing.

He looked around the clearing now. Suula, Dorian and Steith were laid in their hammocks with their eyes closed. They held their backpacks on their laps with one hand resting on their daggers, looking ready to spring into action at a moment's notice. Rauul and Kail were standing watch with Kring, casting sideways looks that betrayed their continuing distrust of him. But the giant was either unaware or unconcerned. He was staring into the forest with other things on his mind; rooted like a misshapen tree. It was obvious the giant was hurting and he didn't believe they had anything to fear from him. He had promised to help Della and Kye believed him. He had met plenty of mean and conniving people and he didn't think Kring was one of them.

He settled back and watched the mist streaming beneath his hammock - a soothing sight despite his initial revulsion. They had told him not to stare into it, but he decided a quick look would be alright. His eyes were barely fixed on it when a deep relaxation swept through him and he sunk pleasantly into the diamond netting of his hammock. Just a bit longer, he thought, as his quick look became a stare. Something was promised by its beguiling glow - something just out of focus. He looked through it until there was nothing in his universe but green mist. It occurred to him then that the pulsing light was changing frequency to match the rise and fall of his chest. Or was it the other way around? His eyes grew heavy, then closed. Soon after he fell asleep, listening to the mist's strange exhalation as it sped beneath him – *hhhhhhhhhh...*

Warning

Della sped through the forest, looking for her rescue party. She was working on the assumption that they followed her from Joebel Pass and was searching in its general direction, weaving a likely path through the trees. She rose from the forest every so often to get her bearings, but soon realised she was drifting north. When she began to suspect another force at work she stopped and focused on a large oak about a hundred yards in the distance. Then she willed herself towards it and relaxed, trying to empty her mind. Half way there she detected a sideways drift that confirmed her suspicion. The shadow didn't want her to find the exorcist and was nudging her off course. She went on, correcting its influence, but the shadow changed tactics – trying to resist her forwards movement, with no care for stealth. But with only a little more focus she pushed through its resistance with ease.

She wondered why this was, given it had taken possession of her twice at school – striking Ismara with her crutch and shoving her to the floor during noon break. And it even made her go out into the storm to search Agelrish for the monster. So why couldn't it take possession of her now and force her back to the tower? She thought about this as she wove through the trees and came up with a plausible theory. The shadow took control of her at school, because she wanted to retaliate; its intentions perfectly aligned with her deepest desires. And when it took her out of the house to search for the monster, it tricked her into thinking it was her idea.

It could facilitate her desires and work against her only with a stealthy infiltration of her mind. In direct opposition it was evidently no match for her.

She was almost to the mountains when she decided to double back and widen her search. But she turned around and froze. The forest to the east was aglow with a green light that was shining up through the canopy.

The mist!

It had been following her to the mountains without her knowledge. She remembered it and feared it; her leg throbbing with the phantom pain of her old poison. And as it advanced towards her she was transported back five hundred years to the night it first appeared, only hours after the earthquake that tore Joebel apart.

She had spent the day helping her uncle treating the injured and freeing others from the rubble of collapsed buildings. That night they fell into an exhausted sleep, only to be woken minutes later by cries of alarm from outside their window. They dressed quickly and went into the street; joining a group of people gathered around a breathless boy. He was babbling about a strange mist he had seen pouring out of the chasm the earthquake created. Behind him a cacophony of panic filled the night, lending credence to his claim.

Someone gasped and they all turned to see a gown of glowing green mist billowing around the street corner; the front edge splitting into tendrils and reaching for them like a grasping hand. The boy bolted away and they followed, mounting the town hall steps with seconds to spare, the mist flowing past them like waters of a flash flood. It lapped against the houses, more like liquid than gas, penetrating cracks in brickwork and sweeping under doors. And in just a few minutes the streets of Joebel were knee deep in mist, its ground floor windows glowing with sickly green light.

The mist had poured out of the Abyss every night since, soaking into the ground at daybreak and poisoning the soil. Every night it reached further west, pushing her people further away from their once great city. The last time she saw it was the night she left the Eastland for good. She was camping with her uncle at the entrance to Joebel Pass and before going to sleep they looked out at the city, watching mist streaming through its streets and lighting up the lower floors of deserted houses. She cried herself to sleep that night. They were about to start a new life in the west, but she was leaving the land of her parents and childhood behind.

This was the first time she had seen the mist in over four hundred years and it was like coming face to face with an old enemy. She watched it roll through the trees, not wanting to be anywhere near it, but knowing she had to be. She resumed her search, but the wax and wane of its pulsing glow constantly stirred the shadows, giving the impression of movement everywhere she looked. On several occasions a fleeting arrangement of shadow suggested a group of people moving through the forest. But when the light bloomed, they were revealed to be nothing more than shrubs; poised in a way that wasn't remotely human. In the end she called off her search, deciding it was time to go back. Griglis was bound to check on her soon and even if she wasn't caught, there was the hardness of the dungeon floor to consider. Her body was transmitting strong feelings of pressure against her shoulder and hip and if she didn't roll off them soon she would end up with terrible sores.

She was starting to angle up when she saw Kring standing in a clearing.

She stopped in front of him, but he rolled his shoulders and yawned, his shining eyes looking at something a hundred yards behind her. In the next pulse of mist, she turned a full circle and counted eight of them: two more standing guard with the giant and another five sleeping in hammocks. She went to the closest and veered away when she saw his wide brimmed hat and throbbing mist stone. She waited to be sure she hadn't piqued his Membrane sensitivity then went to the next hammock where she found Kye; snoring away with his chin on his chest. Less than two feet below him the mist ran west; the occasional tendril reaching up and stroking his back.

She hid in the foliage and whispered his name, knowing he could hear her in Absence, but not knowing how sensitive the exorcist was to her voice. He turned his head, but didn't open his eyes.

'Kye Wake up!' she said, raising her voice as much as she dared.

This time his eyes blinked open and he stiffened.

'It's alright. It's only me.'

She drifted down to hover next to him.

'Della! Are you alright? We found... I saw what they did to you. But it's going to be alright. We're here to rescue you.'

She had planned to give her warning and be straight off. But when she saw the concern and hope in his face she suddenly felt like crying. Oh how she wished it could be as simple as the brightness in his eyes suggested.

'Listen Kye, because I haven't much time. They know you're here and they're sending someone to kill you.'

She jerked back as Kring took two quick steps over and grabbed Kye's arm. 'Who you talking to lad?'

'Don't go,' said Kye, ignoring his question and reaching after her. 'They already know about Absence. I'm sorry Della, but they tricked me into telling.'

She looked at him in shock, but wasn't angry. She could hear the shame in his voice and knew he had done his best to keep his promise. Her secret was out anyway. Her captors knew about Absence and so did Izle. *'It's alright,'* she said. *'I don't think it matters anymore.'*

Kring's sudden movements had alerted the others and in a few seconds the rest of the hammocks were tipped out and the entire company gathered around him.

'The girl? Ormis asked.

Kye nodded.

She drew back, ready to dart away if the exorcist began firing up his draw. But the Membrane continued to rest. 'Ask her where she is and who she's with,' he said. He wasn't seeing her exactly, but he was endowed with some Membrane sensitivity and was looking in her general direction.

She heard the question and answered without Kye needing to relay it.

'I'm in the dungeon of a tower just east of here. There's two torucks and a

man called Griglis. A ghost has been watching you all day and they know you're coming. They're sending someone out to kill you tonight... Make sure you're ready. I have to go now, before they discover me Absent.' And with that she sped off and was over a mile away before most of them realised she was gone.

Inflation

Della raced over the forest, infused with an unsettling mixture of hope and fear. Hope that her warning had been received in time and fear that her Absence was about to be discovered. As she sped towards the tower it appeared from the forest like a chastising finger. *Silly girl,* it seemed to say, *you took a terrible risk and you're going to pay.* And as she drew closer she became ever more convinced that Griglis was boot heeling it down the dungeon steps; seconds away from turning her over and discovering her gone.

She was so focused on reaching the tower, she didn't see the amorphous light that streaked up from the forest. It passed beneath her, warping the Membrane in such a way she rose like a swimmer lifted by a wave. She had barely time to register the sensation before it drew up in her path, taking form like a reflection on water.

It was the spirit Griglis had spoken to from the tower balcony, but this close she was able to appreciate its shocking features. It was mostly head and shoulders and what little torso it had tapered into a long glowing tail. A meagre ration of skin was stretched across the jutting angles of its face and its eyes were black and huge - abandoned mineshafts in which hundreds of wasps were swarming.

'*You escaped!*' it said in a buzzing baritone.

She hung in the air, terrified. Besides her uncle, she had never been this close to another spirit and her soul hummed with its proximity. This close she felt a crazy alternation of attraction and repulsion, as if the two of them were spinning magnets – about to be drawn together or forced apart. It was well known that two spirits could share a haunt no more than two bears could share a cupboard. In close proximity spirits were usually compelled to fight until one consumed the other – a process she had always likened to raindrops merging on a window pane. It was a pretty simile, but one she would never use again.

The spirit regarded her with hungry eyes, but to her surprise it didn't attack. Close as they were it kept its distance, writhing and twisting as if held on an invisible leash. Then it spiralled away and took off in the direction of the tower. Her relief was instant, but fleeting. As the distance between them opened up she realised it was going to report her Absent.

Relief turned to rage and without thought to self-preservation she shot after it. All she could think about was Karkus's shining knife and his promise to cut her again. She was dimly aware of the shadow trying to restrain her, but it only fuelled her anger and she burned through its resistance with molten willpower.

She struck the spirit and they became a twisting ball of light that arced down into the forest, scattering dozens of squawking birds. She clawed and swiped; fingers raking through a buzzing syrup that ran up her arms like pins and needles. Whatever had been holding the spirit back was rendered powerless by their contact and it spiralled around and grabbed her throat - the wasps in its mineshaft eyes swarming with anticipation.

Its mouth yawed open and it bit her shoulder with teeth like icicles. She released a sound that surged up from the tips of her toes and erupted from her mouth like a jet of water from a geyser. It was more than a scream - a sound that could only be summoned by a wounding of the soul. But then through its clamping teeth she felt something worse – a sudden ramping suction which began drawing her in.

She pushed and hammered at its face, twisting and thrashing in a desperate attempt to detach from it. But it held tight and as she drained into it, her resistance began to wane. Her light faded and the spirit's brightened in equal measure; the wasps in its pupils becoming blazing stars. It was devouring her soul and in a matter of seconds she would be nothing more than a supplement to its energy reservoir.

But help came from an unexpected place.

The shadow hadn't wanted this fight, but its fate was inextricably linked to hers and it was forced to act. It rose inside her, detonating in a blast of whispers that streamed through her wound and into the spirit's biting mouth. Its teeth ripped out of her and its head whipped back as if it had tasted something rotten. The whispers streamed into its baggy mouth and it rippled like a hood in a strong wind.

Della was seized by an all consuming hunger and instead of flying away, she shot forwards and bit the spirit's neck. And now it was flowing into *her* – a rush of light and power too wide for her throat. It expanded her in all directions, threatening to burst her at the seams. But she didn't choke or gag. Quite the opposite – she drew it in ever more ravenously, taking great pleasure in the way it filled her.

The spirit didn't resist. It had been incapacitated by the whispers and all it could do was bear witness to its own consumption. Its face was last to go and it stretched away in terror as it funnelled into her - its mineshaft eyes lined with carpets of dead wasps.

When it was gone she hung in the air, bloated with power; pleasure spiralling up her spine and dancing along her limbs. It pooled in her mind, drowning all thought - her uncle, the shadow and her rescue party now of no concern. She laid back and drifted over the mist flooded forest, warm currents blowing through her soul.

Deflation

As time slipped by she began to deflate. The ribbons of pleasure that swaddled her loosened and her bliss bled through the gaps. She cried out as the final exquisite trickles abandoned her, reaching after them as though they were something that could be grasped. An intolerable hollowness opened inside her and the fear and grief she had temporarily banished poured back in. It triggered a desperate and seedy need to devour more spirit energy and she set off in search of another life force to ingest. But after only a few minutes she was struck with the reality of what she was doing and drew up in despair.

She had devoured another soul.

Revulsion twisted her gut and she retched so violently her soul turned inside out. Back in the tower she emptied her stomach onto the floor, bringing a smile to Karkus's face. But the spirit couldn't be expelled like a belly full of spoilt meat. It was part of her now - a vitality dissolved in the very fibre of her soul. Under the cold light of a thousand stars she cried out. It was a harrowing wail that crossed the Membrane and set jungle creatures scurrying for cover.

A few hours ago she thought she was at rock bottom. But there was a lower place waiting for her and she was there now. She had devoured another soul and taken pleasure in its demise. An appalling and unforgivable act. She flew north on an erratic path, pulling at her face and sobbing inconsolably. Her tears were real, but they ran down a face that was many miles away.

Don't cry Little Laurie, she heard her uncle say, using the name he reserved for when she was ill or upset. *Wipe your eyes and look at the stars with me.*

On some level she understood it wasn't really him and just some conjuring of her mind. But she grasped at the delusion like a drowning man reaching for a branch. She looked up at the night sky, seeing his smiling face in the Wagon Wheel Constellation and feeling his arm around her shoulders. He pulled her close and she could smell his sun burnt skin and the earthy redolence of his clothes.

'It's all my fault,' she blubbered. 'If I'd told you about the shadow you'd still be here with me...' She broke off and sobbed again.

Sssshhh. What's done is done and you can't blame yourself. You were scared and the shadow tricked you. You've got to remember that.

'Did you see what I just did? Aren't you ashamed?'

Of you? Never. He smiled and the stars that were his eyes, twinkled with affection. *You were only defending yourself. I wouldn't have it any other way.*

'You used to say the air smelt sweeter when I was Absent,' she sobbed. 'Well what about now?'

Nothing's changed. You're Absent now and the air's as sweet as a breeze over a summer meadow.

She reached for his face, but she might as well have been reaching for the moon. 'Please come back.'

You know it's not possible.

'I can't go on without you.'

But you must.

'What should I do? I'm so empty... So lost.'

We talked about this and you made me a promise, remember?

With her poisoned leg and poor health, she had always assumed she would die before him. Like most people she feared death, but she feared his more. To be left all alone in the world was a prospect she hoped never to face. And a prospect she never wanted to talk about. Such talk was apt to put her into a gloomy mood that could last for days. But despite this her uncle raised the subject periodically, needing to know she would be alright if anything happened to him – that she could not only survive, but lead a happy and fulfilling life without him.

He started one such discussion after a huge storm struck Pebblesham whilst most of the fishing boats were out at sea. By the time the wind blew itself out and the sun broke through the clouds, half the women in town were widows. It was only by a stroke of luck her uncle's boat was on the dry dock for repairs. He ran through the morbid prophecy she had heard many times before; that much of his work was dangerous and if his long years continued, he was bound to fall foul of a serious accident. Simply put, his good luck couldn't last forever. So he made her promise to do two things if he died before her: to live at the hideaway for a full year before making any big decisions. And while she was there; to read the book he had written for such an occasion. She had seen him working on it, but couldn't bear to think about what was written between its leather covers.

Do you remember? he asked again patiently.

She nodded. 'But I'm a prisoner in the tower and I've got this awful shadow inside me.'

But there's still hope. Kye's here with Ormis and they've come to rescue you.

She looked into his face and her tears dried up. 'Do you really think they can help?'

Yes, I do... Now be at peace and listen. He hugged her close and began to whisper one of her favourite rhymes:

Hear the wind soughing through the trees,
Hear the rain pattering on the leaves,

He blew in her face and drummed his fingers on her temple.

Hear the butterflies fluttering through the flowers
Birds and bees going round for hours...

He rubbed his fingertips together, mimicking the sound of tiny wings then pushed one through her hair, making figure of eights on her scalp. She looked over the Eastland in a nostalgic trance, feeling the warmth of a glowing hearth as he pantomimed each line.

...And when you return weary from the lanes
Sit with me and watch the flames.

He finished and she continued to stare into her past, content with the closeness of him.

You'd better go now before they discover you gone, he said after they had drifted many miles together.

'But I don't want to go. If you're not coming, I'll stay here forever.'

But even as she spoke he began to fade.

The hideout Little Laurie...

...Remember your promise.

Then he was gone and it was as if he had never been there. The place where she had imagined his face was now just another patch of cold, star embroidered sky.

But she felt better now.

She looked around and realised she had drifted all the way to the foot of the mountains. She saw the mist rolling up the lower slopes and knew dawn was close. They hadn't discovered her Absent yet, but they would when they tried to wake her up. She turned east and sped towards a brightening horizon, in search of the tower once more.

Spider Costume

    The seven of them waited; pressed up against trees that only minutes ago were supporting their hammocks. They faced outwards from the clearing, a set of eyes covering every possible line of attack. The mist was the only thing that moved and it continued its relentless journey to the mountains, streaming through their legs like luminous broth spilt from a witch's cauldron.
    Kye occupied the same tree as Ormis and his senses were raw with expectation. He had told the others what Della had said, then listened with increasing concern to the discussion that followed. They puzzled over the foolishness of sending an assailant through the mist and Rauul pointed out that even if it survived the trip unscathed, the care it needed to navigate the mist would make it an easy target for their arrows. In the end they all agreed that whatever was coming was unlikely to be a man or a toruck. A number of possibilities were suggested, each of which filled Kye with a different shade of dread. Kail described a creature that had been sighted close to Rockspur - one that hunted solely in the forest canopy, using suckered tentacles to pull itself through the branches. A few months ago it plucked a soldier from a patrol, reaching down from its hiding place and circling his neck with one of its slimy appendages. Yanking him up into the trees like a fish on a line. They got eyes on it as it disappeared in a thunderous thrash of foliage and the last they saw of the soldier was his boots - sticking out of a body that looked like glistening offal. After that Ormis mentioned a flying beast with a hooked beak and sickle like talons that had been known to swoop on patrols and carry soldiers away. And worst of all Kring spoke of huge worms that could sense where you were standing. They would eat away the ground beneath their intended victim until it collapsed, dropping them into its belly. All were creatures that could hunt unimpeded in the mist, but no one could understand how they could have been brought into the service of Izle Rohn.
    Kye gripped the tree whilst his eyes did mileage, jumping around the mist and the shadows of the canopy. It was a cloudless night, but it was hot and his shirt stuck to his sweaty skin. In Agelrish forest the temperature dropped quickly once the sun set. The reverse was true here. He suspected it had something to do with the mist - some heat radiated by its strange

glow. But when he held his hand above its rolling stream he couldn't feel anything.

He looked down at the knife Rauul had given him. With its heavy blade and ornate handle, it was something altogether different to the rusty knife he sometimes used to skin rabbits and sharpen sticks. 'Just in case,' Rauul had said when he handed it to him. But what did he expect him to do? He thought of asking Ormis, but when he looked at the exorcist's face he didn't look receptive to such questions. So he held his tongue and waited, clinging to the tree like a human vine.

When their assailant finally arrived, it came from the north east and was of a nature that hadn't featured in their discussion.

They heard it before they saw it - a series of sprung branches and a rustle of foliage that suggested it had no concern for stealth. Ormis pulled Kye a little way around the bole of the tree and there was a similar reorganisation by the others, until they all faced the same direction.

They got their first look at it in a pulse of mist light; when it was still over a hundred yards away. Kye strained his eyes. At first he thought it was a man. It was the right shape, but covered in a strange skin that seemed to be in constant motion. Before he could discern any further detail Kail loosed an arrow. It cut the air with a whispering swoosh and pierced the figure's chest. There was a strange cracking sound as the arrow passed through it, then a woody *clock* as it became embedded in a tree.

The figure neither swayed nor staggered. It held its pose for several seconds then collapsed as though made of sand.

Kye saw dozens of dark streaks beneath the mist, travelling from the place it collapsed and heading directly towards them. It reminded him of fish schooling in Agelrish Lake. But whatever was beneath the mist couldn't be swimming and as the streaks swept into the clearing, some sixth sense told him they were *scurrying*. He jerked into Ormis with sudden revulsion and grabbed his tunic.

'Be still,' said the exorcist, pushing his away.

Kye turned to follow the streaks through the clearing. They went past Rauul and disappeared behind his tree, but he took no notice; his gaze fixed on the place where the figure had collapsed. He realised then that Rauul hadn't seen it and when he looked around he saw none of them had.

He was about to shout a warning when a figure stepped out from behind Rauul's tree and grabbed him like an assassin. He spun in reflex, striking the heel of his hand into what should have been its face. But his hand disappeared into the shifting structure of its head and the figure stepped forward, opening up and closing around him like a cloak. The others rushed to his aid, recoiling when a pulse of mist light revealed the true nature of their aggressor.

The figure was comprised entirely of spiders; hundreds of thick shiny bodies held together with thousands of interlocking legs - reforming around him like an outer skin. They had already covered his body and were octocreeping over his nose and mouth, shutting his face away. His fingers were wedged in behind those on his cheeks, trying to prize them off. But they clenched in response, holding together like wire mesh.

They tried to free him, eschewing their weapons for fear of causing injury, pulling at the seething mass with bare hands. But they had little success - the spiders clothed him like a suit of chain mail and all they could do was pull him in different directions. Kring was the most effective; crushing spider bodies in his big fists. They imploded with a loud crack, wet innards squirting through his fingers and running off his wrists. Rauul braced himself stoically, grimacing as the spiders closed over his face in an increasingly tighter cowl. From the shifting ensemble's humanoid surface, hundreds of eyes shone with mist light – a collective arachnid consciousness that eyed them with primeval contempt.

Kring got all four hands inside it and began prizing it open, tearing dozens of legs from their bodies. He had just exposed Rauul's chest when the spiders unlocked their little legs all at once and the foul garment collapsed again.

'Stay away from the trees!' shouted Ormis, drawing them together in the centre of the clearing.

'Carrion spiders!' said Kring, jerking his foot when his feet gave false reports of their return. 'I've seen them strip a dead horse in a couple of hours, but I've not seen them do anything like this.' He looked at Rauul. 'Did they bite you?'

'Here and there,' he said, rubbing his neck.

The figure came at them from behind another tree, gliding out of the shadows with outstretched arms - like a mother rushing to embrace her children. There was no movement of its legs but Kye could imagine the groups of spiders it was using for feet, scurrying beneath the mist. It went straight for Kail who took its head off with a horizontal swipe of his sword. It fell to the ground with the sound of a discarded wicker basket and rolled away in the mist. But its body didn't slow. It struck Kail full on with a whispery crackle, making him stagger back into Kring. The spiders that comprised its severed head separated and scurried after it, running up its back and reforming on its shoulders as it enveloped him.

Kring started crushing spiders with his hands again, but as one perished another shifted to fill its place. There seemed to be a never ending supply – a constant stream that came up from a tail that only Kye could see beneath the mist. The others rallied and were getting some combined leverage when the figure fell away again, leaving Kail swatting wildly at his face.

'Over there,' said Kye, pointing into the mist.

'You can see it?' asked Ormis.

He nodded. 'It's right there.'

'Track it with your finger,' he said stepping alongside him.

Kye commanded everyone's attention with his trembling index finger, tracking the clutter of spiders around the clearing. They went between Suula and Kring and when they went behind Dorian his finger stopped moving. The soldier took a step forward, his face betraying what he thought about being the next to wear the spider costume. But a reprimand from Rauul froze him in place. As they swarmed up his back, Ormis ran over and placed his hands either side of his face. When they were covered to the wrists his draw yawned into existence. The spiders clenched and in the relative darkness before the next pulse of mist light Kye saw the ghost of a man wrapped around Dorian's body. It funnelled into the exorcist and the spiders collapsed for the last time. He made ready to track them again, but couldn't see them anymore.

Ormis staggered to the nearest tree and braced against it like a man about to vomit. Yellow light erupted from his face, burnt through the tree and streaked away, lighting up the forest. It separated into streamers as it faded, taking the look of a huge ghost spider, frozen in a pounce.

Shadow and mist light reclaimed the forest and Ormis sagged against the tree. This was the second exorcism Kye had witnessed and it occurred to him they were the only times the exorcist lost his rigidity; the only times he looked vulnerable. No one went to assist him. They kept their distance, just as Kring did the last time. They waited for him to recover and come to them. 'The spiders were bound to the spirit of an exorcist… Izle killed him and used a spirit meld to bind them together.'

They all gawped, unable to comprehend the cruelty of such an abominable act.

J.B. Forsyth

The Old Dog Springs

Kass Riole slept, his mist stone pulsing in a steady rhythm, staining his pillow with a contracting and expanding pool of green light. His sleep was thin. His mind was deeply troubled and even in his dreams it refused to abandon the circumstances surrounding the King's death and the re-emergence of Izle Rohn. It was warm when he turned in and he had decided to leave the balcony shutters open. Gentle currents caressed the drapery and exercised his oil lamps, causing shadows to gyrate on the walls.

His eyes blinked open and the hairs on the back of his neck stood to attention. There was a spirit in his room. Most people would have cowered in response to what he was feeling, but he was a veteran exorcist and he made the transition from sleep to wakefulness with little outward signs. He closed his eyes and rolled onto his back. To an observer he was just an old man shifting pressure around his tired bones. But inside, his mind was narrowing to a fine focus.

He was one of the rare few born with Membrane sensitivity and his years as an exorcist had sharpened and refined it. But even a commoner with blunt senses would have sensed his late night visitor. For the Membrane was bulging so much, it felt as though it was going to tear.

Most professions worked with a medium; carpenters with wood and farmers with soil. Exorcists worked with the Membrane and he focused on it now, reading its tension and pinpointing his visitor's size and location. It was hovering at the foot of his bed and it was easily the most tangible spirit he had ever felt. He wiggled to the edge of his bed and stuck a leg out, as if escaping the warmth of his sheets. In the same way heat diminished with the distance from a fire, so did the power of a draw. He didn't want a spirit this powerful at liberty in Irongate and he wanted to ignite his draw as close to it as possible. He sat up in a groggy pretence of adjusting his sheets and when his foot was planted on the floor he lurched forwards and fired it up.

The bulge in the Membrane puckered and split apart, reshaping itself into a funnel that emptied into his draw. He drew as hard as he could, meaning to surprise the spirit and exorcise it quickly. But it was the mental equivalent of lifting an iron ball with buttered hands and to his dismay it remained fixed in place.

'The old dog springs,' said a voice from the Membrane, *'but he has neither teeth nor claws.'* Invisible fingers slipped around his throat, tightening in a burning vice that severed his draw. It lifted him clear of the bed and he grabbed it with both hands to support his weight. The patch of emptiness at the foot of his bed shimmered like an oven and his eyes bulged as he stared into its boiling nothingness.

'Whatever happened to the great Kass Riole?' it said, turning him in the air as if to examine him. *'To think I once admired you... I came here hoping for a test. But your draw is like that of a child pulling water from a well!'*

Kass kicked the air, the pain in his hip forgotten, his throat pulsing with blocked blood vessels and stars flashing in his eyes.

'Feel my power! I could crush your throat right now and devour your shade as it rises... Leave your sagging flesh on your fine linen for the guards to find.'

The fingers slipped from his neck and he dropped to the bed in a choking heap.

'Perhaps it was unfair to catch you unaware. Perhaps you'd like time to wake up and try again.' There was a deep rumble of laughter. *'Breathe Kass Riole, breathe. This is not your night to die.'*

The air seethed patiently while he rasped for air.

'Who are you?' he croaked when he got his breath under control.

'You know me and you know who sent me.'

'Izle?'

'Very good.'

'What do you want?'

'To humiliate you in front of the citizens you serve and to strip you of your undeserved reputation. After that... Perhaps then I will devour your soul.'

'Where's Izle?'

'Coming... But only after you are gone.'

There was a thudding on his chamber door followed by the voice of a tower guard. 'High Exorcist! Is everything alright?'

Kass tried to shout a warning, but what passed his throat was only a breathy croak. As he raised his breath to try again the spirit drifted away, stretching the Membrane like a tumour moving beneath skin. His bookshelf toppled from the wall, spewing its contents with a thwack and clatter.

The door burst open and one of the tower guards stepped through with a drawn sword. He took two steps, hesitating when he saw him knelt on the bed nursing his throat. Kass waved him away but he crossed to him anyway, either not understanding the gesture or choosing to ignore it.

'Lord Riole, are you alright?'

'Go, quickly... A spirit...'

The guard was yanked from his feet and driven against the vaulted ceiling, his skull imploding with the sound of a crab being smashed on a rock. He fell as a dead weight, thudding to the floor in a spray of blood, his sword clanging to the floor.

'You have languished in the Caliste too long and I am here to slaughter and torment the citizens of Irongate. They will call on you and you will fail them... And when they have lost faith in the Caliste a public spectacle will be contrived to frame your death. Your end is near Kass Riole and it is Izle's pleasure you be forewarned of it.'

The opposite wall came into focus as the seething spirit vacated his room and slipped out through the open balcony. He climbed off the bed and limped to the tower guard, but all hope for him was vanquished when he saw the crushed shell of his skull and the oblique angle of his neck. His name was Arloc and as he stared into the dark pool forming around his head he thought about the wife and three children he left behind. He started for the door to summon help, but when a distant scream pierced the night he limped onto his balcony instead. As he looked across the city a second scream cut the air and a cascade of lights winked on in the market quarter. He hobbled back inside and began to change; a single phrase repeating in his head: *They will call on you and you will fail them.*

Leash

Della returned to find the mist spiralling around the courtyard – pulsing light on the tower walls like an act of worship. She angled into the cobbles but drew up, realising it was a mistake to return to her body the same way she had left it. Rising in its exact location required a great deal of luck and if she came up wrong the fieraks would give her away. So she went through the main entrance and followed the stairs down; descending neck deep into the stone floor at the bottom and inching through the dungeon's iron door. Karkus was still there, fidgeting with his dagger. But to her relief Griglis was nowhere in sight. She shot across the dungeon; her severed ghost head sliding over the floor and repossessing her body with a twitch. Then she rolled over and peeked at Karkus through half open eyes. He was still on the barrel and there was no sign he suspected anything. But it had been a close thing - the fieraks were swarming around her now, flying into her and bouncing off. They had sensed her on the Membrane and if she had been any slower they would have turned her head into a green fireball. She swatted them away and when they lost interest she turned over again, falling to sleep despite everything that had happened.

    She woke gasping in a drench of cold water, wiping wet hair from her face with bound forearms.
    'Wake up little witch. We've got a long day ahead.' Griglis was standing over her with an empty pail. He seemed to have recovered from what had unsettled him and his gaze was steady. 'Something upset your stomach?' he asked, wrinkling his nose in mock disgust at the patch of vomit the fieraks were hovering over. 'Now get up.'
    She rose with an effort, her muscles raw and numb where they had endured the stone floor. And as she straightened, Karkus was suddenly towering over her with his dagger out.
    She screamed and Griglis laughed. 'She thinks you're going to cut her

again,' he said. 'Hold still or he might. He's just cutting the rope. Remember, you've nothing to fear as long as you do exactly as you're told.'

She relaxed as the rope fell away, but Karkus produced another one with a noose at the end. He put it over her head and drew the knot tight to her throat. 'Your leash little witch. It'll go tighter if I need it to.'

He stepped back and the two of them eyed her warily. She shivered under their gaze, her filthy shirt hanging over the sharp ramps of her collar bone and dripping water.

'We walk a dangerous path today,' said Griglis. 'It would be unwise to make a distraction of yourself.' And with that he led them out of the dungeon, Karkus pulling her to the stairway with the first of many tugs on the leash. They left the tower under a clear sky. Dawn was just breaking and the last remnants of night lingered in the west. The other toruck joined them in the courtyard and they filed through the broken gate.

They entered a forest thick with gloom and possessed by a ubiquitous watchfulness that Della remembered well. The Eastland had just gorged on a huge covering of mist and for the moment it was sated – curled up like a giant beast after a stomach stretching feast. But it wouldn't last long. The vegetation was digesting its poison and by the time the sunlight penetrated the high canopy it would be putting it to work, powering the predatory functions of its twisted biology.

Karkus pulled her through the trees like a dog, maintaining enough tension on the leash to keep her on the edge of a run and yanking it whenever she slowed down. Sunlight began its slow invasion of the forest, enriching the colours and bringing the vegetation out of its brooding repose. In one place hundreds of ramsons speckled the forest floor like snowflakes, giving up a garlic redolence as they stomped through. In another place the trees were covered in red moss that shone with an inner light when viewed from the corner of her eye. Birds flapped, warbled and twittered and the breeze soughed gently through sun gilded foliage. It was a trail of wonders, but she was in no mood to appreciate them. Her grief and remorse was a powerful filter and it leeched colour from everything she looked at. To her the forest was nothing but a pencil drawing on damp paper - a drawing apt to tear open with the weight of its own pointlessness.

They had been going the better part of an hour when her interest was piqued by a strange aura, emanating from Karkus. She became increasingly beguiled, forgetting the chaffing rope around her neck and keeping pace with ease. She was reaching out to touch the aura when Karkus stopped to plan a route around some thorny bushes and she ran right into him. His reflexes were sharp and he shot a hand out, grabbing her by the hair and shocking her from her trance. 'Keep your distance little witch,' he said, eyes narrowing as if expecting her to perform some act of witchcraft. But when she continued to stare he set off again, pulling her along behind him.

His aura was no longer visible, but she understood now what she had seen. It was his soul - shining like a tantalising light around the edge of a secret door. But if this was an after effect of consuming the spirit last night, she hoped it would pass. The thought of spending the rest of her days craving the souls of everyone she met appalled her, and she put the notion out of her head by whispering her uncle's rhyme over and over again:

Hear the wind soughing through the trees
Hear the rain pattering on the leaves
Hear the butterflies fluttering through the flowers
Birds and bees going round for hours
And when you return weary from the lanes
Sit with me and watch the flames

Over the next mile the forest changed slowly to jungle. The trees became taller and thicker and the trunks darker. Shade coalesced to gloom and soon only the occasional bar of sunlight reached the ground. The flowers were different in the jungle; alien species she suspected relied more on mist than sunlight. In another time or place the scenery might have delighted her; dozens of new flowers to sniff, press and draw – dozens of new flowers to which she could pin memories of old friends.

But she didn't like these flowers.

They were more alive than was natural. And as they approach some turned on their stems, watching them like lecherous eyes. A patch of wood lilies took particular interest, turning to look with a collective twitch, white petals curling back like straining ears and long stamens flicking out like tongues. They were beautiful and horrifying at the same time and she was glad when Karkus took them on a sharp angle to avoid them.

It was midmorning when they came to a gorge of gargling and spitting water. Bridging the two sides was a huge tree bridge. Its roots were on the near back – a twisted system that looked like the frozen tentacles of a sea monster.

'Rest the witch while me and Argol sort the tree,' said Karkus. 'And make sure you give her some bread and water.' He handed the leash to Griglis and they trudged away to the gorge.

Della slumped down on a rock, exhausted. Her feet were blistered and raw and her entire right leg ached. It was free of poison now, but it was still weaker than her left one. Karkus had made little effort to accommodate her developing limp and she was sure he would have dragged her by the neck had she fallen down.

Griglis took a waterskin from his belt, handed it to her and sat down. She took several gulps; replacing fluid that was now a glistening sweat on her skin and damp patches on her clothes. He followed up with some bread and it wasn't until her mouth started working on it that she realised how hungry she was. When her stomach craved more, she looked at him again. He had another piece ready in his hand, but he was watching her with an unblinking intensity that gave her a start. She took the bread and turned her attention to the torucks. They were positioned among the roots now, rolling the tree along the bank in a series of great heaves, and rocking it back and forth when it became stuck. She knew the torucks were strong, but the tree was enormous and it looked like an impossible feat.

From the corner of her eye she saw Griglis steal a look at the torucks; the way a thief checks a street in preparation for his crime. She met his gaze directly and saw a disturbing fever in his eyes. She got the feeling he was going to pounce, but he didn't. Something was holding him back and when he looked over at the torucks again, she realised it was them. Suddenly, *insanely*, she was glad they were there. Griglis was harbouring some malevolent intention towards her and his only deterrent was the giant who had cut her finger off. She swallowed the last of her bread and looked along their back trail, hoping to see her rescue party emerging from the trees.

'A small company followed you from Irongate,' he said, reading her mind. 'We killed them whilst you slept... I hope you weren't too close.' She sensed a lie, but his words were like a punch to the stomach and he appeared satisfied with what he saw in her face.

Karkus called over soon after and she could tell he didn't like the way they spoke to him. 'Griglis! Get over here now and bring the witch.' The torucks had rolled the tree half a revolution. Karkus was standing beside it and Argol was on top. Griglis rose with a scowl and led her to the gorge where Karkus lifted her onto the tree and climbed up. They waited for Griglis and when they were all gathered on top, Karkus picked Della up beneath a huge arm and hurried across.

They climbed down so quickly on the other side that Della had no time to register the puzzle there. What she had assumed would be a branching tree crown was in fact another root system, just like the one on the near side. And as soon as they disappeared into the jungle, the root systems on both sides began to flex and writhe like two versions of the sea monsters she had imagined. Under a baking sun they worked against the banks until the trunk was reset to its original position. Then they stiffened again - waiting for less wary visitors to chance a crossing.

Absence

You Almost Died Once

Kye leant against the fifth floor balcony, chin resting on folded arms as he looked over an endless forest. Ormis stood rigid and thoughtful beside him with only the tips of his fingers resting against the stone. Sun soaked the balcony but the exorcist seemed to accept it with no more pleasure than he did shade; as if he was unwilling, or perhaps unable to savour its warmth. The parapet was choked with shrivelled vines and wilted flowers, the white petals of which formed a thick litter beneath their feet. Far below, severed vines swayed gently in the breeze.

They arrived at the tower mid-morning and had conducted a full search, finding nothing but barrelled rations and a slurry of vomit Suula attributed to Della. After that, the little tracker had gone east with Rauul to determine Karkus's route while the rest took rations.

Kye was worn out. After Ormis's exorcism the soldiers treated their spider bites and they all stood watch until dawn. It was the longest night of his life and he spent it staring through the forest, trying not to think about what would have happened if Ormis hadn't exorcised the spirit that bound the spiders. Of how they would have swarmed over each of them in turn, biting their exposed skin until they collapsed with a lethal dose of venom. The memory of Rauul's bulging eyes as they crept over his face was something he would never forget. But now, as he rested on the warm coping stones with the sun washing over him, he could have fallen to sleep.

He caught a glimpse of movement in the forest beyond the outer wall and on closer observation saw it was Suula, making her way back to the gate.

'She's the best tracker in the Westland,' said Ormis when he saw him watching her. 'But she's different, don't you think? The way she moves, the way she holds herself, and the way she sniffs the air.' Kye nodded as he followed her around the wall. 'She was assigned to me during my first posting here. We were out tracking a quaggar raiding party one day when she disappeared. We searched for her all day and the next. But in the end we assumed she had fallen foul of the jungle… It's not uncommon to lose trackers and soldiers like that. One minute they're there, the next they're gone – pulled underground or carried away by a silent predator.' His manner was didactic, the delivery of a teacher talking to a pupil he has kept behind.

'Six months later I was called to an incident in the little town of Western Ridge. There were reports of a girl living in the woods who nearly killed a farmer when he happened upon her butchering one of his sheep. We tracked her to a cave littered with bones and stinking of excrement. The girl was there, curled up in a corner, wild eyed and rabid. It was Suula, but she was so taken by the spirit that possessed her, she didn't recognise me.

'I freed her, but it was the most difficult exorcism I've ever performed. It took four hours to draw her possessor and she had to be tied down the whole time. The spirit was that of an Eastland beast – an entity we call a spirit demon. It was woven into her so deep it changed her, imprinting some of its attributes into her physical make up. And even after I pulled it out some of those changes remained. They will likely remain forever, so long did the spirit demon dwell within her. She was a good tracker before, but she's exceptional now. She can smell a drop of blood a hundred yards away and hear a leaf fall from a tree on a quiet day. And don't think I exaggerate. I have witnessed these feats on many occasions. Every three months the Elite Guard call on her to practice escape and evasion, but despite years of refining and developing their skills, no one can evade her a full day. Regardless of terrain and with a half day's head start.'

Kye tried to imagine what kind of creature had possessed her and realised he had glimpsed it in her dark eyes. Not canine or feline exactly, but something in between.

'Now she will track only for me. Perhaps I, in liberating her from the spirit demon have burdened her with a sense of debt. When she is not tracking for me or training the Elite Guard she resides in the asylum. They try to help, but most of the time she simply sits, eating food when it's brought and staring into an invisible reality.' He turned almost fully towards him. 'Spirits are the enemy boy. They are the authors of misery and destruction and it's important you come to understand this.'

Kye was listening thoughtfully and he stiffened at the allusion to Emilie. But Ormis didn't pursue it any further. A silence fell between them and each basked in their own thoughts. When the exorcist spoke again he said something that made no sense to his tired mind.

'You almost died once.'

It took Kye some time to find some meaning in the words and when he did, he was transported to the icy depths of Agelrish Lake where he almost lost his life.

'Am I right?'

He nodded. 'I nearly drowned trying to save Emilie. The man who fished me out told everyone he thought I was dead. Said he couldn't believe it when I started coughing.'

'You passed through the Membrane. But only partially. The man who rescued you must have pulled you back just in time.' Kye was fully alert now, his eyes bright with anticipation. 'And now you have both an affinity and sensitivity to it. It is the reason you sensed the spirit in Galleran Forest; the reason you saw the spiders beneath the mist and the reason you can see the girl in her Absent form.

'Your brush with death has weakened the Membrane around you and you are now a window within it. You can see, hear and feel what others can't – senses that will only strengthen with time. In the end the real world will not be enough for you and the call of the Membrane will become an obsession that could ruin your life... You aren't the only one with such sensitivities. There are others like you. As a group you are more likely to be victims of possession, to become spirit lures or join the ranks of the Caliste. Izle Rohn is one such person and so is the High Exorcist, Lord Riole.'

At first Kye felt the need to deny his new senses. Della had warned him of Ormis's suspicions and alluded to possible consequences. But the truth was, he craved insight into his new nature and as the words rolled off the exorcist's tongue he was rendered spellbound.

'You're lucky I found you when I did - before the people of Agelrish realised what you are. And you are luckier still that you were born in these times. Not too long ago you would have suffered greatly in the dungeons of the Caliste for what you have become.'

There wasn't a line on Kye's face and when the exorcist paused he swallowed a lump in his throat. 'What will happen to me?'

'You'll never see Agelrish again... When this is over you'll be relocated in the north, in a town populated by others like you. It's a good place. It has the look and feel of an ordinary town, but with one crucial difference. It has a resident exorcist whose sole purpose is to keep the town free of Membrane activity. If he does his job and you follow the rules, you'll live a normal life, uncomplicated by your new sensitivities.'

If not for his loveless upbringing he would have considered the prospect of never seeing his family again with watery dread. But he considered it with dispassion now. He thought about his deeper hearing and wondered if he would miss it. The distant voices he sometimes heard were soothing and he often used them to fall to sleep.

'What about Della?' he asked. 'If we ever get her back?'

'We are obliged to take some study of her. Absence is entirely new to us – a talent we must understand. But we have no intention of causing her pain and suffering. Contrary to the prevailing belief, we are no longer the callus torturers of the old days. We will question your friend and when we are satisfied, she'll join you in the north.'

Kye was considering this when Suula appeared behind his right shoulder, so unexpectedly it made him jump. 'They went east at first light and they went in a hurry. The girl's on foot and her gait is erratic. It's likely they're pulling her on a leash.'

Kye didn't like the sound of that. He thought about Della's severed finger again and wondered what else her captors were capable of.

'Tell Rauul to have his men ready,' said Ormis and with that Suula vanished down the stairwell.

Ormis pointed east. 'See where the forest seems to rise,' he said, tracing a north south line with his finger. 'We call it the Step, though there's no actual elevation of land. It's an illusion caused by a sudden increase in the size of the trees. Beyond the Step the forest becomes a jungle that runs all the way to the ancient city of Joebel and the Abyss. East of the Step the land drinks deeper of the mist, magnifying its dangers. If Karkus continues on his present course, we must follow him there. Bear in mind what I've told you and be on your guard more than ever. Now come. We might catch up with your friend today.'

He whirled from the balcony and started down the stairs. Kye took one last look over the Eastland and hurried after him.

Riddle of the Roots

They heard the gorge before they saw it; a faint rushing sound that grew to a watery rumble. A sound that held a welcome promise in the stifling heat of the forest. When at last they emerged from the trees they found Suula waiting on a patch of sun drenched rock. Beside her a huge tree bridge spanned a deep throat of fast flowing water. Its roots were enormous and Kye thought they looked like a nest of giant vipers, frozen in the act of striking. They gathered around her and looked across the gorge, scanning the curtain of jungle on the far side. When a turn of breeze delivered an appalling odour Ormis took a step forward and peered over the edge – expecting to see the rotting carcass of a large animal. But there was only a rage of white water and a scatter of jutting rocks.

'The smell's coming from the tree roots,' said Suula, squatting to examine some marks in the dirt.

But Ormis didn't hear her. His focus remained fixed in the gorge. He was looking upriver to where the water fell over a series of falls and rapids, sending up clouds of vapour that graced the crossing.

Familiar somehow...

'They crossed here not more than two hours ago,' Suula went on, pointing to a spot on the bank. 'They rolled the tree, crossed on its underside then rolled it back again.'

The Elite Guard looked at her with four different expressions of bewilderment.

'Is that possible?' Rauul said sceptically. 'Look at the size of it.'

Kring stepped up to the tree and crouched beneath a thick root. Then he straightened up, face reddening as he lifted it clear of the bank. Rauul smiled and the rest of the soldiers looked at each other in awe. He rocked it, turned it a few degrees then set it down again. 'It's heavy, but I imagine Karkus and Argol made light work of it... Only question is why?'

'It might have been unstable,' Rauul suggested.

'Looks pretty solid to me,' said Kail.

They looked to Suula for insight, but she gave them another puzzle instead. 'I've searched this side and I can't find where it uprooted. And there's no evidence it was dragged here.'

Ormis was only vaguely aware of their voices. He was still looking up river and all he could hear was the roar of the water. Much the same as having a word on the tip of his tongue, he had a memory on the brink of recall. And all at once that strange barrier at the back of his mind started to thin and he saw a woman behind it. She was wearing a sky blue dress; finished with a lace trim that reminded him of clouds.

He spun around and drew his sword, gripped by a sudden certainty that he was about to be thrown into the river. The soldiers were a second behind him, drawing their weapons and whirling to face the cause of his reaction. But they were alone on the bank and except for where the breeze caressed the high branches, the forest was still.

After a couple of minutes Rauul backed up to him. 'What is it?'

Ormis stared through the trees, feeling young and terrified, his sword arm trembling as his body remembered something his mind didn't. The soldiers fanned out and eyed him with concern. They were accustomed to his iron nerve and his current behaviour was well beyond his narrow repertoire.

'It's nothing. I just thought I heard something.'

Rauul gestured to Dorian and Steith, sending them off in the direction his sword was pointing. They went in a low run, searching the tree line and dipping in and out. They returned a short time later and even before Steith shook his head Ormis knew there was nothing there. He had spun to a threat originating inside his head. The black barrier screening off his childhood had sprung a leak and a terrible memory had gushed through.

When they were all gathered again Suula climbed the tree and crawled out on her hands and feet, sniffing at the bark. Half way across she stood and walked back. 'The other end has no crown - just another root system.' They stared across the gorge with their hands raised to shade their eyes, each of them seeing the truth of her words in their own time.

'Well,' said Rauul. 'Whatever's going on, it's a fine place for an ambush.' The soldiers nodded in agreement. It was what they were all thinking. 'We could scout up and down. See if there's another way over.'

Kring grunted and waved at him dismissively. 'There's no time for that,' he said, hauling himself onto the tree and starting over; prompting Kail to notch an arrow and level it at his back. He looked at Rauul who in turn looked at Ormis. Even after his help with the spiders the Elite guard didn't trust him.

Ormis's head was still reeling and he was only distantly aware of what was happening. The strange fear had gone, but there was still an image of a woman in the back of his head. She was wearing a bonnet of the same colour and trim as her dress, but when he focused on her face that strange

fear surged up again...
There was something wrong with her eyes...
'Ormis?... Ormis!'

Rauul's voice jerked him back to reality. He looked up and saw Kring walking over the tree bridge. He also saw Kail, waiting for his signal with a drawn arrow. It didn't take him long to catch up. Kring had taken it upon himself to cross the bridge and the soldiers were suspecting foul play. Wherever he had gone for the last few minutes he was back now and he felt a familiar anger fluttering in his chest. The giant was playing his hand and the only thing that could stop him was an arrow in his back. His mind whirled and in the space of a few seconds he made a decision that nearly went the other way. He shook his head and Kail lowered his bow.

Kring reached the far side and jumped down. He bent to examine the bank in a few places then disappeared into the jungle. Time slipped by and the sun bled heat into the gorge. When he finally emerged from the trees he was a little further to the north. He trudged back to the tree bridge and waved them across.

'Could be a trap,' said Rauul.

Ormis had already considered the possibility and dismissed it. He had been watching Kring closely since he stepped into the road outside Irongate. Evidence of his brother's crimes were hurting him. It was chiselled into his face and hanging on his posture in a way that was difficult to fake. And when the brothers came face to face again, he didn't think it would result in a hurried alliance. Kring had much to say to Karkus and he suspected none of it was favourable. He had been out of sight long enough to have spoken with his brother, but he didn't look fresh from a confrontation. Quite the opposite. He looked relaxed and as he waited for them he even tilted his head to take the sun on his face.

He sent Suula across with a nod of his head. She ran over on tip toes; covering the trunk in a series of leathery kisses. If it *was* a trap Suula would sniff it out. And he spared no thought for her safety. Toruck's didn't use bows and had no chance of catching her. It would be like bulls trying to catch a cat. But the Elite Guard notched arrows anyway, ready to give covering fire if she needed it.

She reached the other side and jumped down through the roots, landing in a puff of dust and sprinting into the jungle. Under a hot sun they waited again. The Elite Guard watched Kring over their sights and he did his best to show indifference, performing several elaborate stretches and even turning his back to their arrows.

When Suula emerged from the shadows and signalled for them to cross the Elite Guard shouldered their bows. They revered Suula's tracking skills and if she said it was safe to cross, it was safe to cross. Ormis gave the order and they climbed the roots and started over the tree bridge in single file. Six unwary visitors - chancing a crossing.

A Burp and a Yawn

Kye inched after Ormis. The tree was wet from rising vapour and the river roared through the gorge fifty feet below him. He was halfway across when the trunk softened beneath his boots.

They all froze.

It split along its length with a leathery creak, separating their feet. A monstrous burp rumbled through the tree and a breath of green fumes billowed out. It was infused with a concentrated dose of what they had smelt in the root system and it was like they had lifted a lid on a bucket of festering meat.

'Everybody off!' cried Rauul.

They rushed for the far bank, but the crack widened. The bark lost all solidity and wrinkled back over wooden stakes – like chapped lips retracting over rotten teeth. And as they ran, their feet were forced wider, transforming their flight into a desperate disjointed waddle.

The crack ratcheted open and Kye's descending foot only just found the side, leaving him fighting for balance with his legs spread wide. He looked down and saw the true nature of the crossing under the full force of the sun. The tree was hollow and its inside lined with razor sharp spines. Filling its belly were the putrefied carcasses of several animals, all ensouped in a curdled green sludge. Huge black cow tongues rose from the slurry, straining to reach him. He had only a few seconds to appreciate the horror before the trunk jerked open and he fell inside.

He splashed down into the vilest filth he had ever known, spewing rank liquid up the sides and disturbing partially digested solids in its deeper sediments. In the corner of his eye he saw the black tongues reaching for him, but his terrified mind refused to focus on them. He leapt up; acute revulsion setting him back on his feet as though he had landed on a hot plate. Fumes rose all around him, green slop slid down his back and dripped off his arms. The stench in the gutter was like a rotten arm reaching into his throat and wiping its putrid fingers on the wall of his stomach. He retched violently in response and the contents of his stomach erupted from him, adding a yellow streak to the green sludge. He grabbed the nearest tooth and pulled himself up, but a veined tongue coiled around his ankle and yanked him back down. It was too much force for the tooth he was standing on and it snapped, dropping him back into the belly of the tree with a thick splash.

With a creak of tortured wood, the tree started to close.

Kye sprang up, kicking at the throbbing tongue that manacled his ankle. He was distantly aware of the others fighting their own battles either side of him: climbing, retching and gasping - slopping around in the foul sludge. The air was like acid now and his eyes watered profusely, blurring his vision. His heart raced and his panicked breaths drew the rank miasma deeper into his lungs. He began to feel detached, light headed and weak. There was something in the fumes; some poison to sedate and paralyse him. A few more lungfuls and he would succumb - ending his days as another putrefying lump in the tree's foul sediments. The trunk continued to close, darkness displacing the sky and reducing it to a narrow strip above him. He saw the snapped tooth floating on the sludge and snatched it up, stabbing repeatedly at the tongue. He inflicted several puncture wounds that sprayed him with black blood and it released him; coiling and thrashing as it disappeared into the sludge.

Ormis appeared in the space between the closing bark and reached down. They clasped arms and the exorcist hauled him up and began pulling him along the top. But they didn't get very far. The roots on the far bank had come to life and were striking at Kring and Suula like the nest of vipers Kye had imagined them to be. The little tracker stood out of reach, but Kring was moving amongst them, huge broadswords flashing in the sun as he lopped them off.

The tree was almost closed when a cry from behind turned Kye around. Steith was sat in the gutter, waist deep in sludge. There was a tongue around his left arm and another around his right leg, fixing him in place. He was twisting desperately as the teeth closed on him, contorting his body to escape their pointed tips. Kye went to help him, but Ormis pulled him back.

'Leave him. It's too late!'

Steith set his jaw stoically, but as a crooked tooth slow punctured his gut, he released a scream that split the air and echoed along the length of the closing trunk. Kye looked away as another tooth skewered his eye and finished him for good. Ormis yanked him on and they made a final dash for the far side.

But the tree wasn't finished with them yet.

It was fully awake now; its first opening nothing more than a yawn. It snapped open again, throwing Ormis into the gorge and dropping Kye back inside. This time he fell onto a rancid carcass, bones snapping beneath him and slurry splashing over his face. He was on his feet in an instant, fearing to be grasped by another tongue. But those closest to him were trapped under the carcass and they communicated their desire for him by making ravenous currents in the sludge. He started to climb as the tree closed again, but snagged his tunic on a tooth. It went beneath his arm as he struggled upwards, tensioning the material and strengthening its hold. Another belch and the stench thickened. But this time, it wasn't too bad. This time there was a promise in the fumes - the same promise he had heard in the mist last night: that everything would be alright if he just relaxed and gave in. Two more deep breaths and it would have been over, but the tooth ripped through his shirt and he pulled free in time. He flopped over the top row of teeth, gasping at the air as black dots speckled his vision.

'Come on Kye!' Kring shouted. 'Get off before it opens again.'

He turned to see the giant on the far bank, gesturing wildly with all four arms. The roots were all gone now - hacked off and lying inanimate at his feet. Head spinning, he crawled towards him, but the tree sprung open for a third time and flung him into the gorge.

He struck the water on his back, plunging through its depths to make firm contact with the riverbed. The cold was a swift antidote to the fumes and he broke the surface with a delicious blast of clarity. The current took him around a bend and when it slowed he lengthened his stroke, searching for somewhere to climb out. But the jungle hung over the river on both sides; knitted together so tight he couldn't see the bank. He passed under a huge bird of prey perched on a low branch. It eyed him coldly and when it lifted a wing to preen its feathers he thought it was going to swoop on him. But it just stared, taking to the air when it was spooked by a sudden thrashing of foliage.

The river widened and he started to panic, but then he saw Ormis lying on his front in a muddy inlet and swam over; pulling himself out as he twisted onto his back.

'The others?' asked the exorcist between hacking coughs; his blood streaked face a testament to his rougher fall.

'I don't know... I didn't see.'

They sat for a time, purging their chests and allowing their breath to settle. There was a rank residue on the lining of Kye's throat that tasted of putrefied meat and he retched several times before swilling his mouth with river water and spitting it out. When he was done he saw that Ormis was staring upriver again. He was in another trance and Kye didn't like it one bit. He didn't know what it meant, but as he looked into the deep darkness of the jungle he wished the others were there.

It was some time before the exorcist came back to himself with a blink. 'We'll follow the river back to Suula and Kring. They're probably looking for us and we weren't carried too far.'

They clasped arms and climbed to firmer ground. But after a few paces along the bank Ormis staggered and fell flat on his face. Kye assumed it was an after effect of the fumes, but when he bent to offer help, something pierced his thigh. He had just enough time to marvel at the feathered dart sticking out of his leg before he collapsed to the ground alongside him.

Puppetry

Kass Riole stood at the front of the crowd watching a wall of flames devouring a row of houses. Behind him a long chain of people were passing buckets of water to soak a shop that was currently untouched by the fire. Hayhas appeared from a smoke screened side street, coughing harshly as his streaming eyes searched the crowd. Kass waved him over.

'How are we doing?' he asked, his voice scraping out of his bruised throat.

'Lord Beredrim reckons it's under control,' Hayhas replied, turning away to deal with a triplet of barking coughs. 'They've pulled down the fletcher's workshop and some of the stalls either side of Stonegrass Lane to act as a firebreak... But we've lost everything north of Farrowgate to the city wall.'

'And what of casualties?'

'Many. At least twenty fatalities.' He moved closer, speaking quietly so he wouldn't be overheard. 'I spoke to a girl who lives on Market Row where the fire started. She was woken by a scream and saw a ghost smashing up some shops...' Another hacking cough. 'It must've toppled a lamp or something.'

'Has anyone else seen it?'

'No. But Altho and Djin are still looking.'

'You gave them my instructions?'

He nodded. 'To reveal but not draw it.'

Kass had called together his resident exorcists soon after the spirit left his bedchamber. He told them everything, not withholding his seeming impotence against it. His plan was to perform a collective exorcism: one man out front and the others gathered behind – their collective draw aligning to form an irresistible force that would funnel the spirit into him. This done they would surround him, using a variation of the purge to strengthen his compression. And when ready, the front man would signal for them to step away so he could complete the exorcism. It was a proven method and one of his favourite teaching tools. But he doubted it would work in this case. Izle Rohn had sent this spirit and would be expecting them to attempt the technique. So either he was confident a collective exorcism wouldn't work, or he had made preparations against it. But he would try anyway. He couldn't think of another solution and he wouldn't stand idle whilst Irongate was systematically destroyed.

Another man ran from the side street in a swirl of smoke.

'Here's Altho now,' said Kass, hoping for some good news but fearing more bad.

As the young exorcist ran towards them he was struck by an invisible force that bent him into a C shape and sent him sprawling across the cobbles. It was a spectacle with only one possible cause and they raced to his aid; Hayhas in a full bloodied run and Kass falling behind in a rolling hobble.

Altho jerked up in single movement and his arms snapped out to the sides, giving him the look of a scarecrow. It was a sight that wronged nature and the crowd recoiled from him.

'Stay back!' Kass shouted. 'Do not touch him!'

His command was unnecessary as the crowd was already backing way. Some were half turned and ready to run, but they remained in place for now; transfixed by morbid curiosity. Altho's eyes opened and flicked between Kass and Hayhas - a movement that was disconnected from expression, giving him the look of a frightened puppet.

To be invested in the order all exorcists had to demonstrate they could fight free of a possession. It was a dangerous test and one nearly everyone failed on their first attempt. Kass had taken dozens of exorcists through the test and was familiar with the early signs of break out. The pupil would usually regain some function that reflected his inner struggle – a twitch, a punch to the air or a string of babbled words. But Kass was seeing no such thing now. The spirit had complete control of Altho and had given him use of his eyes only to project his fear. But at least it was contained and all they needed to do to initiate their collective exorcism was get their hands on the young exorcist before the spirit discarded him.

Altho whipped his dagger out and lifted his arm to the position of a fiddler; elbow up high and the blade ready to play the tendons of his neck. His eyes widened and someone in the crowd screamed. His other arm suddenly broke free of its scarecrow pose and started pulling the knife away. But the blade jerked back and the cycle repeated several times. Finally, his arm snapped down by his side and the blade was left to rest among a dozen nicks that were weeping crimson tears onto his shirt. But again, this was no sign of an inner struggle that had temporarily gone Altho's way. It was showmanship of the most appalling order; the spirit giving him use of his arm only to make a spectacle of him.

Altho took a step backwards and began staggering away - the clomping of his boots on the sooty cobbles the only sound above the roar of the inferno. The exorcists started after him but drew up sharp when the spirit turned the knife, placing the point to Altho's throat. The crowd around him was swelling, people drifting in from nearby streets and pushing forward to see what was going on.

The young exorcist stopped where the heat grew strong. Behind him the fire was devouring a butcher's shop; tendrils of smoke swirling in the breeze and reaching out for him like arms. Altho spoke, but his vocal cords were being operated by his possessor and his voice was an abomination of the air. 'SAVE ME KASS RIOLE, HIGH EXORCIST OF THE CALISTE... SA-'

His voice tore off as something gave in his throat.

Kass stared in a paralysis of impotence. Altho was only nineteen and full of enthusiasm – a charming young man who still lived with his mother and blushed in the presence of girls. The eyes of the city were all around him now, willing him to act. But what could he do? He could almost hear the spirit mocking him: *They will call on you and you will fail them.*

He jumped when a city guard spoke at his side. 'Lord Riole. May we be of assistance?' There were three guards altogether, blackened and worn from firefighting. The one who spoke had a flat nose and the markings of rank on his shoulder.

'He's possessed sergeant. We need to get hands on him, but his possessor has threatened to kill him if we try.' The guard nodded grimly. Kass saw the ash bow slung over his shoulder and it gave him an idea. 'Our only chance is to get rid of that knife. How good are you with that bow?'

'Best in the garrison,' he said, puffing up.

'Do you think you could shoot the knife from his hand?'

He looked at Altho and shook his head. 'It's too close to his throat. But I could take his arm. He'll let go of it then, no matter what's inside him.'

'Okay. Do it now, but leave these two with me. His possessor can only see what he sees, so it's best if you move back through the crowd and come at him from the side. As soon as you get the shot, take it. We'll be ready.' When the sergeant left he turned to the remaining guards. 'As soon as the arrow strikes we'll rush him. Take care of the knife and hold him down while we draw the spirit.'

But as they waited for the sergeant to get in position, the spirit began walking Altho towards the flames again. Kass stood on tip toes searching desperately for his bowman, no longer caring if he gave him away. He spotted him off to the right. His arrow was levelled, but now Altho was moving he was struggling to get a shot. But then he released his bowstring and the arrow flew across the street in a swirl of smoke, skewering Altho's forearm. His hand opened in a reflex the spirit couldn't prevent and the knife clattered to the ground.

Kass and Hayhas raced over, but they were too late.

The spirit walked him into an invisible wall of heat and they were soon forced back with their hands raised to their faces. Altho began to scream. Perhaps the spirit thought it would make a better show if the young exorcist was permitted to communicate his pain through his ruined throat. It was the worst sound Kass had ever heard. And if that wasn't enough, the spirit gave him the use of his arms. They reached forward to escape as his face blistered and his hair caught alight. All the while his legs continued to walk him into the inferno.

'Again sergeant!' Kass cried. 'End his pain!'

Two arrows flew in quick succession, their flights catching fire the moment they pierced Altho's neck and chest. His screams ceased and his arms dropped limply to his side. But he remained on his feet – his whole body blistering as he was transformed into a charred statue. It wasn't until the fire died down that they were able to take him away. But by then, most of the city had been by to see him.

From a window of the Black Witch Tavern, Raphe looked out to where the smoke lifted into the morning sky. He felt the spirit gathering behind him and turned to a patch of shimmering air.

'Is it done?'

'Yes. I killed one of his men while hundreds watched.'

'Good. But no more destruction. What we want now is fear and testimonies.'

A triple knock sounded on the door.

'Go now. The city will provide food and shelter for those made homeless by the fire. Find out where they're based and report back.'

The spirit left and he opened the door to find a plump barmaid holding a tray of steaming food. She was flushed and a thin layer of perspiration covered her face and cleavage.

'Sorry it took so long sir,' she said, flustered. 'Only the cook lives in the market quarter and what with the fire an' all...' She started in, but he blocked her way.

'Don't worry I'll take that.'

'Oh... Alright. If you're sure,' she said, handing him the tray. She frowned as she got her first proper look at his face. 'Are you feeling alright sir? You don't look very well.'

'I'm fine, really.'

'Some's died they say. And many houses gone to cinders... Some'r saying it was a ghost got it all started, tearing up houses an' all.'

'Well let's hope the exorcists can put a quick end to it.'

'Terrible business though,' she said, shaking her head.

'And on the same day as such sad news of the King.'

'The King?' she asked, puzzled.

'You don't know?' He looked past her into the corridor as if fearing to be overheard. 'It might not be common knowledge yet,' he went on in a whisper. 'But I had a walk earlier and couldn't help overhearing two of the city guards…They're saying the King is dead.'

Her eyes widened.

'Dead? Surely not. It can't be true, can it?' She looked at first incredulous, then alarmed.

'Look. I can't be certain. It was just two guards running their mouths. But if you hear talk of it, be sure to let me know?'

'I will.' she said, studying his face again. 'Well if that's all.'

'Thank you,' he said and shut the door in her face.

The maid started down the stairs in a daze. But she was quick to recover and by the time she reached the ground floor she was busting to spread the news. She had one fleeting thought before she reached the first of many receptive ears: despite his denial the guest in room two had looked more than ill - he looked green.

Knuckle Spikes

The sun was low in the west when Argol brought them to a halt by raising a tattooed arm. They were deep in jungle now; the torucks dwarfed by hulking trees that knitted together in a high canopy. Karkus pulled Della close and used a hand on her neck to walk her to where Argol was standing. Griglis joined them and they stood in a tight knot looking into the jungle.

'What do you see?' Karkus asked.

'A dogape,' said Argol. 'Up there in that tree.'

Della saw it then; a thing that moved along one of the high branches on all fours, thickly muscled and covered with black fur. It lumbered to the edge of the branch and sprung away, disappearing in a thrash of foliage. They remained in position for some time, watching and listening until Karkus saw fit to continue. But only a few minutes later they saw another one, or perhaps the same one, edging along a low branch only fifty yards away. This time it spotted them and froze. In the shade of the canopy it was little more than a silhouette, its green eyes shining like poisonous grapes. For a while it simply observed them. Then it tipped its head back, shredded the air with a series of high pitched whines then slunk away. Before the foliage settled they heard the same sound repeated back from several directions.

'Bollocks,' said Karkus, his face darkening as he yanked Della onwards. 'It's alerted the pack... We'll make a stand at that tree.' They bolted towards the huge tree trunk and Karkus pressed Della into a nook between two chest high roots. He gave her leash to Griglis and grabbed his shirt. 'Your life before hers,' he said and forced him down beside her, a hundred threats gathering in his eyes.

'Of course,' Griglis said, wrapping the leash around his hand and wedging himself into the space next to her. He was so close she could smell his panting breath. And it was the smell of decay – the smell of lungs poisoned by mist. The torucks planted their feet in front of them. They took knuckle spikes from their belts and fitted them to all four hands before drawing their blades: swords above and daggers below - eight fine points and sixteen keen edges held out to the jungle.

They listened to the dogapes thrashing through the foliage and glimpsed them darting through the shadows. They organised behind two huge trees and came at them as a tight pack; shoulders pumping as they beat the ground with clawed fists. Della watched them approach from between the toruck's thick calves, but it wasn't until they drew up in a lace of weak sunlight that she fully appreciated their features.

They were apes, but with the jaws and snouts of dogs. Sleek black pelt clothed their muscular bodies, running to a deep bronze where it tufted around their necks and stubby tails. Their faces were crossed with prominent blood vessels and covered with a bat wing skin, stretched so tight it screamed. And this close their eyes were distinctly reptilian – split grapes with a rich midnight filling.

They rose onto hind legs, looking more like dogs than apes as they whined excitedly and sniffed the air. The sound spiralled and narrowed to a pitch that pierced Della's ears like a pencil and ordered every hair on her neck to stand up. She clamped her hands to her head and shrunk further into the nook. It was a weaponised sound – an aural assault that set every bird within a mile radius to the wing. But the torucks withstood it with a stoical grimace; confidence and resolve carved into the jut of their chins.

All at once the sound ceased, replaced by a strange vacuum that made Della nod in the direction of the pack. If she had been standing, she would have fallen flat on her face. And as mighty as the torucks were, they were not immune. As her head nodded they jerked a stabilising foot out; weapons dipping in the air.

It was what the pack were waiting for and they rushed forward, springing up in a solid wave of snapping mouths and swiping claws. The giants swung their swords and stabbed with daggers. The swords cut into the pack, slicing several dogapes in half. But once the power of their strokes was spent, the blades were lost in the surge of bodies; stuck like axes driven too far into wood. The torucks had expected this and before the beasts could bite at their extended arms they relinquished their blades to the black tide and began pounding the front ranks with knuckle spikes. As the collective weight of dogapes drove forward they were forced against the tree, squashing Griglis on top of Della and sealing them in a cocoon of raging flesh and fur. The toruck's arms worked like pistons - spikes and daggers, spikes and daggers. Each spike was two inches long and the row of four on each fist did as much damage as their daggers, especially when followed with a twist of the wrist that opened huge holes in the beasts. One bit at Karkus's neck but he butted it away, breaking its skull with a crack that could be heard over the howls and snarls of its brethren. When another got close to Argol's face he twisted away and bit its ear off, spitting it back in its face and ending it with a dagger between the ribs.

Della was cowering in the nook when a yank on her hair lifted her face. She screamed, thinking one of the dogapes had got through; but it was Griglis and his eyes were blazing with anticipation. Whatever desire had been in his mind when they stopped at the gorge was back again and she could see he was about to act on it. He clamped her in a scour grip and thudded her head against the tree. And before the pain could register, his mind was plunging through hers. Ormis's scour had been unpleasant, but this was far worse. What she was feeling now was nothing less than a violent rape of her mind and she screamed and squirmed under his grip, trying desperately to push him away. But she was wedged in a nook with little wriggle room and his hand remained fastened to her face.

The shadow had been waiting for Griglis to attempt this very thing and when his scour reached the place where it was hiding and began to draw, it didn't resist. It rose like a wind, shifting Della into Absence and funnelling her into him. As her soulless body slumped Griglis released her with a cry of surprise. He had tried to suck a stain from a piece of cloth and had swallowed the cloth instead.

The shadow expanded Della into Griglis and all at once the whole ensemble of his sensation was upon her: the position of his limbs, the dampness of his shirt and even the throb of his arthritic knee. But more than this, she felt his dawning horror as he realised what was happening. The violent scour had rendered her dizzy and disorientated and she could only watch through his eyes as the shadow turned him to look through Argol's legs. At least a dozen dogapes lay dead and dying at the torucks feet, but one of them was working its way forward beneath the melee; split grape eyes glowing above a canine snarl. The shadow forced Griglis onto his belly and crawled him through Argol's legs to meet it. Della felt some resistance, but it wasn't hers. She was still in a paralysis of shock. It was Griglis; trying to take back control of his body. But he was too late. His defences were flooded and his efforts were quashed.

The shadow insulated Della to his sensation like a second skin. What did get through was distant and dulled, but it still felt like she was crawling towards the dogape and not him. As they came together it bit his neck and pulled him back through the pack in a series of jerks. She felt its teeth and those of the others that set about him. And although the sensation was dulled, the pain was immense and she screamed with each new perforation of his flesh – a sound that was two parts him and one part her. She felt claws separating his ribs and teeth behind the muscles of his thigh, scrapping over bone. There was a searing pain in his shoulder then a terrible yanking, over and over again, until his arm came off. Then they were all over him. One moment it was like falling through a barrel of broken glass, the next like being pulled apart by fish hooks. Then all at once she felt nothing and knew he was dead.

Triumphant howls split the air and the assault on the torucks fizzled out as those on the front line rushed to join the feeding frenzy. Most were too late, unable to get anywhere near the spot where Griglis's rapidly disintegrating corpse was being fought over. When they realised this they turned back to the torucks, reassessing them with narrow eyes. They watched for trembling hands and swaying bodies. And they watched the blood flowing from their wounds and how easily they drew breath. But mostly they watched their eyes and sniffed the air, hoping for signs of fear and panic.

But nothing in their assessment gave them any encouragement.

The four armed giants were glaring at them over a heap of dead and twitching bodies, feet set firm and huge frames braced for another attack. Both were marred with several deep wounds, but most of the blood dripping off them wasn't theirs. They watched with interest as the giants moved their arms through a succession of poses that lined up strange markings on their blood slicked skin. They had no idea what it meant, but their primitive intelligence was able to discern that the giants were not only ready for another fight; they were inviting one. After several minutes of silent study two of them crawled forward on their bellies. But they didn't attack. They sunk their teeth into one of their fallen instead, dragging it to a clot of thick ferns where they were helped by others to cannibalise it.

Della hung in Absence in the place where Griglis was being taken apart, still reeling from his scour and the pain of his death. And as the feeding frenzy continued she became aware of the shadow's voyeuristic satisfaction. It was only then that her fragmented mind coalesced and she was able to take charge of herself once more. She pushed the shadow back down inside her and flew back to her body, animating it with a twitch and a gasp. Then as the torucks faced off with the pack she took her chance. She removed her leash, climbed out of the nook and edged around the tree with her back against it. And when she got to the other side she sprinted into the gloom as quick as her wobbly legs could carry her.

Karkus saw her escape out of the corner of his eye, but he remained in place; not even turning to see her go. Drawing attention to the witch would be a big mistake. If the pack got wind of her flight she would be in pieces in a matter of seconds. All he could do now was face off with the dogapes until they moved on and hope he could catch her before the mist arrived. He ground his teeth at her audacity and felt the urge to step forward and stamp the life out of a twitching dogape – the one he head-butted. But he stayed rooted, knowing such a move was likely to provoke another assault. Not that he minded them coming again. He was pumped with a boiling aggression and there was one dogape in particular he wanted to vent on. It had bitten him on the shoulder and was looking at him now with a glint of satisfaction in its green eyes. A look he wanted to wipe off its stupid face with his knuckle spikes. But another round with the beasts would waste valuable time and put the witch out of reach for the night.

When the rightful recipient of his knuckle spikes looked away he took time to examine his wounds. Toruck blood clotted well and he was pleased to see most of them had stopped bleeding already. He snatched a sideways look at Argol and saw that his countryman had fared even better. The two of them had come out far worse from some of their rougher courtship wrestles. He grinned and rolled his shoulders. When the pack moved on they would hunt the witch and when they caught up he would take her ears *and* her nose.

J.B. Forsyth

Leecher

Della was panting hard with her hands braced on her knees. A deep stitch was woven into her side and her legs were howling with unaccustomed use. She looked back for signs of pursuit; but the gloom was empty and quiet. As her breathing slowed she felt the shadow boiling inside her. Karkus was taking her to Izle where it could be reunited with its greater consciousness, and it was furious with her for running away. She had felt its dismay the moment she bolted from the tree, but it made no effort to stop her. Unexpected as this was, she soon understood why. Before she took a dozen steps it rose into her eyes; superimposing images over her view of the jungle and revealing in shocking detail what the vegetation could do to her. There were spitting ferns and poison spike vines, puddles of mist water and blistering deadwood - dangers she hadn't seen or understood. And whenever she put a foot wrong, its fear rose in warning - a mental nudge that steered her to safer ground. More evidence it wanted her alive; that their fates were inseparable.

Now as she recovered in a place of relative safety she felt the full heat of the shadow's anger and hers flashed in response. *Izle!* she said, addressing it with an internal voice. It was the first time she had spoken to it that way and it came to attention like the tightening of clothes worn on the inside.

I know who you are and what you want... You want to be whole again... But you're a bad man and I swear on my uncle's memory I'll do everything I can to stop you. Do you hear me? It's your fault my uncle is dead and I hate you! She was shouting inside her head now and her hands were trembling. But her flash of temper was just that, and once the words were out she realised it was a mistake to provoke it. The shadow boiled and she braced for a punitive response; expecting to be forced to bash her head on a rock or poke her eye out with a stick. But after a long stand-off it simmered down and faded away.

The shadow was infuriated by the girl's oath and wanted to teach her a lesson. She was expecting to get her eye poked out and it didn't want to disappoint her. But the girl would fight and it couldn't win. It had entered her body weak and disorientated; an enfeebled fragment of a greater consciousness. After gathering its faculties, it resolved to reunite with its better part and began influencing her to that end. It scored some minor victories, but the girl's mind was improbably strong and it was soon forced to accept it was the lesser part of their unfortunate union. The way she suppressed and partitioned her thoughts in preparation for Absence was magnificent; a skill strikingly similar to the discipline of containment. It feared that if it was subjected to a sustained application of her talents, it would take hours to resurface; a death sentence for both of them given the dangers all around. So as much as it wanted to teach her a lesson, it resisted the urge. It had to pick its fights and this wasn't one of them. For all the girl's power she lacked the discipline of vigilance and it would continue to exploit this – rising to positions of influence while she was sleeping or overwhelmed with emotion.

Della looked around, suddenly aware of how vulnerable she had been in the last few minutes. The jungle was still quiet, but it was poised; like a trap waiting to be sprung. With her oath to the shadow fresh in her mind she knew she had to find her rescue party.

Her best chance was to seek them in Absence, but she needed to find somewhere safe to leave her body first. She crossed to the nearest tree, hoping to find a suitable hiding place in its low branches. But one of the thick vines that spiralled around its trunk began to creak, turning its flowers towards her. In a matter of seconds dozens of black eyes were staring out from within hoods of orange petals. And dozens more appeared, craning their stems around from the other side of the tree. *Come sit with us little girl,* their collective consciousness seemed to say. *Sit with us and rest for a while.* But they looked like muggers and Della needed no help from the shadow to decline their invitation. She backed away, imagining the vine throttling her - its orange flowers crowding her face as it tightened on her neck.

She spotted another tree with low branches and was half way there when a familiar glow heralded a fresh tide of mist. She planted her feet as it approached, fighting the urge to run. The faces on its leading edge contorted in glee as they broke around her, like school bullies happening on their favourite prey. She thought Ismara would look at home amongst them; her cruel eyes glittering like emeralds and her hooked nose riding the flow like a shark's fin. The mist streamed around her legs, passing through her untreated britches. It dissolved into her skin and her left leg began to throb as it was reunited with its old poison. She studied the mist between herself and the tree, looking for signs of leeching. There weren't any, but the lessons of the Wilderness were hard to forget and she crossed the distance with caution, testing the ground before shifting her weight.

The tree grew at a slight angle and was covered with a deeply fissured bark that was easy to grip. She climbed out of the mist, pulling up tendrils that coiled around her legs, releasing her only when she pulled herself onto the first branch. There was a good hiding place further around the tree and a little higher up - a thick bough with two large knots between which she could wedge her body. She climbed onto it and settled in, relieved to be safe from Karkus for a while. Even if he was foolish enough to walk the mist her tracks would be hidden from him until dawn.

She looked up through the branches and was pleased to see there was hardly any foliage screening her view of the darkening sky. The stars would soon be out and at some point the Wagon Wheel Constellation would pass over. But then she frowned, realising the foliage belonged to a network of vines. The tree itself had no leaves of its own and looked dead.

She sat up, seeing it was one of several leafless trees that ringed a small clearing. Her interest piqued, she crawled along the branch to get a better look. The trees were leaning over a huge spiral of funnelling mist, holding loops of vines up as if in homage to it. She stared into the vast swirl in fearful fascination, trying to see what was leeching it. But all she saw was a circular patch of bare earth. There had to be something down there though; and not knowing what it was made her nervous. It was unwise to rest so close to such a powerful leecher and she was stuck there until dawn.

She crawled back, settled into the knot and started her preparations for Absence. She separated from her body the very instant she began thinking about it – just like she had done at the tower. The cause of such rapid transitions was still beyond her, but she was beginning to suspect it had something to do with the shadow - some consequence of having another consciousness floating inside her.

She soared through the dead branches and saw the tower poking through the forest canopy a few miles to the west. If Kye and Ormis survived last night, they would have tracked her there. She looked around, hoping to find a landmark to lead her back and realising the dead trees were perfect – a huge leafless circle in a sea of green. She sped away, but in her haste failed to notice the gaping hole at the top of the tree. If she had, she might have paused to consider whether the hollowness of the tree was in any way connected to the powerful leecher it seemed to worship.

Wormeye

Kye twisted his hands against his bindings for the third time, but the rope held and his chaffed wrists began to sting. He gave up, slumping against the thick pole he was tied to and looking over at Ormis. They were in a mud hut without windows and its only entrance was a screen of hanging leaves that admitted little light. He heard voices outside; speaking in an ugly language he didn't recognise, but spoken in a tone he did: excitement. And he could hear distant voices beyond them, blended together in an ominous chant.

Ormis was slumped against another support, his head hanging and his legs spread in a wide V. Wet hair obscured his face and his left hand rested in a puddle of river water; his mist stone feeding it regular pulses of sickly green light. His right shirt sleeve was ripped and in the dim light Kye could see a series of scars that ran from his wrist to his elbow. He stared at them for some time before deciding they were old burns; similar to those his mother got from the stove. He wiggled forward and kicked him. The exorcist twitched, but his eyes remained closed and his head continued to hang. He opened his mouth to call his name, but thought better of it. A noise might bring their captors running and he was in no rush to meet them. He shifted back against his support instead, deciding to let the exorcist wake up in his own time.

He tipped his head back to rest against the support and was surprised to see two ghosts watching him from the roof. He flinched down, jarring his neck and setting off a glassy headache.

'Who are you?' he asked when they continued to stare.

'I'm Najo,' said the boy on the left, 'and this is my sister Allie. What's your name?'

'Kye.'

'And you're Twum,' said Allie.

'Twum?'

'It means you've got the sight,' said Najo. 'That you can see us... Is *your friend a soul burner? His ring marks him as one.'*

Kye had never heard an exorcist being referred to as a soul burner before, but after witnessing two of Ormis's exorcisms he thought it was a fitting description. 'Yes, I guess he is.'

'Why do you keep his company? Are you learning his craft?'

'No,' he replied, appalled by the idea. 'We're looking for a girl.'

'We haven't seen a girl in the jungle for a long time,' said Allie.

'She's been kidnapped by torucks and they're taking her to a man called Izle.'

The little ghosts exchanged a knowing look.

'If you mean the soul burner that lives under old Joebel,' said Najo, *'then she's lost to you. For he's involved in things much worse than soul burning. He tortures and torments those he takes into the glass tunnels and we can feel their suffering from many miles away.'*

Kye thought about the spider creature, wondering what else Izle Rohn had created. 'What do you want with us?'

The ghosts giggled. 'We *didn't bring you here,'* said Najo. *'We saw them carrying you from the river and came for a closer look... It's been a long time since we saw anyone your age.'*

'Who are they?'

'Quaggar,' said Najo.

'Cannibals,' said Allie. *'But they only eat their own... You'll be given to Fyool.'*

'Fyool?' He recognised the name, as it was part of the ugly mantra they were still chanting outside.

Ormis moaned and began to stir.

'The soul burner's waking!' Najo whispered, retreating into the roof.

'Wait... Can't you help us?'

But they were already gone.

Ormis opened his eyes and flicked wet hair from his face. 'You alright boy?'

'My head hurts.'

'That'll be the poison from their darts.' He looked over at the hanging leaves and started tugging on his bindings. 'Who were you talking to just now?'

'Ghosts.'

The exorcist studied him. 'How many?'

'Two. A boy and a girl.'

'And they were talking to you? They weren't contesting their haunt?' Kye gave him a puzzled look. 'They didn't fight?'

'No.'

Ormis looked at the roof incredulously. 'Then there must be some black art keeping them apart. Spirits are solitary entities and whenever they cross paths, one will consume the other.' He paused, his expression as black and brittle as charcoal. 'You didn't call them did you?'

'No,' he said with a hint of irritation. He was getting fed up with the exorcist's continuing mistrust of him. 'They were in the roof when I woke up.'

'I expect Izle Rohn sent them.'

'They said they were afraid of him.'

'What else did they say?'

'They saw the quaggar carrying us here from the river and wanted a better look. They said we're to be given to Fyool... Who's Fyool?'

Ormis shrugged and was about to say something when the leaves parted and three chestnut skinned quaggar pushed through. They were squat, with thick sinewy arms and barrel chests. Their bodies were covered with prominent veins that pulsed with mist light, giving the impression they were being struck by green lightning every few seconds. Instead of hair they had grass; mostly long and green with streaks of lacklustre yellow that looked in need of a good watering. The stink of their unwashed bodies was like a physical presence and it raged around the hut.

The one in the middle was the ugliest of the three; snaggletoothed with a missing eye. He motioned for them to stand and after they struggled up their posts he looked them over in turn. Up close Kye saw a worm in his empty eye socket. And as he appraised them with his good eye it flexed and twisted - flicking its tail out and running it along his scarred forehead. But he didn't seem to mind. 'Vistack ik grub,' he said with a wide grin. 'Vishtack ik Fyool.'

Wormeye stepped back and gestured widely. 'Quiprik unt *gruuuub,*' he said, the last word an extended croak of pleasure. His escort stamped their feet in approval, filling the hut with depraved laughter. He gave a signal and they stepped forward, cutting them from the posts and rebinding their wrists in front of them. Then they stepped away, forcing them from the hut with jabbing spears.

J.B. Forsyth

Fyool

They emerged to find themselves in a narrow clearing with a thick curtain of jungle leaning in from either side. They had slept for most of the afternoon and the sun had dropped out of sight - its dying rays now gilding only the very tops of the trees. Crude huts of various sizes scattered the clearing and several low fires burned in between. The area was littered with gnawed bones and teeth, clumps of fur and plucked feathers. Several dead animals were hanging by their feet from a length of vine. One looked like a bird, but the others were so strange Kye had no idea what they were. He couldn't see any more quaggar, but their endless mantra rolled over the crest of a small hill: 'Fyool! ... Fyool! ... Fyool!'

The leaves of another hut parted and Rauul and Kail stumbled out with their own trio of spear jabbing quaggar behind them. The soldiers were damp and dishevelled and Rauul was walking with a heavy limp. His thick britches were ripped down one side and the material was soaked in a big oval of blood that ran from hip to knee. 'They could have tidied up a bit,' he said after looking around the clearing. He was trying to make light of the situation, but Kye took no humour from it. Something bad was waiting for them at the end of their walk and his hands were beginning to tremble.

They crested the hill and saw hundreds of jerking quaggar; pulling their grass hair and shaking their faces at the sky. A frenzy of movement through which they maintained their ominous mantra. They were gathered around a semi-circular stockade, built tight to a rocky bank. And at the centre of the bank was a gaping fissure – a craggy eye that horded shadow.

The spearmen forced them down the hill and tied Kye, Ormis and Kail to separate trees. Rauul was taken closer to the stockade and lashed between two more - his arms and legs spread wide apart. He didn't struggle and only gritted his teeth when they yanked his shredded leg out to the side. When all knots were secured Wormeye produced an animal tooth dagger and waved it in the air.

'Look away boy,' said Ormis and he did, just as Wormeye drew the dagger across Rauul's chest. The Captain of the Elite Guard made no sound, but his head jerked back and his facial muscles worked hard over his clamped jaw. Another quaggar stepped up to him, bearing a large yellow leaf. He pressed it to his bleeding chest, grinning greedily as he collected his flowing blood in its deep folds. Rauul spat in his face, but the leaf bearer hardly noticed; his expression changing little as he licked the offence from his cheek. When he was satisfied he turned toward the stockade and lifted the leaf above his head. It sagged in the middle, dripping trickles of blood from its glossy surface. There was a roar of approval and when it died down he stepped away, allowing a much larger quaggar to move in and swing a heavy cudgel. It shattered Rauul's knee cap with a dull *thwock* and his legs gave way, transferring his full weight to his bound wrists. This time he was unable to keep his pain to himself and he screamed it across the clearing – a sound that was quickly drowned by a depraved cheer. Kye was still looking away, but his blood ran cold and for the first time he began to consider the possibility he was going to die here.

They cut Rauul down and he was taken up by four quaggar and carried to the stockade, his face contorting with agony when their rough handling grated the fragments of his shattered knee. The crowd parted, revealing a gate. They took Rauul through, dropped him in the dirt and made a hurried retreat. But the leaf bearer stayed behind. He approached the crack in the rocky bank, hunkered down as if the darkness within could reach out and grab him. He stuck his hand into the leaf, flicked blood around the opening and threw the whole thing in. Then he backed away to where Rauul was lying and thrust his bloody hands into the air. 'Fyool!'

'Fyool!' the spectators replied, their eyes watery with emotion.

He produced a powder from a pouch and rubbed it under Rauul's nose. The soldier flinched as though struck then rolled away, grasping his knee. The leaf bearer left the enclosure, pulled the gate shut and bolted it. Then he mounted the walkway and joined the others in their chant, all eyes fixed expectantly on the crack.

'Fyool!... Fyool!... Fyool!'

Kye looked into the stockade just as something indefinable shifted in the opening of the crack. Rauul got a better look and began dragging himself away on his elbows. He heaved himself up and hopped to the stockade, where the quaggar were now drumming on the wood; their coarse mantra hushing to a reverential whisper. *'Fyooool! ... Fyooool! ... Fyooool.'*

The inhabitant of the crack began separating from its lair. Fyool's insectoid legs reached around the sides of the opening and pulled its maggot like body out with a sound like jelly slipping from a mould. Its skin was transparent and mottled with purple patches; thin enough under its belly to suggest what its last meal had been. It had six legs with two larger appendages that sprouted from its shoulders and bifurcated into pincers. But its most disturbing feature was its head. Amid a collar of rippling skin folds was an oversized quaggar face, complete with a sprout of filthy grass hair. *'Aaaaah! Vistack ik gruub. Vishtack ik Fyool!'* To the quaggar Fyool was a deity, but to the captives it was a poisoning of the eye.

Rauul turned away and reached for the top of the stockade, but a quaggar boy was having none of it. He hurled a rock, striking him on the forehead and forcing him to stagger away. He took too much weight through his smashed knee and it duly gave way, relinquishing him to the dirt.

Fyool turned towards him, wrinkling its nose and rippling its body. It opened its mouth and slid its jaw forward, stretching strands of saliva between crooked teeth encrusted with green plaque. Then it lifted its huge pincers and clicked them in the air. *'Fyool!'* the quaggar cried reverently, their collective voice brimming with love and adoration.

Fyool hunkered down and ran at Rauul in a disjointed scuttle. But when it was a dozen feet away he jerked up and threw a rock - the same rock the quaggar boy had thrown at *him*. His aim was faultless and it struck the grub god between its eyes with a dull crunch. It emitted a terrible childish shriek and retracted its head so far into its pulpy body, it almost disappeared. Its legs buckled and reversed direction in a cloud of dust; pincers flailing in front of its grimacing face. A howl of disapproval severed the quaggar chant and Wormeye battered the stockade in a paroxysm of outrage.

Kye felt a different emotion at the sight of the retreating abomination. It was a bright and invigorating elation and it ripped through his fear and despair. But just as he was beginning to think Fyool was going to squeeze back into its crack it steadied itself and pushed its head back out with an onerous hiss. Then with a change of strategy it moved sideways like a crab, skirting the rock face and the stockade; trying to get around the back of its resourceful prey. Rauul twisted to follow its movement, dragging himself across the arena in a desperate attempt to retrieve the rock. But it was too far away and before he could reach it, Fyool charged again.

It grabbed his ankle with its pincers and lifted him so high, his fingers groped the ground. Then it thrust its vile mouth upon him, sinking its rancid teeth into the meat of his thigh. Rauul flexed at the hip and began pounding its huge quaggar face. But as it munched on him, his screams were unbridled - a series of dreadful notes that were music to its worshipers' ears.

'Fyool! ... Fyool! ...Fyool!' they began again jubilantly; their eyes feverish with pride. Oh how they loved to watch it feed.

Fyool dropped him and skittered away as though fearing retaliation. It backed up against the stockade and rocked from side to side, its green eyes fixed on Rauul as its jaws worked on a chunk of his flesh; eventually swallowing it with a peristaltic wave that rippled its flabby neck. With growing confidence, it crept back to where he squirmed in the dust, an expression of mad delight appearing on its face.

But it was so focused on its prey, it failed to see what the eyes of its worshipers were suddenly drawn to. Some other creature was emerging from its lair; scrambling out on what appeared to be six fleshy legs, the foremost of which were covered in strange black patterns. It was smaller than the grub god, but its torso was lean and heavily muscled. It had no pincers or quaggar face, just a blunt featureless head that gave it the look of a battering ram. Its appearance ended the recently restored Fyool mantra and replaced it with cries of alarm. Whatever this new creature was, they weren't expecting it.

Once clear of the crack the creature rose onto its rear legs and Kye suddenly saw it for what it was. Its front two pairs of legs were in fact arms and there were swords in its hands. There was a collective gasp from the quaggar and a delicious rush of hope in the captives.

It was Kring!

Fyool's Lair

At the sight of Kring charging toward an unsuspecting Fyool a blizzard of emotion rose in Kye's chest. A few seconds ago he was waiting in line to die, but now his eyes were watering with hope and pride. Ormis was wrong about the giant, and here was the proof. He had tracked them to the clearing and was risking his life to save them.

Kring leapt onto Fyool's back, squashing its fatty body into a pair of translucent globules. It staggered under his weight and when it collapsed he grabbed a fist full of its grassy hair and brought a blade to its throat. It tried to retract its head and when it realised it couldn't, a childish fear came over its monstrous face. For a few seconds the spectators were carved figures, their grass hair stirring in the breeze as they looked on in shock and horror. Then a spear flew from one end of the stockade. Kring turned it away with the flat of his other sword and sent it quivering into the dirt. More spears were raised, but Wormeye barked a restraining command. One of them might strike the grub god and he didn't want that.

'Let them go!' Kring boomed, pointing to their captives. Fyool struggled beneath him, eyes rolling back and pincers reaching for him. But they lacked the range and all they could do was click at the air.

Wormeye either didn't understand or had chosen not to comply. He gesticulated wildly, balling his hands into fists and croaking a barrage of ugly words. Fyool found some new leverage and shifted to get more reach with its left pincer. But as it whipped up Kring severed it with a backhand swipe and it landed in a twitching heap; the stump it left behind pumping foul slurry into the dirt. Fyool screamed and tried to buck him off. The quaggar were ignited by the sacrilege and their grass hair danced around their outraged faces like flames.

Kye saw that Fyool was tiring, perhaps even dying. And seeing this, his hope began to fade. If the grub god died, they were finished.

'Let them go,' Kring repeated, pointing to the prisoners with his sword then raising it above Fyool's head - a threat that needed no translation.

This time Wormeye seemed to understand.

He turned from the stockade and barked a red faced command at the quaggar that were guarding them. Kye flinched when they drew daggers, not knowing whether Wormeye had ordered their release or their deaths. But the guards went straight to work on their bindings and they were soon free.

'Into the passage,' called Kring as they ran to the stockade. 'Suula waits in the back.' The quaggar parted reluctantly, their dirty hands fidgeting with murderous intention. But Ormis threw the crude bolt and they rushed through unmolested.

Kye ran into the crack with Kail, but the exorcist went to Rauul and knelt by his side. The Captain of the Elite Guard looked up at him, his face ashen and his eyes like sky behind thin cloud. His tattered thigh was still pumping blood, but the flow was weaker now. He reached up and pulled him close. 'I haven't got long … I can feel it…' His voice was wispy and it broke off into a series of laboured breaths. 'Make sure I pass.' He fell back and Ormis covered his face with splayed fingers. A dozen yards away Fyool continued to struggle beneath Kring, its face a mask of pain and misery. He sent his scour into Rauul as his soul began to rise and all at once the Membrane was a tangible thing – an invisible fabric that was tearing open around the dying soldier. He drew gently now - just enough to keep his soul in the vicinity of the tear and to ensure he passed. And he went peacefully. He died in a place where the Membrane tore easily and he was ready to go. Ormis waited for the invisible fabric to seal itself over its prize then he was up and running into the crack.

Only Kring remained in the arena.

He was ringed by hundreds of hard faces, all waiting for the opportunity to right a terrible wrong. In one fluid movement he rolled off Fyool's back, lifted its rear legs and began dragging it back to its lair. Fyool tried to resist, but its movements were sluggish and its remaining pincer flapped in the dirt. There was some ugly shouting and spears flew from several quaggar who lacked restraint. They fell short, but before anymore could be thrown Wormeye lashed them with a coarse tongue, bringing them under his fragile control once more.

When Kring reached the crack he dropped Fyool's legs and sprang onto its back, bringing a sword down vertically through its neck and pinning it to the ground. It jerked twice and went still; its miserable expression now fixed on its face. There was a moment of shocked silence when Wormeye stared at his dead grub god in statuesque horror. The only movement in his face was that of its resident worm, its crazy wriggling finally dislodging it from his eye socket. It fell over the stockade and in the shocked silence it could be heard striking the dirt. Then the entire crowd erupted in outrage, howling and screaming as they jumped into the arena. But Kring yanked his sword free and disappeared into the craggy blackness before the first spears clattered against the rock.

    Kye followed Kail through the darkness on his hands and knees. The smell was rank, but after the stink of the tree bridge he found he could tolerate it well enough. After several minutes of blind crawling, when only words of encouragement from Kail persuaded him through some of the tighter spots, they emerged into a large cave. Suula was waiting for them, holding up a sword that burned with a strange green fire. As Kye got closer he could see tiny flies dancing around it. They were feeding off a thick substance smeared onto the blade and their little bodies seemed to be the source of the green flames. He recognised them as fieraks, the same flies Ormis had used to light up the Lady of the Forest. The eerie glow barely reached the cave floor, but it was enough to highlight piles of old bones and half eaten corpses. This was Fyool's lair and it stank of decaying meat. And as he looked around he had a chilling thought: if Kring hadn't saved them they would have all ended up here. They waited in silence and it came as an enormous relief to Kye when Ormis and Kring emerged from the passage.
    'We got in through there,' said Suula, reaching with her sword to illuminate another opening on the far wall. 'It goes for a hundred feet or so then there's a steep angle up to the opening.'
    Kring moved forward, took the sword from her and looked back at the others. 'I'll take us out. The entrance was well hidden, but if they know about it they'll be waiting.' He crunched away through a heap of old bones, dropped to his hands and knees and disappeared into the tight passage.
    Fyool's lair was at the centre of a fissure that ran right through a rocky mound. Its rear entrance was nothing more than a horizontal crack, ten feet off the ground and screened by thick foliage. When Kring reached the opening, he listened for a while before pushing his head through and studying the jungle. The sound of quaggar pursuit was all around them, but it was distant. And once he was satisfied there weren't any in the immediate vicinity he lowered himself down and helped the others out. When they were all gathered beneath the opening Suula took her sword back, wiped the thick substance from the blade and resheathed it. With no feeding source the flies scattered, their tiny flames burning out as they dispersed. She led them away from the rocky bank and into the darkening jungle, through hulking trunks and beneath thick branches. They skirted a patch of ferns, ducking for cover behind an enormous tree root when they heard a sudden thrash of foliage overhead. Suula picked out the source and pointed to it: a lone quaggar sentry climbing down a tree to join the hunt. When he reached a low branch he jumped, but before his feet touched the ground Kring stepped out and separated his head from his body with a single swipe of his sword. His body thudded to the forest floor and his head bounced and rolled. They were all moving again before it came to

rest, his dead eyes staring after them.

They managed nearly half a mile before an ear piercing shriek told them they'd been spotted and with no further need for stealth they stretched their legs in response. But outrunning their pursuers wasn't just a matter of speed. They still had the intrinsic dangers of the jungle to contend with and they were forced to follow Suula in an erratic zig zag. At one place they even had to double back when they came to a fallen tree covered in spitting daisies. This brought the quaggar cries much closer and from that point on Kye ran in a hunch; unable to shake the idea there were spears trained on his back and that at any second he would see one emerging from his chest.

The jungle broke suddenly on a vast muddy expanse with nowhere to hide for miles, but Suula took them on without breaking stride, guiding them along solid islands and firm ridges. The lack of cover pushed them harder, but after a few minutes splashing through the mud the sound of pursuit faded then ceased altogether. They slowed up and stopped, bunching up on a little island of firm ground to look back at the jungle. The quaggar were lined up on the edge of the mud flats, dozens strong and with more arriving all the time. But not one of them had taken a single step onto the flats. They had given up the chase and were staring after them, spears lowered and faces set in stony masks.

'Why did they stop?' Kye puffed. His cheeks were flushed like raw steaks and his skin sleeked with sweat.

Ormis studied them for some time. 'They fear this place,' he said looking around. 'And if they fear it, so should we.' He turned to Suula. 'Can you get us back on the girl's trail from here?'

The little tracker looked across the vast expanse of mud. She was the only one who wasn't panting and she looked like she could run on forever. 'If they continued on the same path they would have walked the jungle north of the flats. If we aim for the north east corner, we could make up some ground.'

The jungle in the suggested direction was so far away, it looked like grass. Ormis looked up at the indigo sky and they all knew what he was thinking. The sun was setting on the Eastland and the mist would soon be on its way. 'Take us there then. As quick as you can.'

J.B. Forsyth

The Mud Flats

Suula guided them around thick mud and past pools of dirty water. Slimy trees grew from the pools – their glistening branches adorned with magnificent red berries that scented the air with a strawberry redolence. Kye had never seen berries so ripe. And they were so dark and bloated, he was surprised none of them had split open. In the distance small otter like mammals were dining on them, jumping great slicks of mud to reach the trees.

The mist appeared when they were about a mile from the north east corner - a billowing blanket that began to distort with currents and eddies as it was leeched down by awakening appetites. And as it swamped the trees, their branches folded up and they sunk into the pools; disappearing with great slurps of mud. Nearby, one of the otter creatures leapt off a folding branch and raced away - vanishing beneath the mist after a series of undulating jumps. They watched for a while, but it didn't resurface.

'We can't stay on the flats,' said Ormis, stepping up to Suula as the mist swept between their legs. 'Can you still guide us?'

She nodded. Whilst the rest of them were watching the approaching mist, Suula had made a study of the terrain with her sharp eyes, committing a large swathe to memory before it was covered. She drew her sword and started forward, feeling the ground with the tip of her blade and sniffing the air. The strawberry redolence was fading now and was being replaced by a flatulent reek that rose from the ground.

They edged after her, knee deep in a vast glowing cloud. And because they were travelling a near right angle to its flow, Kye felt constantly off balance. At one point he thought he was falling and stamped a foot out to stabilise himself. But it was an unnecessary action and it served to do the very thing he sought to prevent – forcing him into a short stumble that almost sent him sprawling. He found it was better if he kept his eyes on Ormis's back. It worked for a while, but his focus was soon drawn to the swirling patterns the exorcist's legs were creating in the mist. He shuffled on with hooded eyes, so mesmerized that when Ormis stopped for Suula to consider their path, he walked into him. He staggered away and would have fallen if the exorcist hadn't grabbed his arm.

'Look at me boy!' he said, taking hold of his shirt and slapping his face. 'Look at me and focus.' The blur of Ormis's face slowly sharpened until the full force of his grey eyes were upon him. 'Has it passed?'

'I think so.'

'What did we tell you about staring into the mist? Don't look into it unless you have to. Keep your eyes moving and you'll have no trouble. Understand?'

He was about to say yes, he did understand, when something caught his attention and he pointed instead. 'Look.' They all turned, but he could tell from their faces they weren't seeing what he was. 'It's the ghosts I told you about.'

Najo and Allie were flying over the mud flats towards them. And as if understanding the difficulty the others were having, they swooped beneath the mist; re-emerging as bright green spectres.

Now they all saw.

Ormis fired up his draw and this time Kye got a greater sense of the medium through which it was acting. He could feel lines of tension joining himself to the ghosts and Ormis. And there was a bowing of material which suggested a force between the exorcist and the ghosts. *You will see, hear and feel what others can't – senses that will only strengthen with time.* The exorcist's words came back to him now and he realised his senses had crossed another threshold, allowing him to feel detailed distortions of the Membrane.

The ghosts drew up fifty feet away, no doubt feeling Ormis's draw. They hung in the air, their green transparencies so close together they were beginning to merge.

'We're here to beg a kindness,' said Najo. *'We saw what the soul burner did for your friend.'*

Kye frowned.

'You didn't see,' said Allie. *'It was after you left.'*

'What are they saying?' Ormis asked.

Kye felt a change in the Membrane and knew the little ghosts were pressing themselves against it. And when Najo spoke again they all heard.

'You helped your friend to pass,' he said, addressing Ormis directly. *'And there was no pain or fire. We're here to ask if you would do the same for us.'*

'Never. Go back to Izle and tell him we won't play this game. Go now, for there is *only* pain and fire for you here.'

'Izle didn't send us and we're not playing games.'

'You're the work of black arts. It's impossible for you to coexist in the same haunt.'

Allie smiled. *'And yet we do. Might there be some things you don't understand soul burner?'*

'You have your answer.'

They drifted away and began to circle around them.

'Move together!' Ormis shouted. 'And be sure we're all joined.' They formed a tight knot - Kring centremost with a huge hand on each of their shoulders.

The ghosts picked up speed, the tension joining them to Kye revolving like spokes on a giant wheel. They spun quicker and quicker, soon generating a physical vortex that blew the mist away; exposing the flats.

What they saw was horrifying. The mud was riddled with the quivering mouths of giant worms. They could see right into the closest ones and they were lined with crooked yellow teeth and filled with swirls of residual mist. There was one in the exact place Kye was going to fall when Ormis grabbed him and it was squelching in its burrow; clearly frustrated by his proximity. It was a sight so sudden and powerful they all shrank from it, bunching against Kring on a small island of firm ground. Kye looked back at all the worms Suula had guided them around and felt sick.

The ghosts slowed and the mist reclaimed the area.

'We call them lurkers,' said Najo. *'And there's hundreds of them. Some big and some small. Some large enough to swallow the giant. The trees are their tails and the berries their bait. When the mist comes they slip down their burrows and up the other side; waiting with their mouths open for prey like you. They won't let you leave. But if you promise to help us, we'll help you.'*

'We'll take our chances with the worms,' said Ormis, strengthening his draw. 'Now be off.'

Kye gawped at him. Given what they had just seen, it was madness not to consider their offer. The ghosts looked at each other and he guessed a similar thought was passing between them.

'Then you'll die,' said Allie. *'They know you're here and they're waiting for you to make a mistake... But their patience has limits.'*

They drifted away, getting dimmer as the mist evaporated from them. Kye wanted to call them back, but the exorcist was gripping him hard and his resolve was quarried into his stony face.

'Have they gone?' he asked after some time. Kye didn't trust himself to speak and simply nodded. The way he felt now, he could have pushed him into the nearest worm hole. 'If you see them again, tell me right away.' He turned to the rest of them. 'We came this far in ignorance. It should be no different now... Suula, take us on.'

The little tracker didn't hesitate. She set off straight away, feeling through the mist with her sword and sniffing at the air. And when she discovered a worm, she circled her sword above it, marking its position in their minds. Ormis followed fearlessly – his easy footfalls a screaming mismatch to the danger all around him. The rest of them couldn't muster the same indifference and shuffled forward as if on tightropes, every blind step a heart pounding act of faith.

Lurkers

The stars came out as they laboured across the flats. Suula's nose was more than equal to the task, but her route to the trees was tortuous and they made slow progress. Where the worms became too concentrated or the ground too soft, they were forced to walk frustrating stretches that ran parallel to the trees or directly away from them. And at every step the worms became more restless, squelching and slurping beneath the mist in anticipation of a wrong step.

About a quarter of a mile from the trees their concentration was broken by a loud stuttering suction. They froze – all heads turning to the sound. Fifty yards to their right the ribbed body of a worm was rising from the flats, its wet flanks glistening with reflected mist light. And as they watched, they were all reminded of Allie's parting words: *'... they're waiting for you to make a mistake... But their patience has limits.'*

The worm was more than twice Kring's height when it stopped rising. It swayed in the air and lolled towards them; its quivering mouth hanging like a loose pocket. Then it splashed down into the mud, wafting mist into rolling spirals and coming at them; propelled by a sickly wave that rippled the length of its wet body. The urge to flee was enormous, but they remained rooted to the spot. There were dozens of gaping mouths hidden beneath the mist all around them and a misplaced step would drop them through a tube of teeth.

The worm made a direct line for Kye, but Kring lifted him off his feet, putting him down safely behind him and drawing his swords. He welcomed the worm with his steel; hacking with vertical strokes. And with a drum beating rhythm, he sliced it open, separating it into two bloody flanks that flopped either side of him. But the worm rippled forward without slowing, oblivious to the devastation of its front end. Kring was half way through it when its underbelly, unable to pass his planted feet, folded back on itself and lifted out of the mist like a toothed tongue. He stepped over it without pause, but the release of pressure allowed the base of the worm to surge forward, pushing the others away. They were each forced to take a couple of blind steps and it was only through sheer luck they found firm ground. The worm stopped only when Kring had hacked all the way through to its tree like tail. By then his face was covered with sword splatter and the worm's twitching flanks were curled out of the mist like the ends of a toothed scroll.

They looked around and saw more worms – rising from burrows, splashing into the mud and rippling through the mist. And it was clear the next one to arrive wouldn't be on its own. Suula had been pointing out the locations of the nearest worm burrows, but in all the excitement Kye had forgotten where they were. He wondered why they weren't rising like the rest and was chilled by a sudden understanding: they were waiting for the other worms to push them into their open mouths. The situation was desperate and when he looked at the others for guidance, he saw the same thoughts mirrored in their faces. To fight was hopeless, but to run was madness.

It was during this paralysis of indecision that Najo and Allie returned. They sped in from the west and circled them again; drawing the mist into a vortex and exposing the mud flats. And in a matter of seconds, they were surrounded by a six-foot wall of rotating mist that encompassed dozens of worms.

'Let's go,' said Kring, stepping around Suula and bounding away between two writhing mouths. Kye and Kail went straight after him, leaving the little tracker alone with Ormis. The exorcist's turbulent eyes flicked back and forth between the ghosts, his mistrust rooting him to the spot. But his hesitation was brief. There was no denying they were worm food if they remained there and with a nod to Suula they sprinted away.

They raced around the burrows and the ghosts kept pace, keeping them in the centre of the vortex. But there was no calm in the eye of the storm - only a constantly changing arena of worms. They made good progress to begin with, easily outrunning those that were rippling over the surface. The worms relied on the mist to blind and hypnotise their prey and without it they were severely disadvantaged.

But they weren't without options and soon changed their tactics.

Some began positioning themselves at right angles to their run; emerging from the vortex as monstrous barricades they had to go around. When two of them began levering themselves together to form a continuous barrier, Kring charged. He dropped his shoulder and slammed into the nearest one, bowing its ribbed belly away and preventing it locking mouths with its partner. He held it while the other ran through and slid off, sprinting after them. Soon after a baby worm appeared. It was faster than the others and came straight at Kye. It would have been completely hidden under a blanket of mist – a tube of teeth with the potential to bite his foot clean off. Kring ran up behind him and launched it off his boot. It turned end over end and disappeared over the vortex.

Their luck ran out when they were confronted by a solid wall of tightly packed worms. How far it extended to either side they couldn't tell, but the jungle was now tantalisingly close and it loomed over the mist. Kring looked over the top of the worms as the rest of them bunched around him.

'There's dozens more behind!' he said. 'Stand back while I cut through.' He began hacking through a worm, but it didn't open as expected. This time he was cutting across instead of along it, and the worm was able to stop the wound opening by pressing it together with peristaltic waves that travelled inward from both ends of its body. And after a dozen vicious strokes, one of his blades became stuck and he had to use three hands and a boot to pull it free. Behind them a semicircle of converging mouths was fast approaching.

'On top quick!' he said, sheathing his swords and drawing daggers. He plunged them into the worm's slippery flank and used them to climb onto its back. Then he helped the others up – Ormis's leg just escaping a puckering tube of razor sharp teeth. From the top they could all see the extent of the blockade – a dense, haphazard arrangement of worms with patches of mist trapped in between.

'We'll have to go across the top,' said Kring, before jumping to the next one. He landed well, but lost his footing on its slimy surface and fell onto its back with a wet slap. He stabilised himself with his daggers, rose to a crouch and waved them over. They jumped over one at a time, grabbing his spare arms and arranging themselves behind him. Najo and Allie moved forward, bringing a single tree inside the vortex.

The worm flexed and arched, trying to throw them; but they were gathered on its relatively stiff middle, away from the ferocious whipping of its tree like tail and writhing mouth. Kring leapt onto another worm whose long axis was aligned with the direction of the trees. He laid prone on its back, upper arms hugging its glistening girth while his lower arms reached back. They jumped over, grabbed his hands for balance and trampled over him.

Kail was last to jump. He sprang clean, but the worm flicked its tail and he landed off centre, slipping off and disappearing into the mist. They stared after him, seeing in their mind's eye the toothed belly into which he had fallen. When his hand appeared, Kring swung down and grabbed it. He pulled and Kail screamed over a sickening crunch. He shot out of the mist, but there was only half of him. Kring let go and he windmilled over them, his severed waist spraying blood. He landed upright with a wet thud, head above the mist and neck hinged back; dead eyes trained on the stars.

But there was no time to contemplate the horror. Suula ran along the worm and jumped off. From Kye's angle it seemed like madness, but he straightened to see her land in an area free of mist. Najo and Allie moved the vortex forward and a whole line of trees came into view. In seconds they were following Suula's lead, jumping down and sprinting between the last few worm holes.

They stopped in the relative safety of the jungle. The ghosts slowed their rotation and the vortex collapsed, allowing the captured mist to continue west. They looked back over the mud flats and saw hundreds of worms moving across the surface like black maggots in a poisonous gas. The blockade was dispersing, but they weren't pursuing. Some of the worms were already slipping back into their burrows – bodies bending into the ground and rear ends whipping into the air.

Kye looked for the ghosts, keen to express his gratitude. But he was shocked to see Ormis leaping at Najo and drawing him in. He shouted at the exorcist to stop, but his protest wasn't needed. A blur of light shot through the trees, severing his draw and spinning him off his feet. Allie grabbed her brother as his elongated spectre took back its original form and they sped off into the jungle. The exorcist sprang up, sweeping his draw around in an attempt to recapture him, but he was already beyond reach.

'They saved our lives!'

'Is that what you think? They led us to a blockade of worms! Kail's dead because of them and the rest of us are lucky to be alive.'

Kye was stunned. The exorcist had it back to front and upside down. If not for Najo and Allie, they would all be dead. 'They just wanted you to help them.'

'And you believed them. This is what I was talking about this morning. Your affinity to the Membrane is growing stronger and it's clouding your reasoning. Spirits are not your friends!'

Kye battled against his gaze and soon realised there was nothing he could say to change his mind. He turned away in a huff and folded his arms.

The little ghosts watched the exchange from behind a tree, and when it was over Allie turned to her brother. *'I can't believe he was going to burn you, after we saved them from the lurkers. He won't help us no matter what we do.'*

'What about Kye?'

'He doesn't have the skill of the soul burner.'

'But he's Twum and strong with it.'

'So what?'

'We could ask him to try.'

They studied Kye's back, considering his potential.

'Even if he's willing,' said Allie, *'the soul burner won't let him.'*

'We could get him alone?'

'How?'

'They came here looking for a girl. We could find her and offer to bring them together. We could make a bargain without the soul burner hearing.'

Allie was horrified. *'But he said she was being taken to the glass tunnels? We agreed not to go there.'*

'Then we'll just have to find her before she arrives.' He reached out and their hands merged in a blur of light. *'You saw how easily that man passed. The Last Place just opened and he funnelled in… The Last Place Allie! How long have we wanted it? We might never get a chance like this again.'*

The doubt melted from Allie's face – no argument could stand against talk of the Last Place. *'Alright,'* she said, her spectral face brightening with hope. *'Let's go.'*

They set off hand in hand, flying through trees and gliding over the mist.

Horror in the Hollows

Della watched from the top balcony as the mist billowed through the courtyard gate and swept around the tower like a wave breaking on a lighthouse. When it reached the back wall it began to rotate clockwise around the base; a current that would continue until dawn when the mist would sink through the cracked cobbles and soak into the land.

She had found no sign of her rescue party in the tower and was beginning to entertain the possibility they were all dead – slain by the assassin Griglis sent out. But to believe it was to abandon all hope; to accept a stark reality in which she was all alone in the Wilderness with only the shadow for company. A reality she couldn't face. So she dismissed the idea and set off to find them. If they had tracked her from the tower the next place to look was the gorge and she took a path in its general direction, searching for the break in the canopy.

Less than a mile from the tower, something encircled her neck and arms. She spun around, expecting to see another spirit, but the sky was empty. She pulled at the invisible nooses and when her fingers slipped through, she realised what was happening: something had found her body!

She forced herself to relax and tuned into the sensations. Whatever encircled her neck and arms was thin and woody and there was a rough friction travelling the length of her back. She fitted it together and realised she was being pulled along the branch by a pair of vines. An image of the mist leecher flashed up in her mind, its swirling eye tightening with predatory anticipation. And although her body was several miles away she felt its blood run cold. She shot off in the direction of the dead trees, her imagination already suggesting a range of imminent and horrible deaths.

She gained height and found them easily. The lack of foliage allowed the mist to light the area like a beacon and she arced into it like a spent arrow, her blurring spectre reforming above the empty knot. The vines had dragged her to the trunk and now with one great tug they yanked her up against it; so hard she felt the crack of her head and thump of her heels.

She ran her eyes up the tree and was struck by a new terror when a pulse of mist light revealed a gaping hole into which one of the vines disappeared. She shot forward, reanimating her body with desperate kicking that served only to twist her around, bringing her face to face with the rotten opening as she was hauled up to it. Another vine appeared from the shadows and when it began to encircle her legs she kicked ever more frantically, fearing the loss of her remaining freedom. But the vine made a wide loop around her legs and simply tightened, squeezing them together at the knees. Then she was tipping; legs lifting away from the trunk and her head pivoting over the lip of the opening. She got one last look at the star studded sky before she was pulled upside down into the dark hollow of the tree.

The vines took her down through a column of humid air – two pulling and one lowering. She was much bigger than the prey they usually snatched from the branches and the hollow trunk barely accommodated her. She jammed her boots against the sides, but the brittle lining simply crumbled, giving up a splintery dust that fell about her face; making her cough and splutter on what little air she was able to gasp through her strangled throat. Sharp splinters ripped her clothes and hundreds of unhoused wood beetles crawled over her exposed flesh in a desperate attempt to find new homes. Blood rushed to her head and lights flashed behind her screwed up eyes. Panic and terror consumed her and with every jolt of progress she gave up a silent scream, expecting to be shredded against the tree's sharp lining or swallowed by whatever waited in the darkness below.

But she wasn't alone in her peril.

The shadow hadn't guided her safely through the jungle only to hide away while she was being torn apart. It rose within her, channelling her panic into rage and speaking words her terrified mind was primed to obey. *Go down there and kill it! Go down there and kill it before it tears you apart!* She shot out of her body and down the rest of the trunk, drawing up in a huge cavern beneath the tree's root system. The space was lit by a rotating funnel of mist that spiralled down from the ceiling and soaked into a huge gelatinous mass. A network of vines ran out of it in all directions; some slack and some taut, but all running into cracks in the cavern wall or disappearing into the ring of root systems that covered the ceiling. This was the leecher beneath the clearing and it wobbled and swayed with the movement of its myriad vines. And as she took in this eerie underworld the vine gripping her neck yanked again, its resulting vibration distinguishing it from the others.

She flew at the leecher and hammered it with her fists. Her blows raged through the Membrane with the same power that had launched a toruck into the air, but all she achieved now was a series of ripples that ran across its gelatinous flank. The shadow realised how futile such an assault was and pushed her forwards, through the spiralling mist and into the leecher's vast body. All at once she was imbued with the full composite of its sensation: its wobbling flesh, the slimy suction that fixed it to the floor and the movement of the many vines that ran through its body. She could feel the way they were arranged in the jungle – spiralling up trees, hanging in loops and snaking through the dirt. Through millions of hair like sensors, she could feel worms wriggling in the soil and insects scurrying across bark. She felt the sudden bowing of branches that signalled the alighting of birds and could differentiate these movements from those caused by the stirrings of the breeze. She could feel the flowers on its vines and realised she had seen them before. They were the ones with the hooded orange petals that had craned their stems to look at her – the ones she imagined throttling her to death. Their black stamens were embedded with primitive light sensors that were now *her* eyes, relaying low resolution images of the jungle to her from hundreds of different angles – a confusing kaleidoscope that suddenly focused into one coherent view. The leecher was so deeply connected to its surroundings it was like she had taken possession of the jungle itself, and nothing moved within a mile radius she wasn't aware of.

She felt no resistance to her possession. The leecher lacked the faculties to detect such an invasion and its basic functions ran on regardless. She could feel the prey in its vines making steady progress through the jungle and down hollow trunks. From their shapes and sizes, she could tell most were rabbits and squirrels; or whatever grotesque equivalents passed for such things this side of the mountains. She identified her limp body as the largest amongst them and it was now exiting the bottom of the tree and angling into the cavern. She felt a split in the leecher's side and got a sense it was some form of mouth, opening to receive her. And with just seconds to spare she took control of the vine, lowering her body to the cavern floor and releasing it.

But she wasn't finished yet.

She needed to make sure the leecher couldn't grab her again and she had to make it pay. She was still blazing with rage and it was being fuelled and poisoned by every wisp of mist that soaked into her; turning it into a hateful vengeance that demanded discharge.

She gripped the jungle and pulled hard. The vines tightened and the leecher's insides were drawn in a hundred different directions. The net force lifted its body and it was only the slug like suction of its underbelly that kept it from detaching from the cavern floor. She pulled harder and felt something go: a single vine ripping out of the leecher's body with a wet spurt. Encouraged, she followed up with several vicious clenches that resulted in a satisfying series of snapping vines and internal tears. Some vines whipped across the cavern floor and some bowstringed, cutting through the leecher like cheese wire and causing it to emit a gaseous hiss she hoped was a scream. Above ground the jungle thrashed as though it were being exercised by a vicious wind. Branches bent and bowed -

snapping and splintering where the force upon them was too great. And she would have gone on until she had torn every last vine out of the leecher, but something within its sensation caught her attention.

Footsteps...

...Two pairs.

...Heavy animals with a bipedal gait.

She relaxed and turned the orange flower heads towards them. The image she received was blurry, but there was no mistaking the four armed figures that were edging through the mist.

Karkus and Argol!

Only then did she imagine the kind of havoc she was causing above ground. If the torucks were here; then they must have been close when the mist came. And they were walking it because they thought the disturbance had something to do with her. Her anger turned cold, sharpening to an icicle she could have thrown at them. Karkus had cut her finger off and now it was his turn to pay. She felt the shadow's dismay as it read her intention. It had saved her from becoming the subterranean horror's next meal and it wanted her back in the torucks' possession. But she was in control now and she pushed it down as easily as swallowing a yawn.

Surrogate Arms

The torucks waited for the dogapes to cannibalise their dead then faced off with them until they skulked away. But sensing a ruse they remained at the tree until they were sure they weren't circling around. It was the returning birds that gave them the greatest confidence and as soon as the evening chorus began again they started after the witch. Karkus assumed they would catch up with her quickly - that they would soon find her mixed up with one of the innumerable hazards that populated the deep jungle. But as they followed her spoor ever further he was forced to rethink. Somehow the witch had run right through some of the most dangerous parts of the jungle; in one place weaving through a patch of grass traps and in another jumping a razor snare *they* almost got caught in. It was an incredible achievement and in the end he put it down to witchcraft. But her tracks were easy enough to follow and all signs indicated that they were gaining on her.

About a mile into their pursuit they came to a place where she had stopped; presumably to catch her breath. He grinned as he stared into the darkening jungle, knowing she was beginning to tire. But his grin disappeared when a familiar glow appeared in the east, marking the arrival of the mist. In just a few seconds the witch's tracks would be covered and they would be forced to terminate their pursuit until dawn. He spat into the mist as it broke around him and cursed, gripping the hilt of his dagger hard enough to ripple the cords of his forearm. So close. He set his feet, thinking things might have been different if he'd provoked the dogapes into another fight and killed them all.

But the waiting didn't last very long. Only a few minutes into their vigil the jungle exploded into life a hundred yards ahead of them – the branches of a dozen trees bowing and flapping as if they were being shaken by an invisible hand. And such was the violence some of the branches began snapping off and falling to the ground. They drew swords and braced, expecting something to charge at them from the direction of the disturbance. But nothing did. The trees continued their tantrum and there wasn't anything in the maddening mix of mist and shadow to suggest a cause.

'Could be the witch,' said Argol.

It was exactly what Karkus was thinking. They were close and there was a good chance she was involved with, or even the cause of what was happening. 'Better take a look, it's not far.'

They crept forward, feeling beneath the mist with their boots and swords. Halfway there the trees suddenly relaxed and the foliage sprang upwards and settled. Nearby, a patch of orange flowers twisted on their stems. They'd had front row seats for the disturbance and it was like they were scowling at them for spoiling the show. Karkus ignored them and scanned the jungle; his eyes glinting green with reflected mist light. Where the centre of the disturbance had been, the jungle canopy was thinner and only a web of bare branches screened the star speckled night. Mist glow climbed the trees in pulses, but revealed nothing of interest. It didn't mean there wasn't anything hiding there though. He had spent enough time in the jungle to know he couldn't trust his eyes. Seconds ran into minutes and a pregnant silence cored his ears out.

Finally, he waved Argol close. 'What do you reckon?'

'Whatever it was; it's got wind of us.'

Karkus thought hard. There was something waiting up ahead and there was a high probability it was the witch. He thought about the way she lifted Rox off his feet and launched him through the air. She had real power and he would be a fool not to respect it. He could no longer use her body as leverage and if she came at them in spirit form, they were finished... But the dangers of the deep jungle were all around and *she* would be a fool to leave her body to its mercy. 'If she's mixed up with something, this might be our best chance to snatch her.'

They crept forward, sweeping their swords through the mist like blind men with canes. When they reached the trees they separated and began to climb. Karkus's thick fingers found easy purchase on the deeply fissured bark and he made good progress; his back and arms rippling with the effort. At the height of mist glow he looked like a monstrous insect - another abomination in a wilderness replete with them.

He climbed onto a wide branch and scanned the shadows. But there was no sign of the witch or any clues as to the origin of the disturbance. He climbed to another branch a little higher up and further around – one with a deep nook between two thick knots. The perfect place for a girl to hide. From there he saw a clearing where a huge leecher was sucking down an enormous swirl of mist. The black eye at its centre glared up – daring him to jump in.

He walked back along the branch and scanned the adjacent tree for Argol, meaning to alert him to the leecher's presence. He clapped eyes on him in a pulse of mist light and saw he wasn't alone. There was a vine rising behind him, like a cobra making ready to strike. He brought his hands to his mouth and mimicked the call of the Quollo bird, but his warning was too late. As his two tone signal cut the silence the vine whipped Argol across his back and neck. He didn't see what happened next because the vines on *his* tree suddenly came to life, the shadows around him shifting chaotically with their movement.

He started down at once, taking no time to make sense of it. In the jungle, hesitation was the second biggest killer after curiosity and lightning reflexes were often the only difference between life and death. But he was too slow. As he jumped to the lower branch one of his boots was swiped by a vine. He fell forwards and struck the branch with his chest; folding over it like a sack of corn and emitting a ragged blast of air. For a few seconds he was totally incapacitated and all he could do was grip the branch and gasp. Black creepers were reaching for him from all directions and there was a twelve foot fall into the mist. He took another breath and slid off, landing in a crouch and springing up awkwardly, his swords appearing in a graceless flurry. The jungle clenched and buried vines bowstringed out of the mist, spraying dirt and forming a three dimensional web around him. He stomped forward, hacking at the vines as others threaded through the web and flogged his shoulders. Argol thudded into the mist a few feet away. He was set upon by a tangle of vines that pulled him to a rotten tree stump. They yanked several times in quick succession and the stump collapsed, swallowing him whole.

Now the entire jungle was reaching for Karkus. The vines came from all angles, whipping and tripping, coiling around his limbs and trying to pin him to the ground. But he kept his head, wielding his blades with precision; severing thick creepers and forging a steady passage through the web.

Deep below ground Della worked her surrogate arms. Karkus was getting away! He was the one who cut her finger off and the one she wanted the most. But he was hacking through her vines and she could feel her elaborate trap falling away. She stretched out as he slipped beyond reach, straining so hard the leecher lost its grip on the cavern floor. It peeled away like a leech and for a time could only quiver in the air. But she knew her chance had passed when his footsteps faded beyond perception.

Della was furious.

The mist was funnelling into her, fuelling her poisonous rage. She squeezed the toruck in the tree stump, trying to pulp him. But he was wedged in a narrow hollow and the vines snapped, sending her berserk. She pulled and pulled until the leecher's body split into a hundred parts and the cavern was splattered with its foul blood. And without the leecher's hunger to draw it, the mist above ground stopped funnelling and all that remained in the cavern drifted down, forming a thin blanket on the floor. Her infusion of poison came to an end and so did her rage. She left the leecher's lifeless body and swept into her own, pushing herself up and staggering across the gore splattered floor. She found a root system and climbed up, squeezing out through a rotten opening when she reached ground level. She tried to stand, but feeling sick and dizzy she fell back instead, banging her head against the tree and falling unconscious into the mist.

Absence

Old Friends and Bad Deeds

Slumped in the fog Della dreamt…
She was sitting on the grass in front of the hideaway. Sunlight baked her shoulders and caught in her eyelashes like golden threads. Her uncle was behind her on the stoop, fixing his boots and improvising a song about the mouse who chewed a hole in them. Nearby, perhaps taken by the tune, a tree sparrow began a cheerful accompaniment; chirping notes that were like sugar on the air.

She looked into the woods and was surprised to see dozens of her old friends walking through the trees or engaged in various activities; all seemingly unaware of one another's presence. Amongst them was Rayle Oakley; riding his white horse up a narrow trail. When he saw her he stopped in a bar of sunlight and raised his hat, offering her the crooked smile she had once fallen for. As she smiled back she noticed Jobby Morrit. He was crouched by a tree with his back turned. She saw the hammer and chisel in his hands and realised he was carving another one of his trademark faces. She screwed her eyes up, trying to make out whose face it was. Most of Jobby's carvings had landed him in trouble. He liked to carve village folk, but he had an eye for imperfections and a talent for accentuating them. He leaned back to get some new perspective and she saw it was *her* face; captured in a fit of laughter. He was working on her eyes now, rubbing blue dye in with his fingers.

She turned to see Aarron Hibble, kicking through fallen leaves. He had outgrown his shirt and britches and she could see at least two inches of creamy skin below his sleeves and above his boots. His extreme height had inspired his tormentors to nickname him The Monster of Maidenwell. For the two years she lived on his lane they were each other's best and only friend – a relationship that earned *her* the nickname The Monster's Crippled Frog; later shortened to The Crogg. Aarron's stature reflected a size of heart and depth of character she hoped someone else had come to love after she moved on. He walked with his head down now; in the characteristic hunch he adopted to make himself shorter, but made him look old and sad. She shouted his name and he straightened up, offering her a shy smile and a wave.

She looked around at her other friends, some of whom had lived lives separated by centuries, but were gathered now under the same sun. Her eyes settled on Dondalie Flack. She was squatting at the foot of an ash tree, dressed in a blue frock topped off with a pink knitted hat. She was holding her hand out, offering a pile of nuts to three glassy eyed squirrels that were sitting on a branch above her. The bravest ran down and went to her in a rolling run. It drew up on its hind legs, snatched a nut from her palm and scattered the rest before darting back up the tree on little claws. Della smiled as she recalled the tea parties Dondalie set out for her cats, the big old shire horse she kept in her scullery and the knitted knapsacks she used to carry her favourite animals around. She was wearing one now and there was a ferret's head sticking out. It was looking up at the tree, eyeing the squirrels with great interest.

Now she saw little Annie and it was like the sun was rising in her heart. Annie was picking flowers to make perfume; her golden hair glowing like a halo. Her cheeks were flushed and her bowed legs were strong and chunky. Annie was bright and healthy - untouched by the cough that would eventually kill her. With a proud smile she raised a tiny fist, showing off a bouquet of little pink and white flowers. She lost her balance and fell onto her behind, blessing the air with a yurp of laughter. Della laughed back. She was in the deepest place of her heart, surrounded by the people who set it alight.

A black and white face pushed itself under her arm and nuzzled her side. She laughed again and ruffled the fur behind Bojoe's ears. He welcomed her attention with a hanging tongue then sprang away. He yapped playfully at little Annie and tore past her into the woods, zigzagging through her friends and nearly taking Aarron's legs out from under him. But as she watched him race deeper into the woods the smile dropped from her face. A wall of green mist was suddenly in his path. She jerked up and shouted a warning. But it did no good and he disappeared into it.

She stood and called to her friends, pointing out the danger and seeing that the mist completely encircled them. But no one heard. They smiled and waved and she could only watch as one by one the mist swallowed them up. Rayle Oakley went first, his white horse disappearing from back to front, his wry smile never faltering as it faded into thickening mist. Below him Jobby Morrit continued to work on his carving, oblivious to the way the mist turned the blue dye in her eyes an emerald green. It took the rest of them in quick succession and little Annie was last to go – swallowed up while picking daisies.

She realised her uncle had stopped singing and spun around. He was gone and so was the hideaway. She was alone on a shrinking patch of grass, within a tightening wall of mist. And all of a sudden she felt cold. But it wasn't the kind of cold she could wrap up against – it was like she was freezing from the inside out.

She called out for her uncle - over and over again, eventually screaming his name. There was movement behind the mist and she stepped towards it, thinking it was him. Her eyes strained, widening when the mist thinned, revealing what was in it. Her uncle *was* there, but he was *everywhere*. In one place he was on his back with a dagger in his chest and in another he was hanging by his neck from a tree. And there were many more of him, stretched out in all manner of ugly deaths. She gasped and shut her eyes. When she opened them again there was a dead toruck in the mist, slumped against a tree with his skull smashed in. A short distance away another one was crumpled in the wreckage of a rotten tree stump, covered in blood. She turned from these new horrors to be confronted by another. The encroaching mist had recreated the face of the spirit she had devoured, depicting its final moments. She closed her eyes again and covered her head, unable to bear such stark reminders of her dark deeds...

For a time there was only darkness, then she heard a voice from somewhere far above. *'Is she alive?'*

'I can't tell.' replied another. *'But it's nearly dawn and if she's been here all night, she's had a good dose of mist.'*

She rose to the voices and opened her eyes. She was back in the jungle and there were two spirits hovering above her. One was a girl and the other a boy, and they were watching her like mourners.

'Are you alright?' asked the girl. *'We met your friend Kye and we're here to help.'*

Della stared vacuously and made no reply. The mist had poisoned the higher functions of her mind and all that was left was slave to her physical need. An intolerable vacuum ripped open inside her – an electrical hunger that craved the delicate light of the little ghosts and the all-consuming bliss it contained. Her eyes sharpened like those of an eagle who had woken to find a pair of sparrows in its nest.

She tore forth in Absence, grabbing the ghost girl and biting her neck. But as she connected with her energy a blade of light sliced through the Membrane, separating them. She spun away and turned back just in time to see the boy ghost disappearing into the jungle, pulling the girl by her hand. She shot after them, her bottomless hunger clenching miserably with missed opportunity and her eyes gleaming like emeralds.

J.B. Forsyth

Feral Wraith

Kye was looking across the mud flats when dawn broke and the mist soaked into the land. The last of the worms had wriggled into their burrows hours ago and now they were pushing glistening tree tails up through the muddy pools; spreading fake branches that were adorned with a fresh crop of voluptuous berries. He could smell the strawberry redolence strengthening on the air and despite knowing what the berries were growing on, his stomach rumbled.

Without hammocks they had spent the night on their feet, shifting weight from one foot to the other in a constant flow of mist. Kye's back and legs ached, but he didn't wish for his hammock. With the proximity of the worms and the memory of Kail's severed body still fresh in his mind, he couldn't have closed his eyes, let alone fallen to sleep. Kring wandered over early in the night and asked if he was alright. He was close to tears when the giant gripped his shoulder, but he fought them back and sent him away with a wobbly lip. After that he passed the night in sulky thought with his arms folded and a frown on his face. Ormis was wrong about Najo and Allie, just as he was wrong about Emilie. He sensed no badness in the little ghosts and no deception in their request; their sincerity as obvious as the stone the exorcist was using for a heart. Without their help they would all be dead and how Ormis could think otherwise was an infuriating mystery.

The exorcist called over now and for the first time in hours he turned from the mud flats. The western mountains were gilded with dawn light, but the jungle was still a haven for shadows and it would be some time before the sun penetrated its canopy. In the thin light the others looked haggard, but he sensed they weren't done yet. He could still imagine Suula sprinting back to the mountains; Kring laying waste to a quaggar army and Ormis firing up a powerful draw at a moment's notice. Tracker, warrior and exorcist. If nothing else, he was in good company.

He was walking over when a meteor of light arced down through the trees and came straight at him. He ducked in reflex, but it stopped without striking him, forming a familiar figure when its tail caught up.

'Najo!'

'Your friend's right behind me -'

The little ghost was struck by a second meteor, becoming a raging ball of green and white light that was so bright, Kye was forced back with his hands to his face. Ormis rushed over, creating a great spasm of Membrane as he plunged his arms in and began to draw. The light elongated in response; resolving into two spirits. With cringing horror Kye realised the second spirit was Della, but she was more shadow than ghost now. Her eyes were feverish emeralds in black sockets and her arms were like the raking branches of a leafless tree. Najo was twisting violently in her grip, but she held tight and their lower halves entwined, creating a corkscrew of green and white light. And in the same way Kye had felt Najo's honest intentions, he could feel Della's malevolence radiating like heat.

Ormis strengthened his draw and Kye took another step back. His Membrane sensitivity was strong now and it felt as if the exorcist was gripping the jungle and pulling it towards him like an elaborate tablecloth. But Della gave no ground. She appeared mindless of the danger and focused entirely on Najo – her blazing eyes spewing spectral mist over his terrified face. Their combined thrust pulled Ormis forward and he was forced to lean back, his planted heels making deep grooves in the dirt. When he began to stagger, Kring rushed up behind him and knelt, fixing him in place with two muscular arms. His draw ramped up again and to Kye it was like the rising pitch of a note already high enough to shatter glass. The effect was immediate and Della began to funnel into him.

Kye was paralysed by the sight, unable to make sense of it. Della had become something from a nightmare - a feral wraith of mist and shadow he hardly recognised. He knew something terrible must have happened for her to undergo such an appalling transformation and he was rooted to the spot by the horror of it. She was the only person he felt a connection with since his sister's death – the only person who could understand and sympathise with his new sensibilities. Only an hour ago he had been thinking about the new life Ormis had planned for him and the possibility of Della joining him in it. He had set his hopes on the idea and now that prospect was vanishing before his very eyes. A swirl of indignation rose in his chest and without the slightest idea what he was doing, he stepped into her.

J.B. Forsyth

Deeper Empathy

It hadn't taken Della long to catch up with the little ghosts and when they split up she followed the boy without hesitation. He was the one who had denied her, so he was the one she would take first. She pursued him for several miles, becoming increasing infuriated by his sprightly manoeuvres. Whenever she got close, he would cut away at a sharp angle or loop over her. In one place he stopped so suddenly she overshot him by a dozen yards and by the time she realised what was happening, he was opening up a huge lead again. He even tried to lose her by going through the ground. But she stayed close enough to feel the grooves he created on the Membrane and she followed him as easily as she did through the air.
They had put several miles of blurring jungle behind them when all of a sudden he seemed to give up; arcing down and drawing up like a runner catching his breath. She took her opportunity and swooped, so preoccupied with her malevolent intentions she didn't notice the shadowy figure he started speaking to. She hit him at full speed and his light folded around her like an electrified sheet. She clawed him as he billowed away. His blissful light was clothed in a thin layer of Membrane and she was determined to puncture it. She could already feel its tantalising power, tingling up her arms from where her clawing fingers were raking him. But then something gripped her ankles and a sudden rushing force, much like a wind, began drawing her backwards.
She turned to see a man the girl in her near dead heart would have recognised straight away - a man whose determination was carved into the hard angles of his face. She tried to pull free, but he was joined to her by the strange wind and she could only drag him through the jungle. But then a giant appeared from the shadows and fixed him in place. The man's drawing force increased and it was like slipping down a slope with an ever increasing gradient. In a matter of seconds, she knew it would be too steep – a vertical precipice over which she would surely plummet. But then a boy walked out of the shadows; his face brightening in the light of her

terrified prey. He stepped into her and it was like a window opening on the Membrane. It presented her with an irresistible means of escape and she took it; letting go of her prey and funnelling into him.

She planned to take quick possession of the boy and run him into the jungle - far enough to be safe from the man with the strange drawing force. So she went into him hard, meaning to smash through any resistance. But there wasn't any. Instead of fighting he welcomed her in a spiritual embrace, drawing her deeper than she planned to go. She backed up, trying to fit into his limbs and make him run. But she was too deep to take effective control and all she managed were two disjointed steps after which he collapsed to his knees and fell forward. Bright light flared as he struck the ground, then his raw consciousness enveloped her; his memories and emotion soaking into her mind…

In one memory he was being lifted from a bath and wrapped in a towel into which his name was sewn beneath a big white rabbit. There was the scent of lemon perfume when his mother kissed his cheek and the dreamy warmth of her lullaby in his tiny ears. In another she saw his sister slip from a rope swing into a glistening river and felt him laugh so hard it put stitches in his side. She saw them walking home with the sun on their backs, their clothes dripping as they cut through a field of blazing barley. In another she felt his exhilaration as he raced from Farmer Fon's orchard with his friends, apples spilling from their pockets and rolling down the lane. His memories were floating in his raw nature and the ensemble was completely disarming - like running from a stormy night into a sunny afternoon.

But there were darker memories here too…

She saw the red face of his stepfather as he beat him with a hard bristled broom and felt the deep scratches on his forearms as he protected his head. She saw his mother's drawn and loveless face when he went to her for comfort and felt the shock of her bony fingers when she pushed him away. She saw how the loss of his sister hung off his mother like a weight and how every day she blamed him with her eyes. She glimpsed fragments of the terrible dreams in which he relived his sister's drowning and saw some of the cruel twists that woke him up in a cold sweat. And she felt the guilt stitched into those dreams and his belief they were due penance for allowing her to run onto the ice. She saw how his friends began to reject him and how he was shunned by the village. She felt the infected wounds of that rejection; his crippled self-worth and the aching hunger in his heart. And behind it all was his promise to himself: that if he ever had children of his own - to hold them close and fill their hearts with happiness.

In the space of a few seconds she understood the boy more than he would ever understand himself, and his name was Kye. She floated up; out of the deep place where he kept his memories and into the part of him that dealt with conscious thought. Here he was contrasting two images: a girl with ringlets of golden hair and a shred of shadow with crocodilian eyes. He was confused and dismayed; trying to understand how these disparate images could be the same person. She saw flashes of imagery as he worked on the riddle. He was remembering the girl staggering through a dark wood and her grief playing into his head in a form he thought of as deeper hearing. And now he was seeing her appear to him in a gaol cell as a ghost...

The girl was her!

Della's identity came rushing back as she relived the moment she told him her secret through *his* memory of it. And now she understood how bad he felt after being tricked into disclosing it. She felt his determination to save her and how much it pained him to see what she had become. His compassion was enormous and it was like being hugged on the inside...

Now she was back in her dream. The mist was all around, but now Kye was there. He reached out and when she took his hand the mist blew away. But then, as she looked into his hopeful brown eyes they widened in alarm. She felt fingers pressing into his face and a terrible scouring force plunging through his mind. It was the man she now remembered was Ormis and he was coming for her. His draw was vicious and she was unprepared. He wrenched her from Kye's grip and she could only look down at his shrinking face as she was drawn from him.

She gusted into the exorcist and his draw collapsed on her from all sides, compressing her into an increasingly smaller space. She fought against him to no avail and in a few seconds couldn't move at all. It started to get hot, really hot and she soon realised *she* was the source of the heat...

Smaller and smaller...

Hotter and hotter...

She screamed and started to burn...

Kye opened his eyes and saw Ormis's splayed fingers retreating from his face. He scrambled to his feet, but before he could take a single step, Kring dropped to one knee and grabbed him around the waist. 'Get off me!' he yelled, feet sliding in the dirt. When it was clear he was going nowhere he shrieked at the exorcist who was standing with his back to him. 'Don't do it! Let her go! She's better now!'

'It's for the best lad,' said Kring, his voice low and full of genuine sadness.

'Get off me! You don't understand. I was helping her.' Spittle flew from his mouth and his legs continued to kick, refusing to give up.

It was only when he heard Della's screams that the fight went out of him. The multi-coloured light of her exorcism blazed out of Ormis in dazzling streamers, burning up the dawn shadows as they twisted away.

There was the virginal white of lily petals and the unblemished blue of a summer sky. There was the vibrant green of spring pastures and the rusty gold of autumn leaves. And there was the blood red of a lover's sunset and the heart-warming orange of a winter hearth. For a few seconds the jungle was ablaze with the wholesome colours of her character and they blew through the Membrane like a dying breath. Kye's mourning for his sister, although terrible, was drawn out over many months. But what he felt now was a compressed grief, almost too much to bear. The streaming colours were a sensory eulogy that spoke directly to his heart, threatening to burst it at the seams. It was the saddest and most overwhelming experience of his life and if Kring hadn't been holding him up he would have collapsed in a heap. And when the light disappeared and its afterimage faded into the shadows, he felt like he was fading with it. He sagged in the giant's grip, his hands trembling and his legs wobbling like a new-born foal. Della was gone – burnt down into raw energy and dispersed on the Membrane. He glared at the exorcist as tears coursed down his cheeks. What Ormis had done felt like a sacrilege of nature - as if he had pulled the plug on goodness itself, allowing it to drain away.

When Kring released him his legs weren't ready and he dropped to his hands and knees. The giant offered a hand, but he slapped it away.

'You killed her!' he bawled at the exorcist, each word like a flaming arrow shot at his back. 'You heartless bastard! I hate you! You never gave her a chance.'

It was some time before Ormis turned to him, his face dark with morning shadows. And if he hadn't been so consumed by emotion, Kye might have seen that Della's exorcism had affected him in some uncharacteristic way. 'You saw what she had become,' he said in a voice that was almost a whisper.

'She was still there... I was helping her!'

Ormis recovered and took two furious steps towards him. 'Is that what you call it? What you did was madness! Didn't I warn you against such impulses?'

'You never gave her a chance,' he repeated, his furious face rivalling the exorcist's scowl.

'A chance to what? Gorge on the boy spirit and come back at us bloated with power? Your friend didn't deserve what Izle did to her, but her suffering is over now.'

His eyes were shining with such intractable righteousness that in the end Kye looked away. Ormis didn't understand – would never understand. All of a sudden he felt a compulsion to get as far away from him as possible. So when the exorcist finally stalked off, he took several steps around Kring and sprinted away.

Madness

Kass Riole stared into the green light of his mistlamp. The Caliste had been using the lamps for over two hundred years now, after it was discovered that Eastland mist continued to swirl and glow if it was trapped in glass. This it seemed to do indefinitely; with no deterioration in the intensity of its light. The only change was: it stopped pulsing the moment it was isolated. No one knew why this was so; but his favourite theory was that the pulses were generated by a power residing in the Abyss – a power which the separated mist could no longer be influenced by. But despite this loss it retained much of its hypnotic quality and as he brooded on his thoughts he stared into its green swirls as he would the flames of an open fire.

He had returned to the Caliste two hours ago, forcing himself up the Cragg's four hundred and eleven steps in order to carry out his required study. The office of the High Exorcist was built into the eastern end of the battlements and one of its walls was a bulging grey mountain face. Its natural light came from two windows. One offered him a view of the main gate through the cloister and the other; a fiery depiction of the setting sun in stained glass. The room itself was sparse; cleared out of most of his furniture when he became a permanent resident of Irongate Tower. All that remained now was an ornate chair and a desk he hadn't wanted. They were hand carved and embellished with symbols of his order – bespoke furniture the craftsman had no doubt regarded as appropriate for the High Exorcist, but which *he* regarded as uncomfortable pretension. He shifted in the chair now, wondering whether Izle Rohn had once suffered its hard angles as he contemplated his dark deeds.

There was a knock on the door and Hayhas came through. 'The people have got wind of the King's death and half the city's been out on the streets demanding confirmation. Lord Beredrim addressed them an hour ago and told them he died in his sleep.'

Kass tore his eyes from the mistlamp and scraped his chin. If the people of Irongate had heard about the King's death; someone must have told them. He was well aware that secrets separated from people like oil from water; but the men he had entrusted with the information were not the sort to run their mouths. 'Did he give a date for the burial?'

'In three days and the first Reader Ceremony the day after that.' Kass nodded. Three days was the traditional period of mourning. 'I spoke to Solwin about the recall and he thinks it'll be a while before everyone's back. Amris and Farim have been working in Galthro and should be back tomorrow. But the others are much further afield. Pavro's way out at Pebblesham - investigating a haunting in some tidal caves.'

Kass sighed. 'I don't think it'll make a difference anyway. For a collective exorcism to work one of us will need to fix the spirit with a draw, and after today I don't think that's possible... It's too clever to get caught in the open and you've seen how quick it transitioned to possession. It swept into Altho and there was barely any latency before it took control of him. It was sent by Izle and I've no doubt it's one of his fifteen. It knows our methods and it knows what our options are. What's needed is something radical... Something it won't expect.'

Hayhas raised his eyebrows and looked at the book on his desk. 'Solwin said you'd been browsing some interesting shelves. Find anything?'

He had indeed, but it wasn't something he expected Hayhas to approve of. He had come to the Caliste to lay hands on this book and had even wasted precious time smuggling it past the librarian. Over the last hour he had read one particular section over and over again. He rose from his ornate chair and rotated the book towards Hayhas. The leather cover spun on the oak table and in his near empty office it sounded like a dragon, shifting in its sleep. With a sweep of his hand he invited him to look, then shuffled out from behind his desk and limped to the stained glass window.

Hayhas watched him go. But when it became clear Kass had no more to say, he went to the table and bent over the text; squinting to focus on the faded letters.

'*Meld exorcism*,' he said and straightened up. Kass made no response and continued to look down into the city through a strip of yellow glass; wondering where the spirit was hiding and how long he had to prepare. 'I don't understand.'

'It's the only way to weaken it.'

'But you'd need another spirit; and of similar potency.' Again Kass was silent, knowing that he would come to it. He felt his eyes on his back and even pictured them widening when he spoke again. 'You can't be thinking... Surely not?'

Kass could hardly believe it himself, but he was thinking that very thing and he used another stretch of silence to confirm it. He had joined the Caliste whilst Hayhas was in training and they had been close friends ever since. Of all the opinions he could solicit on a difficult matter, he valued his the most. And whether or not he approved of what he was about to do, he couldn't do it without first hearing his council. Hayhas had always been one to speak his mind and he turned back to face him, bracing for a forthright response.

'It's madness.'

'Is it?'

'*You* ordered him bricked up.'

'I did. And there was good reason. We weren't learning from him anymore and some were getting hurt. It was only arrogance and a childish need to prove ourselves that drew us to him.'

'You make my case.'

'I need only to draw him and purge him at the right time.'

'*Oh come on!* What did Cudgil say about holding him? ... Something about an asylum in his head. He'll drive you mad.'

'Yet Cudgil kept his sanity. He walked him through the city and all the way up the Cragg. I've been through his notes. A dozen exorcists escorted him, but he didn't use a single one... I won't leave the cell until I'm sure he's safely contained and if I can't do it, I'll think of something else.'

'Let's say you *can* do it. What about the meld? It's only been done once before.'

'I know. With spirit demons in Rockspur Caves. I've been through all that.'

'All other attempts have failed miserably and you want to exhume this technique in the middle of Irongate with thousands of people around. If you fail, we could end up with two spirits - or one of unimaginable power. And what about his indomitability? There's no reason to think it won't transfer to the meld?'

Kass felt the words maul him. It wasn't so much what Hayhas was saying as he had already considered such things. It was more the tone of his voice and his incredulous eyes.

'I don't plan to exorcise him. I'll meld him and bring him back here. If that poses too much of a problem, I could always take him to our holding cell in Irongate Gaol.' He paused, feeling his confidence wilt under his old friend's gaze. 'It's all I have Hayhas,' he went on, aware now that strain and desperation was leaking into his voice. 'You haven't felt this spirit as I have. When it grabbed my throat I felt its fingers *individually*. I didn't think the Membrane could be stretched so thin. It had absolute power over me and when it comes again, it'll be our last chance.' He hobbled back to the desk and swept his hand over the book again. 'Izle won't have thought of this. It is our one recourse and I'm going to take it.'

'What about the girl? We could wait to see if Ormis brings her back. She might have some answers.'

'Now *you* sound desperate. Ormis could be days, even weeks, and this whole episode could be over by sunrise.'

Hayhas studied him for some time and Kass could almost see the machinery whirring in his wise old head. He expected another mauling or at least a trademark puff and was surprised when he simply said, 'You'll need me with you when you draw him.'

'I'll go alone.'

'But the protocol -'

Kass waved a hand dismissively. '- I'll take the risk. There've been one hundred and eight recorded visits resulting in one broken arm, a sprained ankle and five admissions to the asylum.'

'But those numbers are based on his visitors following protocol – going in two at a time. It says nothing about the risk of going alone. And the two-man rule's not just about safety. It's to stop him using his visitors to walk himself out.'

'Izle went alone.'

'And look how he turned out. There's a good chance those visits had something to do with what happened to him.'

'We can't both go. I need you down in the city with Djin.'

'What for?'

'I want you to find Beredrim and get him to loan you half a dozen men. Use them as you would our own; in preparation for a collective exorcism. Let the spirit think that's our plan. I'll join you as soon as I can.'

Hayhas puffed. 'Are you sure you can even get down there and back up again? You're an old man with a rusty hip and a bad heart.' There was a familiar brightness in his eyes and Kass knew he was on board.

'I got up here didn't I?'

Hayhas smiled. 'Very well then.'

He felt a weight lifting from him and only now realised how important his support really was. He stepped forward and grabbed him by the shoulders. 'Thank you old friend,' he said through a lump in his throat. 'Madness can be a lonely place.'

J.B. Forsyth

Dungeon

The arched iron door that led to the dungeons beneath the Caliste was set into the west wall of the cavern, behind its cloistered courtyard. It had rested on its hinges undisturbed for more than twenty years and it squealed now as Kass pulled it open and stepped through; casting the green hue of his mistlamp down the stair lined throat beyond. He locked the door behind him and started down, squinting into the shadows as they fled before him.

The warren of caves and passages beneath the Caliste were for the most part a natural feature of the Cragg, but they were extended and developed as a prison under the infamous Lord Hygol; for use as a place of interrogation, torture and death. He reached the bottom and hobbled into a cavern. There was a large mistorb on a high ledge - the last of many spherical lamps once used to illuminate the dungeons and it glowed on its perch like a bewitched eye; as bright as the day it was set there, a hundred years ago.

The cavern was once the main guard room, but it had been stripped of everything except a number of small barrels that were stacked against the wall. He grimaced at them and wondered if they had ever been used as a receptacle for severed fingers. Barrelling was one of the worst atrocities his order had presided over; a mass punishment reserved for communities found guilty of witch harbouring or in repeated breach of doctrine. A barrel, marked on the inside at a level deemed to reflect the seriousness of the crime, was placed in the centre of the offending town at dawn and collected at dusk. And if it wasn't filled to the mark with severed fingers, the exorcists would make up the difference by cutting thumbs. In small towns the practice was devastating – leaving whole communities with only three fingers. And children weren't spared. Historians agreed it was the increasing frequency of such atrocities that pushed the people of the Westland into the years of revolt that ultimately reformed his order.

Kass hurried through the cavern, refocusing on the work ahead of him. He left by another passage with cells on either side. All doors were open and there was a key in every lock. Years ago, the belly of the Cragg was home to over two hundred inmates. But those days were long gone and so were all the prisoners… Except for one.

He swept by the empty cells without so much as a glance into their dark interiors – shadows shrinking back from his mistlamp and insects scuttling into cracks. He passed confidently across two intersections then hesitated at the third before turning right. With the slightest movement of his lips he counted doors until he arrived at the ninth. He stepped through this one; casting light onto walls that hadn't felt it in years. Besides the shackling hoop set into the floor, the cell was empty and there was nothing to distinguish it from any of the other cells he had passed; except that it was the ninth.

He went to the rear of the cell, set his mistlamp on a rock shelf and took up position over the shackling iron. He grasped it with both hands and pulled, grimacing against the grating of his hip. There was a scraping of rock and a square section of floor lifted free. He heaved it clear. The stone clonked down and the metal ring clanged - sounds that fled like escapees, only to be gobbled up by the hungry silence of distant corridors.

He retrieved his mistlamp and fed it to a black shaft; illuminating the top of an iron ladder. He clamped the handle between his teeth and climbed down; the cold iron rungs progressively numbing his hands. When his boots struck rock he stepped off into a semi-circular cave. Three cells had been cut into its curved wall and there was a half mined opening that contained the tools of its forging.

The middle cell had been bricked up on his orders - to keep people out rather than to keep its resident in. But he was here to open it up again. He set his lamp down carefully, considering for the first time the consequences of breaking the glass and having to find his way out of the dungeons in complete darkness. He selected a sledge hammer from the stash of tools and planted his feet in front of the brickwork. He swung hard; striking a clean blow with its heavy face. But the wall didn't give. He swung twice more in quick succession. The first blow loosened a single brick against the mortar and the second knocked it right through. Encouraged, he battered the wall until his breath ran out and his forearms were ringing like bells.

He lowered the hammer and leant on it while he surveyed his demolition. The pine and rose petal aroma of alushia sap filled the air – liberated by mortar dust that was settling in green swirls. The opening he had created looked like a toothy grin and as he stared into its ominous black mouth, he reconsidered his purpose here. Hayhas had called it madness and perhaps he was right.

The entity that waited in the cell was known within the walls of the Caliste as the Indomitable Spirit. But to the common man he would always be known as the Butcher of Baker's Cross. Setting aside books concerning the five disciplines, no other subject occupied as many shelves in the library as the Indomitable Spirit. The boundary between knowledge and ignorance was a natural place to apply the mind, popular with the novices and masters alike.

In life the Butcher was a spirit lure – a common calling for those with Membrane sensitivity. Most lures were discovered and dealt with before they caused too much trouble. The heightened spirit activity they generated gave them away, and given a few days a competent exorcist could usually triangulate their location using Membrane trails. But the Butcher knew this and he evaded detection by staying on the move – practicing his arts as he travelled the Westland. He settled in Irongate after mastering his craft and by then he was able to create trails that confused the resident exorcists for many years.

At some point he began taking his spirit summoning much further than most – drawing them inside and risking possession in order to imbibe their secrets. He began to profit from his work by using what he'd learnt from the dead to exploit the living. He blackmailed murderers, thieves and philanderers; extorted businessmen and courted widows. And by the time of his arrest he was one of the richest men in Irongate.

But his intimate spirit probing was also his undoing. He held them for too long and they left an impression on him – reshaping part of his mind in their image and character. As spirits came and went he relinquished more of himself to this process, until he was but one personality in a growing congregation. He struggled to control their many voices and in the end they drove him mad. Soon after he crossed another line, drawing animal spirits that engendered him with blood lust, compelling him to commit a string of brutal murders in Baker's Cross.

He was caught under a full moon, biting the cheeks off an eviscerated barmaid as she lay dying in the snow. He didn't run when the city guards approached and it took four of them to hold him down whilst an exorcist scoured him. Out of his depth and in his own words *disturbed* by his scour, the exorcist ordered the guards to carry him up to the Caliste, where senior exorcists worked on him for five days. It was only when the great Cudgil Orgra finally drew and purged the spirit inside him that they realised he wasn't possessed at all. The entities they had toiled to extract were all a part of the Butcher's own multifaceted soul and when Cudgil ripped it out; he died instantly.

But that wasn't the end of it.

Reports soon reached the Caliste of a spirit terrorising the streets of Baker's Cross. After a three-day pursuit and a difficult collective draw, they realised they had hold of the Butcher again. He had survived the exorcism and returned to his old haunts. Cudgil brought him back to the Caliste where it was agreed a second exorcism should be attempted in a special cell coated with alushia sap, through which spirits are unable to pass. It didn't work and after years of fruitless study and failed exorcisms they were forced to conclude that he was immune to them. The cell Kass stood before now had been built to hold him permanently and he had resided here ever since.

Hayhas had called his plan madness and he had to admit it was recklessly ambitious at the very least. In theory he could use the Butcher for a spirit meld - but Theory and Practice weren't identical twins. Theory stood for inspection in bright sunshine, with short sleeves and polished buttons. His scruffy brother Practice, slouched in the shade; his long coat full of hidden pockets in which any amount of surprises could be concealed. Mentally, he had given the scruffy brother a good going over; dragging him into the light and turning out as many pockets as he could find. It would have to be enough. He reached into the gaping brickwork with his mistlamp and stepped through.

The Indomitable Spirit

There was about three feet of space between the other side of the brickwork and the door of the cell. He produced his key and turned it in the lock. Three keys had been made, but the whereabouts of the other two were unknown – a situation which had factored strongly in his decision to brick it up. The iron door whined as he pushed it open and he stepped through into a small antechamber. He closed it behind him and turned to face another door, beyond which was the Butcher's cell. The antechamber had been deemed a necessary fail safe in case the Butcher managed to trick his way out, and like the main cell it had been treated with several coats of alushia sap. The protocol that Hayhas had got so worked up about, dictated that no one visited the Butcher alone; the antechamber's doors were opened one at a time; and the visiting exorcists conducted thorough scours of one another on their way out. This ensured that if the Butcher took residence in one of them, he was discovered before he could truly escape. Kass had broken with this part of the protocol by coming here on his own, but he adhered to another section now by raising his draw to the required threshold before opening the second door and stepping into the short passage that fed the cell. He closed it behind him and raised his mistlamp; illuminating hundreds of leather strips that hung from the ceiling. They yielded as he walked through them, whispering against the stone floor and clicking softly as they closed around him. The pine and rose petal aroma strengthened with his every step as the alushia sap with which they had been treated was released into the stale air. The strips were a physical barrier to the Butcher; an ingenious way of keeping him from entering the antechamber when the inner door was opened.

When the last strips swung together behind him he sidled along the cell wall, knowing that stepping into the open space was inviting the Butcher to throw him against the rock. But then he stopped…

Something was wrong.

The cell felt empty. He couldn't feel the Membrane and that meant there was nothing moving, or even resting on it. He produced a small phial from his breast pocket, pulled the stopper out and held it up. But instead of buzzing to life the little fieraks lining the bottom slept on.

The cell *was* empty.

He stepped away from the wall and pointed the open phial at all four corners of the cell. But still, the fieraks were unmoved. He was just beginning to consider the appalling possibility that the Butcher had escaped when something struck him beneath both hands, liberating the phial and the lamp from his grip and sending them smashing to the floor. He watched with dismay as the mist bled from the lamp and seeped into the fissures of the stone floor. A second later he was plunged into darkness.

Oh what a fool he'd been.

He flinched as his Membrane sensitivity fired up, indicating a powerful presence right behind him. He braced for a blow, but none came. The fieraks started to buzz and the cell began to brighten with a green light.

'*Who are you old man?*' asked a voice that was like slivers of ice on the Membrane; the voice of a woman caught drowning babies. Kass turned. Towering above him in an aura of excited fieraks was a spectre who was easily seven foot tall. She had a bald head and a rudder like nose that channelled the malevolent glare of her black eyes. Her shoulders were narrow and gowned in a cloak that hung over her jutting collar bones and impossibly thin frame.

Kass shrank from her; losing the last of his fragile composure. This was not the face he had expected to see. But with the Butcher of Baker's Cross it was best not to presume anything. 'How did you -?'

'- *Evade your detection and the appetites of your pet flies?*' A hideous smile crossed her face. '*Do you think we've been idle in this stinking prison? We've learnt much by fermenting what already exists in our minds.*'

We instead of *I*. Kass had forgotten how the Butcher referred to himself. To him the many personalities of his divided mind were separate entities. The spectre drifted to the far side of the room where she faded into blackness once more.

As Kass inched back to the wall a broad shouldered man materialised in the middle of the cell. He was much shorter than the woman, with a pocked face and square jaw. But his eyes were ice blue and *cramped;* like drops of sea water through which hundreds of drowned souls were peering out. This was the prisoner's true form – the Butcher of Baker's Cross.

'*The Witch of Winter Wood*,' he said with a grin. '*Beautiful isn't she? Your order burnt her at the stake during a snowstorm; right outside this city. She hates exorcists more than the rest of us put together.*' He drifted away then turned back suddenly. '*Tell us old man, where is your High Exorcist?*'

'Gone. Disgraced. Expelled from the order more than twenty years ago and hiding in the Wilderness.'

The Butcher threw back his head and laughed and it was like the laughter of an entire theatre released into the cell. *'Then you are Kass Riole. Yes. Kaaaaaas Rioooole. Forgive us for not recognising you. Twenty years is a long time and your whiskers are now white.'* The Butcher lunged forward, appraising him with bulging maniacal eyes. *'We told him to kill you,'* he said, drawing back. *'Now you are here and he is not. Don't tell us Riooooole. You command now in this black rock - highest among your soul burning fraternity.'*

'Correct.'

The Butcher revolved, revealing the witch's face where the back of his head should have been. But he completed the revolution with a new face.

'Do you recognise him Riiiooole?' he said, using the man's mouth to speak the words.

'No.'

'He's one of your ancestors - Hobe Riole was his name. Hanged for cutting a fair lady's throat. But not before siring the boy that would become your great grandfather. We thought you'd like to meet him.'

'Hello,' said the face.

Kass paled. He was well aware of the games the Butcher liked to play; but he was still taken aback by this chilling diversion.

'He told them all he was very sorry as he stood on the scaffold. But his fake remorse was for the benefit of his mother who crumpled in his stepfather's arms as they adjusted the rope on his neck.'

'What I really thought,' said the man, *'was that I should've cut out off her face and worn it as a mask.'*

The man's delivery was so cold and sincere that it turned Kass's blood to ice. His head rotated to reveal a snarling wolf which lunged forwards, snapping its jaws in front of his face and making him jump half way up the wall.

'Boo!' said the wolf with a wink of its eye. Then it drew back and laughed in that terrible discordant blend of dead voices; its tongue hanging inanely from its mouth. It morphed back into the Butcher, but now he was wearing wolf paws. He drifted forward, his face expanding and distorting until it seemed to Kass like he was looking at him through a fish bowl.

'We wonder. Have any of your grandfather's predilections filtered down the generations to you?... Do you harbour a secret desire to butcher your students and dance through the halls in garments made from their skin?' Kass stared into the Butcher's huge eyes, unwilling to facilitate this line of inquiry.

'So the reason for your visit? Have you come to exorcise us Riiiole of throat cutter's lineage? You have, haven't you? We could feel the wax and wane of your draw the moment you stepped in. And we can feel it now, building inside you like a wave... Tell us, what makes you think you can

succeed where others have failed?' Kass made no reply. He stood flat to the wall, watching and calculating. The Butcher had sensed his draw, but it was protocol to maintain one in his presence. A way of preparing the body for a sudden spiritual assault; much like a fighter bracing his abdomen for a physical blow. *'Does your aged frame house a power of which we should be wary? Or are you just an old fool? And this wavering of your draw. Is it poor control or the resting tremor of a has been that should have given up his mist stone years ago?'* He twitched in ridicule and an idiotic grin appeared on his face.

The Butcher was more sensitive than Kass remembered. He was well aware of the tiny fluctuations in his draw, but was surprised he could sense them. If anything though, it helped his situation. He didn't want to be seen as a threat; on the contrary, he wanted to be seen as vulnerable. The physical fitness required to draw the Butcher was many years behind him, so the only way he was going to get hold of him was to get him to attack. And once he had hold of him he was confident he could contain him. His draw had weakened over the years, but his grip on a captured entity was still the spiritual equivalent of a bear trap.

'Why don't you come here and find out?' he said, realising only then that it might be a mistake to challenge him directly. No one had visited him in a long time and a confident challenge would make him cautious - suggesting he was here to try out a new purge technique.

The Butcher's grin fell away, but against all hope he stared at him as if considering his offer.

Come on, come on, thought Kass. Maybe the direct approach would work.

But it didn't.

He drifted away instead.

'Hang him by his bowels,' said a boy.

'Call the crows to peck out his eyes,' said a girl.

'Well if you're not here to exorcise us Krrrriole,' said the Butcher, turning back, *'why are you here?'*

'To ask a question,' he lied.

'Then out with it.'

'What business did Izle have with you?' He had prepared the question as an ostensible reason for his visit as it was the obvious question to ask. He wanted to appear as an inquisitor rather than a threat. His plan was to engage him in conversation and direct it in a provocative way.

'Ah,' said the Butcher. He floated into a corner and a hundred hushed voices began speaking all at once. Kass couldn't understand what was being said, but it sounded serious. The Butcher dimmed to a deep shade of maroon and he bent over as if in secret conference with the voices. It ended abruptly and he turned back with a crafty smile. *'We will speak of his business, but first we must know why he was expelled.'*

'He was abusing his position. Using his scour to enslave those who had placed their trust in him.'

'And you had him arrested?'

'We tried. He fled into the Wilderness with those already bound to him. We went after him, but in the end we thought him dead. Another victim of the jungle.'

'But you were wrong, weren't you?'

Kass nodded and the Butcher drifted to the opposite corner, gripping his ghostly face. When he turned back his eyes were bright and mysterious.

'How many of your order did he enslave?'

'Fifteen. All of whom fled with him.'

The Butcher jerked and his face morphed into that of a little girl. *'Sixteen,'* she whispered, putting a finger to her lips. *'But don't tell him we told you.'* Her image flickered, once, twice and Kass got the feeling she was a part of his personality he was trying to suppress. Finally, the Butcher won out with a twitch and he never saw her again.

'We will tell you what you want to know,' he said, drifting back over with blazing eyes. *'And it will be our pleasure. Because we want you to know that we orchestrated your predecessor's fall from grace.'*

Kass felt his focus waver once more. He had always believed that Izle's visits with the Indomitable Spirit were motivated by obsession with mastery, but the Butcher's offer suggested there was more to it... Or was this just another game?

'Like many before him he came to exorcise us. To validate himself as the greatest amongst your order. From the moment he knew of our existence he could not rest. He purged us again and again, but always we remained - an ever deeper splinter in his boundless ego...' Kass's interest was piqued by this unexpected turn in the dialogue and the answer to his question now seemed to be of primary importance. *'... He didn't take it well. And after a while he started coming on his own, resorting to more drastic methods that the rest of you would not have approved of. He drew us and held us; studying us with internal scours as if we were a riddle to be solved. But it was all he could do to stay sane and he achieved nothing. Achieved nothing because it was our game all along. Our game!'* His voice rose triumphantly and his head produced a foam of faces.

'*Kill him*,' said an old lady with a squint.

'Spill his insides so we can lick up his blood,' said a little girl.

'Sixteeen!' said a man with a finger to his lips.

'Riiole high, Riiole low, what's going on he don't know,' sung two little girls who sunk back into him in a fit of giggles. *'Reeole pee 'ole, stick it in his keyhole.'*

Kass wondered if Cudgil had seen some of these faces when he first drew the Butcher or if these were different ones. In one of the reports he had just read, Cudgil said it was like the whole city had joined them for his exorcism.

'*Let me tell you something,*' he said, reclaiming his face. '*We are not so different you and we.*'

'I think not. You are a rapist and a murderer and we have nothing in common.'

The Butcher laughed with genuine mirth. '*You have a point Riiiole. You have a point indeed.*' He stared into space, his eyes bright with cherished memories. '*Blood is such a special fluid don't you think? Sometimes bright, sometimes dark. And you can never tell how it will flow from a person until you bite them. Will it trickle or gush? Or will it spurt or spray? You should see a puddle of it steam like hot piss on a cold day... But you misunderstand our point. Our skills and methods are much the same. We are both manipulators of spirits. The only difference is you spit them out. We could have taken your path Krrrriiole. Exorcisms are not difficult and we have done many ourselves. We would have been great, perhaps greater than you. Spirits gravitated to us like bees to a pretty flower and we could vanquish a legion of spectres without leaving this prison. But we can't see the point of destroying something of such potential. Can we?*' In response to this the Witch of Winter Wood appeared briefly and shook her head, her black eyes swirling beneath her hairless brow ridge. '*Each one a mine of knowledge and experience. Each an enriching addition to our community of minds. And if we come across any that displease us we purge or ingest them... You have your books Reeeeole... We have our minds.*'

'It's forbidden.'

'*Forbidden by whom?*' said the Butcher, spinning into a vortex of colour so bright Kass had to shield his eyes. '*Forbidden by men, not by nature! An arbitrary law of your beloved Caliste. Such rules limit your progress and stunt your growth. The time we spent beyond these walls, we spent preying on lost souls and taking their skills and memories for our own. And now we are them and they are us.*

'*We know things that would fascinate you Ree hole – like what the Baby Killer of Barrowey did with all those little bodies and why King Rothway's daughter ended up hanging from the city gate by her intestines... No? Too macabre for your taste. Well maybe you'd be interested in knowing who set that fire in your library or who has the other two keys for my cell?*'

Kass felt his heart skip at this last. He truly would like to know who had those keys but he wasn't about to take the Butcher's bait. He kept his face straight, feigning disinterest.

'*Still no? But I think there is one among us whose story you won't be able to resist.*' He paused and his eyes brightened with an excitement that seemed to infect all those drowning souls within them. '*A girl who fascinates us still. It was her story we used to corrupt the great Izle Rohn.*'

Kass felt a sudden twist in his gut and he got a feeling that some dark unknown was about to step out from behind his ignorance.

'Will you hear her story Kass Riole?'

Kass had come here with plans, but the importance of what he had to say was written in the air and he couldn't leave without hearing it.

'Tell it Butcher.'

His face lit up as he glided to the centre of the cell and he looked like he was going to explode with excitement.

'We found her in the mountain village of Lyell during our travelling days,' he began. As he spoke his face morphed into that of a girl with corn coloured locks and blue eyes. *'Laurena is her name - though she has gone by many others in her long life. We stopped for the night, renting a pitch in the field behind The Tickled Pig tavern. But before we went to sleep we cast our net in the hope of catching some local delicacy. We were hoping to attract the ghost of a local boy who we were told had wandered too far from home and had been eaten by a wolf. But it was the girl that came and we weren't disappointed were we?'*

'No we weren't,' said a little boy who replaced the girl for a few seconds. *'It was like she had a hundred story books in her head.'*

'It soon became clear that she wasn't an ordinary backwater ghost,' the Butcher continued. *'We passed her on the lane a few hours earlier and her ghost came to us while her body still breathed! Have you ever heard of such a thing Riiiooole? Or even read about it in your dusty library?'*

The blood drained from his face. He *hadn't* heard of such a thing until yesterday, but now he knew with utter certainty, he was talking about Della.

'She's the reason you cannot purge us. She is a child of the old world and during her short visit we used what was in her to make us immune to your pathetic purges.'

Kass twitched and his draw fizzled away to nothing.

It lives!

The Butcher watched him with relish.

'It is her story we want to share with you now. She was born to this world a long time ago, and her parents came from another world altogether; forced to flee across the universe from a race called the Uhuru... Did you hear that Riiiole of the Cragg? The uuuuniverse,' he said this with an air of grandeur; punctuated by a gasp of wonder from his internal entourage. *'We can see it as clear as day. As if we were crouched on the mountain ledge instead of her.'* His face morphed back into the girl's and this time her eyes were lowered as if fixed on something far below. *'Listen to her story Riiiiole,'* he said and then added in a voice charged with childish inspiration. *'Oh and we'll use her voice to tell it; you'll like it better that way.'*

The girl started to talk. Her voice was youthful and bright, but she recited her story in the third person. It gave the rendition a creepy puppet like quality that raised the hairs on the back of his neck and sent a cold disquiet through his bones. He had sent men across the mountains to look for this girl and now, through an odd twist of fate, she was standing right before him.

'It is night and she's hiding on a mountain ledge. Her uncle is injured and she's supposed to be resting with him. But after witnessing the exodus from their camp she was compelled to follow. Her leg throbs with poison and it was only with gritted teeth and sheer force of will that she reached this place.

'A man appears from a rocky channel below. Another appears behind him and then another until there's a whole row of men marching up the pass. Higher up, seven elders await them – four women and three men. And their leader Gallianos is with them. He wears the Creator Stone around his neck and it shines with an inner rainbow of colours -'

'- It is the very stone that hangs from The Reader today,' the Butcher interrupted; like a child who can't wait to share an insight, *'But it is*

smaller around his neck.'

'On route,' he went on as the girl, *'they sling their weapons into a rocky gully and shout something. It's a word she can't make out, but they shout it from their hearts. They gather in a deep bowl of rock. She begins to count them, but gives up at a hundred and fifty when they start to mingle. She recognises Mr Thenyon - a woodcutter who lives on the outskirts of Joebel and Tom Denny, the baker's apprentice who once pushed her into a river playing tig. The men embrace and the sound of clasping hands rings around the mountain. Eventually Gallianos raises an arm and they grow solemn and still. "A great pestilence has gathered at the foot of the mountain," he says. "A great pestilence that has driven us from our homes and into these mountains. Tomorrow it will rise from the foothills and take what's left of us.... Men of the new world, tonight you give your lives..." His voice hitches and wavers and she can see that he weeps, '... so others can live on... Long will your descendants heap honour and gratitude upon you." Two men set down a large iron pot of liquid. They queue up, fill the cups they are carrying and spread out. A toast is made and the word they cried before rings out again. This time the word is clear as it is spoken with the power of their collective voice: Eternity!*

'Heads tilt back as one and the liquid is drunk. Not a single man falters in the act. Silence claims the scene - the men as still as statues. Minutes slip by; then almost as one their knees buckle. Some drop like stones, others stagger and collide, but soon enough, a tangled mass of bodies covers the rocky bowl. Movements catch her eye, the twitches and convulsions of those nearest to her and she realises some of them are still alive. Gallianos grasps the Creator Stone and holds it up. The jewel flares and her senses are slain by a crippling force that infuses the air.' Her voice wavered and she morphed briefly into the wolf, who began to whine and cower, its paws covering its head.

'We struggle to tell this part,' said the Butcher, taking his original form, *'because the stone's power was so great it burned the experience into her mind allowing us to relive it. We have felt the Wakening at your ridiculous Reader Ceremonies, but the power of the stone is much more than that. If there's a god of creation, she was in its presence.'*

His eyes glazed over and his face morphed back into hers.

'Her heart quickens and it is like she exists outside of herself, her life suspended while the jewel does its work. There is movement from the twitching pile of men as an invisible force begins to manipulate them, lifting and twisting their limbs and separating them from their bodies. There are no cries of pain, but the stillness of the mountain is profaned by the tearing and ripping of flesh and sinew. Deep into the night the work continues. Gallianos holds the jewel up and his arm never falters. The seven elders that stand with him are as rigid as the rocky outcrops on which they stand.

'Scavenger birds are drawn by the carnage, but they soon settle on ledges; transfixed by the spectacle. By the time the cold eye of the moon looks directly down on the rocky bowl, bones and flesh have been separated and they rest in a pool of blood that looks black in its light.' The girl's eyes opened wide, bursting with excitement. But Kass understood it was the Butcher's emotion he was seeing and not hers. *'The Creator Stone breaks and fuses the bone, raising an enormous skeletal frame from the grisly soup. Its skull is formed from several pieces coming together all at once and her heart misses a beat. Suddenly the skeleton seems sentient – the owner of the power that created it. She shrinks down on the ledge. In its empty eye sockets, she senses the presence of a pitiless god.*

'Organ tissue rises up and packs the frame. One huge mass, the size of a boulder disappears into its chest. She realises it's a heart, forged from the individual hearts of the fallen men. Muscle and tendon follow - wrapping and layering the bone; empowering its joints. The pool of black blood is drained dry as the skinless titan draws it up through its feet. Eventually all that remains of the men is a litter of clothes and folded material she realises is skin. This latter comes together now in huge swatches that rise up and wrap the giant figure like bandages.

'Now it is done and it stands there like a child born of the mountain - a titan whose proportions and features are the average of the sacrificed men. There is hardly time to appreciate it before Gallianos throws his hands up and a shock wave thunders through the mountain. Silence. Then a double thud from its chest. It lives!'

The Butcher's face came back and his eyes were full of wonder. *'I wish you could see it Riole. It is our favourite memory.'* He clutched his hands to his chest, looking like a love sick maiden thinking about her betrothed. *'A memory we value more than all the rest put together. It's so vivid and raw - more beautiful than blood on freshly fallen snow.'* His eyelids flickered and he shivered with pleasure, his spectral form glowing through several shades of red and orange.

'Gallianos finally lowers the stone,' he went on, his face blinking back into that of the girl's. *'The elders fill their cups in the iron pot and return to him. Now they* drink. *But this time they die. Gallianos removes his mantle and lays it over each in turn. Their ghosts rise through it and disappear into the titan's head. When the last of them vanish, he holds the Creator Stone against the mantle and it turns to ash. In its place is a spectral mantle which he draws around his shoulders before dropping to his knees.'*

Not since he was six years old had Kass been so rapt by a story and as the Butcher went on all other thoughts melted away in the periphery of his mind.

'He remains there for the rest of the night, pouring out his grief at the foot of his creation. It is not until the moon sets and the sun glazes the tips

of the mountain that he pushes himself to his feet. He looks up at the titan and there's some silent communication between them. High above two eyes open... With movements as sure and smooth as any man it reaches into the gully where the men cast their weapons and picks up two enormous swords. There has been some magic in that gully she hasn't seen. It takes Gallianos in one massive hand and thunders away down the pass. She climbs down from the ledge and hobbles out onto a rocky spur that gives her a clear view across the plains and her heart quails at what she sees.

'*Smoke drifts across the Eastland as the homes of her people burn. Gathered against the foot of the mountains is an Uhuru army. A race that had, until a week ago, existed in her mind only as a result of the stories told by her parents and teachers. Now the Uhuru are here and her parents are gone; lying unburied beneath the drifting smoke.*

'*Below her the titan is crashing down the mountain towards the army, bounding off great precipices and sliding down banks of shale - breaking off great boulders that tumble after it. On a rocky outcrop she sees Gallianos and his robes are flapping in the wind.*

'*The titan lunges from the mountain and thuds down amongst the Uhuru, setting about them with its twin swords. A second later she is hit by another shock wave – a blast of pure terror that radiates from the Creator Stone. A weapon designed to strike fear into the hearts of its enemies. Even though she stands high above the battlefield the urge to flee is immense. But she watches, trembling; barely able to hold her water. The Uhuru do not flee. She knows they resist with the power of another stone: a green gemstone full of mist and malice. Green fire erupts from their ranks, but the titan is unharmed. A skin of white spirit light emanates from it, deflecting the enemy's attacks around its body so it appears to fight through a twisting mesh of fiery green veins. The smell of burnt butter is carried up to her on the breeze.*'

'*Isn't that odd?*' said the Butcher. '*That the coming together of the two great powers should smell like something as mundane as burnt butter.*' His face flickered over hers and he sniffed hard, closing his eyes as he savoured the smell. Then the girl was back again.

'*The titan smites the Uhuru, carving and trampling, and it is as if they raise their bright magic only to celebrate their own death. She sees two of their giant snakes. The distance has shrunk them to the size of worms, but it doesn't stop her leg from throbbing. One of them disappears under the titan's foot – its tail whips up and spasms before one great sword cuts it in half. It rages amongst its foes, never tiring or faltering, slicing through great swathes of Uhuru with every swipe of its heavy blades. Eventually it stands alone in a stain of carnage.*

'*Now it strides across the plains toward Joebel. It stops in the centre, knee deep in houses. At its feet is the rat hole from where the Uhuru poured - the portal they forged from the other side of the universe. It discards its swords, kneels and reaches in. White fire erupts from its arms, becoming so bright she loses sight of Joebel entirely. She feels the mountain quake and when the light dies, the portal is closed.'*

The Butcher's face reappeared and his eyes were brimming with gleeful expectancy.

'You lie,' said Kass in a voice that betrayed his groping mind. He had been so drawn into his story that his draw had fizzled away again and for the last few minutes he had been completely vulnerable. He knew the Butcher had sensed it, but he seemed more interested in his reaction and was staring at him with a childish satisfaction.

'You doubt me? So did Izle. We have told you what was in her mind and nothing more; but if it is a delusion, her imagination is better equipped than reality itself... What's the alternative? That the titan, or The Reader as you call it, is a selector of kings, dropped from the sky to serve the Westland?' He shook his head with contempt. *'Do you really believe that Krass Riiiiole?*

'The last command Gallianos gave the titan was to protect the Creator Stone and to allow only those with noble intentions to access it. That's why it was mistaken for a selector of kings.'

Kass's mouth opened, but no words came out.

'Izle believed her story,' he smirked. *'But there again he had no choice. While he was trying to purge us, we were busy imbuing his mind with her story. In the end he saw it as we do and it became an obsession that drove him to test himself at a Reader Ceremony. He never stood a chance and I knew it. Izle failed because the titan saw the selfish purpose within him... He didn't take his rejection very well did he? You all thought his reaction was due to injured pride, but what really irked him was he knew he would never get his hands on the Creator Stone. He came back to us in frustration and anger and we consoled him by telling him there was another way.'*

'And what way is that?'

'Protection of the stone was not what the titan was created for. Oh, it performs such function well enough, but we suggested to him that it wasn't infallible. Gallianos gave it this guard duty – the afterthought of a mortal man and not a design of the Creator Stone itself. We convinced him he had the power to trick The Reader. Was it not a basic skill of the exorcists to resist an invasion of the mind? To compartmentalise thoughts and feelings and keep them out of reach of a would be possessor? Wouldn't that work with The Reader? Couldn't he simply hide from its scour?'

'Why didn't *you* try?'

The Butcher laughed. *'We did! But we were rejected. Go look at the records if you don't believe us. They say we're mad and perhaps they're right. Look at us Kass. We are not one voice, but many. And we couldn't all hold all our tongues under its glare. In truth, we don't know if it's possible to fool The Reader. We only suggested it to keep his interest while we worked on him. We advised him to strengthen his mind with forbidden arts and sent him back up to the Caliste like a sickness.*

'If Izle's back, it's to go before The Reader again. He might even try to kill the King to initiate a ceremony.' Kass stiffened and the Butcher grinned. *'He's already killed him hasn't he? It's written all over your face... If he gains possession of the Creator Stone, he'll destroy your noble edifices. And it will be all our doing.'* He swept an arm in front of him like a magician completing his trick. *'This is our legacy Kass Riole! You have imprisoned us here in this tree sap prison and in return we have poisoned one of your finest men and turned him loose.'* The Butcher's face was bright with triumph; the dead congregation behind his eyes united in pleasure. *'Well Riole, what do you think of that?'*

Kass's mind was reaching out in several ways at once. The death of the King made sense now. A Reader Ceremony was imminent and with the Caliste out of the way there would be no one to stop him getting a reading. Kass had much to think about, but it didn't change the purpose of his visit. His priority was still Irongate's rogue spirit and the Butcher remained his only hope.

'An interesting tale, but no doubt a delusion of your sick mind.' The look of self-satisfaction plummeted from the Butcher's face. 'You believe you're the greatest spirit lure that has ever lived. But you are not. Granted, you were formidable in your own time, but now you're nothing more than a historical sideshow. There's a different world outside this rock and your talents have been surpassed by many. The spirits we put in the cells either side of you make you look like a fumbling child.'

'Liar!' He turned his head left and right, looking through the walls of his cell. His surface boiled like lava, pushing out dozens of faces and swallowing them again.

'You were once feared, but now you're pitied. You say I have no control over my draw, but look at you. You have no control over yourself.' The Butcher rippled and bulged, his face twitching as he tried to suppress the rising turmoil inside him. Kass stepped away from the wall and grew tall.

'You asked me if I housed a power of which you should be wary. Now's your chance to find out. I came to purge you. To free this cell up for one greater than you. There are others that could do it, but I needed to fill a quiet time when I had only my thumbs to twiddle. You are housekeeping forgotten - housekeeping overdue.' His voice rose as he spoke, exuding strength and confidence. Not a single note of fear crept into it, for there was none in him. He was bristling with the vigour of youth and it was coursing through his veins.

The Butcher stared at him, stunned.

'What...? The Butcher of Baker's Cross hesitates. Do you fear to strike an old man with a wobbly draw? An old man who visits you alone... They say you fear no exorcist. But you fear me now, don't you? Come here Butcher and bring your congregation of ghosts.'

Our Game!

The Butcher frothed and fizzled like butter in a hot pan. He drew back with a snarl of rage and bore down on him in a blast of spirit wind that should have lifted him from his feet. But Kass was ready.

The theory of Membrane dynamics proposed that the souls of the living were contained in pockets held together like the puckered end of a drawstring bag. His draw had been building behind the neck of that theoretical bag and as the Butcher flew at him he loosened the drawstring, turning the bag into a windsock for his gust; welcoming rather than resisting his assault. It was well timed and he managed to confine most of his momentum to the Membrane. But a tiny fraction leaked through and it struck him like a battering ram, sending him flailing against the wall. His heart stuttered and he gripped his chest. *Not now. His body couldn't fail him now.*

He wrapped him in his draw and pressed down on him from all sides. The Butcher fought ferociously, trying to expand into his head with a fountain of insane voices that would have flooded a lesser mind.

'Is that your heart knocking on the Membrane Peehole?'

'I think you're dying! Three seconds left to live Kriole. Three, two, one, BOO!'

'Don't brag, you're the King of the Cragg.'

'Sixteen!'

'Shshshsh.'

The trick was not to fight the voices; but to let them spiral away while maintaining steady pressure with his draw. If he entertained so much as a single voice, the Butcher would take possession of him.

'Warm blood steaming on cold snow.'

'Absent when present and present when Absent.'

'Reach up and scratch out your eyes. Do it now! ... Do it now! ... Do... It... Now!'

'The Creator Stone in your hand; the titan in your power.'

Absence

The voices faded as he bore down, partitioning the Butcher from the rest of his mind. He imagined gagging and binding him with a succession of mental knots. The last one he wove through the rest and left loose. Tightening it would purge the Butcher and he didn't want to do that just yet.

He turned around and leant against the wall, steadying his breathing and waiting for the pain in his chest to subside. His mistlamp was broken, but he still had his mist stone. It pulsed on his finger, bleeding its poison light onto the wall – a green abscess in the black belly of the mountain.

With only the stone's light to guide him he groped his way through the antechamber and up the iron ladder. He conducted a series of internal scours as he moved through the dungeons, making sure the Butcher wasn't wriggling free. It was always better to tighten the knots as they came loose rather than wait for them to drop off altogether. But to his surprise the Butcher was perfectly still within him. So still, it was hard to feel him there at all. With each scour he became increasingly concerned. Contained spirits always fought against their bindings. *Always.*

He felt his way back to the old guard room and the welcome glow of its mistorb. Moving quicker now he climbed the stairs and stepped back into the fresh air of the Caliste. With no business left in the fortress he went straight to the gatehouse and descended the Cragg. He leant heavily on the iron handrail as he went, stopping several times beneath torch lit horrors to catch his breath and conduct further scours.

Night marinated the city below him; soaking into narrow streets and sheltered doorways. Here and there lamp light bled from windows - the only sign of the city's nervous inhabitants. But it was to The Reader and its magnificent jewel that his gaze was drawn. With the Butcher's story fresh in his mind, he looked at them with new eyes; wondering how much of it was true. It was a story he needed to pick apart - a story he would need to document and share with the upper echelons of his order. But he knew he might never get the chance. If his plan failed and he died tonight, no one would ever hear it.

He made it down the steps and walked into a brace of city guards at the first corner. 'Lord Riole!' said the larger of the two. He had a flat nose and a face full of freckles.

'Sergeant Falc.'

'Are you alright Lord Riole,' he said looking him up and down with concern.

Kass was weary and his hip felt like a ball of broken glass. His hair was thick with ash and his face smeared with soot. The robes that hung off him were soiled and creased. So little was there about his appearance to set him apart from the cities beggars that he would have forgiven the sergeant if he'd walked right by and tossed him a copper moon.

'Just a little tired is all. It's been a long day... Is the curfew in place?'

Sergeant Falc nodded. 'They went straight home after Lord Beredrim's speech and there hasn't been a single breach. It's as if it was self-imposed. Which I suppose it is. Nobody wants to come out after what happened earlier.'

He was about to give some reassurance when the soldiers flinched back from him. 'Lord Riole. Are you sure you're alright?'

Kass frowned. 'Why?'

'Your eyes... They clouded over for a second.'

Kass turned his mind inwards and conducted a deep scour. The guards flinching back from something in his eyes suggested the Butcher had come loose. But once again he found him resting easy in his restraints. Something he had said came back to him now: *'Do you think we've been idle in this stinking prison? We've learnt much by fermenting what already exists in our minds.'*

He refocused on the guards, understanding how his scour must have looked to them. One moment he was talking to them, the next he was in a trance. 'I'm sorry about that,' he said with a smile. 'I felt a little light headed, but it's passed now.' The guards seemed to accept this explanation. Like most people they viewed the exorcists as a strange bunch, prone to odd behaviours that were beyond their comprehension. 'Tell me, what's happening with the people displaced by the fire?'

'Many have been taken in by relatives, or those with a good heart and room to spare. Some had nowhere to go, so they've bedded down in the old barracks - neigh on a hundred of them.'

'Do they have food and blankets?'

'Plenty.'

'And what are they saying this evening?'

'They're scared.' He hesitated and glanced at the other guard.

'Go on sergeant, you can speak freely. What do they say?'

'Begging your pardon Lord Riole, but they say the Caliste has no power over this spirit... That it's beyond you.'

Kass smiled. 'After what they witnessed today who could blame them? But you can tell them we still have hope.' The guards smiled back and nodded their heads, trying to communicate faith, but failing miserably. 'Now if you'll excuse me, I've got urgent business with Hayhas.'

'Of course. Good evening Lord Riole.' The soldiers stiffened respectfully, then disappeared around the corner.

Kass intended to take a direct line to the market quarter, but his feet took him on a winding course that brought him out on Reader Way. He started to cross, but for some reason he stopped. Then, with a feeling like the ground was moving instead of his feet, he did a ninety degree turn to face The Reader. It stood in its enclosure, visible from the waist up; its westward gaze cutting through the darkness a hundred feet above him. He stared at its face. Its vigilant expression was the same as always, but the

warm iridescence of its jewel seemed to caress its visage with new appeal.
'*The Creator Stone!*'

He started towards the enclosure, his appointment with Hayhas forgotten. As he drew closer the cobbles beneath his feet softened and broke up, becoming a narrow mountain trail. He blinked and all of a sudden he was approaching a rocky depression filled with the twitching bodies of hundreds of men. He walked on spellbound as The Reader was constructed before his very eyes. An invisible force tore the bones from the bodies and sent them spiralling into the air; fusing them into an enormous skeleton. The sagging flesh followed, packing out its frame as it drew a huge pool of blood up through its feet...

The enclosure walls reappeared, materialising out of thin air fifty yards in front of him. Two sentries stood in the shadows by the gate – still as stones.

Why had he come here?

'*To see it!*'

He veered away from the enclosure and climbed the steps of the adjacent tower. Two more sentries flanked the door and as he passed between them he gave neither the friendly acknowledgment they had come to expect from him. Once inside, he cut straight through the base of the tower to a door that opened directly into the enclosure. He stepped out onto the cobbles and looked at The Reader with new understanding.

'*The flesh and bone of over three hundred men.*'

In the light of the Creator Stone, he could just make out the rocks between its feet – the throne upon which only fifty-one men had been allowed to sit.

'*The mantle is hidden amongst those rocks. I should see if it's there.*'

He streaked across the courtyard with a feeling of urgency, oblivious to the guards on the walls. One of them saw him and whistled down.

'*The mantle will give you control of The Reader and access to the stone. What hope is there for the city without it?*'

He was about to cross the Threshold of Consciousness when a guard sprang in front of him, levelling a sword at his neck. 'That's far enough.' Another guard ran up behind him and tapped his shoulder with the tip of his sword.

'Lord Riole!' said the first guard in sudden recognition. 'To go before The Reader is treason.'

All at once Kass snapped back into reality. He stared at the Threshold of Consciousness then looked up; realising with dawning horror where he was and what he had been about to do.

'Are you alright Lord Riole?' he asked without lowering his weapon.

Kass gawped. The Butcher had wriggled free of his bindings and walked him here and if he had taken a few more steps The Reader would have killed him. He remembered the city guards flinching and realised they had seen him coming loose. He should've listened to Hayhas. This really was madness.

'Lord Riole?'

As the Butcher's mocking laughter filled his head, he bore down and tied him up again.

'So close don't you think?'
'You can't hold us Kriiiiole.'
'Like we told you before. This is our game!'

And then one last voice, spoken in a conspiratorial whisper:
'Sixteen Kass Riiiiole... Not Fifteen.'

That number again.

Then the voices were gone and the Butcher was still once more. But this time he was taking no chances. From now on he would keep his draw active, maintain a constant pressure on his mental knots. The Butcher had come loose with an act of spirit escapology that was way beyond his understanding, but he would do everything in his power to prevent it happening again.

'Lord Riole? ... Lord Riole!?'

He looked at the guard, arranging his face in an expression of weary confusion. 'Keren isn't it? I can't understand how I got here... I must've walked in my sleep.'

''Tis treason,' Keren repeated, though now there was a tremor in his voice.

'There's no treason without a king,' Kass lied.

Keren looked at him – his training no doubt thin on how to deal with those in higher authority who transgressed the rules. He looked at the other guard for guidance, but found no help there.

A shout turned their heads. 'Lord Riole come quick,' called one of the tower guards as he came running across the courtyard. When he saw the swords levelled at him, he stopped and drew his own. 'What's going on?'

'Nothing. It's just a misunderstanding,' he replied, raising a hand to show he was alright. The Enclosure Guard were sworn protectors of The Reader and its protocols, but the Tower Guard had sworn oaths to protect the King and the Lords. 'Why do you seek me?'

'Hayhas sent a messenger. The spirit's turned up at the old barracks and it's smashing the place up.'

Kass looked at Keren and could tell he wasn't going to write this off as a misunderstanding. He knew the protocols of the enclosure guards well enough to know he was supposed to arrest him and send word to Marshall Beredrim. It was only his rank that was giving him pause. 'Let me go to face this spirit. I give you my word I'll present myself to Lord Beredrim the moment I'm done...You know who I am and where I reside... People are in danger and I'm the only one who can help them.'

The guards shared an uncomfortable look over his shoulder and in the end some tacit agreement passed between them and they lowered their weapons.

'Thank you,' said Kass. He whirled away and followed the tower guard out of the enclosure, leaving them staring after him.

Meld

Kass hobbled after the guard, calling upon him several times to slow down. For the most part the citizens of Irongate were locked tight in their homes and only the weak light that shone out from the edges of their doors and the corners of their windows gave them away. The shops and taverns were completely dark and their black windows seemed to gobble their reflections as they streaked by. Near the market quarter the smell of smoke strengthened and they were soon passing rows of burnt out houses. Distant shouting amplified with every step and before long they could hear smashing glass and splintering wood.

He arrived at the old barracks to find it awash with lamplight and teeming with the dispossessed. The drill square out front had been appropriated by the Trader's Guild many years ago and furnished with dozens of makeshift markets stalls. Many of these were now part of a ramshackle structure that had been erected next to the barracks to accommodate those who couldn't fit inside. There were perhaps sixty people in the square now and to a man they were frozen in place with their heads tipped back; all looking at an enormous spirit. It had been revealed by dozens of fieraks and they were buzzing around it excitedly, feeding on its energy.

The spirit's face was gaunt and feverish and its skull deformed; covered with knuckles of bone that had ripped through its hairless scalp. Supporting its head and in sharp contrast to its emaciated face was a thick neck and a set of broad shoulders that tapered away to a snaking body of spectral smoke and flame. If the spirit really belonged to one of the fifteen exorcists Izle took into the Wilderness, he had changed so much he was unrecognisable.

In one clawed hand it held a man by the ankles. The man's features were bludgeoned to a pulp and his body kinked by a myriad of fractures that made him hang like dough. Kass stared at this vaguely human form with horror, realising only when he spotted a pulsing mist stone that it was

Djin. The spirit had used him to smash the market up and in all likelihood, a loud crack he had heard before turning onto the square had been his skull, impacting one of the broken stalls.

Lord Beredrim and a dozen city guards were braced shoulder to shoulder; their weapons raised instinctively, but uselessly against it. Hayhas stood in front of them and as he approached he could feel his draw. It was a respectable draw for a veteran, but it was having little effect. The spirit was rippling under its influence, but it remained fixed in place.

'Shut down your degenerative draw old man,' it roared in a voice like distant thunder, *'and send for Kass Riole.'*

Kass pushed his way through the crowd. 'No need. I am here!'

The spirit's eyes widened with glee. It threw Djin's broken body over its shoulder and swatted Hayhas away with a contemptuous backhand, sending him crashing into a stack of boxes. Then it snaked through the air until it hung over him.

'At last your champion steps out of the shadows in which he has been hiding,' it said, addressing a sea of terrified faces with a sweep of its fiery arm.

Kass had used his time climbing back up through the dark dungeons of the Caliste to think about what he would do when this moment arrived. A meld exorcism had been performed only once before, when two exorcists released their contained spirits in close proximity. The spirits' natural affinity brought them instantly together and into a contest that was concluded when one consumed the other. The victor, temporarily subdued by an acute glut of power had been drawn and purged without putting up any resistance.

But Kass knew the same process could never work here. There were two key differences between that spirit meld and the one he was about to attempt. For one, he couldn't simply let his spirit go. The Butcher was an anomaly resistant to exorcism and who knew what else. There was no guarantee he was prone to the same spiritual magnetism that attracted all other spirits to each other and he could not, would not, risk him fleeing the scene.

The second difference was that the spirit he had come to exorcise was free. The exorcists that performed the first meld simply let their spirits go, allowing them to rise and mix like vapour. Such a gentle release would do little to serve him here. The spirit had promised him a spectacular and public end and it was gathering itself to crush him.

For *his* meld to succeed he had to ensure the spirits made contact whilst at the same time protecting himself from a physical assault. The only way he could do both was to purge the Butcher with all the force he could muster. To use him as a weapon.

He began to tighten his knots, squeezing him to the brink of purge and then holding him there. The strain was enormous, the mental equivalent of holding one's breath to near unconsciousness. In a matter of seconds, he would be forced to loosen off or burn him up with one last constriction.

'People of Irongate, your High Exorcist swore an oath to protect you. But he can no longer fulfil it. He has grown old and idle and is no longer worthy of his position. I claim this city as my haunt and there's nothing he or anyone else in his black fortress can do to stop me. People of Irongate look upon your High Exorcist for the last time.'

The spirit gathered its flaming smoke to strike, but as it raged down Kass purged his prisoner. The spirits collided in a flash of light and the spectators shrank away with their hands shielding their eyes. A shock wave shook the Membrane and those normally numb to it, felt it for the first time in their lives.

The impacted spirits blazed into each other, spreading out in a disc of light that curved towards Kass like a mushroom cap. Transparent arms of spirit light reached around the edge, giving the impression he was being attacked by a giant spectral squid. But when the glare faded and the people saw him standing his ground within it, they raised a cheer.

But it was a short celebration.

The tentacles withdrew into the curved disc and the light sprang away, reforming into its component spirits. The Butcher coalesced into a raging figure with multiple heads and the fire spirit swatted at him like a cat on its back. It grabbed at the heads with fiery claws, biting their faces with grotesque distortions of its mouth. But as it bit down, the heads sunk into the Butcher's spectre, only to be replaced instantly by another. Among them: a toothless old lady with baggy ears; a little boy with an eye patch and a young woman whose long hair swirled around as if blown by a violent wind. Hobe Riole rose from the place where the toothless old lady disappeared; his eyes bright with delight as he attempted to throttle the spirit. A giant eagle appeared briefly to peck at the spirit's eyes and when it was grabbed by the neck the wolf replaced it, biting and clawing as if on a hot plate.

As the struggle continued the Butcher resolved into a single figure: The Witch of Winter Wood - her shining crow eyes bulging in her masculine skull. Beneath her hooked nose, her square jaw worked itself to a blur trying to find purchase on the spirit's neck. But it held her off – gripping her throat with a smoke-flame hand. Then all of a sudden, it spiralled around behind her; clamping its mouth on the back of her neck. The witch shuddered and the congregation inside her screamed in pain. She tried to rip it away, but it held fast and started sucking her in. Her spectre began to distort and flicker and in one juddering wrench she became the Butcher himself; his eyes wide with the knowledge of his imminent demise. His face imploded and he disappeared into the spirit like an inhalation of vapour.

The spirit twisted towards Kass as though meaning to rage down on him again, but all aggression suddenly drained from it and it sagged in the air, closing its eyes. Kass had expected the Butcher to win, but it didn't matter either way. His plan had worked. The spirits were melded and the victor hung vulnerable above him; temporarily incapacitated by an influx of raw energy. And all he had to do now was step forward and draw it. Once it was contained he could take it to the alushia cell in Irongate Gaol and attempt its exorcism at leisure.

But he hadn't come through the process unscathed. When the Butcher's purge light had connected with the spirit a terrible back stream force had raged through his soul. And now instead of rushing forward to draw it he dropped to one knee, clutching his chest. There was a rush of boots across the cobbles then an arm around him.

'Kass? Surgeon! Over here now!'

It was Beredrim's voice, but he seemed to be talking from miles away. Time for drawing the spirit was running out and if he didn't act soon the meld would have achieved nothing. He started to rise. But there was no air in his lungs and an invisible vice was crushing his chest. He had just enough time to appreciate his greatest failure before the colour drained from the scene and his thoughts turned to sludge. He collapsed into Beredrim's arms; his dead eyes staring at the sky.

Beredrim lowered Kass to the cobbles. He would mourn his friend, but he was a man with responsibility and he packed his grief away – to be taken out at another time. He rose to face the spirit. Kass had subdued it; but it was stirring now. His protocol for dealing with ghosts was to evacuate their haunt and keep people out until the exorcists arrived. But this spirit had been raging over the whole city and didn't seem to be restricted to a haunt. And as for help; he couldn't expect any in the near future. Kass and Djin were dead and it looked like Hayhas was unconscious. The eyes of the people were on him now. He was their only hope, but he had never felt so impotent. The sword he held was useless; nothing more than a symbol of his willingness to fight.

He was about to order the square cleared, when a man pushed his way out of the crowd. He was wrapped in a thick travel cloak and his boots clomped confidently over the cobbles.

'Move back all of you,' he said, striding past Beredrim to where the spirit sparked and billowed like a volcanic ash cloud. He braced himself in front of it, hands balled into fists and head bowed in concentration. The spirit began to ripple and distort. He drew its fire-smoke tail towards him and the moment it touched his chest, it funnelled into him. His hands became glowing mittens and he thrust them into the air, orange fire blazing from his fingertips; so high and bright that noon shadows were cast across the city. Even The Reader was touched by the light and for a short time it looked like a regular man, warming himself by a campfire. The light burnt out and the man sagged in the resulting shadows.

Beredrim rushed to his aid, but he raised an open palm, declining assistance. 'Is it gone?' he asked instead. The man nodded and when he turned, he got a better look at his face. There weren't many exorcists these days and he would have said he knew all of them. But he didn't know this one. A little strange he thought, given the man's evident prowess. 'Well done. The city's in your debt.'

'The exorcism was easy. Lord Riole did the hard work.'

Lord Riole thought Beredrim. Didn't the exorcists refer to him as High Exorcist? 'What's your name? I don't believe we've met.'

'Ri Paldren,' said the man, offering his hand. 'I got word of the recall this morning and came as quickly as I could.'

Beredrim shook with him. 'And you were just in time. My gratitude once again.' They stood together in silence as Kass was lifted onto a stretcher and taken away. Beredrim was so saddened by the scene he was totally unaware of the indifference with which the newcomer watched him go. 'Who ranks now the High Exorcist has fallen?' he asked.

Ri hesitated. 'That would be the High Exorcist's aide.'

'Hayhas. Yes of course.' He looked over to where a surgeon was attending him. 'But it looks like it'll be some time before he's back on his feet. The spirit gave him a hefty backhand before you arrived... Can I ask a favour of you?'

'Of course.'

'When the recall's complete, I'd like you to report back to me?'

'I'll come as soon as I can.'

Beredrim thanked him again then strode away to the barracks.

Raphe pushed through the crowd, tolerating their applause and the occasional pat on the back. He had assumed the name Ri Paldren to keep his true identity a secret. If Lord Beredrim was to check the name he would find it on the Caliste's investment register. But the real Ri Paldren was wrapped in a bloody blanket and going cold in a dank cellar.

He left the barracks behind and set off along the first of many streets that would lead him to the Cragg. The High Exorcist's demise had not gone entirely to plan. His use of the Indomitable spirit was totally unexpected; a bold and brilliant tactic that would have worked if the old dog's body had been as strong as his mind. But it wasn't, and in the end they had achieved their goal. This morning the city's faith in the Caliste was broken, but it had been spectacularly restored tonight. The difference now was Kass Riole was dead and they were in charge. He picked up his pace and when he got a glimpse of the Cragg through an alleyway he thought of Solwin; wondering if the old librarian pleaded for his life when he was dragged to the battlements to be thrown off.

The Last Place

Kye surprised Kring when he bolted away and he even got a few seconds head start on Suula, who gave chase the instant she heard a twig snapping under his sprinting feet. He ran on a near straight line; his thudding boots broadcasting his unwary flight to a sentient jungle that primed itself in response. Strange creatures shifted in their burrows; flowers opened deadly pollen sacks and dozens of creeper vines looped down from low branches or snaked along the ground. He ran on oblivious; his eyes streaming and his grieving heart boiling with anger. The only thing that mattered to him now was getting away from Ormis and the scene of his monstrous crime.

It wasn't long before he was seized by a creeper. It coiled around his ankle as his boot came down; jolting him back as he ran on. Fortunately, his momentum was sufficient to break free and he stumbled forward in a low run, ducking a swiping branch that would've raked his face open. As he recovered his rhythm he looked over his shoulder and saw Suula right behind him; short arms pumping like pistons and her dark eyes fixed on him with predatory purpose.

He sped up in response, taking a line through a patch of violet flowers that coughed up a cloud of pollen. Their green stems stuck to his britches and within a few steps he was ripping great clumps out of the ground. He slowed, taking several panting breaths of rising pollen. The jungle began to blur, but he staggered on; tearing free of the flowers with a rising nausea. He was so disoriented, he didn't see the steep bank in front of him and he ran right out over the top. Where his feet expected firmness there was only air and when his boot found the incline, he fell forwards. The bank was studded with rocks and tree roots and their harsh edges pummelled his tumbling body. The last four feet were near vertical and he rolled off the edge; thudding to the ground with a violent huff of breath. He squirmed onto his back, face furrowed with pain.

When he opened his eyes he found himself staring up into two transparent, blurry faces. 'Lie still and the dizziness will pass,' said one. He could do nothing else and as the swirling nausea subsided, the little ghosts crystallised above him.

'You're lucky,' said Allie. 'If you hadn't escaped those flowers, you'd be turning to sludge right now.'

'Stay where you are boy!' came another voice, lancing through his head. He pushed up onto his elbows and saw Ormis glaring down from the top of the bank. And through Allie's transparency, he could see Suula working her way down; picking a path between several burrow like openings - too big to belong to rabbits.

'Your friend survived his exorcism,' said Najo with bright eyes.

'What?'

'His fires failed and her ghost remains.'

Kye sat up, feeling some of his anger returning. 'Why would you say that? I saw what he did to her.'

'So did we. But her light came together and now she's whole again.'

Kye's head swam – more with confusion than with pollen. 'Came together? I don't understand.'

'Nor do I,' said Allie, her face glowing with wonder. *'But it's true.'*

'Then she might still be alive!'

Najo frowned. *'No. She was dead when we found her.'*

'You don't understand. She's different. She can leave her body without dying.' The little ghosts exchanged a worried look. 'It's not the pollen - my head's clear now. I know it sounds crazy, but it's true. If she survived the exorcism, she could still be alive.'

The ghosts looked at one another again, but this time he couldn't read their faces. *'We could take you to her,'* said Najo, *'and you can see for yourself.'*

Suula was working her way past the last of the ominous openings. In just a few seconds she would reach the ridge from where she could jump down.

'Hurry up and decide Kye. If you're coming you've got to come now.'

With no time to think, he stood up and steadied himself against a final swish. 'Okay. Take me there.'

'Stay close,' said Najo as he floated away. *'You've pricked the jungle's ears and now it listens.'* As if on cue, the glistening snout of some strange creature poked out of an opening. But after sniffing the air it disappeared back inside.

He ran after them, squelching along the muddy channel at the foot of the bank and staying well clear of the openings. He limped heavily to begin with, but he'd sustained no major injuries during the fall and soon relaxed into his stride. Ormis didn't call after him – the risks of shouting this deep in the jungle were too great, but he could feel the exorcist's furious gaze scorching his back.

The little ghosts led him on, instructing him when to jump and when to duck; when to slow down and tiptoe and when to sprint. He didn't hesitate in his flight and by the time they stopped at the foot of a massive tree, he had opened up a substantial lead on Suula. Breathing hard and sticky with sweat, he looked around.

The area was littered with twigs and leaves, snapped branches and severed vines. It looked like a strong wind had blown through; but only a small area was damaged. A dozen feet to either side the foliage was untouched and the jungle floor devoid of leaves. On closer inspection the earth around the tree was scarred with narrow trenches; as if dozens of roots had been ripped up. He could smell moist dirt and something less pleasant behind it – a meaty odour that seemed to rise from the ground.

Najo pointed. *'She was slumped against that tree.'*

Kye squatted to examine the area, but what he saw made his heart sink. There was a vague impression in the dirt that could have been made by anything. He turned back to the ghosts and was taken aback by the way they were looking at him. Their eyes seemed to be on fire and their light had dimmed to a moody purple. He straightened with a spurt of fear and spun around; certain he'd been led into a trap and that someone or something was about to spring from their hiding place and seize him. Nothing did. For the time being at least, they seemed to have this part of the jungle to themselves. But if this wasn't a trap, what was it?

'We can see you don't believe us Kye,' said Allie. *'But she* was *here. I swear it. If you're right and she's still alive, your tracker will find her.'* The ghosts took one another's hand and he knew they were about to reveal their reason for bringing him here. *'We thought if we helped you, then you'd help us.'*

'To do what?'

'To pass,' Najo said, brightening with the words.

Kye shook his head in disbelief. 'I'm not an exorcist.'

'But you're twum, and we felt what happened when you took your friend inside. You stretched the spirt plane so thin, we felt the Last Place calling.'

Kye was stunned. 'I was just trying to help her. I don't know what I did, or even if I can do it again.'

'You don't have to know,' said Allie, drifting closer. *'We just want you to try – to open up and let us in.'*

'Then what?'

'Do what you feel is right. Please! Your tracker will be here soon.' There was a dreadful pleading in her voice and a wild desperation in her eyes. What they were asking him to do was insane, but he felt pity for them.

'Okay. I'll try,' he said, his heart quickening with the decision.

The ghosts looked at each other, shocked that he'd agreed to it.

Somewhere in the distance there was a rustle of foliage, signalling Suula's imminent arrival.

'Let my sister go first and I'll follow if there's time.' He wrapped her up in a bright embrace, then she broke away and drifted towards Kye.

He steadied himself, but couldn't help taking a step backwards as she passed into him. It wasn't like it had been with Della and as their souls merged, he started to panic.

'Don't fight her,' said Najo from a thousand miles away. *'Just relax and let her in.'*

Somehow, after a few disorientating seconds he managed to do just that and all at once he felt like a puddle upon which Allie's reflection was settling.

But what was he supposed to do now?

Suddenly, bizarrely, he was remembering Lady Demia's lesson on traditional dance. She had positioned his arms before stepping aside for one of the older girls, who placed herself against him in a way that made his cheeks glow. When they started to move, his legs felt wooden and all he could manage was a clumsy shuffle that made the other girls giggle. Lady Demia silenced them with an angry rebuke, then told him to just relax and let her lead. He took the advice and after a dozen steps he was dancing like the best of them. He decided to let Allie lead him now and closed his eyes, turning his mind over to her. What resulted was another memory - her memory; and it played out as if it was his own...

She skipped up the path towards her crooked house, letting out an exaggerated, *'Aaaaw,'* as an acorn struck the back of her head. She turned and watched Najo slip through the branches of a large oak and drop to the ground.

'Race you to the swings,' she said as he straightened up. She whirled away and sprinted around the side of the house. There was a trim lawn at the rear and a thick woodland beyond that. Two elms stood apart from the other trees and it was from a thick branch of each that their swings were suspended. She had a good start and sprang onto hers before Najo was halfway across the lawn. She leant back with a cry of victory and kicked herself forward. But as she swung back again, her smile vanished. Najo had stopped running and was frozen in place - his saucer eyes focused over her left shoulder. She twisted to follow his gaze, but didn't get to see the monster before it ended her life. She heard it bounding through the leaves and a second later there was an enormous crunching pain.

A brief period of blackness...

Now she was looking down from a considerable height. Below her, a hunched form was crouching beside her broken swing. Its humped back was covered with a ridge of spines and its scaly skin bled streamers of green mist. She watched as its head jerked back and the last of her body disappeared into its excited mouth. It swallowed hard and looked across the lawn with hooded eyes; dropping down onto its cracked yellow belly and bracing on muscular forelimbs.

Her brother was rooted to the grass along the line of the monster's gaze. His shoulders were slumped and his hands shaking. His face was bloodless; his eyes glassy and silled with tears. On claws like rakes, the monster heaved itself across the lawn towards him, leaving currents of mist in its wake. Its nostrils flared and the long spines on its back swayed like boat masts. It leapt and her brother went down in a frenzy of slashing claws. As its ranks of slimy teeth went to work on him, his terrible screams scraped the air.

There was a smash of plates and through the kitchen window she saw her mother running from the house. When she looked back, all she could see of her brother was his forearm - hanging limply from the monster's mouth. As it worked its jaw, Najo seemed to wave goodbye before disappearing into its gullet. It fixed a considerate gaze on the house as if wondering whether there was another meal waiting inside. But then it turned away and bounded back to the woods; its flanks distended with large chunks of their little bodies. It nudged the broken swing with one blood soaked shoulder, leaving its varnished seat twisting on a single rope.

A moment later Najo materialised beside her.

Now they watched together as their mother streaked around the corner. She ran across the lawn; drawing up sharp when she reached a patch of grass covered with splotches of dripping blood. She saw the twisting swing and ran to it screaming their names, dropping to her knees when she discovered a much greater spillage of blood and clutching her chest as if dealt a mortal blow. She remained there for a time, body shaking and chest heaving. Then with a guttural moan she pushed herself to her feet and disappeared into the trees in a hysterical run.

They watched their mother stagger through the woods until well after dark. Watched as her voice hoarsened with desperate maternal cries. And they watched until she collapsed in a ditch many miles from home.

Kye got flashes of memory now...

He saw how their mother had been found by a woodcutter, shivering and wet. He saw how the villagers spent a whole week looking for them; and their grave faces when the search was called off. He saw how they haunted their old house; watching their mother's grief leach her like a cancer. And he saw them reveal themselves in a bid to ease her pain; an act that served only to deepen her distress. He saw their mother die a lonely death only days before the advancing mist reached their door; her natural passing robbing them of the reunion they were hoping for. And he saw the woodland becoming a jungle that enveloped their empty house; penetrating its mortar and wrestling it down to rubble. He saw, he saw and he saw and his eyes streamed with it.

As he took Allie's pain to heart, he became acutely aware of the Membrane. It was under extreme tension now; pulling away from him in all directions. A depthless void tore open in his chest and he flailed and staggered; feeling himself draining into it. But then he realised it was Allie; separating from him and flowing into the opening. It was the Last Place and he felt her relief as it received her.

When she was gone he opened his eyes, inviting Najo to follow with a wave of his hands. He wasted no time blending with him; but despite his longing for the void he held back on the brink, filling his mind with a whisper of gratitude before funnelling in: *Thank you Kye.*

Absence

A Tortoise Robbed of its Shell

Ormis ran behind Suula, breathing hard and struggling to match her pace. Kring was falling further behind, his broad chest heaving and his bald head glistening with beads of sweat. By his reckoning they had chased the boy for nearly a mile. Suula had taken them around several noose vines, a patch of sneezing willow herb and the trapdoor of a large pit spider. Under normal circumstances, Kye would have fallen foul of these dangers within seconds; but he had seen him talking to thin air at the foot of the bank and knew the ghost children were guiding him. He didn't know what game they were playing, but if Izle Rohn sent them it wouldn't end well. He had warned Kye repeatedly about meddling with spirits and all evidence to date suggested his warnings had floated straight through his head. Whatever the boy hoped to accomplish with his reckless run, he was doing a good job of alerting the jungle. And as he ran on, he cursed Kass Riole's decision to send him.

In part he was angry at himself for not keeping a closer eye on the boy. He should have expected him to react like this; for such reactions were common in those who witnessed the purge of close friends. But the girl's exorcism had left him reeling and he hadn't been in his right mind.

An exorcism was rarely a clean process and between the draw and the purge, transient blends would sometimes occur. Such blends were the precursors of possession and he had been taught to deflect them around his mind, so they ran off like water. But the girl had taken him over during her expulsion and instead of purgefire, chains of flowers had erupted from him. The thawing of his emotions underwent a sudden acceleration in that moment and it was like a sheet of snow was sliding off his heart. The feeling hadn't lasted long though; fading with the flowers and disappearing altogether when the boy started running his mouth. But whatever change was upon him, it had crossed a boundary and his competence to perform his duties was now in question. He had been wide open to the girl - a shameful vulnerability through which she could have possessed him. And when they got back to the Caliste he would disclose his inadequacies to the High Exorcist and submit to whatever rehabilitation he deemed necessary.

Suula stopped and when he puffed up alongside her, she simply pointed. Kye was standing at the foot of a dead tree in a patch of ravaged jungle. His eyes were closed and a broad grin was marooned on his face. The expression was inane - an expression at odds with his own thunderous scowl. Suspecting a trap, he fired up his draw; using its Membrane tension to cast around for signs of the ghosts. Kring caught up, unsheathed his swords and began circling the tree.

Ormis felt nothing in his draw to suggest the spirits were close, but when he saw a thin mist rising from Kye's chest, he charged over. He didn't know what was going on, but he was determined to put an end to it. He thrust a spanned hand into his face and pushed him to the ground. Then with his anger firmly in charge, he flouted the protocols governing the scour, expanding into him like a blast of air into a paper bag. Kye yelped and squirmed, but he held on long enough to prove him pure. He hauled him to his feet and glared into his glassy eyes.

'What did you do?'

'I helped them,' replied Kye triumphantly.

'Helped them how?'

'To pass!'

'That's impossible.' The idea that the boy could perform anything close to an exorcism was absurd.

'Well they're gone and it doesn't matter what you think.'

It was too much for him - the boy's petulant words were like thistles in his ears and he struck him with a whipping backhand that sent him staggering away. He fell heavily and curled up as if expecting him to follow with a boot.

'Get up! I'll not strike you again. What I *should* do is leave you here. You'll regret your stupidity when the jungle takes a closer look.'

Kye got to his feet and faced him with childish defiance. 'Della's alive. Her light came back together?'

A look of exasperated incredulity crimped his face. 'Is that what they told you?... You saw what happened. Without a soul she's dead. Those ghosts beguiled you and brought you here for who knows what purpose.'

'Look over there and see for yourself,' he said, pointing to the base of the tree where Suula was already squatting.

'She *was* here,' the tracker said. 'Less than an hour ago.' She straightened and peered into an oval hole at the base of the tree. 'Came out of here and sat for a while.' They watched as she surveyed the area, bending and sniffing, sifting through the debris and picking up severed vines. 'The torucks were here as well. They were seized by the jungle and one of them was dragged into that rotten stump and didn't come out. The bigger of the two escaped, but came back later to carry her away.'

Kring stiffened, his eyes turbulent with a new sadness.

'See!' said Kye. 'What would he want with her if she's dead?'

'*Proof* she's dead,' said Ormis. 'If she's important to Izle, his word won't be enough.' He turned to Suula. 'There's nothing more to be gained by going on. Take us back to Rockspur.'

'You can't just leave her?' Kye protested.

'She's dead.'

'But you don't know that for sure!'

'Lower your voice or I'll gag you. You've already stoked the jungle with that reckless run.'

As he spoke a line of uplifted earth about six inches high ran out from between two trees and came at them. Kring stepped forward to meet it, turning one of his swords point down and stabbing it into the ground. The burrower veered away and Ormis gestured after it: *see*.

'We'll return with more men. Perhaps there'll be a chance to recover her body.' He turned from Kye and spoke to Suula. 'If we hurry, we might beat the mist.'

Suula started away, but when Ormis pulled Kye's shirt to get him moving, he saw that Kring was still rooted to the spot. He was staring east, along the line of his brother's footprints.

'Kring?'

'I'll not be going with you.'

'But you must.'

'Must I? I've seen plenty I need to speak to Karkus about. I'll continue east till I find him.'

Ormis called after Suula, signalled her to wait then walked to the giant. 'We'll return with fresh men.'

'And let his trail go cold? Giving him time to slip further into the dirt? No, I'll go on while there's still hope.'

Ormis studied him.

He had no authority over the giant now. Kring's heart and mind had already gone ahead to Joebel and nothing he could say could keep the rest of him from following. He had wanted him arrested at the Wall. Not because he suspected him of involvement in the girl's kidnapping, but out of concern that family loyalty would steer his hand.

But he no longer believed that.

The evidence of his brother's crimes had stricken Kring like an illness. He had to go on - to see what had happened to Karkus and to understand it. He couldn't take back his iniquities, but he could serve sentence on those responsible.

If they parted now, he might never see the giant again. Despite their close company over the last two years he had never allowed their relationship to stray beyond the boundaries of work. Kring was warm natured and good humoured, but he had conversed with him through a sheet of ice - treating him like a disposable accessory. He had been blind to this before, but he saw the truth of it now.

They were all waiting for his response - no doubt expecting him to leave the giant with a blunt farewell or to rebuke him for going on. But in that moment he felt a rare squirt of sympathy. It was a delicate thing, but it was enough to jam the cold cogs that usually dominated his thinking. 'If you're going on, then I'll go with you.'

Kring's face was a picture of surprise. 'That won't be necessary. You take the lad back. I'll make my own way.'

'What good are your swords against spirits? You might need me.'

Kring held him in a lengthy appraisal. His offer had broken with form and he felt something new forming between them. 'Alright,' he said finally. 'Together then.'

Ormis turned back to Suula. 'Take the boy to Rockspur and make a report to Lord Formin. Have him assign you a dozen men and bring them to Joebel.'

'You can't send me back!' said Kye. 'You brought me here to help her!'

'At Lord Riole's behest! He wasn't to know what a liability you'd be.'

'But if she's alive I could still help.'

Kring stepped over and placed a big hand on his shoulder 'You should go. You've showed great courage to come this far and you should be proud.'

Kye had come to like the giant, but his gentle words sounded patronising and he slipped his grip, dropping to the ground and folding his arms. 'I'm not going anywhere. And if you want her to take me back, she'll have to carry me.'

Any other time Ormis would have frothed at such puerile stubbornness. But for now that side of him was strangely absent. He had no doubt Suula could drag the boy to Rockspur by his ears, but he could see by her face she had no appetite for it. She wanted to go on to Joebel as much as Kye did.

'A boy has no place here. There's only four of us now and Joebel's a dangerous place.'

'Please don't send me back,' said Kye. His voice was watery and tears were running down his flushed cheeks. 'I came to help you find Della and I don't care how dangerous it is. I've got no friends or family worth having and there's nothing left for me back home.'

A few minutes ago Ormis would have heard insolence in the boy's words, but all he heard now was selfless courage and he felt it in the centre of his chest. His supressed emotions were breaking through his hard exterior and he felt soft and naked - like a tortoise robbed of its shell.

'Very well. We all go... But there can be no more games. Give me your word you'll do as I say.'

Kye's tears were shocked into cessation and it was as clear as the blue sky above him he wasn't expecting him to give in. 'I promise,' he said, wiping his face with his sleeve.

'Then get up. We've wasted enough time already.'

He sprang to his feet in a show of keen compliance and without another word between them they set off for Joebel.

J.B. Forsyth

Silk Ribbons

Della was purged from the exorcist ablaze; her essential faculties reduced to streamers of energy that snaked across the Membrane. Her light faded as she became more dispersed and soon disappeared altogether – spread out so thin she should have dissolved into the Membrane and passed into the forever darkness on the other side. But she was still bound to a living body and as such she did not pass. She began to condense; reappearing like a cloud of mist and coalescing to a ball of light so bright, it sent jungle creatures scurrying and flapping away. She cooled, taking form like a goddess born from a fallen star.

From a black oblivion came a rush of disparate images; flashing through her mind as quickly as pictures could be revealed on a deck of fanned cards. Memory and understanding followed; cementing together in a gasping sense of self. She opened her eyes and was nearly blinded by light. The last thing she remembered was Kye taking her hand and the mist blowing away. It had felt like everything was going to be alright; but then the exorcist drew her out of him and burnt her in his fires.

Was she dead? And was this the afterlife on the other side of the Membrane?

The mists were no longer poisoning her mind and her thoughts were running clean and pure - the way they did when one of her mist fevers lifted. A dreamy hope began to blossom. If she was dead and this really was the Last Place, then her uncle might be here. With joyful anticipation she began searching for him. But everywhere she turned and however far she went there was nothing but bright white light.

Her search was approaching desperation when she began to feel physical sensations. First a pressure in her belly and a tightness around her legs, then the feeling of her arms hanging in the air and her head lolling from side to side. She drifted with this sensory puzzle – trying to fit into it.

And in a matter of seconds, she was wearing it. Her body was being carried by someone with muscular shoulders and huge hands...

Karkus!

But the only way she could be feeling this was if she wasn't dead.

The possibility appalled her. The pain she suffered during her exorcism was the spiritual equivalent of being thrown onto a raging fire. But now it was all behind her, she hoped it had served its purpose. The good life had died with her uncle and now more than anything, she wanted to be with him again.

As if waiting for her suspicions to arise the light began to fade, revealing what was hidden behind it. She drifted forward to take a closer look and was surprised to see a tree. It was the first of many to emerge from the featureless expanse and in a matter of seconds her true environment was revealed. It appeared first in grey monochrome, but as she turned a full circle it came alive with vibrant colour.

Oh no, please no! It can't be...

But it was.

She was in the jungle and its creepy flowers seemed to be mocking her for thinking otherwise. And to top it off she could hear the whispers again and they were carrying her east, towards their source. She flew out of the stream, but something took her in again.

The Shadow! She still carried the shadow!

She moaned and started to cry. What kind of cruel twist was this? The shadow had survived her exorcism and now it was guiding her to its master. In a sudden fit of fury, she willed herself back out of the whispers and took off at a right angle. But after a mile or so she stopped. What exactly was she was planning to do?

Go looking for Kye again?

The idea appealed to her. Their spirit blend had forged some deep connection between them that could never be undone. He immersed her in his fundamental nature and through his memories she glimpsed the experiences that shaped his character. In the space of a few seconds she came to know him from the inside out, unfettered by the barriers of custom and formality. She had risen to where he was thinking about her and his compassion blew the mist right out of her mind. He infused *her* then – appearing in the refuge of her heart – on the lawn outside the hideaway, around which her old friends were gathered. And for as long as she drew breath he would remain there - one of those special people she would remember with a flower if she ever got the chance. But seeking him out again would be selfish. He had risked too much for her already and she wouldn't involve him anymore.

She thought about flying back over the mountains and realised it would only delay the inevitable. Izle had her body and she had his shadow. She couldn't flush it out with a herbal remedy or cut it off with a knife. She had sworn on her uncle's memory to do everything in her power to prevent him becoming whole again, but it was an oath she was going to break. The shadow was a stain on her soul and if the only way she could be rid of it was to go to him, then she would go. So with a dreadful reluctance she flew back to the whispers and allowed them to carry her east.

After a few miles the jungle thinned and she was soon drifting over the vast expanse of vegetation that smothered the ruins of Joebel - an intricate weave of vines and flowers that was interrupted only by the occasional jut of stone columns and the long depressions of overgrown roads. The flowers shone brilliantly in the midday sun and from her perspective it looked like the Wilderness had laid a wreath on the old city – an admission that the people whose land it had taken were worthy of remembrance. But she knew it was romantic thinking and was fully aware that if she took a closer look at the flowers, she would see the horrors lurking behind them.

She watched the scene speed by with great sadness. The bones of her old life were hidden under the vegetation and after five centuries she still hadn't put them to rest. Somewhere down there her mother had sung over her cradle and her father had taught her to swim. Somewhere down there she had once played tig, chalked cobbles and skipped rope. Somewhere down there she had spent many hours, first in frustration and then in exhilaration, learning the secrets of Absence from her parents. She plugged the sentimental hole that was opening inside her. If she succumbed to such thinking the whispers would carry her to Joebel like an army of ants and she would be nothing more than a stunned victim, riding their backs.

As she neared the city centre there was a sudden change in her physical sensations. The pressure in her belly disappeared, replaced by a feeling of falling that terminated with a thudding impact on her back and skull. Big hands manipulated her arms and legs and a cold surface pressed against her skin. For the second time she closed her eyes and puzzled out the sensation; eventually concluding that Karkus had dropped her onto a stone slab. The whispers grew stronger now; from the sort heard across a room to those spoken into an ear. There was an excitement in their mantra and she knew Izle was looking at her.

Up ahead; protruding from a thick lattice of vines was Joebel Clock Tower – the highest point in the old city and a landmark she had been able to see from her bedroom window. Its face was marred with lichen and its rusty hands were seized at twenty-five to one - the time the Uhuru poured from the glass tunnels. Beyond it she could see the vast gape of the Abyss and the ruins of the eastern half of the city, perched on the other side.

Joebel Town Hall was hidden beneath the waxy leaves at the base of the clock tower and she could almost see Izle's whispers rising through them. They were stronger now and she could feel his frustration woven into them. He was trying to reel her in; the same way the spirit lure had done all those years ago behind the Tickled Pig Tavern. But to her surprise and satisfaction she resisted him, easily. She sank through the roof and emerged into the space beneath.

The whispers ceased.

The hall was once a bright atrium, but now it was a dark cavity; lit only by the low light of a wall mounted alushia torch. Its twelve windows had lost all but a few shards of the stained glass that once filled the space with colourful light and were now entry points for bristling clots of jungle. Her body was laid out on a granite slab at the centre of the hall. Her clothes were filthy and torn; stained with blood and covered with splinters of wood. Her left hand hung off the slab and the stump of her little finger glistened in the weak light. The sight allowed her to connect more directly with her physical sensations and she gasped. Her body was a landscape of cuts, bruises and stings and it sang out in pain. If her uncle had been alive, it would have crushed him to see her like this.

Karkus hulked alongside the slab, the wide sweep of his shoulders unmistakable even from above. But it wasn't *his* presence that dominated the space. The whispers were gone; but in their place was a silence that seemed to suck the air into the shadows at the back of the hall. She stared into this soupy blackness and discerned a figure. There were no hairs on the back of her neck to stand up, but the feeling swept through her much the same.

'You have something that belongs to me... Something that ails you... Come down and I will relieve you of it. All will be well for you then.'

His words floated up like silk ribbons – words meant to disarm and seduce her. And they almost succeeded. She started to drift down; wanting to be relieved and believing all would be well. But then she detected the malice woven into his silky voice and froze; the reality of the situation becoming clear. Re-joining her body most certainly meant death. But that wasn't what bothered her.

The man with whom she had shared her long life was gone and she was teetering on the edge of a huge pit of grief. There might be life to be had if she ever climbed out, but she would always have her conscience to bear. Conscience, her uncle used to say, was the great modifier of life's pleasures. It could harden a pillow, take flavour from food and leach colour from the day. Since his death she had killed a toruck, ingested a spirit demon and tore a leecher into a thousand pieces. Worst of all she was responsible for the lynch mob that killed him. Her conscience was irredeemably stained and death would be a welcome escape.

But she hesitated because she didn't think Izle would kill her right away. She suspected that once he relieved her of the shadow he would punish her for taking it. And then he would study her. He knew about Absence and would keep her alive until his interest was satisfied.

'Come child. Relinquish your burden and let the light back into your

heart.'

She decided that was exactly what she was going to do. As soon as he began to draw the shadow she planned to retreat into the deepest memories of her heart – to the woods outside the hideout where she would be reunited with her uncle and her old friends again. And there she would hide; cut off from physical sensation and numb to any punishment or torture he cared to inflict. She would reside there in a nostalgic absence - until her body gave up and she passed away.

Della drifted down and slipped back into her body for what she hoped was the last time. She didn't see Izle rush from the shadows; but felt his fingers pressing into her face the moment she reconnected. But she was expecting this and was already retreating into her mind as his scour reached into her. As she sank down the shadow rose from its hiding place and passed through her like a black bubble. It connected with Izle's scour and she experienced a moment of sheer bliss when he drew it out and her soul ran pure.

His scour withdrew momentarily, plunging back into her with terrifying vigour. Izle was reunited with his shadow - a man remade, burning with rekindled power. His dreadful suction pursued her deeper and deeper and soon her imagination fashioned it into a huge grasping hand. When his fingers fastened on her she sped up, slipping his grip with a series of sharp twists and turns. But in the process she began to panic and when at last she arrived in the deepest part of her mind, she dissolved not into the refuge of her heart, but into a dark memory instead – the last place she would have chosen to hide.

Twenty-Five to One

Laurena walked along a dirt track, feet squelching in her boots and damp clothes clinging to her like a second skin. She had risen early that morning – throwing herself into her chores so she could spend more time with her best friend Anilie. Only Anilie had forgotten to do the same and was still in bed when she went knocking. Her mother let her out to play, but just as they found the rope swing the older boys told them about, she was called in to her neglected chores. Laurena had been bitterly disappointed, but the sun was high and now she was more than happy to saunter through the pastures with its warm apron on her back. If her mother was in the kitchen when she got home, she could help her make pastry or mix batter for a cake. And if she wasn't needed; she would find her father and help him to chop wood.

She jumped a stile and started across a field of cows, who lifted their heads to stare. She stuck her tongue out at the nearest one and was skipping away when a breeze started up. It began so suddenly she turned in reflex; expecting to see what was causing it. She pressed on, but looked around again before taking a dozen paces. Something was wrong with the breeze. It wasn't waxing and waning as expected, but strengthening gradually and she was soon leaning back to avoid being blown over; holding her hair to keep it out of her face. Her clothes started to flap and a chill rose in her damp legs. What had begun as a gentle breeze a few seconds ago was now a storm force wind and she was beginning to lose her feet; crossing the field in long disjointed strides. She went up on tiptoes and took off – blown into the hawthorn hedgerow on the far side of the field. Its defences yielded, bending and snapping with the force of her impact, its thorny projections ripping her shirt and scratching her skin. And still the wind strengthened as though it meant to mince her in the hawthorn's woody lattice. She screamed, but the sound was ripped away before it reached her ears. A strange charge came into the air and a thunderless lightning streaked the sky. But it was like no lightning she had ever seen. It was a luminous, reptilian green; a colour she would loathe for the rest of her life.

The wind ceased and the hawthorn sprang back. She pulled free, tearing her clothes and scratching her face. Several cows had been blown into the hedgerow either side of her and some had crashed through the perimeter fence into the next field. Most were picking themselves up, but some were clearly injured; mooing in distress as they laid on their side. She saw her neighbour's barn and froze. Its whole roof had been blown off; one of its walls had collapsed and a large cloud of straw was settling on the wreckage. She thought of her parents and started to run.

She jumped over another stile and raced across a meadow. There was a stretch of woodland blocking her view of the city and all that was visible was the clock tower. Its big iron hands were set at twenty-five to one, but as she ran on the clock face became obscured by rising smoke. Closer still, there was screaming and shouting. At first she assumed they were the cries of the injured and those coming to their aid, but then she heard a few notes that chilled her blood – sounds more suggestive of slaughter than the aftermath of a strong wind.

Her home was in a glade just outside Joebel, at the edge of a small wood. She arrived at a sprint, but drew up when she saw what had become of it. A large pine tree was lying across the house. The building had collapsed under its weight and two walls had blown out; spewing broken furniture across the grass. Her bed was sticking out of the wreckage and her bookcase was resting on top – books and drawings laid out on the mattress as if on display for some crazy house sale.

Her father was knelt out front and her mother was cradled in his lap.

She went to them in slow dreamy steps. The cries from the city were louder here, but she didn't hear them. All she heard now were his dreadful sobs. She came before him and stopped. He didn't look up, and gave no sign he even knew she was there. His head was hanging and his shoulders jerking as he rocked her mother's floppy head in the crook of his elbow. Her long chestnut hair hung over his forearm; soaking in an expanding pool of blood. Blue eyes looked out of her loose face, but they no longer sparkled with maternal love. They were cold and lifeless and they speared her with a fixed, unseeing gaze.

'Mum?'

She screamed - a long chilling note that brought his head up with a jerk. He also wore a face she didn't recognise. His expression was all emotion and through his streaming eyes she was able to see his bleeding heart. His mouth worked, but he could find no words for her and in the end he just buried his face in her mother's chest.

She looked at them, unable to process what she was seeing – the levers of her mind suddenly jammed and rusted over. But then, as though surfacing from an underwater swim, she tuned into the sounds that were now all around her. The screams and shouts were closer, accompanied by clashing metal and splintering wood. She was incapacitated with shock and couldn't respond, but then a single word of warning blasted through the trees and it struck her father like a slap.

'*Uhuru!*'

His looked up, his face remoulded with fear. 'They've found us!' he said, scanning the woods. 'We've got to get you safe.' He looked down at her mother and back toward the city. Then with great reluctance he laid her down, closed her eyes and kissed her forehead. He froze in place, looking at her for the last time. Then after what seemed like an eternity he sprang up, grabbed her hand and pulled her away. 'Come on now. As quick as you can.'

But she pulled free. She wasn't ready to go yet.

She went back, reached into her mother's shirt and drew her necklace out. It was a simple thing: a set of wooden animals her father carved and threaded with string; a courtship gift her mother never took off. She removed it under his grieving eye; fingers trembling as she picked the knot. Sounds of fighting were becoming louder, but he made no attempt to hurry her. When it finally slipped free, she bundled it into a fist and kissed her cheek. Then she took his outstretched hand and raced away with him.

They were almost out of the glade when a guttural cry went up behind them. 'Faster now!' he gasped, almost pulling her off her feet. They tore around a bend and cut directly into the woods. 'We've gotta get to Uncle Jarl's as quick as we can… There's a shortcut over the river.'

J.B. Forsyth

Washed Up Tree Root

They ran from the woods and sprinted across a wide strip of grassland to get to the river. But after a few bounding steps her eyes were drawn to the sky. Its blue expanse had taken on the texture of cloth and something was pressing through from the other side. It resolved into a huge hooded face with blind eyes and she got the impression it was searching the land. A new dread plumed in her chest and forgetting the threat behind her, she began pulling her father back to the trees.
'What are you doing?' he yelled, yanking her on. 'We can't hide. We've got to keep moving.'
As she lurched forward the scenery started to blur and his handhold began to stretch away, as if her whole arm was elongating. Her footfalls lightened and she was soon rising from the pasture and pedalling the air. She looked up, knowing the face was drawing her and realising she was dreaming. She had retreated into her memory to hide from Izle, but he had found her there. The face in the sky was a representation of his scour and he was trying to draw her out. It was working too. The dreamscape in which she was hiding was sliding away like a silk sheet and in a few seconds it would slip off completely.
She started to panic and saw this was accelerating her detachment and speeding her ascent. The face was growing bigger and its blind cloth eyes were focusing on her. When a huge hand reached out, she forced herself to relax, using the skills of Absence to fall back into the dream. She focussed on the distant sensation of her running feet and her father's grip at the other end of her elongated arm. There were several minutes when nothing changed – when the power of her imagination matched his draw. But then the ground firmed up under her boots and her arm snapped back to its normal length. When she opened her eyes she was scrambling down a river bank - the face in the sky and the knowledge she was dreaming, instantly forgotten.
Her father splashed into the pebbly shallows and helped her down.

They waded towards a cluster of rocks that offered an easy climb up the far bank; but after a dozen sloshing steps they froze. Coming around the bend was a monstrous snake, pushing a wave ahead of it. Its endless body was at least six foot across and its head was crowned by a corona of warty horns. Scales rippled like overlapping shields and a luminous green mist rose from their black joints. As it crunched and clicked over loose stones it fixed them with lidless eyes and flicked out a glistening forked tongue.

A rider was hunched behind the central horns. His face was an abscess and his eyes, pockets of darkest night. He extended an arm with splayed fingers, generating a crackle of air that lifted the water in a fine spray. An invisible force enveloped them, fixing them like posts and allowing them only the freedom to draw breath and move their eyes.

The snake stopped twenty yards upriver, but its bow wave broke around them and splashed up on their chests. The smell hit them next and it was the stink of a corpse, rotting in a tidal pool. The rider swept his hand over the snake and it froze in place. He slid off its back and splashed down. He was tall; over a foot taller than her father, but his body looked unnaturally stretched – like an afternoon shadow come to life. His uncovered flesh was the colour and texture of fried egg white and his tattered clothing was as black as his eyes – a fabric that lacked any crease or fold, giving the impression those parts of him were missing. When he spoke his words scraped out of his throat; like clawed animals emerging from a rocky tunnel.

'Where is the Creator Stone?' he asked her father, waving a hand to return the use of his vocal chords. She glimpsed a shard of green gemstone buried in his palm and realised this was the source of his power.

'Destroyed.'

The snake rider grabbed him by the throat and threw him onto the rocks. He landed with a sharp cry and a crack of bones and rolled onto his side, face screwed up in a mask of agony. She started over to help him; or at least she thought she did. For the magic permitted no movement and her response occurred only in her mind.

The gangly rider sloshed through the water and lifted him by his neck. 'I know it's close. Tell me where it is?'

'I told you,' he replied through his strangulated throat. 'Destroyed!' He was fully released from his paralysis now and stood on tiptoes - one hand gripping the rider's wrist and the other holding his side.

'Watch closely,' said the rider, turning to one of the overhanging trees. He reached towards it and curled his fingers into a fist. As they came together the tree began to wilt - its branches shrivelling and blackening; its foliage drying up and falling like ash. The spectacle was accompanied by a high pitched creaking that gave the impression the tree was screaming, and when he was done it hung over the river like a withered claw. 'Tell me where it is or you'll suffer the same,' he said dropping him onto the rocks again.

'Never!' he replied, spitting a clot of blood at his knees. He was repaid instantly. The rider lifted an arm; there was a hum in the air and her father began to scream. It was the worst noise she had ever heard - the worst she would hear in all her long years. She would have shut her eyes and covered her ears, but she was still paralysed and all she could do was angle her gaze away. Not far enough though; for she could still see him suffering in the unfocussed corner of her eye. A single tear broke through the magic, streaking down her cheek and dripping of her chin.

'Look at your arm and see what has become of it,' said the snake rider as he writhed in agony. 'Tell me where the Creator Stone is or I'll shrivel your child; sicken her limbs one by one and twist her into a deformity you wouldn't recognise. What's more I'll fix your unblinking eyes on her transformation so you can see why she screams.' Her father released a horrible pleading cry. 'Where is it! Tell me and spare her.'

But he said nothing more. He closed his eyes and flopped on the rocks instead.

'Very well. You've made your choice.' The rider used his magic to turn his head towards her and open his eyes – so wide she saw all of their whites. Then he lifted an arm and spread his bony fingers. The air hummed and crackled, but before he could strike her with his wilting magic, a surge of light shot out of her father and hammered into him. His jaw exploded and he spun away, arms flailing and his magic deflected into a patch of river. But she wasn't spared. The water turned green and as it ran around her right leg she felt something that wasn't liquid soaking through her skin and into her bones.

The snake rider staggered backwards, grabbing his ruined face and blowing green gas. A second blast of light lifted him from the river and impaled him on the splintered end of a broken branch. He grabbed at the protruding wood as if trying to pull free, but then his arms dropped and he went limp.

Her father appeared, overlaying the snake rider with his transparency. She had seen him in Absence many times, but had never seen him strike anyone before. Interaction with the material world they referred to as influence; and he had taught her to avoid it at all costs.

'Are you alright?' he asked, looking at the green water running around her leg. But she was still paralysed and could neither test her leg or open her mouth to answer him. When he looked into her face again he saw her eyes widen in alarm. He whirled around; but too late. The rider had lifted his arm and now there was a vicious crackle of the air that warped her father's abandoned body all at once; transforming him into something that resembled a washed up tree root. His ghost blinked out of existence and the snake rider sagged once more; never to move again.

She stood rigid, staring at the place where he had disappeared, struck now by a blossoming grief her paralysed body was unable to act upon. There had been no time to register the loss of her mother, but she felt the loss of them both now and for the next few minutes it scooped her out, transforming her into a hollow statue.

It was only when the snake flicked its tongue out that she snapped back to reality. She looked at the snake and the snake looked at her. Then she blinked and felt the rawness of her dry eyes. They had both been frozen by the rider's magic and it was beginning to lose its hold on them. A few seconds later she could move her tongue and soon after turn her head. She was thawing from the top down and when her chest and shoulders were released she began shaking with fear and grief.

She attempted to run away when the snake raised its head from the water. But only her upper body had been released and all she could do was twist at the waist. It watched her with its carmine eyes, its head swinging side to side in a lethargic arc and dripping water from its underside. It drew back suddenly and struck at her – a movement so fast she saw only its product: a gaping, fanged mouth that filled the whole scene. It snapped shut inches from her face and whipped back, its forward momentum checked by a body still leaden with magic.

She flinched away in reflex, but her lower legs were still fixed in the river like posts and she hinged back on her knees, grasping at the air as she fell into the water. She resurfaced, but wasn't able to rise on her vertical shins and went under again. With water rushing around her face she hugged her knees and heaved herself back up, then stood there coughing and spluttering as she watched the snake. It was looking at its body now, trying to understand why its back half was fixed in the river and raising waves of water as it flexed and coiled; trying to pull free. But when it caught sight of the impaled rider it slithered over and without the slightest hesitation sunk its fangs into him, dislocating its enormous jaw to swallow him whole. And as its old master travelled through its body in peristaltic waves it turned its focus back to her.

She pulled desperately at her frozen legs, looking like someone stuck in deep mud instead of water. She would be released from the magic soon, but so would the snake. It was swishing from side to side now, each undulation moving further down its body. When her legs eventually came free she staggered back, triggering it to strike again. Nearly all of its body was free of magic now and this time its lower jaw bumped her chest and knocked her over. But perhaps sensing its fading opportunity, it didn't retreat this time. Its open mouth strained against its body like a dog on a leash and it inched forward in pace with her splashing retreat - its vile breath puffing out a stinking green miasma. She got back on her feet and fled, feeling the first pulses of pain from her poisoned leg. She scrambled up the far bank and in a racing hobble, set off to find her Uncle Jarl – the man with whom she would spend the next five hundred years…

J.B. Forsyth

A Dangerous Acquisition

Izle broke his connection with a gasp. He had spent more than an hour bent over the girl and his fingers had made imprints on her face. He pushed himself to his feet and considered the dishevelled enigma before him. Despite his best efforts she had resisted his draw; retreating into her mind like a rabbit down an improbably deep warren. She had lost him in the twists and turns, but he had found her eventually; the whole of her consciousness wrapped up in an elaborate memory. He had applied himself to her extraction with resurgent ferocity, but to no avail. It was like she had dissolved into the memory – a trick he would never have thought possible; and one he begrudgingly admired.

How such a wretched girl could stall his plans and resist his draw was both sobering and infuriating. But it wasn't a complete surprise. He had learned of the girl's existence during his visits with the Indomitable Spirit and had even spent time tracking her down - researching old census records and making enquiries in places the Butcher suggested he look. But he had pillaged the girl's mind before his imprisonment and his information on her past whereabouts was so old, it was virtually worthless. If she had stayed in any of the places he listed, it was well beyond the living memory of the current inhabitants. But he had discovered a tantalising lead in the valley town of Harbrook.

The late warden was a diligent record keeper and in one of his browning log books he found several entries concerning a carpenter who had settled there with his niece. The girl had been lamed by a snake bite and walked with a crutch. The warden was suspicious of the man as he could provide no references. But he allowed him to work there for a probationary period during which he proved his worth and was granted permission to stay. They became popular and well respected members of the community, but one night they vanished without a note or a word to anybody – their possessions abandoned in their river side log cabin. It was the girl and her beloved uncle, he was sure of it. He had checked the records of all the villages within a fifty-mile radius, hoping to pick up their trail. But he never found another mention of them. In the end, he had found her when he was focused on other things – crossing his extended consciousness as he spoke to the shapeshifter.

In the last few days he had learnt much of what she called Absence; experiencing it first hand through that part of him trapped inside her. When she left her bed to search for the shapeshifter he had simply observed – feeling the internal adjustments she made to leave her body. It was a skill he might never have learnt, if he had to force her to teach him. But through their blend he had learnt it instantly. When she fell asleep in the gaol he took her into Absence without waking her up. He didn't need the pathetic colour separation method she used; for he was quick to see it for what it was: nothing more than a focusing aid for her weak mind. He had found such preparation unnecessary, gleaning the shortcuts intuitively and performing Absence in a fraction of the time. Whether he could do it in his own body was yet to be proved. But it wasn't much different from his extended scour technique, which he was now beginning to think of as a tethered Absence.

There was still a lot he could learn from the girl: the secrets of longevity, the origin of the Creator Stone and the history of her people. But there was no time; a Reader Ceremony was imminent and his men were in position. The problem was, she was too dangerous to put aside until later. For as he learnt from her, she had, at least subconsciously, learnt from him. She could now leave her body in an instant, as if the shortcuts he had used to take her into Absence were mental doorways he'd left open for her. This, combined with enough power to throw a toruck against a tree, made her a significant adversary. He could not allow her to take leave of her body again and now after years of searching for her he had to kill her.

He slipped a dagger from his robes, but before he could draw it across her throat his hand was stayed by a fresh wave of bitterness. The girl had jeopardised years of preparation and simply bleeding her delicate throat would not satisfy him at all. So with another idea in mind, he turned to Karkus. The toruck dwarfed him; but what contrast there was physically was reversed mentally. To Karkus he was an omnipotent and infallible power, whose will was inseparable from his own. And if he were to command it, he was sure Karkus would drop to his knees and pull his own throat out with his enormous hands - a theory he might one day take pleasure in testing.

The subjugation of the torucks had been key to his plan. He had lured them from Rockspur with a plume of smoke, funnelled them into a glue bog to render them a captive audience. From the edge of the bog he had turned them with a projected scour – a process that proved more difficult than he expected. The toruck mind was surprisingly robust in areas concerning loyalty and righteousness and they had thrashed and cried as he took down the noble edifices of their mind. But by the early hours they were his. Since then they had been his eyes and ears in Rockspur and Irongate. Karkus was going to be his personal bodyguard once he was back in the city, but after the girl's kidnapping he would have to lay low for a while. Another thing to thank her for.

He spoke to Karkus now, though the channel he had carved in his mind.

'Her body clings to life and her soul hides deep inside. Take her to the chute and throw her to Gomsa. He should be ravenous by now. But understand this: she cannot be permitted to leave her body again. Keep a blade to her throat and if she so much as twitches you must kill her immediately. I'm flying west now to Irongate. When you're done here, return to the Tower of Misrus and wait for me to send word.'

He watched Karkus lift the girl from the slab and disappear into the glass tunnels. It pleased him that she would end her meddling life as ballast for Gomsa's stomachs. There was a small chance that she would resurface once Karkus dropped her down the chute; but Gomsa would be waiting and she would be far too occupied to be any trouble. He smiled. The more he thought about it, the more he hoped she would be awake for her final moments.

Absence

Glass Tunnel

The jungle passed by unseen to Kye's whirring mind. His head throbbed with a clamping headache and he was sure Ormis had ruptured something with his rough scour. But he didn't care. He would gladly suffer ten times worse for what he had done for Najo and Allie. He had helped them to pass and it had been the best feeling of his life. Not a physical pleasure, but a deeply satisfying and wholesome one. Now he knew how to help Emilie and as he walked on, he vowed to return to the lake and give her the painless escape she had been robbed of. The only problem was Ormis. He had promised to burn her up in one of his barbaric exorcisms and there was nothing he could say to change his mind. So he had decided to run away as soon as they got back over the mountains and find his sister before Ormis did.

The jungle gave way to a new type of terrain, populated by huge towers of vegetation that ran either side of a wide lane. Each tower was different and some were beautiful to behold. The flowers on one had petals like peacock feathers and throbbing egg yolks for hearts. On another, the flowers were as white as royal bed sheets; their long stamens blowing bubbles that caught little rainbows of light before they burst – forming a snaking vapour that caressed the leaves.

But some of the other towers were downright sinister.

One was covered in a beard of cottony fibres which barely hid a colony of bloated slugs. Another was a stinking wall of palmate leaves through which horn shaped projections grew; their open ends swollen like lips and glossed with crimson nectar. He saw several insects disappear inside; but none came out.

As they travelled between these strange towers he started to think of them as sleeping giants, and once the idea took hold he began to hear the bubbling of their guts and the restless fidgeting of their creaking joints. What followed was a feeling of being watched. He glimpsed surreptitious movements in the corner of his eyes, but when he looked there was nothing to see. With every step along this creepy avenue, he expected a flowered structure to split open and a grotesque hand to snatch him inside.

His first look at the Eastland after coming through the Wall had left him feeling cheated. Lady Demia had done a full lesson about the Wilderness, painting a picture of a twisted land, full of dark and dangerous horrors. But he didn't feel cheated anymore. The Wilderness *was* a land of horrors - she just hadn't told them about their beautiful costumes.

Ormis caught him goggling and tapped his chest; giving him a look he had no trouble translating: *Stay focused boy, this is no place for nonsense.* The exorcist had agreed to let him go on in an uncharacteristic moment of weakness. But whatever had come over him was long gone and his grey eyes were as hard as ever. He snapped out of his daydreaming and continued with renewed concentration, paying more attention now to what was going on upfront.

It wasn't long before the jungle started to close in and they had to weave around thick cobwebs that hung from squat black trees; staying well clear of the red eyed residents that were hiding in the web flowers. Most of the obstacles looked benign: stems of long flowers bobbing in the breeze and gnarled roots sticking out of the ground. But with the memory of the shredder still fresh in his mind, he complied without question when Suula signalled for him to duck or give something a wide berth.

He began to see masonry beneath the vegetation, realising the structures were in fact overgrown ruins and the spaces in between, ancient streets and alleyways. He saw several balusters of a stairway in one and the top of an arched doorway in another. And as he was staring he stumbled over some broken cobblestones.

They slowed as they progressed, Suula spending more time looking around and twitching her nose in the air. The smell of flowers had gradually strengthened and now it was a cloying redolence that seemed to be hindering her. When she stopped he thought it had blocked her senses completely, but then he saw the big hole beyond her.

She signalled for them to wait, dropped to the ground and crawled forward to peer inside. The rest of them watched whilst the sun baked their necks; listening to the drone of insects. She reached into the hole, took her arm out and sniffed at her fingers. Then, after listening for a few minutes she got to her feet and waved them over.

Kye was surprised to see the hole was in fact a tunnel; cut straight into the ground at a steep angle. The walls were made of green glass - flawlessly smooth and unblemished by lichen or moss. A set of steps were hacked into its base. The crude cuts went right through the glass and into the clay and the treads contained crystalline splinters of the smashed material. There was a muddy paste on the lip of the first few and he realised this was what Suula had been sniffing at. He counted the steps; but the tunnel descended quickly into shadow and his eyes failed at fifteen.

'They went in no more than an hour ago,' she said. 'There were traces of the girl's blood back at the tree, but I can still smell it in the tunnel. Fresh blood. Most likely from wounds reopened by rough handling. She's still alive.'

Kye beamed. He hadn't doubted Della was still alive; but Suula's confident confirmation still felt like a weight lifting from him. He saw an altogether different reaction on Ormis's face. A casual observer would have seen indifference in his stony countenance and rigid posture, but Kye had been around him long enough to know better. There wasn't much to go on: a slight tip of his head and a faint clenching of his jaw - but he could tell Ormis was stirred. He had just been told by his most trusted source that the girl he had exorcised was alive. Kye expected him to challenge her, but to his surprise he just stood there, staring into the tunnel.

Suula was the only one left with a backpack after the disastrous river crossing and she slipped it off now and took a little pot from one of its inside pockets. She thumbed off the lid, stuck her fingers into a greasy paste and smeared it onto her short sword. Kye was struck instantly by the smell - the same rose-pine redolence his britches smelt of before he fell into the tree monster. She removed another pot and sprinkled what appeared to be dead insects onto the grease. When they started to buzz, he realised they were fieraks. They began crawling over the blade, each one igniting with a familiar green light. The lights strengthened and merged, becoming a single flame that encompassed the entire blade. Then the fieraks were taking off, whizzing around the sword and dipping into the grease whenever their glow started to fade.

'Their light is weak and so is their heat,' said Kring, putting his hand into the flame. 'See.' He treated one of his big swords in the same fashion, then did the same to a dagger and handed it to Kye. 'If you move it too fast you'll lose them,' he said, swishing his sword to demonstrate. The fieraks were left behind by the sudden movement and for a split second there was a perfect teardrop of flame hanging in the air. But then the flies swarmed after the blade and it collapsed in a green blur. 'Move it nice and slow if you want them to keep up.'

They waited while Ormis treated his sword then gathered at the rim of the tunnel.

'Once we start down we'll communicate with hand signals and whispers only,' said Suula. 'Voices will travel far and true along glass walls.'

Kring went in first, followed by Suula, Kye and Ormis. Shadow enveloped them and the sounds of the jungle soon faded away.

J.B. Forsyth

Runaway Sundial

They descended in cautious steps with their flaming swords held out in front of them. As the gloom thickened, flecks in the glass wall began to reflect their light and it was like they were travelling through a barrel of twinkling green stars. The gradient levelled out and the steps ended, delivering them to a passage of similar dimensions. Kring took them on, stopping where the tunnel was joined by others so Suula could decide which way to go. Some of the openings were plugged with rocks. Kye's first thought was that the tunnels had collapsed, but an overhead swish of Suula's sword revealed their glass ceilings to be intact. The others exchanged a knowing look and without a word between them they continued on. The side tunnels had been blocked up on purpose - to keep something from getting out.
 The passage ended abruptly, spitting them into a natural cavern. Its proportions were out of reach of the fieraks' weak light, but the sound of their boots was suddenly snatched away; suggesting a large cavity. They fanned out and soon arrived at a waterline that stretched away to either side as far as they could see.
 Kye took an instant dislike to the water and when Suula pointed to indicate Karkus had gone in, he felt a rising panic. The water seemed to be watching them and the thought of wading through it filled him with dread. But Suula didn't hesitate and she went in on tiptoes, rippling its brooding surface. When she was knee deep she turned back and squatted, holding an arm out to suggest they proceed in a chain. They linked up with Kye at the back and started forward; their reflections distorting in the sloshing water.
 Kye followed with rising dread and with every step he became more and more certain something bad was about to happen. He had once played a game in which he had to walk as far as he could with his eyes closed. It looked easy, but after a dozen steps there was always the feeling of something looming in front of him; an obstacle that was never there when he opened his eyes. He had a similar feeling now, but with his eyes wide

open. With every churning step he felt an invisible peril gathering in front of him; a feeling that became so strong he planted his feet, bringing the rest of them to a stop. Ormis turned back, inquiring after his behaviour by raising his brow. None of them noticed the unnatural speed with which the water settled. In less than a second it was a flawless mirror; reflecting their flame lit faces to perfection.

Ormis regarded him with atypical patience. But just as Kye was thinking how to communicate this sense of imminent danger, it left him - just like it did in the game, when he opened his eyes. He shook his head in the end, deciding it was just his imagination running riot – a symptom of being in such a dark place so far underground. Despite this Ormis continued to interrogate him with his eyes and it was only when he shook his head for a second time, he seemed satisfied. He turned away and they started moving again; sloshing gently forward through an ever increasing depth of water.

The surface crept up their legs and when it breeched the top of Kye's boots, it poured into them like a slurry of ice worms. He cried out in revulsion and flailed backward, yanking out of Ormis's grip as the sound echoed around the cavern walls. The others were quickly around him, swishing their light over the water as they searched for the source of his reaction. When nothing was found, Ormis grabbed his shirt. 'Out with it now!'

'The water... Can't you feel it?'

But before the exorcist could reply, the water began running away from them and they were forced to brace against the flow; poised like four paddlers in the retreat of a spent wave. In just a few seconds the cavern floor was bone dry and they were left listening to the frothing rush of gathering water.

The cavern lit up, revealing an enormous foaming claw that covered most of the far wall. At its centre was a ten-foot glowing fish eye. Its golden iris was alive with crimson capillaries that streamed in from the edge and emptied into a merciless black pupil. The eye clenched, focusing on them for a few seconds before it blinked out of existence.

'Run!' Ormis bawled. But the water was already crashing down and it struck them like a thunderous waterfall, hammering them into the cavern floor. Kye went head over heels in the turbulence, losing all sense of up and down. The vileness he had felt in the water was all around him now and it was like he was brushing past a huge fish covered with millions of crawling parasites. And he sensed another presence trapped between its scales – a man with a screaming face who seemed to be reaching for him...

He swallowed some of the water and coughed it out, but the parasites were inside him now and they were squirming into the membranes of his nose and throat. His chest tugged for air and he knew that in a few seconds, he would be forced to take the foul liquid into his lungs.

The water fell away just in time and he dropped to the cavern floor on all fours, gasping for air and soaking wet. But he didn't stay wet for long. The water began to separate from him; coming together in a network of trickles that raced down his body and sped away in rivulets. What little he had taken into his throat slipped from the corner of his mouth like threadworms and he jerked back, slapping at his face.

He heard coughing – a series of deep breaths and explosive expirations that could only belong to Kring. He looked around for him and saw a succession of green lights flickering on in various places. The water had washed the fieraks from their blades and now they were returning to feed on them. He went to the nearest light, found his dagger and swished it through the air. Ormis stomped out of the darkness and grabbed his shirt again; his hard face apple green in the weak light of his own blade. 'What about the water? Quickly now!'

'There's a big fish in it and a man too – like with the spiders.' He swatted himself as he spoke; some part of him refusing to believe the parasites were gone and sending crawling sensations all over his body: the corner of his eyes, behind his knees and between his toes.

Ormis seemed to accept this and he turned away to stare after the departed water. Another green flame approached and Kring's hulking form materialised beside it.

'Suula?' asked Ormis, and when the giant shook his head he whirled away and called her name. But there was no answer. 'It's got her!'

They ran to the rear of the cavern and discovered a twenty-foot-high barrel of frothing water, rolling backwards against the wall.

'It's drowning her,' Ormis shouted over the roar, thrusting an arm in and hurrying along its rolling face. Kring joined him, plunging his two left arms in shoulder deep and searching in the opposite direction. Kye stepped forward hesitantly, wanting to help but afraid to reconnect with the parasites. But then, in the widening space between the exorcist and the giant, Suula's arm appeared at the base of the barrelling water and began to rise. He leaped forward to grab it, but he wasn't quick enough and she arced away and disappeared over the top.

'She's here! I saw her!'

Ormis and Kring ran back and plunged their arms in either side of him. The giant took a quick side step and lunged, his entire top half disappearing in a huge froth. He jerked out with Suula's spindly wrist gripped in his thick fingers. Her head appeared with a gasp, but her body continued upwards with the flow and when she finally came out, he had to step back to catch her. As she collapsed into his arms the eye ignited on the under surface of the barrel. It rose like a merciless sun and this close Kye could see the thread like parasites squirming in its iris. They had taken its prize and its liquid focus seared them with a promise of imminent reprisal.

They turned from its brightness and ran for the glass tunnel; Kring throwing Suula over his shoulder and sprinting ahead. But half way there Ormis shouted them back.

'Not the tunnels! It'll drown us... If there's a spirit in the water, it must be purged.'

The eye blinked out, leaving them clustered in weak flame light. In the darkness to either side the water rushed by and came together somewhere in front of them with a thunderous clap. The eye reappeared in what was now an encircling wall of water and it was traveling anticlockwise; causing their shadows to rotate like a runaway sundial. After several circuits Kye turned to Ormis with a dreadful verdict.

'It's looking at me.'

'Why you?'

'I don't know.'

Ormis watched it come around again. 'You saw the man in the water and he saw you. Now he's unsure what to do.'

Kye looked into the eye and saw the exorcist was right. There was a waxing and waning of its terrible glare that suggested uncertainty. But when its light became steady and the ring of water began to tighten on them like a glistening noose, he knew its mind was made up.

'Prepare yourself,' said Ormis, striding away as he tracked the eye. He broke into a run as it appeared over his right shoulder and dived in, extinguishing its light and plunging the cavern into darkness.

Water Skin

Kye stared after him, listening to the ring of water as it tightened around them. When it appeared in their flame light, its curved face had grown so high he couldn't see the top. He stepped back and bumped into Kring.

'Steady lad,' said the giant, placing a firm hand on his neck. 'Save your breath 'til the last second then swim out as hard as you can.'

The water drew ever closer, whipping up a cold breeze and spinning like a tube of black glass. They bunched together in what was now a tight column of air; watching their reflections grow larger and closer. Kye got a good look into his own horrified eyes before the water hit him like a wet slap; ripping him away from the giant and drawing him into its powerful vortex.

It rolled and twisted him, making it impossible to do anything that resembled swimming. The water was dark and cold, but there was no sign of the giant fish and no sign of the man trapped inside it. He bumped into something that could have been one of the others and when he reached for them the water collapsed again, dumping him on the cavern floor.

He saw Ormis staggering through the water, holding his throat. The eye was a fiery puddle beneath him; the water above it domed up to his knees and covering the rest of him in a transparent suit that appeared to be drowning him. Kye splashed over and started swatting at his face; trying to channel air to his mouth. But it was like trying to make a dry spot on a shallow river bed.

Ormis stared out of his watery mask without seeing him. His focus was turned inwards – engaged in something more important than his lack of air. Suula and Kring were soon helping - the little tracker pawing the water like a burrowing rabbit and the giant swiping at it with paddle sized hands. But the eye was generating a steady current to replenish what they splashed away and their combined effort was to no avail.

Kye felt a sudden net-like sensation around his shins and jerked back in reflex, high stepping out of the water in fear of becoming caught. But when the net began to move, it passed straight through his legs. It drew in toward Ormis and the eye domed up until it hung off him like a blazing skirt. Another tug on the net and the eye disappeared. The water poured off the exorcist and he collapsed to his knees, gasping for breath.

Suula retrieved a flaming sword and Kring pulled Kye away. 'Give him space lad, he's not finished yet.'

Kye understood then that the net-like sensation had been Ormis's draw; its Membrane tension somehow confined to the water. And the sudden tug, the moment it won out – pulling the presence from the water like a tablecloth yanked from under dinner plates. Now Ormis was fighting the spirit as he fought for air, coughing and thrashing in a screed of water. This exorcism was in a different league from those he had seen before and he began to feel like a spectator to a schoolyard brawl. He had taken an instant dislike to Ormis that had only deepened over the last few days. But as he watched the struggle unfold every fibre of him willed him to victory.

Ormis became still and Kye took another step back; fearing what it meant. The battle was over, but the outcome was yet to be revealed. There was no way of telling if the exorcist had bested the spirit and as the seconds ticked out he was imbued with a terrible certainty: that he was about to turn his head and glare at them with a pair of glowing fish eyes.

But to his relief Ormis braced on his hands and knees and began purging the spirit in a fiery blast of red and gold light that streamed from his face and fanned out over the wet floor. When it ran beneath Kye, a series of images flashed up in his mind: a dark dungeon where splayed fingers were reaching for his face; a group of men standing in a jungle choked ruin; and a putrid swamp with shallow waters that barely hid its scaly resident. These were the burning memories of the man in the water and they ran through his head with context and meaning. He was seeing the moment Izle took control of him; his arrival in the ruined city of Joebel; and the monster to whom his master bound his soul. Stitched into every scene was his pain and a bitter sense of betrayal. Kye's heart had cheered when his purgefire erupted from the exorcist, but as it dissolved into the Membrane, he hung his head in shame. He had celebrated the exorcism of a man whose only fault was misplaced trust - another victim of Izle Rohn.

Ormis sat back on his heels and drew several deep breaths. His damp hair hung over his face and his wet clothes dripped into little puddles beneath him; giving him the look of an exhausted sailor after a shipwreck. 'Ceppra was his name,' he said between breaths. 'Izle bonded him to the water and the creature living in it.' Then he fell onto his hands and sagged.

Tragic Canvas

Without the spirit to tame it, the water drained away into cracks and fissures, leaving only the odd pool where the floor held a depression. Kye remained with Ormis while Kring and Suula searched the far end of the cavern. The exorcist was sitting back with his eyes closed now. He seemed to be practicing some kind of recuperative meditation and in the green light of Kye's fully restored sword flame, he looked like a graveyard monument. When he finally opened his eyes and got to his feet he did so in the manner of a man twice his age. He had beaten the spirit, but had spent something of himself in the process. Kye watched awkwardly as he stripped, wrung his clothes out and dressed again. When it was done he stood there damp and dishevelled; lacking any of the arrogant rigidity that usually defined him.

'There's another tunnel,' said Suula when she returned with Kring. She led them to a circular opening in the far side of the cavern where the floor sloped down – a tunnel with the same glass lining as the one they entered from. Kring took them in with his sword held horizontally – creating a low fierak flame on his blade. Ormis took the rear guard, but he wasn't up to it. He was swaying as he walked and his eyes were glassy and fixed – like someone trying to stay awake after a week without sleep. Kye looked back several times in concern, but to his increasing dismay the exorcist didn't seem to be getting any better. His plan was to run away from him as soon as they got back over the mountains; but right now, here in the darkness of this underground passage, he wanted to see the return of the exorcist he hated.

The tunnel curved and they discerned a faint light coming from somewhere around the bend. A little further and the sound of heavy footsteps brought them to a halt. Kring lifted a hand in a stay gesture and continued alone, pressed tight to the inside wall. There was a short silence followed by a whine of metal and a loud clang. The giant turned back to them and mouthed a single word: *Karkus*. Then he repeated his stay gesture and disappeared from sight.

Kring stepped into a small cavern lit by two wall mounted alushia torches. Along the left wall was a stockpile of barrels and beyond them two wooden doors. In the centre of the space was a crude oak table, attended by three stools and covered with dirty pots and utensils. On the right wall, four feet above the ground was a hole in the rock - its iron cover wide open on its hinges. Karkus was bent in front of the opening with something under his arm. He squinted – trying to make sense of what he was seeing. But then his brother shifted and the light illuminated the face of the kidnapped girl as he fed her to the hole.

'Karkus!'

His brother spun, drawing a sword and letting go of Della's legs. They fell limp, bending at the knee and hooking over the rim. 'Kring!'

'They told me you'd broken your oaths and that you were in league with a renegade. They said you murdered gaolers in cold blood and kidnapped a girl… I told them it couldn't be. But now I see the truth of it with my own eyes.'

Karkus took a step towards him, a tight lipped smile splitting his stubbly jaw. 'I did all they say and more.' His words were flat and cold – a blunt confession served on a platter of ice.

'What's happened to you?'

'We've been fooled,' he said, his eyes bright with passion. 'The people of the Westland are not our allies. They would see us destroyed and our great city taken for themselves. The spirits that plague us were loosed by the same exorcists they sent to rid us of them. Izle challenged them and they chased him out. We must return him to power so the spirits that scourge our land can be expelled forever.'

'Is that what he told you? Is that all it took to drive you to this wickedness?'

'Wickedness?'

'You murdered unarmed men, kidnapped this girl and cut her finger off.'

'She's a witch with a black heart!'

'She's a child!'

'More like a weapon of the Caliste. She killed Rox – lifted him off his feet and smashed his skull against a tree,' he said, stepping back to the hatch. 'Sound like a child to you? She's a witch and you're too late for her.' He lifted her legs and she slid from sight.

Kring took a step forward. 'Where does it go? What's down there?'

'A fate she has earnt.'

Kring stared at him aghast. 'What did he do to you brother? You were a man of honour! A man of renown!'

'I've chosen my path.'

'But it's over for you. Soldiers from Rockspur are on the way. You've got to give this up.'

'Must I?' he said, drawing a second sword.

'You would fight me over this?'

'You and all that follow,' he said and lunged, his huge frame galvanised in a split second, his twin five-foot blades scything the air.

Kring was taken by surprise and was barely able to parry his vicious barrage. Metal clashed and their layered echoes knifed off the walls. The swordplay was so rapid the fieraks couldn't keep up and they chased their energy source, creating spirals of glowing green light around the blades. Kring was no match for his younger brother and was soon forced back to the tunnel where a flurry of blows put him off balance and dropped him to one knee. It should have been over then. Karkus broke through his defences and drew an arm back to deliver a blow meant to lop off his head. But before he could swing, Suula rushed from the tunnel and leapt onto his chest, stabbing with her dagger. He reeled back and crashed into the barrels; sword arms flailing as his lower arms prized her free and hurled her across the table. She crashed through the clutter of filthy pots and slid off the other side, cracking her head against the wall and settling in a motionless heap.

Kring got to his feet and stepped into the cavern again. An appalling sadness flooded his heart. The brother he knew was gone and any hope of returning him had evaporated during their exchange. He had seen into Karkus's eyes and there was nothing in them he recognised. He looked over his shoulder and saw Ormis behind him – sword drawn and ready to fight. But the spirit in the water had drained him. He looked fragile and weak and if Karkus got the chance, he would make short work of him. He pushed him back into the tunnel with a broad stroke of his arm. 'Go. Take the boy and run.' Ormis started to protest, but his patience was now as short as the exorcist's had ever been. He shoved him again – sending him staggering against the tunnel wall. 'Go now! Get the lad safe.'

He looked at Karkus and knew only one of them would leave this place alive. Whichever way it went; he couldn't win - the outcome for him was either death or insufferable grief. But if he died the boy and the exorcist wouldn't be far behind. They had a head start, but Karkus would soon hunt them down.

Not for twenty years had he bested his brother in combat. Not since Karkus's first entry to the Zilgar games had *anyone* bested him. His chances were grim. But if he was to have any chance at all, he needed to fight with conviction. So, as his fingers tightened on his swords he hardened his heart, locking away all thoughts of the brother he loved and mustering his blood lust. He took another step into the cavern and glared at the other toruck whispering, '*You are not my brother.*'

As they faced off, he felt the God of Battle descend. It was said Toragin kept a gold framed painting of all violent contests upon the walls of his infinite halls. Battle was art and Toragin its artist. But he wasn't the sort to stay behind his easel. Toragin liked to influence his creations, reaching into the scene to twist an ankle here or cramp a sword arm there. Sometimes he favoured daring and flair and sometimes he punished them. But mostly he let the art guide him; falling into a creative trance so deep, he didn't know how his work would turn out until it was finished. It was a notion about which Kring had always been fond and as his senses brightened for battle, he imagined a fresh canvas stretching over the cavern.

Karkus upended the table onto Suula with the tip of his sword and moved to the centre of the space, kicking the stools away. The little tracker had stabbed him where his chest knitted to his left arm and the wound was bleeding profusely. But he came straight at him, huge blades whispering through a series of savage, tree-felling arcs. Kring met each squarely, the muscles of his forearms singing with each bone jarring collision. He was forced back again, but this time Karkus didn't push his advantage. He sidestepped instead, stealing a glimpse around the bend of the tunnel for more would be assassins.

But Kring learnt something from the exchange. The wound Suula dealt him had gone deep. Karkus was an upper- left- hander and hundreds of sparring sessions had taught him to expect a devastating onslaught from that side. But Karkus's blows were significantly weaker on the left and as they squared up, he saw a corroborating sign: the tip of his left sword positioned lower than the right. He lunged with a flurry of blows and Kring turned them all away - six whooshing questions met with six jarring answers. Fierak light streaked and spiralled around the blades in ghostly trailers that seemed to worship their swordsmanship.

Kring countered with a ferocious combination that forced Karkus into several high parries with his injured side. Metal rang in a series of colourful shrieks; each successive note silencing the last. He finished with a vicious overhand and a cross body swipe he threw his whole body into. Karkus blocked both, but his injured arm collapsed and all four blades slid together – *Shhhhhyk.*

With their steel locked, their fists flew like pit fighters. Kring took three hammer blows to his torso, but it was tensed like iron with the strain of the brace and he was only distantly aware of the thudding impact. He got two of his own through, both to Karkus's injured side. But then, out of nowhere, an explosive uppercut to his jaw sent him reeling away. He thudded against the wall, losing all sense of his surroundings. But to his surprise Karkus didn't follow up. He came to his senses and saw Ormis brandishing his sword in the entrance of the tunnel – threatening to attack. The stubborn fool had ignored his instruction – a decision that had drastically reduced his life expectancy.

He stepped away from the wall and swished his swords. The fieraks were left hanging for a second then settled back on the greased blade; creating a flame that ran up and down as he angled the steel. If there had been spectators to the contest, one of them might have suggested the little flies had judged the swordplay and decided their allegiance. But Kring had no such thought. He knew it was the whim of Toragin that counted. The God of Battle was elbow deep in paint and the look of his finished canvas was far from decided.

He was breathing hard now, but Karkus was too. Torucks were built for strength and power, but were quick to tire. His brother was younger and fitter and the longer this went on, the worse his chances. His injuries were usually muted in the heat of battle, but Karkus had done a good job on his jaw and it was grating like broken glass. He was encouraged to see the last exchange hadn't been completely one sided though. His shoulder was hunched in a protective spasm and the tip of his left sword was now pointing downwards.

Karkus's spare hands went to his hips and whipped out a pair of daggers. It was a significant move and one he couldn't replicate - his own daggers in the seat box of a distant wagon. Swords above and daggers below. It was how his countrymen fought in full battle mode. The Dance of Eight was usually a short one, for there was just too many moving parts and skill had to give ground to luck. But to raise the weapon count when it couldn't be reciprocated was a cowardly act - one his countrymen would spit over their shoulders at.

He knew how it would go now. Karkus would try to get close so he could put his daggers to use. His only chance of staying in the fight was to keep his distance. But Karkus surged forward like a cavalry horse; forcing another brace with a flurry of blows that culminated with a pair of diagonal down strokes. As soon as they were locked, Karkus stabbed with his daggers. He slapped one of them away, but wasn't so fortunate with the other. It pierced his forearm between two bones and came out the other side. He knew his brother's next move was to yank it, so with a roar of pain he turned his forearm, taking the blade with it and forcing Karkus to lean sharply to stop his wrist from breaking. He took a sidestep and stood on a broken stool leg which slid away beneath his boot. He lost his balance and the brace collapsed, leaving him wide open. Kring didn't hesitate. He turned the tip of his flaming sword and buried it in his chest.

Karkus dropped to his knees and his weapons clanged to the cavern floor; blood gushing like water from a punctured dam. He fell and the twelve inches of steel projecting from his back scraped across the stone. Kring yanked the dagger from his forearm and dropped down beside him. He turned his head so they were face to face and spoke his name in a splintery voice. But the light in Karkus's eyes was already fading. Despite his broken jaw he roared his name; roared it until his brother's pupils were dead moons. In a fit of disgust, he pulled his sword free and threw it across the cavern. The wound he had inflicted was right in the centre of a large tattoo: a soaring eagle with the sun in its mouth. It was the Krogan family emblem and he had the same one on his own chest. His name was under one wing and his brother's the other. He lifted one of Karkus's limp arms and held it against his own, aligning a special set of symbols: *Brother I love thee*. Then he enveloped him in a four armed bear hug and started to wail.

When news of the brothers' battle reached the toruck homeland it was this scene they imagined on Toragin's canvas. All agreed it was one of his saddest works. They had expected the God of Battle to paint many great canvases of the brothers Kring and Karkus. But never one like this. They said when he was done, Toragin took the tragic canvas and hung it in a place he rarely chose to walk – a dim and dusty corridor in a quiet corner of his endless halls.

Gomsa

Kye and Ormis watched the fight from the shadows of the tunnel, rushing into the cavern when Kring started to wail. Ormis went to Suula and Kye to the gaping hole in the wall. They had ignored to giant's signal to stay back - creeping forward in time to see Della disappearing into the hole and to hear Kring asking where it went. *A fate she has earnt*, Karkus had told him and as Kye peered in, the words repeated in his head.

The hole was the top of a narrow chute that fell away into complete darkness. It offered little to his eyes, but it gave richly to his nose. An invisible odour boiled over its rim, speaking to him of spoilt meat and excrement. He reached in with his flaming sword, chasing the darkness further down its throat and calling her name. But there was no answer.

He turned to Kring who was now rocking back and forth with his brother across his lap; the eerie creak of their leather the only sound in the cavern. Kye wanted to comfort him, but he didn't know how. He had felt the same need to comfort his mother when they lost Emilie. For weeks after she just rocked in her chair; body wasting away and eyes more sunken with each passing day. He went to her once – slipping an arm around her waist and laying his head on her shoulder. But she pushed him away so hard he knocked a table over and broke a vase. So now, he stood there as a bystander to Kring's grief – wanting to comfort him, but not daring to.

Ormis bent over Suula and put an ear to her mouth. 'She's alive,' he said, rolling her onto her side. He went to listen at the wooden doors then joined him at the chute.

'I could climb down after her,' said Kye.

'No. We'll find another way and go together.'

'But it might be too late then.'

'Remember how she was when you last saw her.'

'But I got through to her –'

'- Enough! We'll go down together.' The exorcist hadn't recovered from his battle with the water spirit yet, but he was getting there. He whirled away and went back to Suula who was beginning to stir. Kye watched him go and with a surge of indignation, he grabbed the iron hinge and heaved himself into the chute. Ormis raced back to pull him out; but he shuffled down out of reach.

'Come out now! You don't know what's down there.'

'Della's down there.'

The exorcist thrust himself in to the waist, grabbing at his collar. But Kye slipped his grip and moved further down. 'Go then, if you must. But don't touch her and don't even think about calling out. Wait at the bottom for us to find you.'

He started down, feeling blindly with his boots. The gutter of the chute was slippery with slime and its steep angle promised a rough slide if he lost his grip. In places the slime was so tacky he had to peel his hands free and his skin was soon sore with it. When his left foot slipped he braced against the wall, ripping his shirt and scraping ribbons of skin from his forearms. His heart jumped into his mouth and for one terrible moment he imagined he was falling through a toothed worm. The idea was so strong that once his boots found purchase again, his shredded nerves propelled him several feet back up the chute. He came to rest in a cold sweat and considered going back up. But he thought of Della and brought his panic under control. He forced himself down again – a miserable decent during which his muscles burned like fiery knots and his flimsy resolve threatened to buckle. But then the chute levelled off, delivering him into a deep dark expanse. He straightened his cramped body and swished his flame through the shadows...

The smell of meat woke it up.

It unfurled six intestinal feelers, oozed from its crack and flowed across the cavern top until it was suspended over its feeding chute. There was a body on the floor. The darkness was too complete to see it, but it was able to pinpoint its exact location by smell alone. It sniffed deeply through its many cavities and released a longing gurgle. This one was different to the quaggar they normally threw down. And it was female – most likely a girl. Her sweet smell infused its tubules; teasing its empty stomach sacs and drenching them with anticipatory secretions.

When it heard clashing metal echoing down the chute it flinched away, sliding several feet into its crack. It listened for a while, wondering what the sounds meant, but it wasn't long before the rising aroma enticed it back again. It lowered itself until it was connected to the top and bottom of the cavern like mucus stretched between fingers; then it detached its suckers and slopped down beside her. With no thought to consequences it licked her face. The salty taste of her sweat exploded on its tongues and a hunger of enormous proportion raged through its body. And only with a tremendous call on its waning will power did it stop itself from enveloping her.

It had to think about this...

This could be another test and it didn't want to fail again...

The last time Izle threw a quaggar man down, it was ordered to let him escape. It was a test of discipline it hadn't been equal to and in a spasm of excitement, it tore his leg off when he started running for the light. Izle had expressed strong disapproval, leaving it to reflect on its failure and nurse its grumbling stomach sacs. This time it would try harder. Pleasing its master brought great tranquillity to its mind and great peace to its dreams. And Izle had promised it could go back to the surface once it passed his tests. It longed to move through the trees again and to hunt its prey through the jungle canopy.

But it shouldn't have tasted her. Resisting would be twice as hard now.

It was about to whip a tongue out for a second taste, when it heard voices in the chute and someone climbing down. It thought about sliding up to see who it was, but then it remembered the time it reached through the hatch at the top and snatched one of the quaggar without permission. Izle had punished it for doing so – reaching into its mind and stirring things around until it was sick. So, tempting as it was to go up and take a peek, it slid up the cavern wall instead and expanded across the ceiling.

The sound of descent grew closer and soon it could hear the puffing of breath and the occasional grunt of exertion. A faint green glow appeared at the base of the chute; growing in strength until a figure backed out with a flaming sword. It was a boy and his scent suggested his flavour was similar to the girl's. The flame on his sword was painfully bright after the long darkness and when he began swishing it around, it retracted its most sensitive eyes and shrank into one of the larger cracks.

As it watched, it remembered how Izle used fire to capture it - setting its lair alight and channelling it into his trap. It had burnt six of its feelers trying to escape and it didn't want to experience pain like that again. It felt the tightness of those old burns now as it stared at the boy's flickering flame. The colour of its dancing tongues was green, but it expected they would hurt just as much as the orange kind. Perhaps worse.

It wondered why Izle had sent these new people and why he allowed one of them to bring fire. Until now they had been dropped down the chute and left to grope in the dark. All it usually had to do was make itself known, then follow them through the tunnels; perpetuating their terror with the occasional slimy caress. Fear seasoned their blood and if it held off long enough their flesh was delicious. So why did this boy have fire? Was it another punishment for its previous failure? Or another test? It decided the best thing to do was to wait and see what happened.

Kye thought he saw movement in the shadows above him and flinched down, raising his sword to cast weak light on the rocky ceiling. He saw nothing on the cracked and fissured surface to justify his fright, but he studied it for some time before lowering his blade. The deep crevices had a starved feel and as darkness reclaimed them, he imagined them yawning open.

He took two steps away from the chute and found Della lying motionless on the floor. Her eyes were closed and her hair was stuck to her face in matted strands. Her clothes were shredded and torn; gaping wide enough in places to reveal wounds beneath. She looked terrible… she looked dead.

He dropped to his knees and shook her. But her shoulder was bony and cold and he snatched his hand away; convinced he was shaking a corpse. He steadied himself then remembering how Ormis listened for Suula's breath, he leant forward and did the same. At first there was nothing; but as he brought his ear closer to her mouth he felt the gentle currents of her breath. *Alive!* he thought with immense relief. He shook her with more confidence and whispered her name. But she didn't respond.

Somewhere in the darkness in front of him something spattered onto the cavern floor. He jumped to his feet in one giant pump of his heart and thrust his flame at the ceiling. But there was nothing to see. His first thought was that it was water - seeping through the rock and dripping down from cracks in the ceiling. But it didn't sound like water. Whatever had splatted onto the floor was thicker - perhaps even a droplet of the tacky substance that lined the chute. It was not a comforting thought. He stared into the thick sediment of darkness beyond his trembling sword, trying to see what his beating heart insisted was there. Ormis had told him not to move Della, but the black hemisphere above him had taken on the feel of a gaping mouth and all at once he felt vulnerable. He bent, grabbed her legs and pulled her to the wall next to the chute, knowing he would feel better with solid rock against his back.

When he straightened up he saw markings on the wall – extending away on either side of the chute as far as he could see. Some were carved or scratched and most were filled with some kind of paint. But the scrawl was so erratic, it proved difficult to read. He studied a small area and eventually picked out a few words. In one place was written, *Help me*; and in another, *I am a man*. And there was one word that appeared all on its own, over and over again: *Gomsa*

He followed the scrawl a few paces along the wall and found another tunnel. But as he thrust his flame in another sound made him spin around – that of a thousand fish slopping around in a giant bucket. He raised his sword in reflex and this time saw something glistening in the retreating shadows. He remained there for a time, frozen – not daring to lower his sword. He looked at Della and knew they couldn't stay. Ormis had told him to wait, but they couldn't stay here with some anonymous horror lurking in the ceiling. He decided to carry her into the tunnel. It was next to the chute and he thought there was a good chance it led to one of the doors at the top.

He sidestepped back along the wall to Della and realised there was a problem. Hours spent humping corn sacks for Mr Febula had built strength into his frame, but he reckoned he would still need both hands to hoist her against the wall and position her on his shoulders. And that meant putting his sword down. It would only be for a few seconds, but the idea of lowering his light and bending his back to the slime-dripper appalled him. So for a while he just stood there, staring into the darkness and summoning the courage to make his move. When he was ready he stepped away from the wall and swished his sword through the air; casting light around the cracked ceiling and hoping to drive back whatever was hiding there. It seemed to work. In one deep cavity something shrank back with a thick gurgle – the sound of bubbling snot, sniffed up a giant nostril.

He sensed his chance and took it. He leant his sword against the wall, grabbed Della by her shirt and hoisted her against the rock – plunging their upper bodies into the hungry darkness above the flame light. Then he bent at the hip and she flopped over his shoulders just as something bubbled and slurped above him. He snatched his sword up and straightened, thrusting its quivering tip in the air. His light revealed only empty cavities, but with Della across his shoulders he was unable to see directly above him. As he backed into the tunnel another thick droplet splattered onto the floor in the exact spot he had been standing. Once inside, he braced himself; expecting the cavern's slimy resident to drop into the entrance. But nothing appeared. He knew it was there though, hanging from the ceiling just beyond the threshold of the tunnel, for it was dripping more of its thick mucus onto the floor: *splat... splat... splat*. In the end he convinced himself that whatever was in the cavern had decided to stay. Nevertheless, he backed down the tunnel another fifty yards before turning around and hurrying away.

It waited for the boy to leave then slid down the section of wall he illuminated with his fire. Darkness had reclaimed the markings, but it pushed its wet membranes against the rock, feeling the deep engravings and using its sense of taste to visualise those filled with blood. On some level it understood the markings were symbols, representing thoughts and ideas. But it couldn't decipher them. It remained stuck to the wall for some time; pulsating with stomach cramps as it started to remember...

It remembered a city built around a colossus and a house on a cobbled street with a red door and a window box full of flowers. And it remembered a woman with gentle brown eyes who sung lullabies and kept her hair in a yellow bow. Terrible longing raged through its hearts. It let out a sorrowful gurgle and peeled itself from the wall. These were the memories that gave it the nightmares, compelling it to carve the markings and fill them with blood. In another life it had once been a man. Izle Rohn turned that man into the abomination it was now and with time it forgot all about him.

But the sight of the inscriptions brought it all back...

It remembered the day it was bound with its new body – how the man it once was screamed and thrashed at the sudden horror of wearing his new feelers. How he retched at the roll of his membranous stomachs and the hideous stink of his secretions. It remembered how Izle mitigated his revulsion with soothing scours and how he taught him to tame the primitive intelligence that inhabited his new body. With time *he* had become *it* and the man it had once been faded into the back of its mind.

It learnt to coordinate its suckers and feelers - to collapse and elongate its cavities so it could slurry through narrow passages or stretch into a lumpy mat. When the first quaggar was dropped down the chute a formidable hunger took over and it brought its strange limbs to bear gleefully, tearing off chunks of him and stuffing them into its mouths. There was great pleasure as the flesh stretched its stomach sacs, but deep disgust followed and it heaved half the body parts back onto the cavern floor. With time its disgust faded away - no match for the constant demands of its ravenous bellies.

The man he had once been refused to fade entirely and would often step forward in its mind, reminding it of how things really were. Twice it tried to kill Izle for making it into such an abomination and twice it failed – its master punishing it with painful scours and periods of starvation. It felt a fresh wave of anger now and clenched so hard some of its bladders leaked onto the wall. Next time Izle paid a visit, it would try to kill him a third time.

It slid over to the tunnel as something more urgent resurfaced. Its stomachs were hurting badly now. When the boy lifted the girl against the wall her sweet redolence wafted up to the ceiling – an aroma so exquisite it spilt from its hiding place and slid over to them. And if the boy had been a second slower, it would have taken them both. It was already detaching its suckers when he raised his flame and it had to use every ounce of its remaining suction force just to stay in place.

It stretched out now, covering the mouth of the tunnel like a tumorous skin. It sniffed deeply and gurgled through its mucous clogged air pipes. The smell of them was beginning to fade. This might well be a test, but it didn't care about pleasing Izle anymore. Its hunger was enormous and it would sate its bellies with them before they reached the door. But it had to be careful. It didn't want to get burnt again, so its first task was to separate the boy from his fire. With a gurgle of anticipation, it set off, pouring into a deep channel in the tunnel wall and beginning to flow.

J.B. Forsyth

The Abyss

Kye hurried away with Della yoked over his shoulders. The tunnel was narrow enough for his weak light to reach both sides, but what he saw wasn't comforting. The walls and ceiling were deeply fissured and there were gaping holes that revealed other passages running parallel to his own. He went past these with a spurt of fear, thrusting his flame in to deter anything that might be lurking inside.

After a while he began to rethink the wisdom of using the tunnel. It had taken a number of twists and turns, but hadn't angled upwards yet. And now with every step he became ever more sure he was moving further away from the cavern at the top of the chute. He stopped and considered waiting for Ormis. But as he stared into the darkness he heard a strange noise. At first he thought it was a distant waterfall, but when it got louder he knew he was mistaken. It was the sound of rushing sludge and it was coming straight for him. All thoughts of waiting for Ormis evaporated and he began to run - no longer bothering to check the fissures with his flame.

But the sound soon caught up with him, becoming a bubbling and squelching slurry that filled the tunnel's walls and ceiling. He froze - his mouth suddenly dry enough to store salt. Something whipped out of the darkness and struck his wrist. He yelped and would have dropped his sword if not for his white knuckled grip on it. He saw something that looked like a length of sheep gut and slashed at its snaking tip. It withdrew into a hole where something much larger shifted in his light – a glistening flank covered in warty tumours and blinking pockets that might have been eyes. It slurped away, but a sinister gurgle told him it hadn't gone very far.

He stood there shivering with fear; his heart beating so hard he felt it pulsing in his ears. Cold sweat wrapped him like a damp towel and he gripped Della like a talisman. He backed away, but struck something hard and spun around with a sharp cry – certain the thing in the walls was behind him. But what he discovered was a wedge of rock that forked the tunnel. He looked into both passages and cursed - the choice he had to make, too big and too final. He considered calling for Ormis, but the thought of raising his voice deepened his fear. The silence in the tunnel had a terrible liquid quality and he couldn't bring himself to ripple it. His lip quivered and his eyes began to well. In any other situation he would have sat down and cried; but the idea of giving up on Della hardened him. He took several deep breaths and walked a short way into both tunnels. The air in the right one was fresher and he hurried down it without looking back.

It watched the boy go. The choice he made was a good one - though not for him. At the end of the right hand passage was an endless fall or an impossible climb. He would go there and look; but in the end he would come back. All it had to do was curl up and wait. It wouldn't be easy though; for the smell in the tunnel was maddening. The boy's skin was leaking a cold sweat that was now seasoned with terror – a good sign he was ready for eating. It found the opening of its favourite ambush cavity and drained in with a slurp that echoed through the darkness.

Hope leapt into Kye's heart when he saw a light at the end of the tunnel. As he got closer he saw what looked like a muddy bank topped with grass. But it wasn't until he arrived at the end of the tunnel that he realised what he was really seeing. For what seemed like an age he could only stare; fully possessed by the spectacle in front of him. When the spell broke and he remembered himself, he spun around with a cold rush - sure his distraction had allowed the horror in the tunnels to creep up behind him. But the tunnel, at least as far as the daylight allowed him to see, was empty. He lowered Della to the floor, propped her against the wall and looked out again.

He was standing on the edge of a great chasm and what he had thought was a grass topped bank, was actually a sheer cliff face topped with jungle ruins; perhaps a full mile away. Ormis had mentioned an abyss when talking about the mist and he realised this was it. He took a step forward to peer over the edge and was at once gripped by fear. The chasm dropped to an impossible depth, so deep the two sides seemed to converge. If there was a bottom, he couldn't see it. And there was something down there, some invisible force that began to appeal to his new senses. He became aware of the Membrane and felt it bending over the sides of the chasm, stretching away to somewhere a million miles beneath his feet. His knees felt suddenly weak and he stepped back from the brink, letting out the breath he was holding. The whole thing seemed alien - something outside of nature.

He checked back over his shoulder then looked out over the chasm again. The cliff on the other side was pocked with a number of openings, all at various heights. One of them was directly across from him and he realised it might once have been a continuation of the tunnel. It wasn't too far below the forest and he thought if the same was true for his side, he might be able to climb up. So he laid down and pulled himself forward until his head was sticking out over the edge.

The first thing he saw as he looked north along the cliff face was a waterfall. It arced over the top of the Abyss and disappeared into a vast cloud of rising vapour in which a huge rainbow was currently on display. He watched in awe for a few seconds, but when he turned to look upward he shrank back into the tunnel with a spasm of horror. All along the cliff, giant tree roots were straining to reach him – the nearest one curling its hairy fingers into the top of the tunnel and feeling around.

He sat up with a sinking despair. He had made the wrong choice at the fork and now there was nowhere left to go. He thought about going back and taking the other tunnel, but his insides balked at the idea. The only sensible plan was to wait for Ormis. When Suula recovered she would have no difficulty sniffing them out. He hadn't washed in days and he was streaked with jungle filth and slick with sweat.

In the light of day Della's appearance was even more worrying. He could see the rawness of her wounds, her chalky face and sunken eyes. He reached over, shook her again and listened for her breath. Alive, but unresponsive. He had come to the Eastland to help her, but what good was he now? She had suffered enormously in the exorcist's purge and he was beginning to wonder how much of her had survived. Maybe all he could expect was a living body without a soul. But the thought made him shudder and he was quick to dismiss it. She had already proved herself to be remarkably resilient and while she drew breath there was still hope.

Time spun out and as the shadows made slow progress up the opposite cliff, he thought about his parents. They would have been told of his involvement with Della by now. Bill would be angry and his mother indifferent. Neither would be heartbroken. And he couldn't imagine either of them traveling to Irongate to get him. The thought hurt, but he had decided to run away from his parents emotionally as well as physically and there was no going back now.

The daylight had weakened considerably when he got up to stretch his legs. The sky was a deep blue in the east and the shadows had climbed out of the chasm, almost to the top of the tallest trees. He didn't realise the significance of this until he looked into the Abyss and was rewarded with a new horror. Way down between the two converging sides was a seam of pulsating green light.

The mist!

Ormis had told him it came out of the Abyss at sundown and he had forgotten all about it. He watched it rise and because he couldn't judge the depth of the chasm, he was unable to judge its speed. But if the mist flowed over the rim at sundown, it wouldn't be long before it swept into the tunnel.

Absence

He regarded Della with a terrible dread, knowing he had to go back to the fork and try the other passage. If they stayed, they would be forced to breathe the mist and if that didn't finish them, the slime dripper would. He looked back over the side. The mist was broadening to a wide strip and he could now see faces on its swirling surface. He fought down his panic and tried to think. Whatever waited in the tunnels - the cavern at the bottom of the chute had to be its lair. The fork wasn't too far back and if he could make it into the other passage he would be moving away from it again. More scared than he had ever been in his life, he hoisted Della onto his shoulder and set off into the gloom.

J.B. Forsyth

Magnificent Canvas

Stinking darkness enveloped him. Fear swarmed him like flies around a carcass and with each hard won surge of courage he could only swat them away for a few seconds. The walls gaped with deep scars - hundreds of black hiding places with the potential to harbour a slippery horror. He stepped quickly past the shallow ones and stabbed the deepest ones with flame. Despite his fear, he knew he couldn't afford to be too cautious. If he probed every last crack, the mist would catch him before he reached the junction and they would never escape. But the more hiding places he left unchecked, the more nervous he became and he took to spinning around every few steps to stare into the darkness - sure something was about to slip from an overlooked fissure. Going forwards became increasingly hard. The shadows grew thicker and more reluctant to give way and with each step they retreated over ridges and cracks in such a sly way they courted his imagination; conjuring black feelers and bringing him up short with his heart climbing out of his throat.

He reached the junction and buttonholed around it; his back tight to the dividing wedge of rock. A few steps into the new tunnel he began to speed up in the knowledge he was moving away from the slime dripper's lair. But after several more steps he froze. The stink of the thing had never gone away, but in the last few seconds it had become concentrated enough to make him gag. Had he gone wrong at the junction and taken the tunnel back to the cavern? Even if he had, the smell had never been this bad. It was as if the source was all around him now. He spun around twice, sweeping his light over a section of wall replete with pocks and gashes - some so deep and dark they looked like hollow eyes and mocking grins. He saw no sign of the monster, but the stench was so bad and so intimate, it felt like it was condensing on his skin. With his next breath he inhaled a foul vapour which brought a taste of spoilt meat and excrement into his mouth. He gagged and was backing away as something wet slapped him on the knuckles and knocked his sword from his hand. He watched in horror as it dropped through a crack in the tunnel floor. A teardrop of flame remained for a split second, then it collapsed into the rock as the fieraks went after the blade. Darkness enveloped him with the weight and finality of a death shroud and he could only listen as the sword clattered to its final resting place far below.

The next sound unhinged his knees: a deep two toned gurgle unlike anything he had heard before. But as alien as it was, there was no mistaking its glee. Something huge slopped down behind him; as if some enormous animal were being eviscerated and its guts pouring into the tunnel. In its wake was a waft of air so pungently vile he almost passed out. He wanted to run, but the smell was so debilitating he struggled just to stay on his feet. He heard the thing unfolding its slippery appendages and gripped Della tighter. Something slimy slapped onto his face – like a cloth covered with warm frog spawn. He stood rigid, unable to fulfil the urge to rip it away. It slopped around his face, smothering his nose and mouth. It was a massage of spoilt offal that should have discharged his stomach. But his terror was so great it had seized up his bodily functions like rusty gears.

A mucus dripping feeler fixed on his neck, sucked up a pocket of sweat from behind his collar bone and slipped inside his shirt; coming to rest over his hammering heart. A gurgle of pleasure in his ear now. The feelers withdrew and Kye had a strong intuition of something gathering to strike. But a word jumped into his head – a word his subconscious mind had tucked away for this very circumstance. It was the word he had seen scrawled all over the wall at the bottom of the chute and he spoke it with urgency, forcing it through the choked hole of his throat.

'G...G...Gomsa!'

If he had spoken it a second later, he would have been screaming it from inside a dilated stomach sac – a membrane so thick it would have silenced the sound. But he heard a wet spasm of limbs instead.

'G...Gomsa...That's your name isn't it?' he said, shivering as if he were standing in a tunnel of ice. His question echoed away and a heavy silence pressed in on him from all sides.

'I know w... what Izle did to you.' These were the hardest words he had ever spoken and they came out in a pitch he didn't recognise. 'You w... w... were once a man...' He could hear feelers sliding up and down the walls and a huge mass seething behind him.

As his mind searched for another life prolonging sentence, Kring appeared in an orb of green flame light. At first he thought it was a trick of his mind – a hopeful illusion to ameliorate his imminent death. But then the giant spoke. 'Get behind me quick.' His gaze was fixed over Kye's shoulder and his face was chiselled granite. 'Follow the tunnel. Keep your hand on the left wall and take the first left turn. The door's not far. Go now and don't look back.' Kye tried to, but he was rusted to the spot. 'Go now!

Ormis and Suula await you.' The change in the giant's tone oiled his joints and he squeezed past him, feeling his way along the wall.

The thing saw the giant arrive and it watched the boy go; the word he had spoken still reverberating through its head.
Gomsa.
Yes, it had heard that word before. It was the name it had scrawled all over the cavern wall. It was its... *his* name. The word echoed through its mind over and over again, each time spoken with a different voice. There was the kind voice of his mother, the excited voices of his friends and the scalding voice of his teacher. He saw the busy streets of a city and could smell its spices and filth. He saw a lofty fortress built into a black mountain face and a colossal figure looming over a sea of roof tops. The boy had spoken his name and it had entered its mind like a magic key, unlocking the door behind which the man was imprisoned.

Kring faced the black shape as it writhed in the shadows, listening to its sporadic bubbling as Kye's footfalls faded away. He could have backed away after him, but it didn't cross his mind.

When he saw it gathering to strike the boy he thought he was too late. But Kye had spoken a word that sounded like a name and it shrank back from him. It was clear the boy had reason to think it was another one of Izle's abominations, and if that were true, it would serve his purpose very well indeed.

He sensed the God of Battle enter the tunnel and spread another canvas.

Killing Karkus had shattered his heart. But the pieces had hardened into a cold lump of vengeance. He stared at the thing as it squirmed: unmoved by its foulness. He would hack and cleave his brother's name into it until he could hack and cleave no more. He hoped Toragin had brought a vibrant palette, for he intended this work to be a masterpiece – a magnificent canvas to make his brother proud. With a roar that seemed to startle the abomination he lunged forward.

Kye looked back when he heard the roar and was rewarded with a sight that would haunt his dreams for many years to come. The giant was silhouetted in the light of his flame. Beyond him, something boiled and seethed in the shadows. His eyes strained, trying to make sense of the glistening surfaces that moved in and out of the light and the thick eel-like feelers that projected from the darkness and snaked along the wall. He got a sense of something turned inside out – something stitched together from waste on a slaughterhouse floor. And it was huge. Too big to have flowed through the walls. He remembered the thick slime dripping from the cavern ceiling and the idea that such a thing had been suspended from the rock above him was like an infusion of ice.

He watched Kring leap forward, bringing his blades to bear amongst its feelers and folds. The thing peeled its sticky limbs from the walls and closed around him – the same way some of the jungle flowers closed around insects. The battle raged mostly in the shadows - revealed only in highlights by the erratic swirling of fierak light. He caught glimpses of flailing feelers and rolling wet flanks studded with shining eyes and warty sacs. And he got glimpses of Kring's broad back and cleaving steel. He heard the giant's grunts, the monster's gurgles of pain and the sick sound of cloven flesh.

He didn't know how long it lasted, but he watched until the finish; when the fieraks disappeared and the tunnel was plunged into darkness. He heard Kring one last time – a cry dedicated to his brother: *Karkus!* It echoed along the tunnel, fading into a silence so deep and ominous it rang in his ears.

He stared into the blackness, unsure what had happened. His ears strained, hoping to hear Kring, but he heard nothing. He knew he should go – to use the time the giant had given him to get Della safely away. But without knowing if he was still alive, he couldn't bring himself to leave. So he stood there for some time, summoning the courage to break the silence. '*Kring?*'

He cringed at the sound of his voice, half expecting a reply in the form of a wet feeler on his face. But when silence settled once more, he knew the thing was either dead or gone.

'Kring!'

When there was no response this second time he knew Kring was dead. He turned with a heavy heart and inched along the tunnel – finding his way by sliding his hand along the wall. As he went he remembered Kring juggling by the campfire and his kind words when he helped him with his hammock. And he remembered his elation when the giant crawled from Fyool's lair and saved them from the quaggar. In the darkness he began to cry and with no spare hand to wipe at his tears, they ran down his face and dripped off his nose.

The tunnel angled upwards and after taking the left turn a door opened in front of him. Ormis appeared in the resulting column of light and he rushed by him into the storeroom. Suula was there, sitting on one of the stools with a hand to her head. Karkus was still lying in the centre of the cavern, but Kring had repositioned him. He was on his back now, arms folded over his chest and his tattoos aligned in rows of symbols.

He lowered Della to the floor, rubbing at his neck while Ormis crouched over her.

'She's alive!' said the exorcist in disbelief. He reached down and spanned her face with his fingers. He scoured her for a long time – eyes vacant, body statuesque. When he finally withdrew he gave Kye a black look. 'Her body survived the exorcism, but I can't find her soul.'

It was what Kye was beginning to suspect and he looked down at her with a sinking despair.

'Where's Kring?'

'There was a monster,' he replied through a lump in his throat. 'He saved us.' It was all he could bring himself to say, but his red eyes and damp cheeks told the exorcist the rest.

'Are you sure?'

He nodded and a fresh wave of tear began to flow.

Ormis stood up with a look of genuine sadness in his eyes. He looked like he was about to console him, but a shout from Suula turned their heads. 'Mist!'

She was pointing at the tunnel that led back to the cavern. Ghostly serpents of mist were snaking around the corner and winding their way forwards. Ormis looked at the opposite tunnel and after a brief hesitation he gathered Della in his arms and went to the other door instead. 'In here quick.'

Suula pulled it open and Kye followed Ormis in. The mist was half way across the cavern when the tracker stepped in and closed the door, breaking off a tendril that was reaching after her. It sank down, spreading to a thin layer on the floor.

The room was empty and Kye thought there was a good chance it was a holding cell for whoever or whatever they had been feeding to Gomsa. Ormis lowered Della to the floor then joined Suula at the door, removing his shirt and packing it against the cracks, blocking mist from seeping in.

'We'll see out the night in here,' he said. 'What little gets through will go to ground, but the sun will rise before it gets too deep. Once we get a good seal, we'll take turns holding the girl.'

They passed the night without a single word between them and Kye had plenty of time to appreciate the change in his companions. Suula had lost her feline poise and from time to time she would close her eyes and sway; looking like she was going to faint. And the exorcist didn't look much better. He spent most of the night staring through the door and rubbing at his face. Kye suspected it wasn't just the battle with the water spirit that was weighing so heavily on him – it was Kring as well. Three days ago the exorcist wanted him arrested at the Wall – but he got the feeling he was mourning the giant's death as much as he was.

The mist was halfway up their boots when it disappeared into the rock. Kye was holding Della at the time and he slid down the wall, closing his eyes with great relief.

Man Ablaze

Della opened her eyes three days later. She was in a round stone brick room with an open doorway and four glassless windows. A bright bar of sunlight was streaming through one, warming her from the waist down. Kye was slumped by her side, snoring away with his arms folded and his chin on his chest. But it came as no surprise to her. She knew he was there long before she woke up.

She never expected to rise into her body again. She had fled into her darkest memory, but somehow Kye's voice had found her there; telling her she was safe and that everything would be alright. It allowed her to drift to the place she had meant to go – the sunny lawn outside the hideaway, around which all her old friends were gathered. And when she arrived, Kye was there too – a kind faced bystander who began beckoning her away. In the end he convinced her to leave and she had risen from her memory, reconnecting with her body in cautious increments. When she felt the ridge of his shoulder and heard his laboured breath, she realised he was carrying her. He rested at regular intervals during which she flopped in cool grass, listening to distant birdsong. At those times he shook her and spoke close to her ear - imploring her to wake up. A voice that got louder with every stop. She felt him lowering her to floor a few minutes ago, but he hadn't spoken this time. By the look of him he had gone straight to sleep.

She watched him for a while; taking in his filthy clothes and tangled hair, wondering why he had risked so much to help her. But she was pleased he was here now and the nearness of him was calming. The last time they were together in the flesh, she had thought of him as a troublesome boy who had gotten mixed up in something that wasn't his business. But the merging of their souls had forged something new between them. They had connected on a deeper level than nature normally allowed; the repercussions of which were yet to be revealed.

She decided to let him sleep and tried to raise herself to a sitting position. But her hands wouldn't separate. She looked down and was surprised to see her wrists and ankles bound together with rope.

'You're awake,' said Kye, lifting his head. He twisted onto his knees and regarded her with relief. 'Are you alright? I wasn't sure if you'd ever wake up.'

'I ache all over, but besides that I'm fine.' She raised her hands. 'Why am I tied up.'

'It was just a precaution. Karkus tried to feed you to a monster, but you're safe now.' She looked at him in horror. 'We're back in the tower again. The one they were keeping you in when you warned us about the spider creature, remember?' She didn't know anything about a spider creature, but remembered escaping the tower to warn them they were in danger. It wasn't far from where she devoured one of Izle's spirits. 'We weren't sure what you'd be like if you ever woke up. The last time we saw you...You were all...You know?'

She more than knew. The last time he saw her she was a mist poisoned wraith who tried to use his body to run away from Ormis. She was back to her old self now, but the wraith was a black stain that would haunt her conscience forever more. She looked away, feeling unworthy of his gaze. 'That wasn't me Kye, any of it. It was the mist and the shadow.' She began to cry and tears streaked her dirty face.

He reached out and took hold of her bound hands. His touch was warm and comforting, but for some reason it made her tears come faster. 'I know. I knew you'd be alright once you woke up, but Ormis wouldn't listen and he told Suula to tie you up anyway.' He smiled, but his face collapsed when he registered the fear in her eyes.

'The exorcist's here!?'

But before he could answer, she heard someone bounding up the tower's stairwell.

Him!

A liquid cramp gripped her body. In the exorcist's purgefire she had suffered an agony that surpassed any she could have imagined - an unearthly pain that seared the fabric of her soul. And now he was coming for her again. She jerked to her feet, stiffness and fatigue fleeing her bones like startled crows. She made for the nearest window and was brought down by her ankle bindings. But she was up again in a flash, shuffling away from Kye who was grabbing at her shoulders and pleading with her to stay calm. She managed to get to the window, but he held tight; preventing her from climbing out. There was a hundred-foot drop at the other side and she would have jumped rather than face the exorcist again. She spun around as his boots thundered up the last few steps, flattening herself to the wall; chest heaving and fingernails clawing the stone.

As the exorcist charged into the room time slowed down. To her he was a man ablaze – his eyes, the tips of black skewers upon which he would roast her again. She felt the crushing oven at the centre of him reaching out and her terror was so great she began rising into Absence. But Kye slipped his hand into hers and she felt the bond between her body and soul strengthen again.

'Wait!' he said, stepping in front of the exorcist and holding up a warding hand. 'She's back to herself and you're frightening her. She thinks you're going to exorcise her again.'

Ormis watched her squirm against the wall, searching her face for the truth of his words. 'What's your name girl? ... Out with it now.'

She made no reply. Her breath was rapid and she couldn't fix words to it.

'Go on tell him,' Kye said, squeezing her hand. 'It'll be alright.' Somehow his voice reached into her panic and she managed to get her breathing under control.

'Della.'

'What's the last thing you remember?'

'Returning... to my body... Feeling Izle pressing his fingers to my face and... taking his shadow back.'

The Membrane tension collapsed and the oven she had imagined inside him ran cold.

'You survived an exorcism,' he said with utter disbelief. 'How is that possible?'

She didn't know, but she gave him her best guess. 'I was Absent... not dead.'

'Anchored to this world by living flesh,' he said and behind his eyes she could see this strange new concept fighting for acceptance within his chiselled beliefs. 'What you can do defies the teachings of the Caliste. I cannot begin to understand it; but understand it we must. When we return to Irongate you will be detained until our interests are satisfied... But I assure you we are no longer the barbaric order most people still believe us to be and you'll be treated with respect. If you co-operate there should be no reason why you can't continue with your life in a way that pleases you... But before I leave this room I need to scour you again.' Della's fear spiked and she squeezed Kye's hand and shook her head. 'You've been in contact with Izle Rohn and you have to be proven pure.'

'Let him do it,' said Kye. 'Then he'll leave you alone.'

'I can't. You don't know what it was like.'

'He brought me here to help you remember. Please Della. Let him look if he needs to. If Izle's left something inside you, he can help.'

She looked into Kye's eyes and saw he truly believed what he saying. And she knew there was no escaping it anyway. If she didn't comply, the exorcist would force his scour on her and it would be much worse.

'Alright... But I need to prepare.' He nodded his agreement and she slowed her breathing, siphoning Kye's calmness through his hand. 'Okay. I'm ready.'

Ormis stepped forward and spread his fingers over her face. She winced and flinched back, bumping her head on the hard edge of the window. There was no heat in his scour, but it was an ordeal nevertheless. He stayed in her mind much longer than he did the first time, switching between draw and scour in an effort to dislodge anything that might be hiding inside her.

'That's enough,' she heard Kye say from a great distance. 'You're hurting her.'

A moment later the exorcist withdrew and he stepped away. 'I know about the whispers and the shadow you took from them. We searched the caverns and tunnels beneath Joebel, but there was no sign of Izle. The toruck's that served him are all dead and besides you I have no lines of inquiry. I can see you're distressed, but you need to tell me everything you know right away. We think Izle killed the King and we need to know what his plans are.'

The death of the King was news to Kye and Della and they exchanged a look of horror. King Lyrus was widely admired and they were both stricken by the news.

'Go on,' said Kye, 'Tell him.' His hold on her was firm and reassuring and his voice leaked into her like sunshine. She relaxed further, peeling away from the wall and taking the air deeper into her chest. Then with a flush of courage, she looked the exorcist in the eye.

'The shadow was part of him and it was like he was dissolved into me.' Ormis nodded as if he knew as much already. 'He sent the monster to get it and when it failed he sent the torucks to the gaol. Once he got me to Joebel he took the shadow back, but I knew he was going to punish me and so I retreated inside my mind. That's all I remember.'

'Why was the monster in Agelrish in the first place?'

'I don't know.'

'Did you learn anything of their plans?'

She shook her head.

'You must have seen or heard something!' he said with a flare of frustration. 'You were with them for days.'

Perhaps there were clues if she had been looking, but she was preoccupied with grief the whole time. 'I'm sorry,' she said and meant it. On the matter of stopping Izle, they were well aligned.

Ormis paced the room, talking to the stone floor. 'If word has got out the King is dead; there'll be three days mourning before the first Reader Ceremony begins.'

Della gasped - her eyes widening with stunned recollection. A clear memory jumped into her head, transporting her in place and time. Its implications washed through her like a wave, drowning all remaining fear and leaving something more powerful in its wake - an ancient sense of responsibility so great her body tingled with it. 'He means to go before The

Reader.'

Ormis stopped pacing and turned to face her. 'I don't think so. The boy told us about your vision of a Reader Ceremony. But Izle tried once before and was rejected. He has sunk so far into the dirt since then that the Reader would lop his head off if he so much as stepped into the enclosure. What you saw was probably wishful thinking.'

'He'll do it anyway.'

The exorcist narrowed his eyes. 'Why so?'

'He thinks he can hide from it.'

'Nonsense!'

'He hid from you didn't he?'

'When?'

'At the tree house when you scoured me.' Ormis glared. 'He hid from me for a long time before that – putting ideas in my head without me knowing. And he did it while he was divided and weak. Now he's whole again and more powerful. He might think he can hide his true self from The Reader?'

She saw the square peg of her reasoning penetrate the round opening of his ear. There was a tightening of his face, but he raised no argument against it. 'Even if such a feat were possible, how would it serve him to become King? Once his identity became known, Marshal Beredrim would arrested him. No one is above the law in the Westland.'

'He won't be able to.'

'Why?'

And there it was: a question that would require her to lay bare a lifetime of secrets if she were to answer it. They looked at her and she looked at them – one an exorcist and the other a potential spirit lure - the kind of people she had been running from her whole life. In the short time she had known them, one had nearly killed her and the other had saved her life. If Izle knew a way to trick The Reader he had to be stopped and now her uncle was gone, they were the only people in the whole world who could help. Whether she liked it or not, she had to trust them. So, hoping she wasn't making a big mistake, she opened her mouth to answer…

J.B. Forsyth

Revelations

'There's much more to this than you know,' she began. 'Absence permits me to leave my body, but it serves in other ways too. It allows me to purge pain and disease and it extends my life, keeping me young... My real name is Laurena and I was born in Joebel over five hundred years ago. I witnessed the creation of The Reader and I felt the earthquake that tore open the Abyss.'

Kye's jaw dropped and Ormis's eyes took on the shine of blown glass.

She paused, allowing time for her revelation to settle. She expected the exorcist to erupt, but he said nothing. His face was an unreadable mask, his body as still as The Reader itself. She saw now how much he had changed since they were together at the gaol. His face was drawn and his clothes hung in dirt caked folds. He was no longer in possession of his broad rimmed hat and his hair was unkempt and matted together in greasy clumps.

'My people are from a different world – a planet just like this, orbiting a star in the Wagon Wheel Constellation. Many years ago they found the jewel that hangs around The Reader's neck. We called it the Creator Stone for some believed it was the womb from which the universe was born. My father once asked me to close my eyes and he put it in my hand. When I opened them I was staring into an endless depth of stars through which my eyes could have fallen forever – a thing of such power and beauty we thought it lost or discarded by a god.' Her voice strengthened as she spoke - the mere thought of it imbuing her with courage.

'A second stone was found within days of the first. That one I haven't held and wouldn't wish to. For where there was light and creation in the first; there was mist and malice in the second. The stones were separated and studied. My father was among those who studied the Creator Stone and they learnt much from it - not least the secret of Absence. But their greatest discovery was the stone's power to create what was in its user's mind. The problem was: to create what you desired, you had to think of it with extreme focus and clarity, and if your mind wandered the results could be disastrous.

'We tried to make livestock, but the cattle clustered together with sad eyes and died in agony within a few days. Their proportions were never quite right and their meat had an odd taste no one liked... We created buildings that were unstable or made of alien materials that hummed when you got too close. Worst of all, someone created a mountain range right over one of our cities, killing thousands. After that, our leader Gallianos forbade its further use. He said fallible men weren't supposed to wield the power of gods and it was a mistake to even try.

'Those studying the second stone became secretive and after a few weeks they disappeared altogether. When they reappeared it was clear their stone had power too, but it had poisoned them body and soul. We called them the Uhuru - an ancient word that means empty souls. They tried to take our stone and there was a long war that nearly destroyed both sides. In the end we escaped, using the Creator Stone to create a portal to this world.'

The exorcist was a statue of himself and there was no way of telling what he was thinking. But she went on regardless. Her words flowed confidently and she never faltered. It was a history she had discussed hundreds of times with her uncle; a history that was documented in a little book he had written at the hideaway and a history she knew inside out.

'We lived on the Eastland plains for many years before the Uhuru found us. They used their stone to make their own portal – appearing from tunnels of green glass they burnt into the rock beneath the city. Hundreds poured out, killing my people wherever they found them. Many died that day – including my parents. The survivors were beaten back to the mountains. On the eve of our inevitable defeat and with the prospect of the Creator Stone falling into enemy hands, Gallianos decided to use it again - to create the titan you call The Reader. At first the image in his mind was denied. What he tried to create was a titan that would act in our interest, but the stone wouldn't produce it from thin air. It showed him such a thing could only be made with the flesh and blood of healthy men.

'He spoke to my people and told them what he had seen in the stone. With the Uhuru army gathered at the foot of the mountain and defeat only hours away; every last able bodied man volunteered to sacrifice themselves for its creation. Lots were drawn and those selected were led to a place high on the mountain. What happened next I saw with my own eyes... They drunk something that knocked them out and Gallianos used the stone to build the titan from their bodies. When it was done, the drink was taken by seven elders, whose rising souls were passed through his mantle and used to give it consciousness. The next morning Gallianos sent it down the mountain to where the Uhuru were camped - his mantle allowing him to communicate with it. In less than an hour it destroyed the Uhuru and sealed the portal between our worlds. Afterwards Gallianos took the titan west and hid it in thick forest. The battle with the Uhuru was won, but he told my uncle he was appalled by the sacrifice and repented his use of the stone. He gave it to the titan to protect and hid the mantle in the rocks between its feet – hoping never to need it again.'

Still no reaction from the exorcist. He hadn't even blinked. Kye looked like someone watching a magician's trick and there wasn't a wrinkle on his amazed face.

'In the following days we returned to Joebel and started rebuilding. But we were soon struck by a second disaster from which we never recovered. A huge earthquake shook the city one morning and it was torn apart by the bottomless chasm you call the Abyss. We thought it had something to do with the Uhuru portal – either it hadn't been sealed properly or our old enemy had forced it open again. And when their poisonous mist rose from the Abyss that night we fled, fearing their return. They never came – but the mist eventually forced us over the mountains. We settled in the Westland and soon the old war and the origin of The Reader were forgotten... But if Izle knows about the Creator Stone and the mantle, you'll be powerless against him once they're in his possession...'

As her words ran out she expected the exorcist to speak. How much of her story was written in the old library of the Caliste she didn't know, but judging by the glassy shine of his eyes, there was very little. It wouldn't be easy for a man like Ormis to take on board what she had said. He was one of those men whose knowledge was engraved in stone tablets and who required a hammer and chisel to write over it. But before he could speak, she began again. With her story out she felt years of fear and indignation bubbling in her chest; demanding to be heard.

'There's something else I want to say while I still have the courage.' He permitted her to go on with a nod that was barely perceptible. Kye sensed how hard the next bit was going to be and squeezed her hand in support.

'The first ghosts appeared shortly after the Abyss opened. Before then there were no such things. People lived and people died. There was no after. Some blamed the forging of the portal – saying it brought the spirit plane closer to our world. The ghosts of those that died in the earthquake were the first to rise and the panic they caused hastened our departure. The further west we went the more dispersed we became – living in small communities we had to fortify against the horrors that started coming out of the mist. Fear and superstition poisoned our minds and we began to distrust our neighbours and friends - a path that eventually gave rise to the exorcists.'

Her tone changed to one of accusation and she squeezed Kye's hand.

'For most of our lives my uncle and I have been hiding from exorcists - in fear of what you might do to us. We were in Irongate when the first stones were laid in the Caliste, and in Hanlow when extracts of the Witch

Laws were nailed up in every village.' The next words were anathema to her and she recited them with venom. *'The coupling of spirit and host can only be undone in death; the pain of which must transcend earthly suffering if the bond between them is to be broken, the spirit banished and the host to find peace.'*

She got a reaction from Ormis now. His face twitched and his lips separated with a short, gasping breath.

'Those words have haunted me a lifetime and if another passage has caused more pain and suffering, I haven't heard it. I've seen women *slow torn* by horses roped to their arms and legs and children staked out for starving rats. I've seen an old man wrapped with glowing bands of iron and a young girl sanded to a pulp with deadwood. Atrocities inflicted by friends and neighbours who, despite the screams, were convinced they were doing a good deed... Your order claims to have changed, but has it? I'll do all I can to help you stop Izle getting his hands on the Creator Stone. But when all is done, I fear you'll lock me up in your black rock until you've taken everything I've got left.'

She was trembling now, but she forced herself to look the exorcist directly in his eyes. She wasn't sure how he would respond to this, but his reaction was a complete surprise. He blinked and whirled away, hurrying to the door and disappearing down the stairs without a single word.

'It's the truth Kye.' she said when his footsteps faded away. 'Do you believe me?'

'I think so... But it means you're very old.' He squinted, pretending to make some difficult calculation. 'Maybe five times as old as Lady Wiblow.'

She remembered the old widow who lived in a row of little white houses on Agelrish Ridge and smiled. 'Maybe six,' she said with a sparkle in her eye.

He laughed and she did too. It seemed absurd after all she had just said, but it was born more out of relief than humour. She had unfurled a festering secret and thrown it to the wind. And in that moment she didn't care where it came down or what the consequences might be. She felt light and liberated - an absence in her own skin quite different from the Absence she knew.

And it appeared Kye had accepted her for who she was - just like that.

She could see it in his eyes and feel it in his touch. He was the first friend she had no secrets from and despite everything, it felt good.

Vision

Ormis leant against the tower wall, trying to get his emotions under control. He was standing on the very same step Griglis had run to three days earlier, following a very different, but equally revelatory experience with the girl. After hearing voices at the top of the tower he had rushed up the stairs two at a time, priming his draw as he went. He had expected to find the living embodiment of the black wraith he exorcised two days ago, but he found only a frightened girl instead. She was paler and thinner than when they first met in Agelrish woods – but the same girl nevertheless. She had survived his exorcism unharmed and unchanged. There was precedent for this. The Indomitable Spirit's immunity was well documented, but as inexplicable as his talent was, the girl had surpassed him – surviving an exorcism physically as well as spiritually.

Her story was as tall as the tower he was leaning on, but he believed every word. Her extraordinary talent lent credence to it, but it was more than that. He was an interrogator of spirit lures and lynch mobs – work which brought him face to face with deceivers every day. He had watched her closely as she spoke, but there wasn't anything in her face or manner to suggest she was lying. If anything – the truth had radiated from her like heat.

But astounding as the girl's revelations were, it was her recital of the old Witch Laws that struck him a blow. There was only one known copy of the first Witch Laws and it was kept in a hallowed corner of the Caliste's library – one of a number of priceless books Solwin kept under lock and key. A book that could only be viewed with the old librarian looking over your shoulder to assure its pages were spared unnecessary wear. He was familiar enough with the passage the girl had recited to know she had spoken it word for word. Not as though she was reading it from the text – but as if it were burnt into her mind.

The extract was from the Principle of Pain Purification, an idea later rejected and renounced by the Caliste. But the girl was right – it was a superstition that had motivated many atrocities over the years and still continued to. By the time the Caliste retracted the principle it was too late. The idea was fixed in the collective consciousness and no amount of denouncements had been able to erase it.

He first heard the Principle of Pain Purification when Lord Riole read it aloud in a cold classroom and it had filled him with a disabling mix of grief and resentment that came from nowhere. The girl's recital had triggered that strange vulnerability again – an emotional turmoil that had only strengthened as he fled down the steps. Now, as he fought to get himself under control he was struck by a vision. In the foreground was an abandoned market with vegetables strewn over the tables and scattered on the cobbles. Beyond the stalls was a brick building with a smoking chimney. A dead man was slumped against its wall and as he looked into his vacant eyes a terrible scream lanced from the chimney.

He dropped to the steps, clutching his chest. There was some great horror in his vision - some deeper meaning just out of reach. His life before the orphanage was screened away behind a mental cliff face that had been crumbling over the last few months and the girl's recital had brought it down in one great landslide; allowing him his first look behind. He closed his eyes and saw a woman wearing a lace trimmed blue bonnet. Her features wouldn't resolve, but he knew with sudden certainty it was his mother.

All at once he felt small and desperately bereft...

The vision dissolved into a background of courtyard walls and he started to feel better. When Suula came through the gate he pushed himself to his feet and tried to cobble together some presence of mind. There was much left to do and he wouldn't let what was going on inside his head interfere with it. If the girl was right and Izle was heading for the city, he had to get there as soon as possible.

'The girl's awake,' he said as she sprang onto the steps beside him. 'You can untie her if the boy hasn't done so already... Bring them straight down, I want to be at the Wall by nightfall.'

Her dark eyes lingered on him for a second, then she disappeared into the tower.

Pssst

Ormis separated from a bustling crowd and climbed the steps of the Black Tower. At the top, one of the guards stepped forward and placed a hand on his chest.

'Sorry, but Lord Beredrim's receiving no visitors today.'

'I bring important news. If you send word, I'm sure he'll make an exception.'

'Orders are clear. He's not to be disturbed – by anybody.'

'But -'

'- Look. There's been some big changes around here the last few days. You might want to try back tomorrow.'

Ormis held the guard's gaze. There was much he had to speak with Lord Beredrim about that couldn't wait. But Rauul had personally trained the Tower Guard and there was little chance of these men disobeying orders. So he pushed down his irritation and turned away; hurrying back down the steps and disappearing into the crowd.

The Night Earl watched him go; signalling an accomplice who fell in behind him. There were other exorcists due in the next few days and there was a substantial purse on each of their heads. But this one was to be kept alive - ten times as many silver moons for his safe delivery. He had wondered what was so special about him; but hadn't dared to ask. For the men from whom he had taken this contract made his skin crawl and when they spoke, their voices echoed in the back of his head. On fulfilment of the contract he would receive more money than he made running the street gangs in a whole year. But if truth be known, it wasn't the money that motivated him to put so much of his own time into seeing it done. Though he would never admit it to anyone, he feared the consequences of disappointing his current employers and had already decided never to do business with them again. He swaggered away to find some shade, stealing an apple from a stall and fixing the seller with an icy glare; daring him to

Absence

complain.

    Ormis pushed through the crowds. He had returned to a city much different from the one he left behind. The Reader Ceremony was underway and the streets of Irongate were suffocating under the weight of visitors. The sun was scorching a path across an unblemished sky and it was showing no consideration for those that braved the streets – baking their heads and immersing them in a thick blanket of stale air. Permits had been granted to merchants and artisans from far afield and their stalls were set up in rows along the full length of Reader Way. He passed one behind which a grinning man was whittling miniature Readers from blocks of sycamore – his knife flashing in the sun as he made a series of confident cuts. There was a small army of finished products set up in rows in front of him, all of varying size and price. The next stall belonged to a huge apple of a woman, dressed in a bright red and orange dress. She offered him a toothy smile and drew a hand along a rail of shiny silks. But she read his disinterest and her hopeful eyes were quick to find a more promising prospect in the clot of people behind him. Outside The Moon and Cobbles, a group of red faced men were quaffing ale from silver tankards. A street girl was attending one; pushing her fingers through his curly brown hair while three ladies at a nearby table looked on in disgust. As he passed the inn, the crowd pressed him against a boy with a dirty face and opportunist eyes. He gave him a knowing look, but his pockets were empty and he made no attempt to protect them. It would be a good day for the boy though – as there was much to gain for quick little fingers in a tight flow of unwary visitors.

    He turned onto a quiet street that led directly to the Cragg. A little girl was leaning out of an upper floor window, moving her blue frocked doll so its button eyes could follow him along the street. As he passed beneath, she waved its hand – but he didn't wave back. Further on, a bald man was slumped in the doorway of a watchmaker's shop. A quick glance at his tattered cloak and filthy stubble marked him as a beggar and a sign on the shop door above him read: Back at noon tomorrow. He had found a comfortable place from which to solicit spare change. But it was a poor choice as all the money was flowing up and down Reader Way. As he walked by, the beggar lifted his head. 'Pssst'

    He didn't slow or even look in his direction. He had never been one to encourage beggars and wouldn't have tossed him a coin even if he'd had a pocket full. But once he was past, the man got to his feet and called after him. '*Ormis.*'

    He turned and after a deeper appraisal spoke his name. 'Hayhas!'

    'Come quickly. You're being followed.' And without further explanation the shabby exorcist walked past him and hurried down a narrow alley.

Ormis looked back down the street and saw a man ducking into a doorway directly below the little girl. She was leaning further out now; angling the doll so it could see where he was hiding. But Ormis didn't wait to see if he would reappear. He backed up and ran after Hayhas, catching him up at the end of the alley. They jumped a wall, crossed several back yards and were soon making their way down a street lined with houses that had been razed by the recent fire – black ruins that still smoked and smelt of charred wood. Hayhas turned onto a narrow street and after a quick look back to ensure they weren't being followed, went to the red door of a timber framed house and pushed it open. 'Quick. Before we're seen.'

Ormis ducked in and stepped into a scullery. Hayhas hurried in behind him, bolted the door and gestured for him to sit at a table. 'You've heard the news?'

'At the Wall.'

'Kass was my oldest friend. My only friend if truth be known.' They locked eyes and Ormis could see the depth of the old man's sorrow. Someone else might have gripped his shoulder or offered words of condolence. But his noble emotions had gone back to sleep and sympathy was temporarily beyond him.

'I don't know how long we've got, so I'll get straight to it... I was the first to confront the spirit the night Kass died. It was sent by Izle and we suspected it might even have been one of his fifteen, but its skull was deformed and its spectre composed of smoke and flame. I tried to draw it, but it was like trying to lift a boulder with a strong sniff and when Kass arrived it swatted me unconscious...

'I woke in the infirmary and one of the orderlies told me he'd caught someone pressing a pillow to my face. He challenged him and he jumped through a window and ran off. Still weak and unable to get out of bed, I sent word to Lord Beredrim, requesting he pay me an urgent visit. But he never came. The next morning Atto came to see me. He was answering the recall, but the gate guards told him I was in the infirmary and he decided to look in on his way to the Cragg. I shared my concerns and sent him to alert the others. He was to return as soon as he was done, but when he wasn't back by nightfall, I began to fear the worst. I think I sent him to his death that morning Ormis, I really do.' He rubbed his face and shook his head. 'I knew I had to get out of the infirmary, so I shaved my head, swapped clothes with a dead man and left. I came straight here. This is my sister's house and it's the only place I felt safe.

'Kass thought Izle had an end game in the city and what I've seen over the past few days confirms it. I saw men I don't recognize going up and down the Cragg and two of them broke into my home and turned it upside down. What's more, I got a good look at the man who exorcised the spirit after Kass collapsed. They're saying he's an exorcist and in a way they're right – only he's another one of Izle's fifteen. He calls himself Ri Paldren now and he comes and goes from the Black Tower like he owns it.'

He stiffened as a group of men passed by outside, shouting and laughing. 'I'm getting out of the city with my sister tonight. They're asking questions and it won't be long before someone points them in this direction. I stayed only to warn you. We've got more men coming in for the recall, but I should be able to stop them before they reach the city... Now tell me your news; Kass told me about your assignment.'

'Izle's been living beneath Joebel, on the edge of the Abyss. We think he turned Karkus and his men in much the same way he did the other fifteen and sent them to kidnap the girl. We rescued her, but Izle got away. We think he's here now.'

'What did he want with the girl?'

'Kass told you what the boy said she could do?'

'He did. Is it true?'

'It is. She calls it Absence and it's the reason she got mixed up with Izle in the first place...' He recounted the girl's tale, beginning with her encounter with the monster and how she became host to Izle's extended consciousness. And as he spoke he could see a slow amazement working into the creases of the old exorcist's face. '...Now he's whole again we think he came here for the Reader Ceremony.'

'Why?'

'For another reading.'

Hayhas frowned. 'Whatever for?'

'To take possession of the Creator Stone.'

'The what?'

Ormis repeated everything Della told him at the tower now. Hayhas listened without interruption, but this time he looked affronted; as if each word was unravelling his reality. And when Ormis finished he leant back as if from an enormous meal. 'That's some tale.'

'Do you believe it?'

'Do you?'

Ormis nodded.

'I don't know what to say; it's almost too much to hear all at once. But if it is true, how does he plan to take the stone? The Reader rejected him once already.'

'He's not been idle with his time. What he practises now is nothing you would recognise. Not only can he project his scour, he's developed a way to bind spirits to jungle creatures. And he's been using the souls of his followers for this purpose – presumably to ensure their loyalty. We were attacked by two of them. One was bound to a clutter of spiders and the other to a monstrous fish and the water it was swimming in. The girl thinks he's here for another reading. She believes he's found a way to hide his foulness from the Reader and I think we should take her seriously.'

Hayhas puffed and shifted in his chair. 'Today's the second day of the ceremony and no one of any substance has been up yet. It's been open readings, but with one difference - the hopefuls have to register at the tower and they've been allotted times... New rules decreed by Beredrim they say. But I think this Ri Paldren's behind it. Most of those who've been up so far have been; how can I put it? ... Of interesting pedigree. But it's proved popular with the people and letting a bunch of drunks and petty criminals have a go certainly adds spice to the proceedings....' He broke off suddenly, his eyes widening. '... He'll attempt it tonight.'

'Why?'

'There's talk in the city about a man with a chance. He's a woodcutter from Abroath – a humble man who was bullied by his friends to come. And it's like most of his village is here to watch. I heard one of them telling how he rebuilt the local school after it was destroyed in a storm and how he took his neighbour's young sons on when she passed away. Sounds just the sort don't you think? He's up tonight and I reckon Izle will be right in front of him. If he's heard the same talk, he won't risk this woodcutter getting in before him. He's probably been waiting for someone like this to come forward so he can take his reading while the walls are packed.'

'We have to stop him.'

'I agree, but how?'

'Expose him. Have him arrested.'

'By whom? If this Ri Paldren character has got some kind of influence over Lord Beredrim, he's got control of the city guard. We try anything like that and we'll be staring out from behind bars... If they don't kill us first.'

'Then I'll kill him before he sets foot in the enclosure.'

Hayhas studied him. 'Sounds good to me, but I don't think it'll be that simple. He'll be well guarded and you'll have to find him first.' He got up, shuffled to a cupboard and took out a bundle of clothes. 'If you're to have any chance of getting close to him, you'll have to change your appearance. These beggar's rags have been working so well for me, I thought I'd get some for you.' He threw them onto the table. 'When you dress like this people look straight through you. It's like you're invisible... Go on, put them on.' Ormis wrinkled his nose, but started to change without protest. 'Take that mist stone off while you're at it... And that walk of yours. It's too stiff. You need to tone it down a bit and shed some authority.' Ormis stepped back from the table when he was done, pulling a loose thread from his frayed cuffs and brushing at some dried food that caked his torn breast pocket. 'Where's the girl now?'

'With Suula and the boy. We took a room in The Daggers and Dice.'

Hayhas frowned. 'It wouldn't be my first choice.'

'Nor mine; but you've got to take what's available during a ceremony.'

'Get Suula to take them to Bilfrey before you go looking for Izle. If she finds the local Farrier and tells him she's lost an old horse – he'll take them somewhere safe. And when you're done here, do the same. I'll meet you there.' They went to the door and shook hands. 'Good luck Ormis. I hope we meet again, under more favourable circumstances.'

'Until then.'

Hayhas stuck his head out and looked up and down the street. 'Quick now, before someone comes.'

Ormis stepped out and strode away. He was halfway down the street when he remembered what Hayhas said about his walk. He tried to relax; to saunter along in the easy way of the visitors when they had all day to kill. But he got the feeling he looked more like those who wandered the asylum and he stiffened into his regular stride; deciding the clothes would have to be enough.

J.B. Forsyth

The Daggers and Dice

Della felt a hand on her shoulder and opened her eyes.

'They brought food,' said Kye. 'And it's not bad.'

She sat up and took the plate he was holding. They were in a first floor room of The Daggers and Dice – a rundown inn currently benefiting from a huge influx of visitors. They had entered via the back door and after being eyed by several rats and a pair of scabby dogs, they were shown to their room by a landlord with a tattooed face and a ring through his nose. There was standing room only in the bar downstairs and although the bare floorboards softened voices to murmurs, they did little to dampen the eruptions of hearty laughter and bad tempered language. Ormis had gone to the Black Tower to see Lord Beredrim, but he had left Suula behind to guard them. She was standing with her ear to the door now, listening to the comings and goings in the corridor outside.

She looked at the steaming stew on her plate and went to work on it. Her appetite was increasing every day and when the thick gravy filled her mouth she realised she was ravenous. She was halfway through before she paused to look up. Kye was laid on his bed watching her. She smiled around the chunk of stringy beef she was chewing and he smiled back.

He had been overly attentive since she woke up at the tower - offering food and water every few minutes and inquiring about her wellbeing. After their decontamination at the Wall, he tried to engage her in conversation. He was full of stories about his adventures in the Wilderness, but her exhaustion had rendered her a bad listener and he had chastised her a few times for not paying attention. She owed him her life, but so far she had given him nothing back.

'I've been thinking about this Absence thing,' he said as she slid her fork back into the stew. 'Do you think you could teach me?'

'I don't think Ormis would approve,' she replied, half-jokingly.

'Well it's not up to him,' he said, lowering his voice as if Suula wouldn't hear. 'I'm asking you. I'd try really hard and I wouldn't give up.'

'I've never taught anyone before, but I don't see why not. But you'd have to agree to certain rules.'

'Like what?'

'Like not frightening people or spying on anyone.'

He looked disappointed and she could tell he had intended to do those very things.

'Alright,' he agreed, but a little too begrudgingly for her liking.

'And you'd have to promise to stop looking at me like that?'

'Like what?'

'Like I just stepped out of a fairy-tale.'

He smiled. 'Okay - I promise.'

It was hard to think about anything beyond stopping Izle acquiring the Creator Stone. But she could imagine spending time with Kye. There was a strong bond between them now and she felt like she had known him a hundred years – the deep connection they shared, bypassing the manners and customs that delay one person's acceptance of another. She never had a brother – but knew instinctively it wasn't like that. And she never had a lover and didn't think it was like that either.

'Okay then. When this is all over I'll teach you.'

'How long will it take?'

'A long time and some people never learn.'

'Why?'

'They just don't.'

'If I'm one of those people who *can* learn, how fast would I be able to go?'

'How fast? ... As quick as any bird you can think of. Any faster and you'd black out.'

'Why?'

'I don't know. You just would.'

'I bet I could go faster.'

She raised her eyebrows. 'Oh really?'

He chewed his lip for a while then asked, 'Have you ever been to the moon?'

She laughed and nearly choked on her beef. There was so much he could ask about Absence and these were his questions: how fast could he go? And had she been to the moon? Typical boy.

'Why not?' he said, looking offended. 'It's the first place I'd go.'

'It's too far. I flew towards it for hours one night and never got any closer.'

'Well I'd keep going until I got there.'

'Then you'd be riddled with sores and stiff as a board when you got back.'

He looked disappointed, but brightened again. 'How far could I go into the ground?'

'As far as you want,' she replied with a frown. 'But why would you want to? There's nothing to see down there but endless darkness... When you're Absent you can fly like a bird – isn't that enough?'

'Suppose so.' He turned onto his back to stare at the ceiling and she smiled; knowing he was imagining this now.

When Suula whipped a dagger out Della jumped to her feet, spilling the rest of the stew onto her grey sheets. A familiar voice spoke through the door and the tracker relaxed. She lifted the latch and Ormis stepped in. He had changed his clothes and was dressed in a grubby cloak with a corn sack tunic and patched britches beneath.

'We must leave at once,' he said, striding over to the window and peering out. 'Izle's got a man in the tower who's got influence over Lord Beredrim and he's working with The Night Earl. There's two of his associates out front and at least one in the bar... And I see another down there in the alley. They're watching us.' He turned from the window and fixed them with a look of grave concern. 'There's a man amongst the hopeful tonight who they say has a real chance. We think Izle will be there to take his reading before him.'

'We have to stop him!' said Della.

'That'll be difficult. Even if we lose these men, there'll be more at the enclosure.'

'If you can get us out of here, I can do it,' she said, feeling a fresh plume of ancient responsibility. 'Izle left me for dead in Joebel and these men don't know what Kye and I look like. If we can get to the enclosure for his reading I can disrupt him in Absence, and it won't matter how well he's guarded.'

Ormis studied her. She could see him struggling with the idea – trying to conjure some logic to keep them together. But what she was saying made perfect sense.

'Alright then. If they capture us all we're finished anyway.' He waved them over to the corner of the window. Below the sill, the ridge tiles on a ground floor extension ran out to a gable end, twenty feet away. 'See the man?' They did. He was pacing back and forth in the alley, looking up at their window every now and again. 'Do you think you can reach him before he calls for help?' he asked Suula.

'It'll be close.'

'Good enough. I'd rather take our chances this way than going through the bar. I'll go after and you two follow as quick as you can... If there's still trouble when we get down there, we'll hold them off while you get clear. Follow the backstreets to Reader Way and try to blend with the crowds. It'll be best if you stay clear of the enclosure until right before the ceremony...'

He broke off and tipped his head as if listening. Della heard the whispers again, rising in volume and filling the room with an ominous mantra. She stiffened and when she looked at Kye, she could see he was hearing them too. They lasted all of about three seconds then they were gone.

'He's here!' said Della.

'How do you know?' Ormis asked.

'The whispers.'

'You heard them again?'

'Didn't you? You looked like you were listening.'

He shook his head. 'But if Izle's close, we can't delay.'

Suula waited for the watchman to look away, pushed the window open and leapt out. She landed in a crouch and raced across the ridge tiles, slates clicking beneath her soft boots as she angled down the roof. The man turned, his face expanding in a grimace of surprise when he saw the dagger in her hand. She jumped down and the two of them disappeared behind a wall; the warning they hoped to prevent, cutting the air in the form of a scream.

They followed in quick succession, but lacking her fearless grace they were forced to crawl across the ridge tiles. Ormis jumped down and found Suula standing over the watchman's lifeless body. He was reaching up to help Kye off the gable end when another man appeared around the corner; the drum of booted feet signalling more on the way. He left Kye to scrape down the wall and went to meet them with Suula. 'Go now,' he called back, 'And keep the girl safe.'

Kye helped Della off the roof, then they jumped a wall together, taking off along another alley.

The man at the corner was joined by four more. They advanced with glinting knives and confident smiles; but their courage wavered when they saw the watchman laid out behind Suula. They drew up and weighed up – looking into the faces of the two they had been hired to detain. The exorcist was dressed like a beggar now, but his eyes were as cold and sharp as a frontier guard. And his tracker no longer looked like the insignificant waif they had assumed her to be. She was poised like a wildcat and there was a suggestion of explosive energy gathering in her frame. All at once they turned and fled, bumping into the walls as they tried to get in front of one another. The Night Earl had given them this contract, but they had decided he wasn't paying enough. Better to face his fury, than mix it up with these two.

Ormis jumped the wall with Suula and they set off along the other alleyway in the opposite direction to Kye and Della. 'We need to get out of the city,' he said as they ran. 'I need to get word to Lord Beredrim and there's an old tunnel in the graveyard that runs beneath the Black Tower.'

Suula frowned. It wasn't just the implausibility of such a tunnel, it was the way he said it – as if the idea had jumped into his head. She hadn't heard the whispers back at the inn and she didn't hear them now as they followed them along the alley.

Mausoleum

They left by the West Gate, doing their best to blend in with a bunch of revellers as they passed the guards; Ormis leaning on Suula as if suffering from too much sunshine and ale. The road outside was clotted with visitors and there was a queue of slow moving wagons that stretched away for almost a mile. At first they made slow progress, moving as part of a trickle of out goers; fighting through a tide of people coming the other way. But they soon turned onto a quieter road that ran around the back of the city and delivered them to an ancient graveyard.

'The entrance to the tunnel is hidden in the tomb of the first High Exorcist,' said Ormis, 'But I don't know where it is. You go west and I'll go east.'

They walked beneath a rusted archway, separating where the central path was intersected by an aisle. Suula went west in a light jog, stopping almost immediately to read the legend beneath the marble statue of a grieving wife. Ormis went east, head turning left and right as he checked names, slowing up whenever his eyes struggled with worn inscriptions. But when his aisle was intersected by another he was suddenly imbued with a strange certainty that it would take him where he wanted to go, and he turned onto it without hesitation. His confidence growing, he went on at a jog, no longer slowing to check names on headstones. He took two more turns and came to what appeared to be the last two tombs in the northeast corner. But then he saw a set of steps between them. He ran to the top and stared down at a wedge of land. A single tomb brooded in the depression – an ivy besieged mausoleum with a crumbling façade, depicting scenes of witch burnings and exorcisms. This was it, he thought with cast iron certainty. The tunnel was hidden inside.

He pursed his lips to whistle for Suula, but was struck by a moment of thoughtlessness after which he decided against it. He hurried down the steps and read the inscription on the mausoleum wall:

Here lies a visionary,
who challenged superstition and formalised the craft.
Here lies a saviour of souls,
who forged order from chaos and gave us hope.
Here lies the founder of the Caliste,
who is finally at peace beyond the Membrane.

Jagh Yorrvin - First High Exorcist of the Caliste

He pushed the iron door and it swung inwards with a squeal - the bottom edge catching on the stone before it reached the full freedom of its hinges. The sun was right behind him and his shadow leapt inside, draping an ancient stone coffin. He stared into the musty interior; feeling suddenly unsettled. He had never seen the tunnel he was seeking – nevertheless he knew it was inside the coffin. But there was no context to his knowing. He puzzled over this before going in, trying to recall an experience on which to hang his knowledge of it. He searched himself for information regarding the tunnels origin, its builders and its purpose. Had he read about it in a book, or seen it in a picture? Or had it been described to him by another exorcist? But there was nothing in his mind other than the certainty of its existence. Some instinct took control of his feet and began backing him away, but he was struck by another moment of thoughtlessness that made him stop. When he came back to himself he was no longer concerned about the origin of the information and all he could think about was finding the entrance.

He went to the coffin and placed his hands on its granite covering. Then he walked his feet back and drove against the floor. The slab shifted in a stuttering groan and the faint redolence of long deserted bones rose from the wedge of blackness it left behind. It was more than a third open when a man stepped into the doorway behind him. Another shadow was cast, but this time it draped his straining back. The door whined shut and clanged in its housing, plunging the chamber into darkness.

'Who's there?' Ormis said, spinning around and whipping his sword out.

'Izle Rohn!'

The whispers that were speaking to the unconscious part of his mind spoke now to the conscious part and it was like a septic membrane vibrating in his head. He lunged forward, swiping with his sword.

'Drop your weapon Ormis. Hear my voice and remember our bond!'

He felt a mental expansiveness - each syllable throwing bolts and lifting latches in his mind – opening doors to memories that had been locked away for years. His arms dropped to his side and his sword clanged to the floor, his violent intentions gushing from him like blood from an amputated leg. He collapsed against the wall and when he looked up there was a pair of mist poisoned eyes looking down at him.

'There's no secret tunnel Ormis... I brought you here only to test our bond... Let the man inside you step forward and become himself again.' His words made no immediate sense, but they were silky and disarming. They went straight to the vault where his noble emotions were locked away and sprung it open. 'Let him come Ormis... let him come.' His stony exterior fractured on a rising bubble of emotion and he groped the wall for support. 'Remember yourself as a boy and see your parents standing before you.'

At first nothing happened, but then he was gripped with terrible longing as the image of them crystallised in his mind: first his mother with her glowing cheeks and big brown eyes and then his father, with his unruly hair and big hands; the honest angles of his face crumpling with a proud smile.

'Recall how a spirit demon possessed your mother and remember the beastly roaring that tortured her throat.' The words penetrated the blackness in the back of his mind like shovels; exhuming long buried memories and turning them into the bright scrutiny of his mind's eye. 'Your father trusted you to guard her while he rode to the Caliste, but you broke your promise and let her out.' He felt his fingers falter on the cold metal of the cellar door and his promise to his father shooting up his arm like an electric shock. 'You were so happy the next day as you skipped beside her, thinking about how pleased your father would be to see her all better again.' He felt the sun on his face, the lightness of his feet and the joyful anticipation of a family reunion. 'But the spirit demon was wearing your mother like clothes and she threw you into the gorge; bludgeoning your little fingers when you tried to climb out.' He felt her rough hands on his back; the sharp shock of his icy plunge and the ringing pain of his battered fingers. 'Your father arrived with help, but when you told him you let her out, it was as if you'd stabbed him in the heart.' He saw the terrible disappointment in his father's eyes, saw him dropping to his knees and pulling at his hair. 'You disobeyed him one last time and followed him to town where men were crowding around the baker's doorway - trying to get a better view of your mother's kicking legs as they forced her into the oven. Your father was slumped against the bakery wall, waiting in death to blame you with his eyes. To tell you it was all your fault for letting her out...' He saw it all again and it wrung his heart out for a second time. He heard his mother's spiralling screams and smelt her burning flesh. He tasted porridge, jam and acid and remembered vomiting on his boots. 'The nightmares plagued you in the orphanage and you woke every night in a soaked bed with your mother screaming in your head. Dreams so bad they kept you separated from the other children. You blamed yourself and burned your arms as penance - holding them over candles as long as you could bear - needing to feel her pain.' His fingers went to the raised scars on his forearms. His mouth quivered, though he generated no sound. *'But I saved you Ormis. Kass Riole told me about the boy he met on the Cragg and I came to the orphanage to help.'*

'You lie...' he managed to say, for he now knew the truth of it. He tried to get up, to run for fresh air; but the voice was endowed with great weight and it anchored him there.

'You told me about what happened to your parents and your wish to avenge them by joining the Caliste. I filled the hollow inside you with purpose and direction and brought peace to your mind... Remember me and remember our bond!'

He remembered; but it was a version of events his younger self had been blind to. Izle had scoured him to assess his suitability for the order and he had submitted to it with enthusiasm. But as soon as they were joined he began speaking into his head, soothing his mind and locking his painful memories away. Izle visited the orphanage for many months afterwards, using a succession of deep scours to bury his emotion and reshape his personality to serve his nefarious designs.

The illusion of his life shimmered like a scene viewed across a desert and then it was gone, revealing the dark reality behind it. His character was contrived and the realisation was like a mental thunder storm - every jolt of lightning toppling the fake pillars on which he was built. Horror and indignation rose from the rubble and he wept tears of despair.

'Easy now Ormis... I want you to remember only so you can forget again.' His voice was divine and paternalistic now – an audible salve that brought a teetering stability to his crumbling mind. *'Accept my voice and all will be well.'* A cold hand reached out and took his weeping face in a scour grip. *'You were the first of sixteen. Your tutors taught you the craft, but I laid your foundations long before you set foot in the Caliste. I didn't know if you would respond to my voice after all this time, but it pleases me you did. You were the one I left behind Ormis... The one no one would suspect. Open your mind and remember me!'*

He could do nothing else and as a result his physical symptoms abated. And soon there was nothing left in his head but a cold anticipation of Izle's next command and an eagerness to comply - the wheels of their minds turning on the same poisonous axle.

'Our reunion would have been much sooner, but your toruck protector killed the shape shifter that was bringing you my voice. You were to locate and kill the exorcists working outside the city and you would have saved me much trouble. But no matter. Stand now and do my bidding.'

Ormis did as he asked.

'The tracker girl who accompanied you – call her to this tomb and kill her. It will serve as proof of our bond.'

'She'll smell you.'

'Then you must convince her you are alone. Do it now. I'll wait

nearby.'

The iron door swung open and he was blinded by a wash of sunlight. He raised a hand to cover his eyes and when he lowered it, Izle was gone.

Suula was reading a faded inscription on a marble dog when she heard Ormis whistle. It was a familiar two toned signal that informed her he had found the tomb. He didn't repeat it, but she had no problem marking its origin and she ran off in his direction.

As headstones and tombs rushed by she reflected on Ormis's strange behaviour over the past few days. Something was wrong with him. A year ago, he would never have taken Kring through the Wall or let his charges out of sight. Then there were his lapses in focus – periods when he would stare into some other reality, snapping out of it with some uncharacteristic decision or command. And on the way to the graveyard it was much worse. He stopped frequently to tip his head, listening to something she was never able to hear – a strange glaze coming over his eyes. She inquired about it the first few times by raising her brow and when she finally asked him what he was listening to, he just shook his head and hurried on as if nothing had happened. Very Strange.

After Ormis exorcised the spirit demon that once possessed her, she had developed a certain attachment to him. She had no family or friends and he was the only person who ever visited her in the asylum. She understood his interest was purely professional, but she had rebuilt herself around his visits and learnt to find peace in his presence. He helped her to engage with the mindsetters who taught her to supress her latent animalistic urges – to walk instead of crawl, to repress snarls and to sleep on a bed instead of under it. Most of all they taught her to deal with the sensory overload of the city. The day Ormis brought her back to Irongate she lost her mind, breaking away and running through the streets on all fours, attacking vendors and smashing their stalls, before climbing into the second floor window of The Black Witch and terrorizing its patrons. She spent a week in Irongate Gaol before Ormis found her a space in the asylum. When she was well enough to work again, he encouraged her to do so. The work was fulfilling, but only if she was assigned to him. In some strange way, she had come to love him.

She picked up his scent, between damp earth and wildflowers. But as she neared the north east corner another aroma hit her and she ducked behind a headstone to scan the graveyard. It was faint - too faint for Ormis to smell it; but it was the unmistakable odour of the glass tunnels.

She went on in a half crouch, keen eyes lancing between the tombs, fingers gripping the hilt of her dagger. She came to some steps leading down to a large mausoleum. Its iron door was open and Ormis was standing in front of it. She twisted her wrist with her index finger extended – the signal for hostiles in the area. She expected him to step back into the shadows and look around. But he showed no concern whatsoever. He signalled back instead – telling her the sunken area was safe. She regarded him sceptically and skipped down the steps on light feet.

'The tunnel's inside,' he said with no inflection. His eyes were red and it looked like he'd been crying. She stepped back from him and turned a full circle, her instincts on fire. The smell of the Eastland was stronger down here and she could almost see it billowing from the tomb.

'They were here. I can smell them.'

'Then we must be quick,' he said and went in. There was a stone coffin inside and its granite lid was rotated slightly, revealing a triangle of sleeping blackness. 'There's a false bottom beneath the bones. It hides an iron ladder that drops to the tunnel…' He trailed off when he realised she hadn't followed him in. 'What's wrong?'

She stared into the dark corners of the tomb. The chamber reeked of the passages beneath Joebel. She drew her dagger and entered, circling around the coffin in the belief she would find someone hiding there. 'They were here only a few minutes ago,' she said when she was back around front.

'Then they must know about the tunnel. May even have used it to get to Beredrim… Come on, help me push this clear.'

She didn't like it - his tone and demeanour didn't match the circumstances. She had just alerted him to the possibility that Izle's men were in the area and he had turned his back to the door and set his shoulder to the cover stone. Her senses were ringing like bells, but her love and trust of him pushed them into the distance.

'Come on. Before they return.'

She looked around a final time then put her weight against the lid. They pushed the great slab in bursts; grating it open inch by inch. When it was half way over and close to toppling, he called a stop. She looked inside and saw nothing more than a set of ancient bones, wrapped in mouldering rags.

'Can you see the handle behind his right shoulder?'

She couldn't. But she was much shorter than him and had to go up on tiptoes to look. She was at full stretch when something sharp and cold penetrated her side, just below her bottom rib. She screamed and arched back in reflex, just as someone lifted her legs and pivoted her over the hard lip of the coffin. The bones were old and brittle and they snapped as she fell onto them. Holding her wounded flank, she grabbed the side and tried to sit back up, shocked at how easily someone had sneaked up on them. There were no sounds in the tomb and she hoped Ormis had dealt with their assassin. She was relieved when his face appeared over the side. But he didn't offer help. He looked down at her without expression, then bludgeoned her fingers with the hilt of his dagger. She yelped and fell back amongst the bones. He watched while she writhed in pain and coughed bone dust. Then he disappeared from view and the cover stone began to grind back into place.

When Ormis was done he turned to find Izle silhouetted in the doorway.

'Very good. Our bond is proven and now we must return to the city.'

'The girl you left for dead in Joebel – she's here. We saved her from your monster. Karkus is dead and the girl is awake. She knows you'll attempt a reading tonight and she intends to stop you.'

There was a long silence and he could feel Izle's displeasure as if it was his own.

'And how does she intend to accomplish this?'

'She'll come at you in her Absent form.'

'Then the girl is to be your sole concern. Find her before tonight's readings and kill her.'

Ormis nodded his approval and left with him. The dust in the mausoleum settled, the only clue to its new resident - a faint scraping on the underside of the coffin lid.

Ceremony

The steps up to the enclosure were choked with people, some of whom hung over the wall like plants in a window box. Kye and Della pushed their way up until they were blocked by a plump man who turned to see who was pressing against him.

'Our mother waits for us,' said Della. 'We're late and she'll be worried.'

The man's face was kind and he smiled. 'Then you mustn't keep her. Make room for the young ones,' he hollered, his gullibility marking him as a visitor. He pressed his flabby girth against the wall and drew a breath that barely changed his diameter. They squeezed by and after some begrudged muttering from the more sceptical amongst them, the people arranged themselves so they could push through. Higher up The Reader came into view: first the rounded slab of its right shoulder and then its head - the underside of its jaw like a mountainous overhang.

At the top a frowning guard stood in their way.

'Our mother waits for us,' Della repeated.

The guard had watched their improbable progress and gave them a weary smile. 'You'll have to do better than that. You might've fooled some folk down there, but I've been hearing this tripe all day... The wall's full. If you're worried about losing your ma, then wait at the bottom of the east stairway. It's the only way down.' He puffed up and looked over their heads.

Kye and Della looked at each other. They had spent a long hot afternoon in Irongate trying to blend in with the crowds and they were tired. When they heard excited talk about the woodcutter who was up next, they assumed it was the man Ormis had spoken of and headed for the enclosure. But half the city had the same idea and they fought hard to get here. For the last hour they had forgotten their manners – pushing and squeezing through masses of sweaty bodies, crawling under carts and sneaking behind stalls. They were so close now and the idea that this guard was going to make them stand out of sight was too much to bear. So when Kye tipped his head to suggest they rush him, Della nodded and they lunged forwards, driving two channels into the spectators.

The guard twisted after Della, fumbled a grip on her collar and lost her to the masses. 'Come back here right now!' he bellowed, standing on tiptoes to watch them squeeze through the crowd. But realising the futility of giving chase, he cursed instead and turned back to the stairway, his face flushing an angry red. He shook his head at those waiting on the steps. 'Kids. If you ask me they shouldn't be allowed up here.'

Movement along the wall was just as difficult as on the stairs. The walkway was no more than six feet wide, but it was packed seven deep in places. The spectators all faced inwards, chatting and laughing nervously; some swaying with intoxication and others rooted with anticipation. The irritability of the streets was less evident up here, as if stepping onto the enclosure wall had some magical sedative effect. They heard no reprimands for their forced passage and except for one or two disdainful glances the people gave way without acknowledging them. The voices were laced with excitement and spiced with dialects from all across the Westland – amongst them the broad drawl of the White Sea Coast and the clipped cadences of the Southern Highlands. Most of those in attendance had spent the day toiling through baking streets and as a result their faces were flushed and their bodies humming with stale sweat. One or two smelt of smoke – a sure sign they hadn't changed since the fire.

They squeezed along the wall until they were out of sight of the guard, then pushed forward to look out across the enclosure. The walls were packed on all sides. Most people stood with their heads tilted back, drinking in the enormity of The Reader and the swirling light of the Creator Stone.

Behind the opposite wall stood the Black Tower - a pillar upon which The Reader could lean if it had the mind to. Half way up, two figures were standing on a wide balcony. The one who looked like a city guard Kye assumed to be Lord Beredrim. The other was dressed all in black and reminded him of Ormis. Neither seemed to share the excitement of those gathered on the wall and they were both staring into the enclosure with the same brooding expression.

'I bet that's Izle's man,' said Kye, pointing.

Della nodded. 'Making sure the ceremony runs to plan.'

Kye looked into all corners of the courtyard, but couldn't see the ten men whose readings were imminent. Two guards stood either side of the posts that marked The Threshold of Consciousness. Another man was fixing a piece of parchment to an easel. He looked at this man in puzzlement before realising he was the Royal Artist. Should one of the hopefuls be chosen tonight, he would be first to give his service. He would sketch the new King's face and copies would be sent to every town in the

Westland.

It was while he was looking at the artist that Kye became aware of a low thud on the air. He turned to Della.

'The Reader's heartbeat,' she said, reading his question from the expression in his eyes. But knowing it made it more unsettling. He became acutely aware of his own heartbeat and there was a moment when he gripped his chest - sure his heart was synchronising with its slow drum. He was adjusting to the feeling when an iron studded door swung open in the base of the opposite wall and a portly guard with a red beard, led the hopefuls out.

The spectators began to applaud.

Kye studied the men as they crossed the courtyard, looking each one up and down. They were an assorted bunch. There had never been a dress code for The Reader Ceremony and some of them had taken full advantage: one was wearing a hat with an orange feather and another a filthy waistcoat with missing buttons. One man had a hole in his shoe and Kye could see his toes wiggling nervously. On the whole they looked like a bunch of revellers who had taken a wrong turn coming out of The Moon and Cobbles.

'Do you see him Della? Is he there?'

'I don't know. I thought it would be easy, but it isn't. I didn't get a good look at him in Joebel.'

Kye looked back into the enclosure, trying to guess which egg was rotten. He had a sudden flash of inspiration and turned to a woman who was looking over his right shoulder. 'Excuse me lady, do you know which one of them is the woodcutter who's got everybody talking?'

'Three from the back,' she said. 'The one with the beard and waistcoat.'

Kye studied him. He was standing calmly, arms clasped in front of his hips and his head lowered in humble composure. He leaned in to Della and spoke into her ear. 'Izle must be in front of him. That narrows it down to seven.'

The guard raised a hand. He waited for the walls to quiet then addressed them in a booming baritone. 'People of Irongate and beyond, you are here to witness the reading of these ten men.' The crowd cheered, but the hopefuls looked like they were waiting to be hanged. The Reader loomed above them - an indifferent participant in its own ceremony.

The guard unravelled a scroll. 'Reading 82 of the 51st Ceremony. Amile Thorban of Irongate - step forward and be judged.'

For this local man there was a cheer from one side of the enclosure and a friendly heckle from the other. But as he walked forwards the walls hushed. He stopped between the posts that marked The Threshold of Consciousness and it looked like he had been robbed of the courage to go further. There was muttering on the walls and just when everyone thought he was going to run, he stepped onto the Judgement Stone. The Reader bent its neck to look down at him. The twisting light of the Creator Stone vanished and the atmosphere was at once charged with the Wakening.

The Wakening had been described to Kye in a hundred different ways - none of which was close to what he was feeling now. A strange fizzing rose from his feet in a wave and travelled up his entire body to sizzle on his scalp. His senses sharpened and crystallized; as if his whole life had been spent underwater and he was breaking the surface for the first time. But most of all there was the sense of being scrutinised - as though the eye of a god had blinked open in front of him. It was an ensemble of sensation that pleased and disturbed him in equal measure. People gasped and several cried out. The Wakening was what most of them were here for - more than the chance to witness the judgement of their next king. For to experience the Wakening was to step out of their humdrum existences and into the realm of the gods, if only for a few heart fluttering seconds. Lady Demia had told his class the hopefuls were advised to urinate before their reading – so their judgement wouldn't be blighted by shame. The whole class had laughed at the time, but he felt no humour in it now.

Amile Thorban jerked as if The Reader's concentrated scrutiny had dealt him a physical blow, then he took a wobbly step back over The Threshold of Consciousness. The Reader straightened its neck to look over the city again and the Wakening lifted. With his reading complete, Amile Thorban was ushered towards the open door, his head lowered and his jelly legs barely keeping him up. Before he got there, two of the other hopefuls broke from the line and fled across the courtyard, just in time to file out behind him. One was the man with the orange feather in his hat and it came loose as he ran, floating down to settle on the cobblestones. There was nervous laughter from the walls and several jeers. But it was light hearted. The Wakening was believed to be overflow from The Reader's scrutiny and there wasn't one among them who knew how they would fare under its full force.

Kye watched them go then studied those that remained. Lady Demia had also told his class that those who were judged were in some way changed by the experience - its divine scrutiny sparking an introspection that built better character. He wondered if that would be true for these men and if it would last beyond their next belly of ale.

Seven remained.

The guard walked down the line speaking to each in turn. He made some adjustments to his scroll and returned to the front. 'Reading 83 of the 51st Ceremony - Dorn Collistone of East Yaridge - step forward and be judged.'

This man went forwards to take his turn. He was tall with a horseshoe moustache, dressed in a blue velvet overcoat with silver buttons – the best dressed by far. The Reader lowered its head and the Wakening infused the crowd once more; its force undiminished by their first experience of it.

This man endured the Wakening to the point of judgement and when The Reader's eyes blazed red, the guard called for him to withdraw. Kye saw him blow out and smile his relief. He would get mileage from the experience - a tale he would recount and embellish until long after his hair grew white.

It was then Kye spotted Ormis on the opposite wall, squeezing between rows of rapt spectators and turning his head. 'Look. Ormis is here,' he said, pointing. 'I thought he said it was too dangerous for him to help us.' When the exorcist stopped to look over to their side of the enclosure Kye risked a wave. It was enough to draw his focus. He gave them an expressionless nod and continued around the wall.

'He's not trying very hard to blend in,' said Kye, frowning at the way Ormis was shouldering people aside. 'If Izle's man looks down from the balcony he'll spot him straight off ...' But Della wasn't listening. Her attention was nailed down in the enclosure – her eyes blazing as she studied one of the remaining hopefuls. 'Do you see him? ... Della ... Do you see him?'

'Two in front of the woodcutter,' she replied without shifting her gaze. Kye studied him. He was dressed in a plain tunic and britches; his hair long and black and streaked with grey.

'Are you sure?'

She shook her head. 'There's just something about him. I can't stop looking at him.'

'What are you going to do? He's second in line now.'

'I don't know. Just give me a minute, I need to think.'

Kye searched for Ormis and was reassured to see he was a third of the way across the back wall now. When the guard called the next name he looked back down into the enclosure. It was the man with the hole in his shoe and with each step he took forward the leather upper of his boot separated slightly from the sole, giving it the look of a mouth. But as the Wakening returned and his judgement began, Kye watched the man Della had picked out, looking for something to confirm her suspicions. But there was little to see. The man stood in line with his head bowed and shuffled forward when The Reader rejected the subject of its current scrutiny. His reading was next. He felt a rising panic and looked at Della, willing her to think of something.

'Looks confident this next one,' said a rough voice behind him. 'But I'll stake a silver moon against two coppers he'll be rejected.' Gambling on the ceremony was forbidden on the walls, but it was rife. There had been hushed bets going on since the guard led the hopefuls out, but with this mention of the man they were watching, Kye's ears pricked up.

'Yeah... I'll 'ave some of that,' said another voice.

'Good man,' said the first voice. 'I don't like the look of him. Looks just the sort to outlaw drink if he became king. And if that happens my friend, I'll not be needing that silver moon.' There was a ribbon of laughter at this.

'Reading 85 of the 51st Ceremony - Arrhul Culshel of Low Banford step forward and be judged.'

'Where in a cow's arse is that?' said someone else. More laughter, quickly dying to silence as the man stepped beyond The Threshold of Consciousness.

Arrhul Culshel or Izle Rohn? thought Kye.

'I have to stop him,' said Della, with panic stricken eyes.

'Okay. But what are you going to do?'

She didn't answer. Before his question was out, her body sagged and she flopped over the enclosure wall. As the Wakening rushed through his body again he put a stabilising arm around her and looked for the exorcist.

Ormis was ten feet away when Kye craned his neck to look for him – a distance he could have leapt across if the walls had been empty. In the boy's eyes was a communication of urgency and a plea for haste – a sure sign they had identified Izle. He redoubled his efforts, driving his shoulder through tight ranks of spectators - hoping to reach the girl before she could act. The Wakening was rushing through him again, but the motivation to do Izle's bidding was strong and it allowed him to keep moving.

But then it all changed.

High above The Reader's eyes narrowed and the Wakening deepened, sending snaking fingers of expectation into the crowd, snuffing out any last murmurs and pulling all faces towards the courtyard. To this he was not immune. The change in the Wakening demanded his attention and his bond to Izle was no longer strong enough to deny it. He took one last step and it was like walking through honey. He came to a stop only an arm's reach from the boy and turned to look into the enclosure with the rest of them - thoughts of murder slipping from his mind.

J.B. Forsyth

Mindscape

Unseen by anyone but Kye, Della streaked into the man. On the journey back to Irongate she had promised herself never to trespass another soul again. But she broke her promise now, without so much as a raised eyebrow from her conscience. Something more important was at stake and an ancient sense of responsibility was at work inside her. She swept into the man at the same time as the Wakening and felt its full force – the difference between standing in front of a closed furnace and enduring it with the door open. As she settled into his skin she readied herself for a fight. But he offered no resistance and she slipped into him as easily as a hand into a silk glove. Perhaps it was her timing she thought – perhaps he had mistaken her to be part of the Wakening.

The Reader's consciousness came into their combined soul and, at least for Della, it resolved into seven faces. She knew these faces. They belonged to the elders who sacrificed themselves to give mind to The Reader's brawn. They dispersed, scouring every inch of his mind with divine appraisal. Della was overwhelmed by their invasive power, but couldn't afford to stay passive. Readings were over quickly and she needed to act right away. So with a tremendous call on her willpower she turned her mind inwards and became part of the scour.

A couple of his thoughts rose through her like bubbles, but both were benign - one a call on himself to stay calm and another a fleeting thought about what was happening on the tower balcony. The first was to be expected, the second, probably nothing more than a wandering of his mind. She searched his feelings and emotions, but found nothing in his mindscape that caused her alarm. Wherever she looked there was nothing but humble serenity. She realised she had the wrong man and her invasion now felt obscenely inappropriate. As The Reader washed through her she felt a sudden pang of shame – that of a child caught trampling flowers by a face in a window. She began to detach from him, intent on leaving him to a fair reading…

...But then she stopped.

The man's composure was all wrong.

She had been witness to many reading ceremonies over the years and this evening's proceedings were a fair representation: the jelly legs, the premature flight of hopefuls and even the wiggling of a nervous toe seen through a torn shoe. The Reader's scrutiny reduced men to quivering wrecks. Even those who became king were seen to shake and in some cases stumble onto their rocky throne. But this man hadn't so much as twitched in the full force of The Reader's glare and he was standing on the Judgement Stone in confident serenity. And what about his wandering thought up to the balcony? Wasn't one of Izle's men standing up there? A crawling current swept up her neck. It *was* him.

'*I know you're in here! Come out from where you're hiding!*' she said, turning her voice inwards on her tranquil host.

Nothing happened – the seven faces continued their scour. She started to panic. It seemed like an eternity had passed since the man stepped onto the Judgement Stone. In a few seconds The Reader would pass its judgement and from what she could sense, the faces were seeing nothing to warrant his rejection. Izle had constructed a lie – an elaborate mindscape of virtue and serenity beneath which his wickedness was buried. '*I know what you're doing. I know you're in here somewhere. Come out now! Come out you coward and face me.*'

She felt a breach in his mindscape that confirmed her suspicions – the lair of a trapdoor spider flicking open in a summer meadow. This was the moment The Reader's eyes narrowed, when all those gathered in the enclosure felt the change in the Wakening. But that world was a million miles away from Della. The faces rushed to the breach, but it didn't open again and they soon dispersed.

'*He's trying to trick you!*' she screamed. '*He wants to steal the Creator Stone.*'

The faces gathered around *her* now, drawn by her outrage - burning her up with their convergent gaze. Her panic deepened. What she was doing was just distracting them. If they were to discover Izle's deceit, she would have to drag him up from his hiding place herself. She tried to sink to the centre of him and it should have been a rapid descent – like water falling through cracks. But she went nowhere. His mindscape was superficial and constructed with mental steel. She felt her opportunity slipping away and went to her final attempt in an urgent fever of anger and indignation. She shifted to the place where she sensed the breach, taking the ring of faces with her.

'*You have to look deeper. He's hiding from you.*' The faces crowded her like a ring of hungry wolves - eyes shining and dangerous. But they didn't do as asked. And why would they? The Reader had not been designed for such purposes. She pressed herself down in desperation, concentrating all her powers of descent onto the breach.

'*Remember me Izle Rohn? My uncle's dead because of you! Come out... Come out you coward... Come out and...*'

Just as it was a mistake for an ant to wander too close to a trapdoor spider, it was hers to press against the trapdoor in his mind and it sprung open, snatching her inside.

If the subject of a fixed gaze could feel heat from it, the man on the Judgement Stone would have been on fire. For every last pair of eyes were trained on him with feverish intensity. An ominous tone was coming into the Wakening and a strange tension was building in The Reader's frame. Its grip tightened on its swords - blanching its knuckles and rippling its forearms. The crowd paled, the excitement of a few seconds ago replaced by a screaming disquiet. They didn't know what was happening and didn't like it one bit.

Della was drawn down through the mist poisoned realm of Izle's inner mind. The Wakening and the faces were gone now, left behind the moment he snatched her away. She went down kicking and screaming, but it did no good. As he took her down, he wrapped and swaddled her with Membrane – compressing her into a suffocating holding cell, much the same as the one Ormis burnt her in. It was almost over and the future of the Westland was now a bleak picture on the under surface of a card, seconds away from being flipped over. Izle was fooling The Reader and he was doing it whilst holding her bound and gagged. She raged against the injustice of it, expanding furiously against the tight fabric of his mind.

A week ago Izle would have held her, but she was a different girl to the one who chanced upon his shape shifter that day after school. Since then she had suffered a series of tragedies and ordeals and she held Izle solely responsible for all of them. But as potent and raw as her hatred was, it was the consequence of her foulest deed that made the difference now. She had consumed one of Izle's powerful servants and she drew on that reservoir of power as her rage reached a crescendo. She exploded like a small star, rupturing his superficial mindscape and all at once The Reader saw him for who he really was.

Izle Rohn extended his neck to look up into the crimson globes that were The Reader's eyes. The sense of divine scrutiny had withdrawn from him, leaving something much worse in its wake. An ominous crackle came into the air and he felt like he was standing at the centre of a gigantic storm, on the brink of detonation. With a fear he had never known could exist in his body, he ran for his life.

Wrath

Through Izle's eyes, Della saw the enclosure walls spin and his focus settle on the main gate. It was shut; but as he raced for it, a guard pulled it open. She was at a loss to understand why, but then she realised he had committed no crimes of which the guards were aware. They were feeling the hostility in the Wakening, but it was no reason to detain him. To them he was just another rejection bolting in fear. She tried to stop him by expanding into his body and stiffening his legs. But all she achieved was a slight stumble. Without the need to deceive The Reader, Izle's mind was stronger than hers and he shrugged her off. He reached the gate, but as he passed the guard she saw a sudden terror leap onto his face. She couldn't see what was happening behind Izle, but she sensed it in the Wakening. The guards weren't going to stop him, but The Reader was. And as he ran through the gate, she left him to his fate.

In the poison mists of Izle's mind The Reader saw the enemy it had been created to destroy and it swung one of its swords back with a tremendous whoosh. But the enclosure wasn't big enough to accommodate such swordsmanship and the end of its blade sliced through a section of the rear wall, lifting great chunks of masonry into the air along with dozens of people. The debris seemed to hang above the enclosure forever before crashing down on others too stunned to get out of the way. The blade continued its arc, catching a glint of dying sunlight before The Reader lunged forward, stamping its foot down between the Royal Artist and the Captain of the Guard. The impact punched through the cobblestone, sending a web of cracks to the walls and jarring them off their feet. The Creator Stone swung away from its chest, sending a path of crimson light towards the gate. The Reader twisted at the hip as it brought the blade down, huge muscles in its calf and thigh bulging beneath its skin. It should have cut Izle Rohn in two as he raced onto Reader Way, but the sword was struck by a streak of light that shot from the tower balcony, nudging it onto a different trajectory. The blade cleaved the densely populated west wall down to its foundation - butchery and stonemasonry in the same savage arc.

The light gathered above the enclosure gate, becoming a spirit of swirling smoke and hungry flames. A head appeared from the chaos – a skull tortured by bumps and ridges and covered in tattered skin. Many of the spectators had seen this spirit before, for it was the same one they had seen exorcised at the old barracks a few days ago. But the exorcism was a sham – a light display perfected in the deep jungles of the Eastland. The spirit had been watching the ceremony from the shadows of the balcony and now as its master staggered along Reader Way, it bolstered itself to deflect another blow.

The Reader straightened up, its perennially calm face clenched around blazing eyes. For centuries the people of the Westland had used it for a purpose other than it had been created for. And they would have continued to, if Izle Rohn hadn't come before it tonight. But now as it brought itself back to full height the people of Irongate were about to realise just how misguided they had been. For the titan they had built their homes around was no chooser of kings. It was a thing of flesh and blood, forged and hardened by magic to slay an army from another world.

Whoever had given the Wakening its name made an apt choice, for a wakening was all it was – nothing more than the gentle yawning of a much greater power. And now, as the titan roared with rage the people of Irongate felt its full force. It was a weapon that The Reader drew from the Creator Stone; designed to rip courage from its enemy. A weapon never meant for use in a city of its creator's descendants. The same black radiance that preceded the titan when it vanquished an Uhuru army five centuries ago; swept through the city now. But unlike its old enemy, the people of Irongate had no magic to mitigate its power.

The Wakening became terror itself; a medium that submerged all those in its field. A forbidding presence crackled in the air and a deathly precipitation condensed on everyone's skin. They tasted blood and smelt roasting flesh. And The Reader's furious baritone swept through their bodies, vibrating bones and teeth and challenging bladder and bowel. Until then the spectators had been anchored in a terrible hypnosis, but now it broke and they ran for their lives.

As the strength of the Wakening increased, so did its radius of perception - an invisible wave that washed over the entire city, taking those oblivious to the events inside the enclosure by surprise. Wherever they were and whatever they were doing, the dreadful air soaked into their bones and took possession of their minds; filling them with an unfocused terror and an irresistible urge to run - to go anywhere to be free of the damp crackle that spoke of their imminent death. People fled in all directions and those not quick enough were knocked down and trampled. Where the surging crowds bottlenecked, people climbed over the fallen, mashing faces beneath their boots and pulling and clawing at those in their way. In some places the pile of bodies grew so high, those who scrambled over them were able to climb into first floor windows. The elderly were forced into a scramble with the rest, swinging sticks and clocking heads; forced into movements well beyond what their degenerative joints would normally permit, setting themselves up for months of pain.

Screams of agony and terror shredded the air, but they were barely heard beneath The Reader's roar. In a bedroom in the market quarter, two children broke from their play and dived beneath a bed as the Wakening washed over them. They clutched one another in a quivering ball, unaware the source of their terror was the real life version of the carved figure they were playing with.

No life was spared.

Horses reared wide eyed and bolted through the masses – some pulling wagons or carts behind them. On Reader Way a rider was thrown, but his leg became caught in his stirrup and his frothing horse dragged him over the cobbles, smashing him into stalls. When a cart crashed into a shop, dozens of exotic birds took to the wing in little cages; tiny hearts bursting in their chests as they flapped themselves to death. From cellars, under eaves and out of cracks in walls, all that crawled and scuttled surged into the light - a plague of insects, conjured in a matter of seconds. Fleas jumped on their hosts and lice crawled rapidly through hair. Even earthworms felt The Reader's wrath and huge numbers wriggled free of the soil, fleeing beneath panicking crowds in a great rippling exodus. In the filth of the alley behind The Lonely Spirit a sleeping beggar woke with a cry, flailing to his feet and grabbing his chest; sure the end of the world was upon him. As he staggered round a corner he went down, overrun by an army of clawing rats coming the other way.

The Wakening raged out from Irongate for over a mile. Beyond its influence, travellers gawped at the chaos down the road: people running into fields of wheat and potatoes; horses bucking riders or thrashing at their harnesses. And beyond them, hundreds of people spewing from the city gates. What they saw spoke to them of a danger they couldn't see, and many fled with the rest.

On the enclosure wall people surged towards the stairwell in a suffocating squeeze that stole their breath and threatened to crush bones to powder. Some were so desperate to get off they jumped the fifteen foot from the wall, suffering broken legs and twisted ankles. Others quivered and went limp, the power of the Wakening stripping them of all self-control. Kye felt the urge to flee, but the crush of people held him as tight as a nail in a block of wood and all he could do was close his eyes and squeeze Della's limp shoulders.

The spirit above the enclosure gate was repaid swiftly for its interference. On the crest of The Reader's roar two gossamer faces shot from its eyes and struck the spirit, sending it into a nebulous spiral of smoke and flame. It was Izle's most powerful servant, but even after its consumption of the Indomitable Spirit it was no match for its assailants. Within a few seconds the faces devoured it with huge distorting mouths and disappeared back into the titan's eyes.

It turned its attention back to Reader Way. Sensing a concentration of the Wakening along the main road, most people had fled into the side streets. Those who remained were either too injured to move, unconscious or dead. Izle Rohn raced through them, stumbling over the litter of overturned stalls. A terrified blind man stepped into his path and he shoved him aside, sending him flailing into an upturned apple cart. The Reader swung its other sword and it came down on an arc that looked destined to fall short. But as its elbow straightened a ghostly light raced down its arm and along the length of its sword, forming a screaming face on the tip of the blade. It opened its hand and the sword flew over the enclosure's front wall and into the city. It entered Reader Way between the shoemaker's and the ironmonger's; a third of its length disappearing into the cobbles like a dagger into a silk lined scabbard. Windows exploded and all those within a hundred-yard radius were jarred from their feet.

Izle Rohn, once the 23rd High Exorcist of the Caliste, was directly in its path and the blade cut him in two at the waist. In the end, without his black arts to protect him, he was just a man – and he died like one. His lower half collapsed at the knees and his upper half slid down the topside of the blade on a streak of blood; dead before he struck the cobbles.

The spirit that guided the blade rose from the ground. She hovered over his torso to ensure no ghost could rise from him, then travelled back up the blade to become a bleak face on the pommel. When she craned her neck the ground groaned, the sword slipped free and it flew back to the Reader's open fingers. It stepped back and straightened on the granite outcrop and the spirit disappeared into its body. Its eyes cooled from crimson to blue and it went back to its familiar vigil; looking out over the devastation as though nothing had happened.

The Wakening lifted from the city and the people looked around; at first with bewilderment and then in horror at what they were doing. Those who found themselves clambering on bodies, climbed off in shame and began helping people to their feet. Others gawped at the blood on their clothes and at those whose hair they were pulling or whose faces they were about to scratch. At first no one spoke and there was an eerie quiet when even the injured and dying made no sound.

Solace

Kye opened his eyes, not knowing what he would see or even where he would be. The Wakening had taken him outside himself and he looked out over the enclosure with a swirling disorientation. A rear section of the far wall and a large section of the gatehouse had been reduced to gullies of rubble, littered with bodies. At the centre of the courtyard was a large depression of cracked cobblestones, so deep he could see great wedges of dark earth beneath. Three guards were getting to their feet and the Royal Artist was rolling onto his back beside his broken easel. Above them, the balcony where Lord Beredrim and his mystery companion had been standing was empty. Beyond the wall, spirals of smoke were lifting into the evening air. The sudden end to the Wakening had left behind an eerie vacuum through which harrowing cries were beginning to carry.

High above The Reader studied the horizon.

He felt the strength coming back into his legs and turned to see the last of the spectators hurry away down the stairs. Only Ormis remained. His head was bowed and there was a dagger in his right hand. Kye stared at the blade. 'Ormis?' The exorcist's face twitched and his eyes focused. 'Are you alright? I think Della did it. I think she stopped him.'

The exorcist looked at her and opened his fingers, his dagger clattering to the stone. Then he looked east – his face betraying some terrible realisation. 'Forgive me,' he said and ran down the stairs.

Della began to stir and like some limp puppet coming to life, she straightened and turned to him. 'Izle's dead,' she whispered, but there was no triumph in her voice. He hugged her and she hugged him back. 'What happened to Ormis?'

'He was here just a second ago. But he was acting strange and went off in a hurry. It must've been the Wakening. I've never felt so scared.'

'I didn't mean for it to happen this way. I should have gone to him earlier – while he was still in line.'

'You can't blame yourself, this wasn't your fault.'

She looked into the enclosure and Kye could see she wasn't convinced. Some brave folk had returned and were already assisting the dozens of injured people that littered the rubble.

'Come on Kye, we've got to help.'

There were more people clambering in by the gate, so they started around to the back wall. They went holding hands, both of them on jelly legs, with an unsettling swishing in their heads. When they started picking their way down through the rubble an enclosure guard called up. 'Hey you.' He was crouched on a huge slab of broken wall, trying to splint someone's leg with an empty scabbard. 'Come here and help me will yer.'

Kye angled towards him, but Della grabbed his arm.

'I've got to go to it.'

At first he didn't understand. But then she looked up at The Reader. 'Why? I thought it was all over.'

'It is. The city's safe now. But it's calling to me.'

Kye felt his stomach clench and his heart rate spike. 'What if you set it off again?'

'I won't. It wants me to go.'

'Do you have to go now?'

'Yes. Before anyone stops me.'

He was about to protest when the guard shouted up again. 'Boy! Are you coming or not?' He waved to say he was on his way then took Della's hand.

'Go on then. I'll be waiting for you,' he said, before turning away and clambering down through the rubble.

Della crossed the enclosure, approaching The Reader in dreamy steps. For the last few days she had thought of nothing else besides stopping Izle from acquiring the Creator Stone. Now Izle was dead and the stone was safe, but for some reason she felt worse. The fate of the Westland had served as a distraction to her bleeding heart and tattered conscience and now she was feeling the pain of them once more. The Reader was calling to her with a promise of solace and she went to it with hope.

But even though it called, she was still subjected to the Wakening and it struck her as she stepped over the Threshold of Consciousness. It spread through the enclosure and there were gasps and wails from all those in its field. They looked up with bloodless faces, fearing an imminent plunge into the liquid terror that had only just left them. They saw a girl standing beneath The Reader and most assumed she had been injured on the wall and had wandered towards it in a daze.

The faces of the Wakening appeared in Della's mind and she welcomed them. She brought her shame into her thoughts, wanting them to see the terrible things she had done and the person she had become. Tears streaked her face as they judged her, but in the end they simply withdrew; taking the

Absence

Wakening with them. For some inexplicable reason, she had been deemed worthy – free to walk upon the sacred ground beneath it.

She went to a colossal foot and stroked her hand along its rising arch, noticing the deposits of soil and dead leaves that were accumulated beneath it. Her fingers found what she was looking for behind the hard swell of its ankle bone: an artery as thick as her forearm, pulsing visibly beneath its skin. She pressed her hand to it and closed her eyes. She had heard its heartbeat as she approached and now she felt its soothing thump travelling down her arm and through her body. The Reader's blood was the blood of her people and as it flowed beneath her hand she heard their voices – the same ones that called her from the wall. And as the people in the enclosure watched, she gave herself over to them.

For a time, it was like floating and when she opened her eyes she was outside her old house in Joebel. It was bright and early and her parents were having breakfast on the lawn. Their talk turned to laughter and they leaned over their plates to kiss. Her father's fingers disappeared into her mother's long hair and the necklace of wooden animals he had carved for her swung free of her shirt. She called to them and when they turned, the picture froze. It was the perfect image: her father's wry smile, his cheek bulging with a crust of bread – her mother's freckled face and shining eyes. It was the last time she saw them alive together and they were happy – expressing their love in a wash of warm sunshine. She had gone to The Reader in need and it knew where she needed to go.

She blinked and was by her mother's side, painting rabbits on a bed board they had brought out into the garden. She turned to her mother and insisted with a six-year old's concern that the mummy rabbit should have one ear pointing up and one pointing down - so it could listen for owls as well as its babies. Her mother laughed, swung her around and tickled her tummy.

Another blink and she was creeping up on her father as he dozed on a river bank – a sloshing pail in her trembling hands. She emptied it on his head, delighting in his gasps as she ran barefoot through soft grass to scale a tree, squealing as her foot slipped his fumbling grip. She looked down, giggling at his feigned anger and the wet hair plastering his face.

And so it went on - a string of sweet and cruel memories: making fairy breath perfume with her mother, learning to swim with her father and playing hide and seek with them both. The Creator Stone drew her most treasured memories, adding colour and details to those that had faded to grey. It was like an infusion of sunlight and each one added a layer of warmth to her empty heart.

Aftermath

Beyond the enclosure the stricken city reeled.

The cobbles of Irongate were strewn with the debris of overturned stalls and people staggered and crawled amongst it. Some simply stood and looked around, unable to comprehend what was happening. Fires blazed in various places – some fought and others ignored. Bereft mothers pushed through masses of dazed citizens, calling for the children they had abandoned, while others were reunited with tearful embraces. The frothing horse that pulled its rider across the city had drawn up with wide eyes, its hooves clocking as a boy cut the battered man free.

Visitors bled from the gates in a steady stream, but they didn't converse in the excited tones that usually possessed those leaving a Reader Ceremony. They left in a hurry, huddled together with family and friends and if they spoke, their talk was hushed and clipped. And as they went they looked over their shoulders at regular intervals, assuring themselves The Reader was still in its enclosure.

Ormis pushed through the melee and out of the gates, his face ashen, his eyes fixed and terrified. He was waking up to a new reality with streamers of a cruel nightmare boiling off him. His bond with Izle was broken, but he was coming to his senses with the knowledge of what happened to him intact. And it was a single image that set him running from the enclosure wall and kept him running now: Suula gripping her wounded side - her dark eyes looking up at him in confusion. He ran with fear and self-loathing, two unfamiliar emotions that gripped him like an illness.

He sprinted through the graveyard, but when he arrived at the steps leading down to the mausoleum he stopped and stared at its open door with rising trepidation. Was he too late? He almost froze – too frightened of what he might find. But he hesitated only a second before lurching forward, knowing he had to go there if there was even a chance she was alive.

He rushed into the tomb and another pang of self-loathing struck him when he saw the stone coffin. He threw his shoulder against the cover, pushing it so far in one grunting effort that it pivoted over the far edge and toppled to the floor. Suula was curled up inside, but she wasn't moving. He climbed in, crunching old bones with his boots and fumbling for her pulse. His fingers were shaking, but he eventually detected one. Weak, but definitely there. He scooped her up and climbed out, then hoisted her onto his shoulders and ran back to the city.

    He carried her all the way, his breath heavy and his heart burning in his chest - guilt and urgency driving him through the pain. He fought through an exodus of thousands and set her down in a line of people who were being attended by a surgeon. Her wound had bled onto his neck and one side of his shirt was soaked with blood.

    'Quickly,' he said grabbing the surgeon as he was bandaging someone's head. 'This one's dying. There's a deep wound in her side and she hasn't much time.' There was a whiney desperation in his voice which he neither liked nor recognised. The surgeon glared at him in irritation, but he accepted Suula's greater need and went to her. Ormis backed away, jerking around when Hayhas grabbed his shoulder.

    'Ormis! Are you hurt?' he asked, frowning at his blood soaked shirt.

    'No. But Suula is.'

    'What happened? We felt the Wakening in Market Cross. Was this Izle's doing?'

    'The girl stopped him.'

    'Then we are in her debt,' he said, looking up at The Reader. 'Is she safe? ... Ormis, is she safe? Are you sure you're alright?'

    He was far from alright, but nodded anyway. 'I left her in the enclosure with the boy.'

    'Then you must go back and get them. Take them to the Caliste, it should be safe now. I saw Izle's men running down the Cragg on the way over. I'll meet you there as soon as I can, but I need to find Beredrim first... Ormis?' Hayhas shook him hard. 'Ormis are you listening to me? Ormis!'

    'Yes, I hear you. I'll get them safe.' He took one last look at Suula and raced off to the enclosure.

    Kye stood in the fractured courtyard, watching Della from between two guards. She hadn't moved since placing her hand against The Reader's ankle – as if some magic was fixing her in place. The sight had inspired the Royal Artist to reset his easel and he was working quickly to capture the scene in the dying light. He was nearly finished and was just refining the details of her face.

    The walls were clear of people now. The enclosure guard were among the first to recover and had worked quickly to remove the dead and wounded. When one of them asked Kye to leave, he pointed to Della and said they were together. The guard gave him a sceptical look and was about to throw him out when the one he had helped to splint a broken leg strode over to corroborate his story. After that he was allowed to stay. When one of them asked what Della was doing, he just shook his head and shrugged his shoulders. The three of them had watched in silence ever since and it was only when Ormis ran up behind them that they tore their eyes away.

'These two are my charges,' the exorcist said. There was blood all over one side of his shirt and Kye thought he looked terrible. His face was white and there was a jittery shine in eyes. His authoritative poise was gone and his fingers worked nervously against each another.

'Walked right up to it she did,' said the guard, 'Right after the Wakening, or whatever it was... And without a care in the world. I don't know what happens now, but we've sent word to Lord Beredrim.'

Della lowered her hand from The Reader's ankle and sauntered over. She smiled at Kye and lowered her head to study the ground, as if simply waiting for them to finish their business. The guards soaked her up with their eyes. She was an enigma to them - a twig of a girl who had walked up to The Reader right after it vented its wrath on the city. They looked at each other for inspiration, but when they saw the others blank face they went back to staring at her again.

'I'll take them to the Caliste,' said Ormis.

The guard puffed up, remembering his responsibilities. 'Hold on now. She can't just leave after what she did. Lord Beredrim will decide what happens next.'

'Lord Beredrim *sent* me,' he lied.

The guard narrowed his eyes. 'Why would he send an exorcist and not one of our own? Strictly speaking, you shouldn't even be here. She'll remain with us until I get confirmation through the chain of command. She'll be safer here than in the city right now.' He had just finished a report on the late Lord Riole's trespass of the enclosure and wasn't keen to start another.

Ormis swelled, summoning a little of his old self. 'What crime has she committed for you to detain her?'

'She wasn't authorised for a reading.'

'That may be so, but she was judged worthy. Doesn't that count for anything? As far back as I can remember the enclosure guard served all who have been accepted. Surely now this girl has authority over you.'

The guards exchanged looks of discomfort. 'But this is different and you know it.'

'Barely. She was judged worthy and a reasonable man would say that trivialises an infringement of the protocols. Lord Beredrim asked me to take her to the Caliste and that's where she's going.'

He beckoned to Kye and Della and started leading them away. The

Absence

guard's face worked and his hand gripped the pummel of his sword - weighing the consequences of letting them go against forcing them to stay. But as they got closer to the gate his motivation for the latter drained away and he relaxed his grip. He shrugged at the other guard and watched them go; already thinking about his next report.

Ormis led them from the calm of the enclosure and into the chaos of the city. Bodies were laid out either side of Reader Way and covered with silk taken from a toppled merchant's cart - fine shrouds of red, green and blue hugging the contours of the dead and shinning in the lamp light. Dozens of people were working their way along the lines, exposing dead faces and hoping not to see their loved ones staring up at them. The injured were there in large numbers, huddled in doorways, propped against walls and bleeding onto the road. Calls for assistance filled the air, but there wasn't enough help to go around. More casualties were arriving from the side streets all the time – one man with a broken leg was being pushed in a barrow and another with a bleeding head carried over someone's shoulder. Further down the street two tradesmen wandered the debris, recovering carved models of The Reader and trampled wicker baskets. Beyond them, a group was gathered around the cleft made by its sword, shaking their heads as they tried to make sense of it all.

Ormis took them right by, turning a corner at The Moon and Cobbles. There was a dazed barmaid leaning heavily against the tavern's doorway and two children leaning out of an upper storey window, crying for their mother. The exorcist ignored all calls for assistance and even shrugged off an old man who grabbed his tunic. Kye stopped to help a number of times, but Ormis pulled him away with increasing irritation. In contrast Della just walked on; seemingly oblivious to what was going on all around her.

They took a quiet street to the arched jawbone at the foot of the Cragg. They hurried up the steps, passing beneath the beastly skulls fixed to the rock face. The city dropped away and it wasn't long before Kye and Della were tight to the handrail and the sounds of the stricken city reduced to an occasional whisper on the breeze. They were puffing hard when they reached the top and entered the Caliste.

The gatehouse was open and the courtyard beyond festooned with shadows. A single green mist lamp glowed in the far corner of the cloister. Ormis signalled for them to stay at the gate, did a quick survey of the immediate area then called them inside. He took the mistlamp and led them through the cloister and into the black dormitories at the rear of the cavern. In a sphere of mist glow, he took them down a long dark corridor and ushered them into a room, placing the lamp on a table between two beds. 'Wait here for a man called Hayhas. He knows where to find you.' Then he left, closing the door behind him.

Kye listened to him striding away. 'Do you think he's alright?' he asked Della. But she didn't even look at him. She was sitting on the bed, staring at the wall. Something profound had happened to her during her contact with The Reader and he could see she was still in the grip of it.

He looked back at the door; biting his lip.

Demons

Ormis staggered along the corridor with only the weak light from the high windows to guide him. He had held himself together long enough to fulfil his responsibilities, but now his charges were safe his demons set about him. His life was a lie; his character contrived and implanted by Izle Rohn - a loathsome garment he had worn for over twenty years. Now Izle was gone that garment was becoming unstitched and the bitter winds of reality were rushing in through the seams.

He heard Izle's laugh echo up the corridor and turned, expecting to see his ghost floating up behind him. The corridor was empty, but he felt a terrible subsidence in his mind and fell to the floor. There was nothing but sand in his foundations and everything he had built on them was beginning to topple. He turned onto his hands and knees, gasping; his eyes huge discs of despair. His ring scraped the floor and he raised the throbbing mist stone to his face; seeing it now as a symbol of the foul arts Izle had used to poison his young mind. He jerked back and tried to yank it free. At first it wouldn't come, but after several brutal tugs it tore over his knuckle, taking a ribbon of skin with it and slicking his finger with blood. He threw it down the corridor and it clattered along the wooden floor. It came to rest beneath a bench, looking back at him like a poisonous eye.

As he stared back, he was overwhelmed with the memories that once plagued his nightmares: smoke rising from a bakery; his mother's screams and the smell of her charring flesh; his father's dead eyed reprimand and the excitement of his mother's killers. He bore the images as if he was a boy again and it was crushing. He remembered everything now: his orphan wanderings towards Irongate; sleeping in barns and stealing scraps; the whipping he received for stealing a farmer's eggs; being found shivering in a ditch by the merchant who took him to Irongate orphanage where he didn't speak for three months, except in the rantings of black dreams.

He wailed at the memories, rocking back and forth with wild streaming eyes. Superimposed on the images was Izle's gloating face and Suula's hurt eyes, staring up from a stone coffin. He vomited – three violent retches that were his body's attempt to purge his crime. But what he had done, couldn't be undone. He pushed himself to his feet and propelled himself down the corridor, tears and spittle streaking his face.

He ran through the cloister and up onto the ramparts, veering and staggering as if his legs had become wise to his true nature and were refusing to serve him. He heaved himself onto the castellated wall and looked out – the tips of his boots overhanging the sheer face of the Cragg. Below him a city of ants scurried around. He looked down at them, feeling none of the heady fear it should have raised. All he felt was a gathering force behind him – the vanguard of an insanity that would drag him off babbling and drooling. But there was a crop of jagged rocks at the foot of the Cragg that would spare him that fate. He inched forward until all his weight was on his heels; putting himself at the mercy of a capricious breeze. He ripped his bloody shirt open and looked at the oath tattooed on his chest:

> *I swear to observe and uphold*
> *the constitution and protocols of the Calista.*
> *To discharge the duties of office*
> *without fear or prejudice.*
> *And to execute the five disciplines*
> *with honour and discretion.*

As he glared at the words he was stirred by a new wave of bitterness and bawled his anguish across the city. Izle implanted the idea for the tattoo, but it was just window dressing to put him beyond suspicion. He clawed at his chest until his skin was in tatters and the words streaked with blood. And when he was finished his arms dropped to his side. He closed his eyes and felt suddenly at peace – the image of his parents alive and happy frozen in his mind. The rocks called up to him now and he stepped into the column of air above them...

But instead of falling he pivoted back on his other heel – grabbed by his belt the moment he stepped out. He twisted and flailed and came down hard; cracking his head on the stone. There was just time before he lost consciousness to see Kye's frightened face leaning over him.

Second Chance

Ormis leant back in the wagon as he contemplated the events of the last month. The 51st Reader ceremony had cast a shadow over the city. Two hundred and thirteen people perished on the night of Izle's Reading, but all who were touched by the Wakening had been affected in some way. Irongate was now a place where people struggled to sleep; the nights continually broken by those surfacing from black dreams. People still drunk in taverns and bought goods in the streets, but laughter and levity were rare commodities. The people were guarded and twitchy, eschewing idle chit-chat to brood in their own dark thoughts. The Reader had shown them just how tenuous their self-possession really was and how quickly they could abandon their children and turn on their neighbours and friends.

The cause of The Reader's reaction was known only to a handful of people, but speculation was rife. A popular theory was that it had become aware of the vice and corruption in some quarters and had decided to show its disapproval. Another theory, much closer to the mark, was that The Reader had been offended by a thought in the mind it was reading, and they reasoned that in ignorance of that thought, the next hopeful risked triggering a similar reaction.

The people of Irongate looked up at The Reader more so than ever, but now they eyed it with fear and suspicion. Throughout the whole of recorded history, the government of the Westland had been built on Reader Ceremonies and king selection. But people had lost faith in these ideas now and as yet there was no appetite for another ceremony. Some were already espousing new ways to choose a king. But until anything was decided, the city was to remain under the control of Marshal Beredrim.

Ormis had spent most of the last month in the Caliste, under the care of a young woman called Hishlee – a skilled mindsetter Hayhas recruited from the asylum. He had submitted to her soothing scour-like treatments and later to a therapeutic dialogue through which he had come to terms with his true identity. He confessed all to Hayhas, first in the ramblings of delirium and later in earnest conversation: his years of fraudulent posturing in the Caliste; the stabbing of his faithful tracker and his intention to kill Kye and Della during the ceremony. To his own ears it was damning; but when it was out Hayhas had smiled sadly and surprised him by offering sympathy instead of condemnation. 'None of it was your doing,' he told him. 'You were doomed the moment Izle set foot in the orphanage.'

    He was visited on a number of occasions by Lord Beredrim, who confessed to have been held under a similar subjugation by Raphe Dilhone – the man Izle sent to infiltrate the tower, who had been going under the name Ri Paldren. He had allowed himself to be subjected to a scour – a procedure Raphe convinced him was necessary after his close contact with the spirit at the old barracks. Raphe's voice jumped into his head, influencing him right up until Izle's death. By the time he recovered he was too late to stop him leaving the tower and despite an extensive search they had yet to find him. Lord Beredrim was tormented by the way he had been used and appalled by his susceptibility to mind techniques – torments Ormis could well understand. Their talks were a catharsis of mutual benefit, helping him to solidify the foundations of his new personality.

    Last week Suula appeared in his dormitory, fresh from the infirmary with a thick bandage on her side. Her visit was unexpected – sprung on him by Hayhas, who knew he would never agree to it. He had supervised her recovery in the infirmary, explaining to her how Izle compelled him to stab her. She listened intently and forgave him - just like that. But when she appeared in his doorway he was struck by a feverish shame, collapsing to his knees and sobbing like a baby. She visited daily after that - inexplicably content to sit in a corner and watch him with her unfathomable eyes.

    The Caliste lost ten exorcists - over a third of their number: Kass Riole, Djin and Altho perished at the hand of the spirit demon and Solwin, along with another six who answered the recall were murdered in the Caliste. Vish Pashgar was now the highest ranking exorcist and was expected to take the position of High Exorcist as soon as he took leave of the toruck king. Until then, Hayhas was in charge of the Caliste.

    Hayhas had expressed his concern that if Vish Pashgar ever learnt of Della's secret, he would subject her to endless tests and experiments. They agreed such a fate would be a terrible injustice given that the entire Westland was in her debt. So with Marshal Beredrim's cooperation they decided to get Della and Kye out of the city long before he returned, and to resettle them in Kambry. It was the right thing to do, but it would be hard to keep her a secret forever. Word was circulating of a mystery girl who walked up to The Reader after its destructive Wakening. The Royal Artist had even done a sketch of her. Beredrim had forbidden the enclosure guards to speak about it and had destroyed the sketch. But there were many who witnessed what Della had done and whose talk he couldn't control. It wouldn't be long before the rumours reached Vish Pashgar and when they did, Hayhas would have some difficult questions to answer.

Ormis volunteered to manage Della and Kye's resettlement; to do everything from drawing up the official papers to the acquisition of the wagon that would take them there. He felt a strong obligation to see them right – something his new nature demanded. But all his presumption had died with his old self and before committing to it, he sought their consent. They agreed without hesitation and he was touched when Kye said he wouldn't have it any other way.

But they had each made one request: Kye to see his sister one last time and Della to visit her uncle's grave. The man he had once been would never have entertained Kye's request, but he agreed to both without reservation.

He kept his word and was pulled up now on a sunny lane outside Agelrish, awaiting their return. When they got back they would head north for Kambry –the town the exorcists had made for those with Membrane sensitivity. It was a peaceful place close to a picturesque river and he planned to stay with them for a while.

He looked at the pale band of skin where his mist stone ring used to be and wondered how long it would take to tan over. He had renounced his oath to the Caliste and was no longer an exorcist. Hayhas had tried to persuade him against it, but he was resolute in his decision. The personality Izle constructed for him had collapsed and the dust needed to settle before he decided what he wanted to do with his life. He was thinking about finding a remote place and starting over with some honest work. He tipped his head back and for the first time in many years, welcomed the sun on his face.

J.B. Forsyth

A Last Hug Goodbye

Kye folded his arms and gripped himself. He stood on a strip of boggy grass next to a clog of fireweed. Their orange flowers were in full bloom; resplendent in the afternoon sunshine. Further back and all around the lake the trees wore their most vibrant green. It was summer to the eye, but it felt like winter in his bones. Something about the lake was leeching the warmth from the air and he wasn't alone in sensing it. He hadn't seen or heard a single bird since leaving the woods and stepping onto the water's edge.

He was about to call his sister for the fifth time when she rose from the lake like an ice sculpture snapping free of the bottom. She caused no ripples he could see, but he felt some nevertheless - ripples of cold that dropped the temperature even further, confirming his suspicion that she was the source of the unseasonable climate.

'Emilie!'

'You shouldn't have come.'

Her voice was a frigid monotone, spoken right into his head. For the last week he had thought about little else besides seeing his sister again, but the chill in her voice almost undid his preparations.

'I came back to help you... To set you free.'

'Go now, while you still can. I am not the person you remember. It's not safe for you here anymore.'

'Just hear me out Emilie.'

'No you hear me out!' she said in a blizzard of voice. *'Your warmth calls to me. It's an unbearable torture and if I come any closer I won't be able to stop myself stealing it from you.'*

Kye studied her, fearing he was too late. She had changed a lot in the time he had been away and was nothing more than a grey sketch of herself. Malnourished was the word that came to mind, but it was an absurd description of a ghost. 'I know and I understand... But it doesn't matter. I've come to help you pass.'

Her eyes widened and she recoiled. *'Why would you say such a thing? Have you come here just to torment me?'*

'I *can* help you. The day you died, I nearly drowned and it changed me. I didn't understand what it all meant at the time – but I do now. I've helped two spirits to pass already and I can do the same for you.'

There was a change in her then – a melting of her glacial eyes and a thawing of her voice. *'Is that true Kye? Is that really true? If this is a joke, it is the cruellest one you've ever told.'*

Kye smiled. 'It is true. You have to believe me. Today could be your last day in this icy prison. Just let me help you.'

She drifted closer and he could see tiny flickers of light in her eyes - the last embers of her soul glowing under a breath of hope. He wasn't too late. Those embers might go out in a few day or even a few hours, but they were there now.

'How would you do it?'

'You just have to come to me. Think of it as a last hug goodbye.'

'What if it goes wrong and I hurt you.'

'It won't.' He took a step forward and held his arms wide to receive her. 'Don't think about it Emilie. Just come.'

'I'm frightened.'

'Don't be.'

She hesitated for just a moment then came, lifting her arms for an embrace that could never be. As his arms closed around her, she melted into him. He gasped and shivered as if he had just dived into the cold waters of the lake. But after a few deep breaths he relaxed, closing his eyes and welcoming her into his mind. He took her down, immersing her in his most treasured memories of their time together: selling their mum's gingerbread from a makeshift stall outside their house; making a den in Agelrish Wood and playing hide and seek in rows of ripe corn - a series of sunny days that still warmed his heart. It triggered her memories too, so they experienced a composite of what was in their shared minds, bolstered and enhanced by details the other had retained. And through his body he allowed her to taste and smell the gingerbread; to feel the webbed shade of their den and to hear the rustle of the corn as they brushed through it.

It wrenched his heart to feel Emilie try to step into each memory, as though they were some real world she could belong to again. He felt the moment she realised it wasn't so - when her joy turned to terrible yearning. He felt her distress as his own and the weight of it brought him to his knees. He felt her need to vent her pain and gave his body over to her, allowing her to wail with his throat, cry with his eyes and beat the ground with his fists. Her anguish had been building from the day she died and the release of it was enormous – almost too much for his body to bear. He fell forward onto his hands and almost blacked out. But somehow Emilie sensed the danger to him and wound herself down to a hollow sob.

He rolled onto his back and felt her grief like a weight on his chest. He began to see and feel how her disconnection from the physical world had bred an obsessive desire of it; and how it drove her to the brink of a moral cliff. He saw these things, felt her pain and understood – his empathy pouring into her like warmth broth. Through it all he became aware of the Membrane, stretching out in all directions from the centre of him – becoming thinner and thinner until it ripped open, revealing the void behind it.

Emilie stopped sobbing.

The forever nothingness she had longed for was right before her. All she needed to do was to give herself to it. But she didn't go straight away. She resisted long enough to whisper through his soul: *Thank you Kye. I love you.*

'I love you too.'

Then she was gone.

He curled up in the grass, crying bittersweet tears into his hands. When he finished he sat up and noticed a starling, perched on a lump of deadwood. It was the first of many birds to return to the lake that day.

Oxeye Daisies

Laurena climbed over the fence, clutching a fist full of Oxeye daisies. She looked up at the sky as she walked out into the field. It was bright and clear - a day her uncle would have said he could see his reflection in. A day to seize or surrender to. She walked to the rectangle of turned earth that was his grave. The villagers had taken his body from their burnt house and buried him in this remote field, miles from the village graveyard. If nothing else, it was fitting. They had never belonged, wherever they went. But she looked around and knew he would have liked it here. There was a fine view across the Vale of Agelrish and birds were singing summer melodies in the hedgerow.

She had been preparing for today for the last week. She had attempted to write a poem to read - to set in words all he had meant to her, *still* meant to her. But she couldn't get more than a few lines down before scrunching it up - the words on the paper too flat and sterile to express what was in her heart. In the end she decided not to plan anything - to just come and let the closeness of him direct her.

She looked down at his grave.

There was an old saying that you didn't go to look at a grave, you went to look through it. And she experienced the truth of it now. The turned earth became a window to their past: walking wild country between new lives, foraging berries and sitting around a campfire beneath the stars. Days without distraction that seemed to go on forever. She felt a mighty rending in her heart and felt the truth of another of his sayings: *Good memories always come with a price - for to recall them is also to mourn them.*

She thought about how time had cheated them, sprinting the good days and crawling the bad. And then all of a sudden it ran out altogether. It was as if the tide had come in while they were playing in the sun, washing over everything they built together and taking him away.

She tossed the flowers aside and dropped to her knees, burying her nine fingers in the cold earth and reaching for him with streaming eyes. *Oh uncle.*

    For five centuries he had been her companion, provider, carer and friend. And now he was gone. She felt her grief unfolding; something so huge her body had no hope of containing it. She gripped the dirt and held on, freezing in place like a dreadful headstone – head tipped back and eyes clenched and dripping. She broke form with a mournful cry that cut through the ambience, setting a pair of hares to flight and silencing the birds.

    For a time, she remained in place, watering his grave with her tears. In the end she sat back on her heels and sagged. The grief she suffered over the last few weeks was a false summit and in coming here she had glimpsed its true peak – a terrible ridgeline she would toil on for many years to come. And she had yet to visit the hideaway and read the book he wrote for her. That would be much harder than today, but she wouldn't go for a while. His memory was soaked into every beam and plank and going there would finish her.

    She looked into the dirt, thinking about the changes she was beginning to feel. With the Uhuru poison gone she was starting to mature - a process in stasis for so long she could feel its resurgence. She wondered if he would recognise her in a few years and the thought choked her up again. She promised herself to come back one day, to talk to him as a woman and show him what she had become.

    She fanned the oxeye daisies over his grave. It was her favourite flower, but one she had never used to help remember someone. Now she knew why: she had saved her favourite flower for her favourite person and for the rest of her life she would see his face in their little yellow hearts.

    She climbed back over the fence and returned to the wagon. Kye was already there and she could tell by his face it had gone well with his sister. He had been so anxious about seeing her again, barely speaking a word on their trip from Irongate. But he looked at peace now, staring out over the fields in calm reflexion. Ormis smiled when she jumped up and with a flick of the reins he set the wagon rolling. Such an expression would have been out of place on his face a month ago, but he had changed a lot since then and it suited him.

    As the wagon picked up speed, Kye turned to her and held out a closed fist. She frowned in puzzlement, but he just nodded at his hand to suggest he had something for her. She put her hand under his and her mother's necklace dropped into it. 'You said you lost it running from the house, remember? I thought I'd have a look for it while I was up at the lake. The bag and your diary were ruined, but I thought you'd want this.'

    She stared at the animal carvings with wonder. She had never expected to see them again. As her eyes welled up he squeezed her arm and went back to looking over the fields. Kye – her new friend and companion. She had already decided to take him with her to the hideaway and teach him

Absence if he had the patience. Her uncle never met him, but she knew he would have approved.

The End

Printed in Great Britain
by Amazon